Introduction

David G. Hartwell & Kathryn Cramer

THIS IS THE SIXTH VOLUME of a series, in which the series is transformed by changes in publisher and format. The first five *Year's Best Fantasy* volumes were mass market paperback originals. This one appears in trade paperback. But that is only the most cosmetic of the changes. We have the new restriction of a shorter book, and therefore fewer words on fewer pages, which means fewer stories. And because trade paperbacks are displayed for sale in bookstores but not in supermarkets and drugstores and such, where most mass market paperbacks are sold, we have decided to alter the mix of our contents a bit.

When we launched the series, we said that in this anthology series, we will use the broadest definition of genre fantasy (to include wonder stories, adventure fantasy, supernatural fantasy, satirical and humorous fantasy). We believe that the best-written fantasy can stand up in the long run by any useful literary standard in comparison to fiction published out of category or genre. And furthermore, that out of respect for the genre at its best, we ought to stand by genre fantasy and promote it in this book. Also, we believe that writers publishing their work specifically as fantasy are up to this task, so we set out to find these stories, and we looked for them in the genre anthologies, magazines, and small press pamphlets. Some fine fantasy writers will still be missing. A fair number of the best fantasy writers these days write only novels, or if they do write short fiction, do so only every few years and sometimes it is not their best work. We will find the good examples and reprint them when we can. And you will find an even broader set of examples from the very fringes of genre, where some of the finest work is being done, in this new volume. We will make further remarks about this in the individual story notes.

It has been an especially fine decade so far for fantastic fiction, and 2005 was not an exception. No one writer made nearly the impact of Tolkien, but Kelly Link's *Magic for Beginners* was listed at the end of 2005 as one of *Time* magazine's five best books of American fiction for the year. That's very spiffy for a writer who makes no bones about her attachment to genre, and for all of the rest of us as well.

The year 2005 was also the year in which the World SF convention was held in Glasgow, Scotland, with a strong showing of fantasy writers. And the World Fantasy convention was held in Madison, Wisconsin, with a notable international contingent. Both conventions, for instance, had large open parties celebrating Australian writers. Literary movements in fantasy such as Interstitial Arts and the New Weird seemed in the process of redefinition and realignment. And the highest paying market for fantasy short fiction, SciFiction.com, ceased publication at the end of the year, as did another prestigious online site, The Infinite Matrix.

There are new magazines, and rumors of more new magazines, but the center of the field was occupied by the few biggest magazines, Asimov's, The Magazine of Fantasy & Science Fiction, and Realms of Fantasy, with the newly redesigned Interzone and its sister publication, The Third Alternative, Weird Tales, and a few smaller fry attendant. The other loci of quality were the original anthologies, which continue to proliferate, and the zines, little magazines of literary ambition descended from, or in partial imitation of, Gavin Grant and Kelly Link's 'zine, Lady Churchill's Rosebud Wristlet, which is still a leader.

Like the earlier volumes in this series, this book provides some insight into the fantasy field now, who is writing some of the best short fiction published as fantasy, and where. We try to represent the varieties of tones and voices and attitudes that keep the genre vigorous and responsive to the changing realities out of which it emerges. This is a book about what's going on now in fantasy. The stories that follow show, and the story notes point out, the strengths of the evolving genre in the year 2005. But it is fundamentally a collection of excellent stories for your reading pleasure. It is supposed to be fun.

David G. Hartwell & Kathryn Cramer
Pleasantville, NY

YEAR'S BEST FANTASY 6

Eating Hearts

Yoon Ha Lee

Yoon Ha Lee (pegasus.cityofveils.com) lives in Jamaica Plain, Massachusetts, with her husband, Joseph, and their daughter, Arabelle, and a glass Klein bottle. Her fiction has appeared in The Magazine of Fantasy & Science Fiction, Lady Churchill's Rosebud Wristlet, Ideomancer, and Shadows of Saturn. She is a section editor at The Internet Review of Science Fiction. She has lived in Houston, South Korea, Missouri, New York, California, and Washington State. In an autobiographical essay about moving frequently between cultures as a child, Lee remarks, "You can go ahead and give me the ruby slippers, but if I clicked them three times, nothing would happen. There's no place like home, all right – I don't have one."

We open this collection with "Eating Hearts," a fine fantasy from The Magazine of Fantasy & Science Fiction, where a major portion of the best fantasy was published in 2005. This story explores in fairy tale form the sexuality of our desire for stories, and our desire to consume fantasy and be consumed by it. It also addresses the subject of cultural displacement, of a narrator who does not feel at home in the reality she inhabits.

THEY TELL MANY STORIES in that land surrounded on three sides by ocean, sometimes of foxes with small sharp smiles, sometimes of rats wearing men's clothing. They tell stories of the magician whose tomb was found empty after his death and of bones that beg for proper burial. Sometimes they speak of their first human king, a son of heaven, and his mother, a bear who had become human by meditating in the deepest and most dreadful of caves.

If they mention the bear's companion, it is to describe her pacing in the darkness, unable to sit still, then running out of the cave in shame, unable to become human.

"It's about not seeing," Chuan explained to her just after he brought the meal to the table. "The perfect magician is all-blind, all-unknowing. No sound reaches a wall to wake an echo; no touch bridges distance." He leaned back against the wall where, Horanga imagined, the cloth of his shirt hung over the hollow curve of his back. He lived in a house in the city, by the river, and long ago the sound of fish swimming endlessly in that river would have distracted her from her purpose.

"Then what do you do in this house?" asked Horanga, looking not at his face or his hands, but at the plate between them. The plate was heaped with tender vegetables, slivers of rare meat, and sliced nuts; over the vegetables and meat and nuts, he had drizzled three different sauces in a tapestry of taste.

"A perfect magician, I said." He smiled.

It was important to understand exactly what Chuan, this latest maker of magic, said to her. To do that, Horanga had to ask insolent questions, which was easy because a woman who came alone to a man's house had no pretense of virtue. She had walked away from her mother's family long ago to seek magic, and since no one in her mother's family would acknowledge her, she sought the more interesting thing: magicians. She was a striking woman, tall like a tree in the moment before wind and snow bring it down, and she had long loose hair and lips on the verge of promises.

Magicians were permitted their eccentricities and their dalliances. So Chuan had bought her new shoes, although she needed them not, and a new umbrella besides, and put a purse of his own coins into her hand, and invited her into his house. An old bargain.

Horanga looked back up at Chuan's face by way of his poised hand and the lines of his arm. She had tasted delicacies from every province, and she understood the importance of this moment. As they ate, the two of them, neither looked away from the other. And as they set down their chopsticks after the last mouthful, Chuan said, "I am, of course, far from being a perfect magician."

This disappointed her. "And why is that?" She knew the coquette's art of gazing down and to the side, of the hesitant touch, and disdained to use it. Such gestures belonged to younger women first of all and to women with shallower purposes most of all. A forthright gaze suited her better.

"The near-perfect magician," he said, "desires a single thing only, when desire he must. He desires it so perfectly that nothing else exists, and this is the root that nourishes his magic-making. At other times, in other places, he may live as ordinary men do. But magic with nothing to distract it from its purpose – that is what he shapes."

"So a perfect magician desires nothing," said Horanga, who believed in stating things plainly. "And everything becomes possible as a solution to the desire he does not have."

"That is it," said Chuan, and his sober tone pleased her. She had spoken with many a magician in her travels, and not all of them had taken her seriously. "You must have a philosophical turn of mind, to grasp it so quickly. Was it to learn magic that you came here?"

"No," said Horanga with perfect honesty, and her gaze moved to the plates whence they had sated themselves. It was her turn to smile, and she averted her gaze to avoid alarming the man with what was in her eyes. "I am not interested in magic so much as I am interested in magicians."

She spoke of a category rather than a particular, but he understood her well enough.

★

Once, a tiger watched outside a window, yearning after human skin and human manners, but knew no means of obtaining them except by eating human hearts.

During the night, when half the moon hung low in the sky and its other half shone in fragments from the city's great river, Horanga said to the man beneath her, "For the desire that consumes your heart, O magician, what would you do?"

Other men had answered this question amid silks, or satins, or furs. She was offended by furs, though she should not be. In any case, they had said the expected thing to a woman above them. Chuan pleased her by saying, albeit in a teasing, dream-laden voice, "Other than this? I might walk blindfolded during the darkest hours, with no star overhead, no path underfoot."

It always came back to darkness above all other forms of deprivation. "Would you go into a cave, a place where no light has ever lived, and no wind has ever blown, and even the water has forgotten its wellspring?"

Chuan reached up to stroke a lock of her hair that would otherwise have fallen upon his face. "A perfect magician would see no need, having mastered all distraction. He would also see no reason why not. But a near-perfect magician – why, yes."

"Into a cave while you have only the scantest of provisions to sustain you, and only a trickle of water?" Her voice grew lower, deeper, descending.

"Yes," he breathed, letting go of her hair.

"Into a cave with no space to lie down, and scarcely enough room to turn around and around?"

"Yes," he said again.

"Into a cave where the seasons blur into one long languid chill, and nothing varies but the speed of your pulse?"

"Yes."

A tiger can only eat so many hearts before they start to taste bitter, then sour, then like nothing at all. By that point, even a tiger's own heart, that rarest of delicacies, loses all savor.

Our tiger, who once watched outside windows, is not incapable of learning this.

Toward morning, when languor had fallen upon them and words returned, Chuan asked his own question. "You only ask about reasons to go into the cave and to stay there. Why not reasons to leave it?"

"You are here, and not in a cave. I should think that the question answers itself."

"And so it does," said the far-from-perfect magician. "How many hearts have you eaten, my dear?"

"Too many," she said, indifferent to numbers, but honest in essence.

"Were they all magicians' hearts?"

"Only later," Horanga said, unsurprised by his astuteness. He was a magician, after all.

"If you are waiting for a perfect magician," Chuan said, "you are looking for the wrong thing. You have a mantle of hair wholly black and you walk upon two legs. You did the better thing by refusing to let the cave consume you, long ago. You wanted to be something other than virtuous, which is to say, you wanted freedom. And you have it, which is one thing more than the mother of that long-ago king ever had."

"It is kind of you to say so," Horanga murmured. "But only humans become perfect magicians through their desire, because they need not become human first. I have discovered no way to eat hearts, of magicians or otherwise, while leaving them intact. I am willing to be enlightened if it does not require sitting still in meditation to find out."

"Nonsense," said Chuan, and took her hand, which had strong, slender fingers and fingernails that were merely fingernails. "About eating hearts, I mean."

Horanga gazed at him in astonishment.

"I have spent this last night demonstrating how to consume a heart while leaving it intact, as have you," said Chuan. "And it seemed to me that you were quite awake for it. Or do you, in the perfection of your desire, have no heart left for me to consume?"

They tell many stories in that land surrounded on three sides by ocean, sometimes of foxes with small sharp smiles, sometimes of rats wearing men's clothing. They tell stories of the magician whose tomb was found empty after his death and of bones that beg for proper burial. Sometimes they speak of their first human king, a son of heaven, and his mother, a bear who had become human by meditating in the deepest and most dreadful of caves.

If they mention the bear's companion, it is to describe her pacing in the darkness, unable to sit still, then running out of the cave in shame, unable to become human.

But the children of tigers, who are sometimes also the children of men, tell a different story.

— *For the tigers in my family.*

The Denial

Bruce Sterling

Bruce Sterling (*www.well.com/conf/mirrorshades/*) lives in Belgrade, Serbia, with his wife, Serbian author and filmmaker Jasmina Tesanović (*en.wikipedia.org/wiki/Jasmina_Tesanovic*). One of the chief architects of cyberpunk science fiction, he has published ten novels and three story collections to date. He has recently reinvented himself as a futurist and design critic, publishing *Shaping Things* (2005), "a book about created objects" as a Mediawork Pamphlet, through MIT Press. Whatever he does, he aims to shake things up. Throughout Sterling's career, part of his aesthetic project has been to put us in touch with the larger world in which we live, giving us glimpses of not only speculative and fantastic realities, but also the unfamiliar reality of the Third World. Sometimes he does this through fantasy.

"The Denial" appeared in *The Magazine of Fantasy & Science Fiction*. Somewhere in the Third World, Yusuf the cooper tries to save his family from a sudden flood. This is what one might call a post-tsunami fantasy, concerning distortions in our perception of reality that we employ to survive disaster. Magical thinking, of course.

YUSUF CLIMBED the town's ramshackle bridge. There he joined an excited crowd: gypsies, unmarried apprentices, the village idiot, and three ne'er-do-wells with a big jug of plum brandy. The revelers had brought along a blind man with a fiddle.

The river was the soul of the town, but the heavy spring rains had been hard on her. She was rising from her bed in a rage. Tumbling branches clawed through her foam like the mutilated hands of thieves.

The crowd tore splinters from the bridge, tossed them in the roiling water, and made bets. The blind musician scraped his bow on his instrument's single string. He wailed out a noble old lament about crops washed away, drowned herds, hunger, sickness, poverty, and grief.

Yusuf listened with pleasure and studied the rising water with care. Suddenly a half-submerged log struck a piling. The bridge quivered like a sobbing violin. All at once, without a word, the crowd took to their heels.

Yusuf turned and gripped the singer's ragged shoulder. "You'd better come with me."

"I much prefer it here with my jolly audience, thank you, sir!"

"They all ran off. The river's turning ugly, this is dangerous."

"No, no, such kind folk would not neglect me!"

Yusuf pressed a coin into the fiddler's palm.

The fiddler carefully rubbed the coin with his callused fingertips. "A copper penny! What magnificence! I kiss your hand!"

Yusuf was the village cooper. When his barrel trade turned lean, he sometimes patched pots. "See here, fellow, I'm no rich man to keep concubines and fiddlers!"

The fiddler stiffened. "I sing the old songs of your heritage, as the living voice of the dead! The devil's crows will peck the eyeballs of the stingy!"

"Stop trying to curse me and get off this stupid bridge! I'm buying your life with that penny!"

The fiddler spat. At last he tottered toward the far riverbank.

Yusuf abandoned the bridge for the solid cobbles of the marketplace. Here he found more reasonable men: the town's kadi, the wealthy beys, and the seasoned hadjis. These local notables wore handsome woolen cloaks and embroidered jackets. The town's Orthodox priest had somehow been allowed to join their circle.

Yusuf smoothed his vest and cummerbund. Public speech was not his place, but he was at least allowed to listen to his betters. He heard the patriarchs trade the old proverbs. Then they launched lighthearted quips at one another, as jolly as if their town had nothing to lose. They were terrified.

Yusuf hurried home to his wife.

"Wake and dress the boy and girl," he commanded. "I'm off to rouse my uncle. We're leaving the house tonight."

"Oh, no, we can't stay with your uncle," his wife protested.

"Uncle Mehmet lives on high ground."

"Can't this wait till morning? You know how grumpy he gets!"

"Yes, my Uncle Mehmet has a temper," said Yusuf, rolling his eyes. "It's also late, and it's dark. It will rain on us. It's hard work to move our possessions. This may all be for nothing. Then I'll be a fool, and I'm sure you'll let me know that."

Yusuf roused his apprentice from his sleeping nook in the workshop. He ordered the boy to assemble the tools and wrap them with care against damp. Yusuf gathered all the shop's dinars and put them inside his wife's jewelry box, which he wrapped in their best rug. He tucked that bundle into both his arms.

Yusuf carried his bundle uphill, pattered on by rain. He pounded the old man's door, and, as usual, his Uncle Mehmet made a loud fuss over nothing. This delayed Yusuf's return. When he finally reached his home again, back down the crooked, muddy lanes, the night sky was split to pieces by lightning. The river was rioting out of her banks.

His wife was keening, wringing her hands, and cursing her unhappy fate. Nevertheless, she had briskly dressed the children and packed a stout cloth sack with the household's precious things. The stupid apprentice had disobeyed Yusuf's orders and run to the river to gawk; naturally, there was no sign of him.

Yusuf could carry two burdens uphill to his uncle's, but to carry his son, his daughter, and his cooper's tools was beyond his strength.

He'd inherited those precious tools from his late master. The means of his livelihood would be bitterly hard to replace.

He scooped the little girl into his arms. "Girl, be still! My son, cling to my back for dear life! Wife, bring your baggage!"

Black water burst over their sill as he opened the door. Their alley had become a long, ugly brook.

They staggered uphill as best they could, squelching through dark, crooked streets. His wife bent almost double with the heavy sack on her shoulders. They sloshed their way to higher ground. She screeched at him as thunder split the air.

"What now?" Yusuf shouted, unable to wipe his dripping eyes.

"My trousseau!" she mourned. "My grandmother's best things!"

"Well, I left my precious tools there!" he shouted. "So what? We have to live!"

She threw her heavy bag down. "I must go back or it will be too late!"

Yusuf's wife came from a good family. Her grandmother had been a land-owner's fine lady, with nothing more to do than knit and embroider all day. The grandam had left fancy garments that Yusuf's wife never bothered to wear, but she dearly treasured them anyway. "All right, we'll go back together!" he lied to her. "But first, save our children!"

Yusuf led the way uphill. The skies and waters roared. The children wept and wriggled hard in their terror, making his burden much worse. Exhausted, he set them on their feet and dragged them by the hands to his uncle's door.

Yusuf's wife had vanished. When he hastened back downhill, he found her heavy bag around a streetcorner. She had disobeyed him, and run back downhill in the darkness.

The river had risen and swallowed the streets. Yusuf ventured two steps into the black, racing flood and was tumbled off his feet and smashed into the wall of a bakery. Stunned and drenched, he retreated, found his wife's abandoned bag, and threw that over his aching shoulders.

At his uncle's house, Mehmet was doubling the woes of his motherless children by giving them a good scolding.

As soon as it grew light enough to see again, Yusuf returned to the wreck of his home. Half the straw roof was gone, along with one wall of his shop. Black mud squished ankle-deep across his floor. All the seasoned wood for his barrels had floated away. By some minor quirk of the river's fury, his precious tools were still there, in mud-stained wrappings.

Yusuf went downstream. The riverbanks were thick with driftwood and bits of smashed homes. Corpses floated, tangled in debris. Some were children.

He found his wife past the bridge, around the riverbend. She was lodged in a muddy sandbar, along with many drowned goats and many dead chickens.

Her skirt, her apron, her pretty belt and her needleworked vest had all been torn from her body by the raging waters. Only her headdress, her pride and joy, was still left to her. Her long hair was tangled in that sodden cloth like river weed.

He had never seen her body nude in daylight. He pried her from the defiling mud, as gently as if she were still living and in need of a husband's help. Shivering with tenderness, he tore the shirt from his wet torso and wrapped her in it, then made her a makeshift skirt from his sash. He lifted her wet, sagging body in his arms. Grief and shame gave him strength. He staggered with her halfway to town.

Excited townsfolk were gathering the dead in carts. When they saw him, they ran to gawk.

Once this happened, his wife suddenly sneezed, lifted her head and, quick as a serpent, hopped down from his grip.

"Look, the cooper is alive!" the neighbors exulted. "God is great!"

"Stop staring like fools," his wife told them. "My man lost his shirt in the flood. You there, lend him your cloak."

They wrapped him up, chafed his cheeks, and embraced him.

The damage was grave in Yusuf's neighborhood, and worse yet on the opposite bank of the river, where the Catholics lived. The stricken people searched the filthy streets for their lost possessions and missing kin. There was much mourning, tumult, and despair. The townsfolk caught two looters, pilfering in the wreckage. The kadi had them beheaded. Their severed heads were publicly exposed on the bridge. Yusuf knew the headless thieves by sight; unlike the others, those rascals wouldn't be missed much.

It took two days for the suffering people to gather their wits about them, but common sense prevailed at last, and they pitched in to rebuild. Wounds were bound up and families reunited. Neighborhood women made soup for everyone in big cooking pots. Alms were gathered and distributed by the dignitaries. Shelter was found for the homeless in the mosques, the temple, and the churches. The dead were retrieved from the sullen river and buried properly by their respective faiths.

The Vizier sent troops from Travnik to keep order. The useless troopers thundered through town on horseback, fired their guns, stole and roasted sheep, and caroused all night with the gypsies. Moslems, Orthodox, and Catholics alike waited anxiously for the marauders to ride home and leave them in peace.

Yusuf's wife and the children stayed at his uncle's while Yusuf put another roof on his house. The apprentice had stupidly broken his leg in the flood – so he had to stay snug with his own family, where he ate well and did no work, much as usual.

Once the damaged bridge was safe for carts again, fresh-cut lumber became available. In the gathering work of reconstruction, Yusuf found his own trade picking up. With a makeshift tent up in lieu of his straw roof, Yusuf had to meet frantic demands for new buckets, casks, and water-barrels. Price was no object, and no one was picky about quality.

Sensing opportunity, the Jews lent money to all the craftsmen of standing, whether their homes were damaged or not. Gold coins appeared in circulation, precious Ottoman sultani from the royal mint in distant Istanbul. Yusuf schemed hard to gain and keep a few.

When he went to fetch his family back home, Yusuf found his wife with a changed spirit. She had put old Mehmet's place fully into order: she'd aired the old man's stuffy cottage, beaten his moldy carpet, scrubbed his floors, banished the mice, and chased the spiders into hiding. His uncle's dingy vest and sash were clean and darned. Old Mehmet had never looked so jolly. When Yusuf's lively children left his home, Mehmet even wept a little.

His wife flung her arms around Yusuf's neck. When the family returned to her wrecked, muddy home, she was as proud as a new bride. She made cleaning up the mud into an exciting game for the children. She cast the spoilt food from her drowned larder. She borrowed flour, bought eggs, conjured up salt, found milk from heaven, and made fresh bread.

Neighbors came to her door with soup and cabbage rolls. Enchanted by her charming gratitude, they helped her to clean. As she worked, his wife sang like a lark. Everyone's spirits rose, despite all the trials, or maybe even because of the trials, because they gave people so much to gripe about. Yusuf said little and watched his wife with raw disbelief. With all her cheerful talk and singing, she ate almost nothing. That which she chewed, she did not swallow.

When he climbed reluctantly into their narrow bed, she was bright-eyed and willing. He told her that he was tired. She obediently put her cool, damp head into the hollow of his shoulder and passed the night as quiet as carved ivory: never a twitch, kick, or snore.

Yusuf knew for a fact that his wife had been swept away and murderously tumbled down a stony riverbank for a distance of some twenty arshin. Yet her pale skin showed no bruising anywhere. He finally found hidden wounds on the soles of her feet. She had struggled hard for her footing as the angry waters dragged her to her death.

In the morning she spoke sweet words of encouragement to him. His hard work would bring them sure reward. Adversity was refining his character. The neighbors admired his cheerful fortitude. His son was learning valuable lessons by his manly example. All this wifely praise seemed plausible enough to Yusuf, and no more than he deserved, but he knew with a black flood of occult certainty that this was not the woman given him in marriage. Where were her dry, acidic remarks? Her balky backtalk? Her black, sour jokes? Her customary heartbreaking sighs, which mutely suggested that every chance of happiness was lost forever?

Yusuf fled to the market, bought a flask of fiery rakija, and sat down to drink hard in midday.

Somehow, in the cunning pretext of "repairing" their flood-damaged church, the Orthodox had installed a bronze bell in their church tower. Its clangor now brazenly competed with the muezzin's holy cries. It was entirely indecent that this wicked contraption of the Serfish Slaves (the Orthodox were also called "Slavish Serfs," for dialects varied) should be casting an ungodly racket over the stricken town. Yusuf felt as if that great bronze barrel and its banging tongue had been hung inside his own chest.

The infidels were ringing bells, but he was living with a corpse.

Yusuf drank, thought slowly and heavily, then drank some more. He might go to the kadi for help in his crisis, but the pious judge would recommend what he always suggested to any man troubled by scandal – the long pilgrimage to Mecca. For a man of Yusuf's slender means, a trip to Arabia was out of the question. Besides, word would likely spread that he had sought public counsel about his own wife. His own wife, and from such a good family, too. That wasn't the sort of thing that a man of standing would do.

The Orthodox priest was an impressive figure, with a big carved staff and a great black towering hat. Yusuf had a grudging respect for the Orthodox. Look how they'd gotten their way with that bell tower of theirs, against all sense and despite every obstacle. They were rebellious and sly, and they clung to their pernicious way of life despite being taxed, fined, scourged, beheaded, and impaled. Their priest – he might well have some dark, occult knowledge that could help in Yusuf's situation.

But what if, in their low cunning, the peasants laughed at him and took advantage somehow? Unthinkable!

The Catholics were fewer than the Orthodox, a simple people, somewhat more peaceable. But the Catholics had Franciscan monks. Franciscan monks were sorcerers who had come from Austria with picture books. The monks recited spells in Latin from their gold-crowned Pope in Rome. They boasted that their Austrian troops could beat the Sultan's janissaries. Yusuf had seen a lot of Austrians. Austrians were rich, crafty, and insolent. They knew bizarre and incredible things. Bookkeeping, for instance.

Could he trust Franciscan monks to deal with a wife who refused to be dead? Those celibate monks didn't even know what a woman was for! The scheme was absurd.

Yusuf was not a drinking man, so the rakija lifted his imagination to great heights. When the local rabbi passed by chance, Yusuf found himself on his feet, stumbling after the Jew. The rabbi noticed this and confronted him. Yusuf, suddenly thick of tongue, blurted out something of his woes.

The rabbi wanted no part of Yusuf's troubles. However, he was a courteous man, and he had a wise suggestion.

There were people of the Bogomil faith within two days' journey. These Bogomils had once been the Christian masters of the land, generations ago, before the Ottoman Turks brought order to the valleys and mountains. Both Catholics and Orthodox considered the Bogomils to be sinister heretics. They thought this for good reason, for the Bogomils (who were also known as "Cathars" and "Patarines") were particularly skilled in the conjuration and banishment of spirits.

So said the rabbi. The local Christians believed that the last Bogomils had been killed or assimilated long ago, but a Jew, naturally, knew better than this. The rabbi alleged that a small clan of the Old Believers still lurked in the trackless hills. Jewish peddlers sometimes met the Bogomils, to do a little business: the Bogomils were bewhiskered clansmen with goiters the size of fists, who ambushed the Sultan's tax men, ripped up roads, ate meat raw on Fridays, and married their own nieces.

Next day, when Yusuf recovered from his hangover, he told his wife that he needed to go on pilgrimage into the hills for a few days. She should have pointed out that their house was still half-wrecked and his business was very pressing. Instead she smiled sweetly, packed him four days of home-cooked provisions, darned his leggings, and borrowed him a stout donkey.

No one could find the eerie Bogomil village without many anxious moments, but Yusuf did find it. This was a dour place where an ancient people of faith were finally perishing from the Earth. The meager village clustered in the battered ruin of a hillside fort. The poorly thatched hovels were patched up from tumbledown bits of rock. Thick nettles infested the rye fields. The goats were scabby, and the donkeys knock-kneed. The plum orchard buzzed with swarms of vicious yellow wasps. There was not a child to be seen.

The locals spoke a Slavish dialect so thick and archaic that it sounded as if they were chewing stale bread. They did have a tiny church of sorts, and in there, slowly dipping holy candles in a stinking yellow mix of lard and beeswax, was their elderly, half-starved pastor, the man they called their "Djed."

The Bogomil Djed wore the patched rags of black ecclesiastical robes. He had a walleye, and a river of beard tumbling past his waist.

With difficulty, Yusuf confessed.

"I like you, Moslem boy," said the Bogomil priest, with a wink or a tic of his bloodshot walleye. "It takes an honest man to tell such a dark story. I can help you."

"Thank you! Thank you! How?"

"By baptizing you in the gnostic faith, as revealed in the Palcyaf Bible. A dreadful thing has happened to you, but I can clarify your suffering, so hearken to me. God, the Good God, did not create this wicked world. This evil place, this sinful world we must endure, was created by God's elder archangel, Satanail the Demiurge. The Demiurge created all the Earth, and also some bits of the lower heavens. Then Satanail tried to create Man in the image of God, but he succeeded only in creating the flesh of Man. That is why it was easy for Satanail to confound and mislead Adam, and all of Adam's heritage, through the fleshly weakness of our clay."

"I never heard that word, 'Demiurge.' There's only one God."

"No, my boy, there are two Gods: the bad God, who is always with us, and the good God, who is unknowable. Now I will tell you all about the dual human and divine nature of Jesus Christ. This is the most wonderful of gnostic gospels; it involves the Holy Dove, the Archangel Michael, Satanail the Creator, and the Clay Hierographon."

"But my wife is not a Christian at all! I told you, she comes from a nice family."

"Your wife is dead."

A chill gripped Yusuf. He struggled for something to say.

"My boy, is your woman nosferatu? You can tell me."

"I don't know that word either."

"Does she hate and fear the light of the sun?"

"My wife loves sunlight! She loves flowers, birds, pretty clothes, she likes everything nice."

"Does she suck the blood of your children?"

Yusuf shook his head and wiped at his tears.

The priest shrugged reluctantly. "Well, no matter – you can still behead her and impale her through the heart! Those measures always settle things!"

Yusuf was scandalized. "What would I tell the neighbors?"

The old man sighed. "She's dead and yet she walks the Earth, my boy. You do need to do something."

"How could a woman be dead and not know she's dead?"

"In her woman's heart she suspects it. But she's too stubborn to admit it. She died rashly and foolishly, disobeying her lord and master, and she left her woman's body lying naked in some mud. Imagine the shame to her spirit! This young wife with a house and small children, she left her life's duties undone! Her failure was more than her spirit could admit. So, she does not live, but she stubbornly persists." The priest slowly dipped a bare white string into his pot of wax. "'A man may work from sun to sun, but a woman's work is never done.'"

Yusuf put his head in his hands and wept. The Djed had convinced him. Yusuf was sure that he had found the best source of advice on his troubles, short of a long trip to Mecca. "What's to become of me now? What's to become of my poor children?"

"Do you know what a succubus is?" said the priest.

"No, I never heard that word."

"If your dead wife had become a succubus, you wouldn't need any words. Never mind that. I will prophesy to you of what comes next. Her dead flesh and immortal spirit must part sometimes, for that is their dual nature. So sometimes you will find that her spirit is there, while her flesh is not there. You will hear her voice and turn to speak; but there will be no one. The pillow will have the dent of her head, but no head lying there. The pot might move from the stove to the table, with no woman's hands to move it."

"Oh," said Yusuf. There were no possible words for such calamities.

"There will also be moments when the spirit retreats and her body remains. I mean the rotten body of a woman who drowned in the mud. If you are lucky you might not see that rotten body. You will smell it."

"I'm accursed! How long can such torments go on?"

"Some exorcist must persuade her that she met with death and her time on Earth is over. She has to be confronted with the deceit that her spirit calls 'truth.' She has to admit that her life is a lie."

"Well, that will never happen," said Yusuf. "I never knew her to admit to a mistake since the day her father gave her to me."

"Impale her heart while she sleeps!" demanded the Djed. "I can sell you the proper wood for the sharpened stake – it is the wood of life, lignum vitae, I found it growing in the dead shrine of the dead God Mithras, for that is the ruin of a failed resurrection…. The wood of life has a great herbal virtue in all matters of spirit and flesh."

Yusuf's heart rebelled. "I can't stab the mother of my children between her breasts with a stick of wood!"

"You are a cooper," said the Djed, "so you do have a hammer."

"I mean that I'll cast myself into the river before I do any such thing!"

The Djed hung his candle from a small iron rod. "To drown one's self is a great calamity."

"Is there nothing better to do?"

"There is another way. The black way of sorcery." The Djed picked at his long beard. "A magic talisman can trap her spirit inside her dead body. Then her spirit cannot slip free from the flesh. She will be trapped in her transition from life to death, a dark and ghostly existence."

"What kind of talisman does that?"

"It's a fetter. The handcuff of a slave. You can tell her it's a bracelet, a woman's bangle. Fix that fetter, carved from the wood of life, firmly around her dead wrist. Within that wooden bracelet, a great curse is written: the curse that bound the children of Adam to till the soil, as the serfs of Satanail, ruler and creator of the Earth. So her soul will not be able to escape her clay, any more than Adam, Cain, and Abel, with their bodies made of clay by Satanail, could escape the clay of the fields and pastures. She will have to abide by that untruth she tells herself, for as long as that cuff clings to her flesh."

"Forever, then? Forever and ever?"

"No, boy, listen. I told you 'as long as that cuff clings to her flesh.' You will have to see to it that she wears it always. This is necromancy."

Yusuf pondered the matter, weeping. Peaceably, the Bogomil dipped his candles.

"But that's all?" Yusuf said at last. "I don't have to stab her with a stick? I don't have to bury her, or behead her? My wife just wears a bracelet on her arm, with some painted words! Then I go home."

"She's dead, my boy. You are trapping a human soul within the outward show of rotten form. She will have no hope of salvation. She will be the hopeless slave of earthly clay and the chattel of her circumstances. For you to do that to another human soul is a mortal sin. You will have to answer for that on the Day of Judgment." The Djed adjusted his sleeves. "But, you are Moslem, so you are damned already. All the more so for your woman, so...." The Djed spread his waxy hands.

The rabbi had warned Yusuf about the need for ready cash.

When Yusuf and his borrowed donkey returned home, footsore and hungry after five days of risky travel, he found his place hung with the neighbors' laundry. It was as festive as a set of flags. All the rugs and garments soiled by the flood needed boiling and bleaching. So his wife had made herself the bustling center of this lively activity.

Yusuf's smashed straw roof was being replaced with sturdy tiles. The village tiler and his wife had both died in the flood. The tiler's boy, a sullen, skinny teen, had lived, but his loss left him blank-eyed and silent.

Yusuf's wife had found this boy, haunted, shivering, and starving. She had fed him, clothed him, and sent him to collect loose tiles. There were many tiles scattered in the wrecked streets, and the boy knew how to lay a roof, so, somehow, without anything being said, the boy had become Yusuf's new apprentice. The new apprentice didn't eat much. He never said much. As an orphan, he was in no position to demand any wages or to talk back. So, although he knew nothing about making barrels, he was the ideal addition to the shop.

Yusuf's home, once rather well known for ruckus, had become a model of sociable charm. Neighbors were in and out of the place all the time, bringing sweets, borrowing flour and salt, swapping recipes, leaving children to be baby-sat. Seeing the empty barrels around, his wife had started brewing beer as a profitable sideline. She also stored red paprikas in wooden kegs of olive oil. People started leaving things at her house to sell. She was planning on building a shed to retail groceries.

There was never a private moment safe from friendly interruption, so Yusuf took his wife across the river, to the Turkish graveyard, for a talk. She wasn't reluctant to go, since she was of good birth and her long-established family occupied a fine, exclusive quarter of the cemetery.

"We never come here enough, husband," she chirped. "With all the rain, there's so much moss and mildew on Great-grandfather's stone! Let's fetch a big bucket and give him a good wash!"

There were fresh graves, due to the flood, and one ugly wooden coffin, still abandoned above ground. Moslems didn't favor wooden boxes for their dead – this was a Christian fetish – but they'd overlooked that minor matter when they'd had to inter the swollen, oozing bodies of the flood victims. Luckily, rumor had outpaced the need for such boxes. So a spare coffin was still on the site, half full of rainwater and humming with spring mosquitoes.

Yusuf took his wife's hand. Despite all her housework – she was busy as an ant – her damp hands were soft and smooth.

"I don't know how to tell you this," he said.

She blinked her limpid eyes and bit her lip. "What is it you have to complain about, husband? Have I failed to please you in some way?"

"There is one matter...a difficult matter.... Well, you see, there's more to the marriage of a man and woman than just keeping house and making money."

"Yes, yes," she nodded, "being respectable!"

"No, I don't mean that part."

"The children, then?" she said.

"Well, not the boy and girl, but..." he said. "Well, yes, children! Children, of course! It's God's will that man and woman should bring children into the world! And, well, that's not something you and I can do anymore."

"Why not?"

Yusuf shuddered from head to foot. "Do I have to say that? I don't want to."

"What is it you want from me, Yusuf? Spit it out!"

"Well, the house is as neat as a pin. We're making a profit. The neighbors love you. I can't complain about that. You know I never complain. But if you stubbornly refuse to die, well, I can't go on living. Wife, I need a milosnica."

"You want to take a concubine?"

"Yes. Just a maidservant. Nobody fancy. Maybe a teenager. She could help around the house."

"You want me to shelter your stupid concubine inside my own house?"

"Where else could I put a milosnica? I'm a cooper, I'm not a bey or an aga."

Demonic light lit his wife's eyes. "You think of nothing but money and your shop! You never give me a second glance! You work all day like a gelded ox! Then you go on a pilgrimage in the middle of everything, and now you tell me you want a concubine? Oh, you eunuch, you pig, you big talker! I work, I slave, I suffer, I do everything to please you, and now your favor turns to another!" She raised her voice and screeched across the graveyard. "Do you see this, Grandmother? Do you see what's becoming of me?"

"Don't make me angry," said Yusuf. "I've thought this through and it's reasonable. I'm not a cold fish. I'm living with a dead woman. Can't I have one live woman, just to warm my bones?"

"I'd warm your bones. Why can't I warm your bones?"

"Because you drowned in the river, girl. Your flesh is cold."

She said nothing.

"You don't believe me? Take off those shoes," he said wearily. "Look at those wounds on the bottoms of your feet. Your wounds never heal. They can't heal." Yusuf tried to put some warmth and color into his voice. "You have pretty feet, you have the prettiest feet in town. I always loved your feet, but, well, you never show them to me, since you drowned in that river."

She shook her head. "It was *you* who drowned in the river."

"What?"

"What about that huge wound in your back? Do you think I never noticed that great black ugly wound under your shoulder? That's why you never take your vest off anymore!"

Yusuf no longer dared to remove his clothes while his wife was around, so, although he tried a sudden, frightened glance back over his own shoulder, he saw nothing there but embroidered cloth. "Do I really have a scar on my back? I'm not dead, though."

"Yes, husband, you are dead," his wife said bluntly. "You ran back for your stupid tools, even though I begged you to stay with me and comfort me. I saw you fall. You drowned in the street. I found your body washed down the river."

This mad assertion of hers was completely senseless. "No, that can't be true," he told her. "You abandoned me and the children, against my direct word to you, and you went back for your grandmother's useless trousseau, and you drowned, and I found you sprawling naked in the mud."

"'Naked in the mud,'" she scoffed. "In your dreams!" She pointed. "You see that coffin? Go lie down in that coffin, stupid. That coffin's for you."

"That's your coffin, my dear. That's certainly not my coffin."

"Go lie down in there, you big hot stallion for concubines. You won't rise up again, I can promise you."

Yusuf gazed at the splintery wooden hulk. That coffin was a sorry piece of woodworking; he could have built a far better coffin himself. Out of nowhere, black disbelief washed over him. Could he possibly be in this much trouble? Was this what his life had come to? Him, a man of circumspection, a devout man, honest, a hard worker, devoted to his children? It simply could not be! It wasn't true! It was impossible.

He should have been in an almighty rage at his wife's stinging taunts, but somehow, his skin remained cool; he couldn't get a flush to his cheeks. He knew only troubled despair. "You really want to put me down in the earth, in such a cheap coffin, so badly built? The way you carry on at me, I'm tempted to lie down in there, I really am."

"Admit it, you don't need any concubine. You just want me out of your way. And after all I did for you, and gave to you! How could you pretend to live without me at your side, you big fool? I deserved much better than you, but I never left you, I was always there for you."

Part of that lament at least was true. Even when their temperaments had clashed, she'd always been somehow willing to jam herself into their narrow bed. She might be angry, yes, sullen, yes, impossible, yes, but she remained with him. "This is a pretty good fight we're having today," he said, "this is kind of like our old times."

"I always knew you'd murder me and bury me someday."

"Would you get over that, please? It's just vulgar." Yusuf reached inside the wrappings of his cummerbund. "If I wanted to kill you, would I be putting this on your hand?"

She brightened at once. "Oh! What's that you brought me? Pretty!"

"I got it on pilgrimage. It's a magic charm."

"Oh how sweet! Do let me have it, you haven't bought me jewelry in ages."

On a sudden impulse, Yusuf jammed his own hand through the wooden cuff. In an instant, memory pierced him. The truth ran through his flesh like a rusty sword. He remembered losing his temper, cursing like a madman, rushing back to his collapsing shop, in his lust and pride for some meaningless clutter of tools.... He could taste that deadly rush of water, see a blackness befouling his eyes, the chill of death filling his lungs –

He yanked his arm from the cuff, trembling from head to foot. "That never happened!" he shouted. "I never did any such thing! I won't stand for such insults! If they tell me the truth, I'll kill them."

"What are you babbling on about? Give me my pretty jewelry."

He handed it over.

She slid her hand through with an eager smile, then pried the deadly thing off her wrist as if it were red-hot iron. "You made me do that!" she screeched. "You made me run into the ugly flood! I was your victim! Nothing I did was ever my fault."

Yusuf bent at the waist and picked up the dropped bangle between his thumb and forefinger. "Thank God this dreadful thing comes off our flesh so easily!"

His wife rubbed the skin of her wrist. There was a new black bruise there. "Look, your gift hurt me. It's terrible!"

"Yes, it's very magical."

"Did you pay a lot of money for that?"

"Oh yes. I paid a lot of money. To a wizard."

"You're hopeless."

"Wife of mine, we're both hopeless. Because the truth is, our lives are over. We've failed. Why did we stumble off to our own destruction? We completely lost our heads!"

His wife squared her shoulders. "All right, fine! So you make mistakes! So you're not perfect!"

"Me? Why is it me all the time? What about you?"

"Yes, I know, I could be a lot better, but well, I'm stuck with you. That's why I'm no good. So, I don't forgive you, and I never will! But, anyway, I don't think we ought to talk about this anymore."

"Would you reel that snake's tongue of yours back into your head? Listen to me for once! We're all over, woman! We drowned, we both died together in a big disaster!"

"Yusuf, if we're dead, how can you be scolding me? See, you're talking non-sense! I want us to put this behind us once and for all. We just won't talk about this matter anymore. Not one more word. We have to protect the children. Children can't understand such grown-up things. So we'll never breathe a word to anyone. All right?"

Black temptation seized him. "Look, honey, let's just get in that coffin together. We'll never make a go of a situation like this, it can't be done. That coffin's not so bad. It's got as much room as our bed does."

"I won't go in there," she said. "I won't vanish from the Earth. I just won't, because I can't believe what you believe, and you can't make me." She suddenly snatched the bangle from his hand and threw it into the coffin. "There, get inside there with that nasty thing, if you're so eager."

"Now you've gone and spoiled it," he said sadly. "Why do you always have to do that, just to be spiteful? One of these days I'm really going to have to smack you around."

"When our children are ready to bury us, then they will bury us."

That was the wisest thing she had ever said. Yusuf rubbed the words over his dead tongue. It was almost a proverb. "Let the children bury us." There was a bliss to that, like a verse in a very old song. It meant that there were no decisions to be made. The time was still unripe. Nothing useful could be done. Justice, faith, hope and charity, life and death, they were all smashed and in a muddle, far beyond his repair and his retrieval. So just let it all be secret, let that go unspoken. Let the next generation look after all of that. Or the generation after that. Or after that. Or after that.

That was their heritage.

The Fraud

Esther M. Friesner

Esther Friesner (*www.sff.net/people/e.friesner/*) lives in Madison, Connecticut, with her husband, two children, two rambunctious cats, and a fluctuating population of hamsters. She holds a Ph.D. from Yale, where she taught before becoming a full-time writer. She was one of the founders in the 1980s of the parody movement, cyberprep. She has published twenty-seven novels so far. Her short fiction and poetry have appeared in *Asimov's*, *The Magazine of Fantasy & Science Fiction*, *Aboriginal SF*, *Pulphouse*, *Amazing*, and *Fantasy Book*, as well as in numerous anthologies, including the *Chicks in Chainmail* series. Characteristically, she is a humorist.

"The Fraud" appeared in *Asimov's*, which published a significant amount of fantasy in 2005 and seems to be less interested exclusively in science fiction per se in recent years. It is not a light humorous story. It is a tale of the Age of Reason, and the death of reason: of the epistemology of cryptozoology, of unicorns, and of self-deception.

THE ROAD DOWN FROM LONDON was still muddy with springtime rains, despite the calendar's protests of June. George Pengallen shifted his weight in the saddle and felt the stab of sores brought on by too many hours straddling a horse whose ample girth seemed better suited to pulling the plow than to the conveyance of gentlemen, even so financially diminished a young gentleman as himself.

The day was warm, the condition of the roads notwithstanding. A sun that could do nothing toward reducing the level of muck underfoot was remarkably efficient when it came to drying out the solitary rider's throat while at the same time conjuring up rills and rivulets of sweat beneath his clothes. George doffed his tricorn hat and used it to fan himself as though he were the commonest sort of country bumpkin and not the darling of a dozen London drawingrooms. Sunshine cut clean lines of shadow beneath his high cheekbones, laid a dusting of fine golden light over the perfectly drawn angles of his face. Given the necessary particulars attending this journey, he had elected not to wear his wig. His badly cropped blond hair stood in want of a proper barbering, a luxury that his starveling purse could ill afford but for which the vanity of his twenty years longed.

Despite his vigorous stirring of the still air with his hat, the heat surrounding him increased. Beads of sweat trickled down from his forehead, stinging at the corners of eyes the bright blue of a winter's frost-nipped sky. He shaded his brow with one hand and peered ahead into the distance, praying to see even a hint that this loathsome journey would soon be at an end.

He was rewarded with the sight of a thin steeple piercing the horizon and, when his mount had lumbered on a few dozen yards farther, with the comforting vista of a village huddled at the church's base. He did not need to consult any written memorandum to know that these were the landmarks he sought. George's memory – well trained by his father's insistence on word-perfect recall of Bible texts from all his children, honed to an unflawed edge by two otherwise wasted years at Cambridge – now unfurled before his mind's eye a *tableau vivant* of the conversation that had followed his last decent dinner in London.

You can not go astray. Lord Edgerton's words played themselves out inside George's head as the image of that florid-faced peer of the realm presented itself in memory so vivid that the young man could almost smell the rancid sweat, stale tobacco, and pungent brandy fumes that always attended his patron as faithfully as a trio of hounds. *Once the village is in sight, you will soon enough come to the road that leads to Munscroft.*

George's remembered self stood with one hand resting upon the mantelpiece of his lordship's library hearth. *There will be no chance of my missing it?* he asked.

None, if you're not a fool. This from Dr. Toombs. He was a small, weedy, bandy-legged man of Lincolnshire blood whose unfortunate pairing of name and profession seemed to have blighted every aspect of his life. George had never heard him speak without somehow managing to cast a withering shadow over the conversation. For all this, he was still Lord Edgerton's most trusted intimate, the man upon whom that peer's judgment relied when he doubted his own.

I hope, sir, that did you take me for a fool you would counsel his lordship not to place so much as a farthing in my trust, let alone a mission of so much delicacy. Perhaps those were not the exact words George had used in the library that evening, but they were what his memory provided.

Dr. Toombs snorted and stretched his legs to the fire, ignoring George's remark, but Lord Edgerton laughed his booming laugh and seemed well pleased with the young man's spirit. Slapping both satin-cased thighs, he exclaimed, *Well said, young Pengallen! Delicacy, aye, there's the very word that nips me at every turn, mousewise. It is that very quality of discretion which I have taken pains to observe in you from the instant of our introduction and which, after some consideration, I now may incontestably pronounce to be admirable, admirable!*

George felt his cheeks heat up, though whether it was from his remembered blushes under his lordship's praise or merely the effect of the June sun, he could not say. There was but little doubt in his mind as to whence his lordship had garnered so favorable an opinion of his prudential nature: Lady Charlotte Weathersfield, none other.

It was Lady Weathersfield who had presented the failed Cambridge scholar to his lordship, which was small wonder to the more perspicacious segments of the London gentry. Lady Weathersfield was widely noised about the town as a collector of handsome young gallants, the brilliance of whose intellects was poorly seconded by the ballast of their purses. Her ladyship's inclination in this regard was, in fact, one of those matters which good society had chosen to keep as a public secret: Everyone knew, but everyone worth knowing treated the information as nonexistent.

As for the young men her ladyship so favored, their reigns inevitably proved to be as brief as those of the Four Emperors. More often than not their insightful minds lacked one critical aspect of development, namely when to keep themselves to themselves. Nearly all of them *would* speak of her ladyship's favors – of the body carnal as well as the body financial – and some would go so far as to vaunt their conquest in the coffee houses. This was entirely unsuitable. Her ladyship was fond, but no fool; she knew that the universities would never let her lack for smart young men, one of whom might actually prove to be discreet. There was no need to endure a man who was anything less than wholly satisfactory, no matter the killing power of his *beaux yeux*. Wherefore her wake was littered with the bodies of the brash and impolitic as she sailed on unencumbered into more accommodating seas.

This was not to say that all of her ladyship's alliances ended badly for the young men. George himself had been some four months in her favor when she presented him to Lord Edgerton, at which point that openhearted and outspoken peer had taken it upon himself to lead the young man a little aside and offer him good counsel. He mentioned the names of three gentlemen, all comfortably placed in the government, one risen to the rank of baronet, and gave George to understand that it had been Lady Weathersfield's soft white hand that had placed their feet upon the first rung of the ladder to preferment. *Please me and you please her,* he said, *for we're old friends. Please her and that's the making of you.*

George's sun-heavy memories of Lord Edgerton and Dr. Toombs and Lady Weathersfield rattled about in his brain, twisting and entangling themselves most horribly as he lurched and bounced along atop his lumpish steed. Dr. Toombs's derisive snorts wove themselves into Lady Weathersfield's most amorous sighs, then were in turn braided up into Lord Edgerton's thunderous roars of laughter. Sunlight on the road before him hurt his eyes. His head began to throb, then to spin slightly as he reviewed the tale that he must tell should he encounter any overly inquisitive parties on the road. This same false history must also do to excuse and explain his presence before the servants once he arrived at Munscroft manor. The common folk were always given to frivolous chatter; it would not do at all should word leak out before he had fulfilled his task to the satisfaction of all concerned.

"I have come at the request of Lord Edgerton to study certain monastic manuscripts in the keeping of Sir Hadrian Ashgrave concerning the supposed medicinal qualities of local flora," George recited for the benefit of his horse's ears alone. "It is his lordship's hope that there may be something preserved in this ancient lore that will prove to be of use in advancing the cause of scientific inquiry in general and of modern *pharmacopoeia* in particular."

Having unburdened himself of this unwieldy bulk of verbiage, he shook his head. The excuse had been of Dr. Toombs's composition. Any servant overhearing such jabber would likely lose interest in anything further George might say, yet still decide to keep a curious eye on the young man's doings.

"We shall have to keep ourselves all the more secure from prying eyes, in that case," George remarked aloud. "That is all there is to it." And with this declaration of intent, he came very near to riding directly past the portal of Munscroft manor.

It was as if he turned aside from the rational world and passed into one fairy-haunted the instant that his horse clopped between the great black iron gates, each with its artful garniture of a gilded gaze-hound running beneath the curve of a crescent moon. The gates guarded an alleyway of trees so old and venerable in aspect that they had likely reached their full growth in an age when their majestic appearance must have drawn the worship of the local Druids. Beneath their heavy branches, shadows lurked and the few flashes of brightness amid the leafy dark might have been a touch of sunlight or the glint of ill-intentioned elfin eyes.

Even the gatekeeper seemed to belong more properly under a bridge, devouring passers-by who failed to read his riddles rightly, rather than minding the roadway to Sir Hadrian's fine residence. He afforded George no chance to rattle through the concocted reasons for his visit, but gnashed his stubby yellow teeth around the equally stubby mouthpiece of a white clay pipe and passed him in.

To his relief, George encountered a far more mundane reception awaiting him when he reached the manor house itself. Either the aged troll gatekeeper had dispatched word of his arrival via dark and mystic arts, or else (more likely) had sent along a boy to run ahead through sidepaths and byways and alert the hall. Whichever the case, by the time George came within hail of the house, a satisfactory number of Sir Hadrian's servants were already in place before the doors, anticipating him.

He was ushered into the house while many hands whisked away his horse and his scanty baggage (save only that one small brown leather box from which he would not be parted under any circumstances), whither he neither knew nor cared. The fellow who conducted him into Sir Hadrian's presence wore his livery as though it were sackcloth, and was in fact such a living exemplar of gloom that George decided here was Dr. Toombs's own soulmate. Together they passed through rooms whose furnishings and ornamentation offered satisfying harmonies of color and form to the eye. George found himself to be so taken up with silent admiration for Sir Hadrian's living arrangements that it was only gradually brought home to him that he was not being led to any particular room but rather through most of the house and out again by another way than that which had admitted him.

The sun was still warm when George's glum Virgil conducted him out-of-doors and into the heart of the manor house gardens. Curiosity became a secondary ache in George's saddle-ravaged bones. He had not been given so much as a cup of water to wet down the dust of travel. If he had allowed this glaring failure of hospitality to pass, it was only because he had expected to be brought before Sir Hadrian somewhere indoors, where the two of them might enjoy refreshment together. But this – ! Oversight easily metamorphosed into insult in George's mind. A man of limited means he might be, but he was still a gentleman; such treatment was not to be borne. By the time the servant conveyed him within the precincts of a small but perfectly kept rose garden, he was nursing the pique of a man far more significant than himself.

The rose garden was journey's end, for here Sir Hadrian himself stood ministering to the fragrant plants as if he were a common hired gardener. It was only a mercy ascribable in equal parts to Heaven and Lord Edgerton that George did not mistake the master for one of his men on the spot. Certainly such a blunder would have been understandable, in the circumstances: Sir Hadrian wore the simple garb of one who made his living grubbing in the dirt of other people's holdings, complete with a rustic's wide-brimmed straw hat. Fortunately, Lord Edgerton had seen fit to take George aside before his departure and familiarize him with his host's appearance by showing him a miniature of the man, for which considerate foresight the youth was deeply grateful.

Sir Hadrian was rapt in contemplation of his roses. It was only when the servant made a great noise of clearing his throat that the older man became aware that he was not alone. His cheerful countenance at once broke into an even more generous expression of joy as he came forward to bid George welcome to Munscroft. As the two gentlemen closed, George was at last able to see that what he had taken for simple gardener's garb was, in actuality, made of cloth too fine for any but a man of Sir Hadrian's rank to possess.

There is no evidence, however seemingly conclusive on the face of it, that can not be made to deceive. Again Dr. Toombs's dour judgment sounded in George's ear. *Rascals and charlatans are more pernicious in this nation than highwaymen, as pestiferous and vile an infestation as weevils in good bread.*

And Lord Edgerton's laugh once more preceded his remembered words:

Come, come, Dr. Toombs, why so bitter? It's not as if you were one of the king's examiners, taken like a plump pigeon by the plausible Mrs. Tofts! Or was her chicanery great enough that you must now take it upon yourself to decry all such possibilities for the honor of the medical profession in general?

In the garden, Sir Hadrian clasped George's free hand in his own, a gesture of such warmth and sincerity that the young man stood charmed on the spot. "You have come! And have you brought – ?" He glanced down at the leather box in George's unyielding grip. "Ah! Excellent." The older man removed his wide-brimmed hat to reveal the white cotton kerchief beneath. The weather had waxed warmer since George's arrival and the rose garden was for choice exposed to the best of the sun's nurturing rays. Sir Hadrian removed the kerchief and used it to mop his streaming face and clean-shaven head while he spoke. "I beg your pardon for this unworthy reception, but I was so eager for your arrival that I left word at the house that you must be brought straightaway into my presence the instant you reached us. Now that you are here, permit me to offer you a more fitting reception. Come! We shall have something cool to drink and something to stay our stomachs. My cook's skills are nothing beside those of Lord Edgerton's man, but I hope you will not find too much fault with the victuals. We live very simply here in the country."

Uttering these and similar sentiments, Sir Hadrian escorted George back to the house where, true to his word, they were served and well served with meat and drink that was simple yet satisfying. They took this refreshment not in the dining room of the manor house, but at a small table in Sir Hadrian's library. George observed closely how Sir Hadrian took especial pains to secure the doors of the room against the potential incursions of household staff. The doors themselves were thick and heavy, proof against the most determined eavesdropper. As for the keyhole, a favored tool of uninvited auditors everywhere, once Sir Hadrian had removed the key itself he stuffed the aperture with the same cloth which had insulated his head in the rose garden. When he had done with these precautions, he took his place at the table without further ado.

When they had done with the cold sliced beef, the bread and cheese and beer, Sir Hadrian sat back in his chair and announced, "So! To business, eh? You have been represented to me as a young man of rich intellectual gifts, a keen, inventive mind, and no patience with quackery. No doubt Lord Edgerton and Dr. Toombs have given you some notion of the problem here facing us all?"

George withdrew a little into himself. "Some, yes," he said, with the merest hint of hesitation. "And I hope with all my heart that this, my unworthy contrivance, may soon provide us with a satisfactory solution." He patted the leather box which he now balanced on his knees.

Sir Hadrian's chuckle put George in mind of a Drury Lane portrayal of that stock character, the Indulgent Father, so much so that the young man mused on whether or not his host had copied that very mannerism from the stage. So theatrical an affectation went well with Sir Hadrian's inclination for masquerading as the hired gardener among the roses. Perhaps there was nothing to it, yet on the other hand...George consecrated this observation to memory, for whatever it might be worth in future, and attended Sir Hadrian's words.

"My dear young friend," his host was saying, "you are too modest. Lord Edgerton has already communicated to me the wonders of your invention. He could not praise it or you highly enough. I am extremely grateful that you have consented to conceal its virtues from the world's inquiring eyes for only a little while longer, the better to serve our cause."

George lowered his eyes. If Sir Hadrian liked to think of him as a humble fellow, he would perform the role to the best of his ability. "How could I do less?" he asked, couching his voice barely above a murmur. "Lord Edgerton has been my patron; I am in his debt. Since he esteems you as his oldest and dearest friend, much concerned with the outcome of the present situation, I consider myself to be in your debt too."

"And in good company, eh?" Again the chuckle, this time with a shade more of the affected about it. Sir Hadrian was nervous and attempting to conceal the fact from his guest and would-be inquisitor. He did so poorly.

"Sir?"

"Nothing, nothing. Well then," said Sir Hadrian. "Has Lord Edgerton informed you *fully* of the conundrum before us?"

"So I hope, sir."

"Tell me then, young man, if you will do so as a favor to my gray hairs – " (Here Sir Hadrian passed one thick-fingered hand over the crest of his perfectly hairless skull and summoned up an ingenuous smile meant to charm utterly) " – what your initial reaction was when he took you into confidence in this...delicate matter."

"My reaction you well may guess," George replied. "I thought that his lordship was pleased to jest with me, a jape based on the late commotion surrounding Mrs. Tofts's grand deception."

"Not so grand, my boy, not so grand as all that." Sir Hadrian reached for the earthenware fruitbowl in the middle of the table and helped himself to a withered apple, a relic of autumn past. Paring it with a penknife he said, "For their vulgar scheme in pursuit of an undeserved pension, Mrs. Tofts and her husband *do* deserve a hanging, and that in short order." He spoke hotly, and for the first time in their brief acquaintance George saw Sir Hadrian in quite another light than that of the affable master of a bountiful domain. There was somewhat of the divinely possessed Old Testament prophet in him now, a transformation as startling as it was impressive.

"Sir Hadrian, you surprise me," George said, leaning forward to engage his host's regard. "Mrs. Tofts's deception was audacious, but hardly criminal to the degree that you suggest. When her stratagem was discovered, she and her husband were sent packing empty-handed, made public laughingstocks. Exposure and ridicule were surely punishment enough, to say nothing of the discomforts that foolish woman must have suffered during the execution of their scheme."

"Think you so?" Sir Hadrian now glowered at George as if the young man himself had been a willing and eager accomplice in the matter of the Toftses' failed cozenage. "I was told that besides your other natural gifts, you were also a young man of imagination. Can you not now bring that reputedly innovative mind of yours to the task of theorizing precisely how deeply that Tofts slut has harmed the cause of true scientific inquiry? Can you not see how her shameless fraud has made our own way out of darkness all the more difficult?"

George sighed and slumped back in his chair. "You are correct, Sir Hadrian, I freely cede the point. I well recall the hubbub that the Tofts case stirred up in the city. A simple country woman who claimed to have been assaulted by a rabbit of human size! Who could credit such a wild tale? And yet, I have seen the bones of giants laid out before my eyes, and the bones of dragons too. Dr. Toombs has some few precious examples of these in his possession; he assures me that all were excavated from English soil. If such things can be, why not a gigantic rabbit? Country folk have a reputation for speaking the truth because they lack the creative faculty for formulating complex lies."

"Spoken like one who has spent little or no time in the country." Sir Hadrian sounded weary. He carved small slices of yellow apple flesh from the peeled fruit in his hand and popped them into his mouth one by one. "And so, of course, when the Tofts trull was later brought to bed of not one, not two, but a whole warren of infant rabbits, that was all the scientific proof any man seemed to need." He spat out an errant apple seed and added, "Fools."

"They were not fools," George maintained, to not a little of Sir Hadrian's surprise. "Or at any rate their judgment in the matter of Mrs. Tofts's miraculous birthings was one that you yourself might have shared with them, given the evidence as they were allowed to view it. If you deem yourself wiser than they, it is only the gift of hindsight."

The younger man was satisfied to observe his host's stunned reaction to being thus gainsaid by someone both many years his junior and nowhere near his social equal. It was a bold stroke, and one which George had calculated on using here at Munscroft as he had used it many times before in London, to as good effect. He had learned early on that slavish toadying was not the way to win favor from Lord Edgerton and his ilk. Unvarnished sycophancy was too common a trait of those hopeful fishies who schooled around the great and the wealthy, gaping after preferment.

Ah, but to be so bold as to hold an opinion other than that of one's patrons, one's masters – ! Nay, to speak in flat contradiction when one had everything to lose by offending them – ! George could not begin to number the ladies and gentlemen of the peerage who had come to treat him with a respect in no way due his pocket nor his breeding thanks to this seemingly artless ploy.

"Is that so?" said Lord Hadrian. "You are *quite* certain that I would have been led the same dance as the rest?"

"The woman was sly and her husband was clever," George replied with a casual shrug of his shoulders. "Besides which, they had obviously resolved to go to any lengths required to establish the veracity of their claims. For her womb to appear to produce rabbits, the creatures must first be concealed somewhere within either the folds of her bed linen or her nightdress and then introduced to the womb itself. For the first stage, I believe she had sewn herself a nightdress of particular design, one concealing many deep and secret pockets, but for the illusion of the birth itself – " He could not repress a shudder at the thought. "It can not have been an experience that was other than painful, and yet she did it many times, for the eyes of many witnesses."

"A determined wench if nothing else," Sir Hadrian muttered.

"Determination will often carry the day against a host of nobler virtues," George said. "As will plain animal stubbornness."

Sir Hadrian grumbled something indistinguishable and got up to retrieve two white clay pipes from a rack near the hearth as well as a Delft jar of good Virginia tobacco. He filled both pipes and passed one to his guest before lighting them with a sliver of kindling wood. The library filled with clouds of aromatic smoke, to George's chagrin. He did not believe that such a censing could be very good for the books, although there were many of his former fellow scholars who assured him that tobacco fumes were a sovereign preventative against the depredations of bookworms and other vermin.

Once Sir Hadrian had taken the first few puffs at his pipe, he spoke again: "I believe that you are right after all, my boy: Had I been one of the first witnesses to Mrs. Tofts's sham I very likely would have been as readily deceived. Ingenuity and guile, both coupled with greed, tsk, where's the honest man can say he'd have the insight to escape the snares such a partnership might lay before his wit?"

"Even the king's own physician was gulled," George reminded him. "His Majesty stood ready to award the rustic charlatans a royal pension when the fraud was finally proven."

"And so easily," Sir Hadrian mused. "So simply it is a wonder none thought of it before the matter came so far. All it wanted was to confine the boldfaced hussy to a solitary room with no hope of communication with her husband nor with any other confidante or conspirator."

"I had heard that she was relegated to a hospital and kept under the eyes of female religious," George said. "This confinement ended in no further births, but rather a full confession, and there was an end to it."

"So, just so," Sir Hadrian agreed. He shifted himself in his chair, then added, "Permit me to assure you, my lad, that our case is nothing like the Tofts affair. For myself, I assure you that I neither seek nor require a pension from His Majesty. As for the notoriety which this matter will no doubt elicit, I dread it. I would be a far happier man were there some guarantee that no news whatsoever of the phenomenon escape the bounds of Munscroft. I am fond of the peaceful life, you see."

"But it will be noised about, sir," George pointed out. "You can not have imagined that it would be otherwise."

"No, of course not." Sir Hadrian took another pull at his pipe and let the smoke escape his lips borne on a worldweary sigh. "Had it been left to me, I would not have spoken of the matter to another soul. But the choice was never mine. She came to me in an unlucky hour, and in worse circumstances. Lord Edgerton was visiting with me at the time."

"His lordship bids me remind you that he is determined to keep his word concerning the absolute secrecy shrouding the matter," George felt bound to interject. "Naturally he has taken Dr. Toombs into his confidence, but no one else."

"No one but you, eh?" Sir Hadrian's kindly eyes recovered a little of their old twinkle. "And your device. How long will it be, do you think, before such wonderful contrivances eliminate entirely the need for men like Dr. Toombs?"

"Never, I trust." George thought the moment apt for another touch of becoming humility. "I am nowhere near his equal in knowledge."

"Knowledge which is old and hidebound, knowledge which must make way for fresh inquiry." Sir Hadrian arose from his chair and knocked the last few embers from his pipe into the fireplace. "Nothing like the new wisdom for which we all soon must praise young men of science like you."

"Thank you, sir." George was already on his feet, having made haste to rise with his host. He mimicked the older man's business with his own pipe, although he found this somewhat difficult to do while still holding fast to the brown leather box. "And now, will it please you that we proceed? Lord Edgerton informed me that your last letter to him spoke of certain changes – ?"

"Yes." Sir Hadrian cut him off brusquely, again looking ill at ease. "The situation has not progressed as I anticipated. We had better settle it soon. Come along, lad, come along. You shall see for yourself." He linked arms with George and hurried him out of the library.

They rushed from the house itself as if Munscroft were aflame. George was astonished by his host's almost youthful fleetness of foot. Stables and herbaries, scatterings of grazing sheep and stands of leafy fruit trees, all passed before his eyes in a blur as Sir Hadrian hauled him along at the quickstep. At last, they entered a wildwood bordering a pasture where grass grew thick and lush. George wondered at this a little, for even a citified fellow like himself knew that Sir Hadrian's stock would fatten profitably on this land. And yet it stood untouched.

The meadow is the moat, he thought, *meant to keep away the questioning eyes of cowherds, and the wildwood is the closely guarded castle. Which means that soon enough I shall behold the princess in her tower.* He was rather proud of the image and resolved to employ it in a poem that he would write to further secure the affections and favors of Lady Weathersfield.

The "tower" turned out to be a rustic cottage in the heart of an old and well-established grove of oak and beech. A tiny vegetable garden had been hacked out of the soil beside the door and a few early shoots of greenery languished in what sunlight could penetrate the overreaching canopy of the great trees. An old woman armed with a hoe labored there, chopping at weeds.

"That is the girl's mother, Madame Christophe," Sir Hadrian whispered, laying a hand on George's sleeve. "They come of a respected Huguenot family although, alas, much diminished. The lady's brother was a silk merchant, a praiseworthy man and an excellent companion. Only death could abrogate the joy I took in his society." He paused, then shrugged. "But that is irrelevant. Let it suffice you to know that when the lady could no longer live in peace on her native soil for fear of religious persecution, she communicated her plight to me. For her brother's sake I welcomed her. She is a widow and has been my guest for upwards of three years."

George gave the laboring Frenchwoman a nervous sideways glance. "She does not seem to be aware of our presence."

"Age has made her somewhat dull of hearing. I'll draw her attention. Hoi! Madame Christophe! We've come!" He bellowed the greeting, causing the older woman to look up from her labors. She did not smile, which George thought a great pity, for she had one of those noble faces whose austere lineaments would be elevated from mere handsomeness to true beauty by a pleasant expression.

But then, what cause has she to smile? he reminded himself, and walked forward with Sir Hadrian to meet her.

Madame Christophe spoke a passable English, only slightly affected by the intonations of her native tongue. "I am pleased to make your acquaintance, Mr. Pengallen," she said, with an unmistakable touch of diffidence not lost on George.

"And I yours, *madame*. I trust that Sir Hadrian has told you of my purpose?"

"He has." Her tongue was ice.

"Then perhaps he has not informed you in sufficient detail. Permit me to assure you that I will offer your daughter neither offense nor the least harm." He raised the box almost to eye level for her inspection. "This device is perfectly – "

"I don't care if you've packed half of hell in that thing!" Madame Christophe spat. Her vehemence came as a blow, and, for an instant, George felt his innards shrink under a gaze as severe and penetrating as that of any judge who had just donned the black cap of the death sentence. "It is no more nor less than what she merits. Do with her what you please." With that she turned her back on him and stiffly led the way through the cottage door.

The interior of the cottage was scrupulously clean, at least as far as George could tell by the scant light which the two small windows admitted. It consisted of a single space which had been divided in two by a crude canvas curtain. Madame Christophe drew this aside with neither comment nor ceremony, revealing a bed whose rich wood, fine workmanship, and ample furnishings made it stand out freakishly from its humble surroundings, like a duchess on a dunghill. There sat the girl, propped up on a monstrous pile of pillows and bolsters, her body heaped with bed linens despite the summer weather. At first George viewed her as no more than his goal, a random shape, a gaming piece awaiting the player's hand, but then his eyes became accustomed to the miserly light and for the first time he truly *saw* her.

She was beautiful enough to make a man forget to breathe. Hair the color of ripe wheat was drawn tightly into a single plait which coiled across her bosom like a golden chain. Her eyes had that same open and artless appearance peculiar to very young children, and yet their emerald depths shone with a look of intelligence and eager inquiry that was both flattering and fascinating. A shy smile curved the corners of her mouth, a charming expression whose brief life was cut short by an abrupt bark of reprimand from Madame Christophe. At her mother's word she immediately lowered her eyes and turned her face away from the two men, a rush of rosy color drowning her pale cheeks.

"My daughter Marie." Madame Christophe spoke the girl's name as if her mouth held a bite of sour plum. "She will answer all your questions; I have told her to do so, although I do not see what good it will do or how it will change her circumstances. We are shamed. I am shamed."

"*Madame*, do not be hasty," George tried to reassure her. "It may be that your daughter's story will prove – "

"She is a *fool!*" The older woman's shout echoed strangely in the confines of the cottage. "Do not mistake me for one as well. I would never have come before our benefactor as she did, with so great a burden of brazen nonsense on my lips."

"But *maman,* it was not –" The girl's protests were weak and quickly squelched by a sharp slap from her mother.

"Be silent! Oh, if only I had been at home that day! I would have taught you the wisdom of a well-governed tongue. But I was in the village, gone to market to satisfy *your* vanity. My lady must have ribbons to deck her dress! And to deck *this?*" With one unexpected movement Madame Christophe seized the bedclothes shielding her daughter's body and flung them aside, revealing the girl in nothing but her nightclothes. The mound of her belly rose up beneath its thin covering of linen like a beehive.

George could not repress a gasp at the sight. In his life he had seen women great with child, but this bordered on the unbelievable. "Sir Hadrian," he said, his voice faltering, "was not Lord Edgerton your guest when this girl came before you with her tale?"

"He was." Sir Hadrian no longer seemed inclined to play the garrulous host.

"But – but that was not three months ago."

"In April."

"And was she so advanced in her condition then?"

"No." The master of Munscroft pursed his lips. "There was not even the slightest swelling of her belly then. These are the changes of which I wrote Lord Edgerton."

"Impossible." George shook his head vigorously, his true mission cast violently from his mind for the moment. "Incredible. To come to such a size in three months' time of the supposed assault – !"

"Yes, incredible." Sir Hadrian looked grim. "Worse than that, plausible only in the face of accepting her story as she tells it. And that, lad, is a thing we dare not do."

"No?" George could not take his eyes from the girl's enormous belly. It exercised a horrific, hypnotic spell over him that not even the perfections of Mademoiselle Christophe's person had the power to break. "Wh – why not?"

"For the sake of science," Sir Hadrian replied, and again George noted the look of nigh spiritual transformation that passed over his host's face. "For the sake of holy reason."

"Sir, how can you say such a thing?"

"How can I say aught *but* such a thing?" Sir Hadrian countered. He turned his attention to the girl in the bed. By this time Mademoiselle Christophe was weeping softly, with scarcely any sound to accompany the limpid tears cascading down her cheeks. "My dear," he said to her in his most kindly, least genuine voice. "My dear, I fear that our young Mr. Pengallen comes to us affected by the second-hand testimony of my good friend, Lord Edgerton. You remember him, do you not? He was the gentleman in my company on the day you burst into my library to recount your ordeal. As I recall, he left us rather precipitously after that."

"Yes." Marie raised her brimming eyes to meet Sir Hadrian's gaze. George thought his heart must stop at so piercingly tender a look. "Yes, I remember him. I am afraid that he – like you – thought me mad."

"Tut-tut, my child, I have never called you mad, have I?" Sir Hadrian patted her hand, under Madame Christophe's flinty eye. "Make no false assumptions. I am a man of science, albeit my specific inquiries have been limited by circumstance to the study of roses. Still, I value above all things the ability to keep an open mind, as does Mr. Pengallen himself. Tell him, I entreat you, in your own words, how you came to be in this condition."

"Yes, speak up, girl." Madame Christophe gave her daughter an ungentle touch on the shoulder. "But do not elaborate. You are in enough trouble as matters stand without decking out your sins in fabrications."

"Hush, madame, let her speak," Sir Hadrian said. "There is no proof as yet to brand her a liar." Madame Christophe only grumbled something unintelligible in her native tongue and subsided into brooding silence.

The girl drew a deep breath that rasped over a quantity of still unshed tears. "It was the fifth of April." Her English was melodious, her lilting accent an ornament rather than a flaw. "Maman had gone to the village, as she has said. I was alone in the cottage and, having finished my household duties, wanted some way in which to pass the time until she might return."

"You might have found some other employment than wanton rambling over the entire countryside," her mother broke in sternly. "Had you given yourself to your prayerbook, you should not now stand in want of God's mercy."

"Madame, I implore you, let the child speak," said Sir Hadrian.

Madame Christophe glowered at him. "She has said too much already. I cannot endure hearing her lies told and told again, and so audaciously! Was it to this end that I begged this humble dwelling of you? When we first came here, you offered to share the comforts of your home with us, but I refused. I feared that if we stayed beneath your roof my girl might attract the notice of some overbold servant. I thought to raise her here, in solitude, far from all the blandishments of men and the temptations of the flesh." She laughed; it was a hollow, bitter sound.

"*Maman, maman,* I swear to you, no man has touched me!" Marie cried, grasping for her mother's hands wildly. "If you will not believe me, then summon a midwife and let her testify to my virginity!"

Madame Christophe drew back from her daughter's pleading gestures as if from the edge of the Pit itself. "Bah! After what you claim befell you, what can be left of your maidenhead but tatters?"

"But I have told you, he never did – !"

"Harlot! Boldfaced whore!"

George felt a great anger growing hot within him. He could not bear Marie's patent anguish, nor to witness her mother's adamant want of pity. He strode up to Madame Christophe, took her firmly by the shoulders, and propelled her toward the door of her own house, saying the while, "Madame, I think it best if I hear the remainder of your child's statement privily."

"Yes, yes," Sir Hadrian said, taking the widow's arm and doing his part to hurry her from the cottage. "He's right, there can be no harm in it, you and I shall be right outside."

"The harm is done," Madame Christophe asserted, but she did not struggle, fearing perhaps to irk her benefactor. Thus it was that George soon found himself alone with the still weeping Marie.

"*Mademoiselle,* take comfort," he said gently, stealing near to her bedside. "I do not come to judge you. I believe you have been judged enough, and over-hastily. Pray continue with your account."

The exquisite girl wiped her eyes with a bit of her bed linens and gulped back her sorrow. "Thank you, sir, you are good to me," she said. "*Maman* too is good, only she has been driven almost frantic by what has happened to us both since I made the mistake of telling Sir Hadrian and his friend that – "

"Forget your good mother," George counseled her, his words warm and wheedling. "Forget Sir Hadrian and Lord Edgerton. Tell *me.*"

"Very well." Like a schoolboy called upon to recite, the girl composed herself, clasped her hands over the parlous swelling of her belly, and began: "I have already told you that I wanted entertainment that day, and so I thought to take a walk in the woodland. I have always enjoyed such rambles. It is quite safe; I once heard Sir Hadrian tell *maman* that his gamekeepers are the terror of tramps and poachers."

"Indeed," said George, but as he feasted his eyes upon Marie's beauty a crooked thought wriggled through his mind: *The gamekeepers guard the land, yet who guards the guardians? Still, if her belly's the work of one of Sir Hadrian's gamekeepers, why would she seek to excuse it with so grotesque a tale? Unless... Perhaps it was not the man who used her, but the master. She is loveliness itself; Sir Hadrian's old, not dead.*

If he enjoyed her person against her will, no doubt he saw it as the natural perquisite of his charity to her mother and herself. And what recourse could she hope for? None. She and her mother are entirely dependent upon him and she knows it. Lesser burdens of the mind than this have driven women mad.

"I came to a lake that lies not far from this house," Marie continued, unaware of how George's thoughts inclined. "It is a place I know well. It is very small, truly little more than a pond, perfectly round and with waters silvery and cool as the face of the moon. I think that it is no natural place, for smooth stones ring the shore."

"Perhaps it is the relic of some long-lost Roman villa," George suggested. "Was it there it happened? By the lake?"

The girl nodded, and fresh tears welled up unbidden in her eyes. "I did not see him approach. I was seated on one of the flat stones, gazing into the water, when I felt a damp warmth on the nape of my neck. I looked up and he was at my shoulder."

"Impossible," George objected. "There, so suddenly, with not even a reflection cast in the water to forewarn you?"

"Nothing." Marie took a deep breath and released a ragged sigh. "At first I did not fear him. He was so beautiful. I had never seen his like in life before. Oh, how he shone! White, whiter than clouds, or new milk, or good bread! Once I saw a picture of such as he, a weaving that hangs in Sir Hadrian's own house. The creature depicted there is a scrawny thing, with a goat's beard and a horn like a peeled twig. Mine was not like that: he was magnificence itself. His horn soared from the center of his brow like a sword made of starlight. I reached out to touch it; I looked into his eyes and saw all my dreams."

George regarded the enraptured girl askance. *No doubt, then,* he thought. *Unless she ends this story by claiming she was raped by Europa's own bull, minus one horn, it is a unicorn she means. A unicorn!*

A unicorn! cried Dr. Toombs. And you did not at once chain her up safe? The girl's a bedlamite or I'm a Turk! His phantom face scowled upon the air between George and Marie as the girl went on to speak of how the beast, her beast, her unicorn, had changed from wondrous apparition to present horror.

She claimed the brute, all unexpectedly, dealt her a hard blow to the temple with his horn so that she fell into the lake. George's recollection of Lord Edgerton mouthed almost the selfsame words Marie now recited for him. The peer's mouth twitched as if he could not resolve whether to recount the story soberly or as a jest. *And indeed she was drenched to the bone when she burst into the library, that much is fact.* She claimed to recall little after that, save only the sight of the creature looming over her through the water, hooves flailing. *Then it lowered its horn to touch the surface of the pool, which sent a sudden heat through all her limbs and then, said she, oblivion. She regained her senses on the lakeshore with no idea of how she'd come to escape drowning. She came to us directly thereafter.*

Dr. Toombs sniffed. *And what of other evidence than that? No sign of bruises? Of blood?*

None. At the time I thought it might be wise to summon a midwife from the village to examine the girl, but Sir Hadrian forbade it.

On what grounds?

What other? The Tofts case. My dear Dr. Toombs, for all Sir Hadrian's piping paeans in praise of reason, he is wholly unreasonable upon that subject. One hearing of the girl's account was enough to send him into fits of dire suspicion. He dreads that the sacred honor of science will be besmirched yet again if word of this gets out.

You mean he believes she intends to follow the Tofts's example in the promotion of her own interests? How, in God's name? Is she determined to birth a herd of unicorns? Dr. Toombs might have laughed then, had it been in his nature. *Bah! Empty fears. Sir Hadrian lives in the country and controls the girl's comings and goings: Who will ever hear of this folderol beyond the bounds of Munscroft if he will not have it so?*

Ah, but you see, word has escaped. Lord Edgerton's eyes sparkled and he touched his chest. *Behold the very vessel of that fugitive word.*

You? You're not fool enough to speak of such nonsense publicly.

You know that to be true, as do I, as does our young friend Pengallen here. Sir Edgerton's specter gestured at George even as Marie described her tearful interview with Sir Hadrian and his friend. *And yet I have written to Sir Hadrian saying that my silence is not...reliable. For you see, I have told him – one man of science to another – that it is my belief that we must keep an open mind in all matters of natural history which remain in scientific question.*

But a unicorn! Dr. Toombs's look of consternation was almost comic. *Insane. Absurd.*

Why? Because you have never seen one? Lord Edgerton was pleased to twit his friend. *You have never seen Virginia either, and yet you easily accept that distant land's existence.*

That is different, Dr. Toombs sputtered. *There is evidence: traders' and travelers' testimony, trade goods, most excellent tobacco –*

Just as there may very well be evidence of unicorns presently dwelling in Mademoiselle Christophe's great belly. Lord Edgerton grinned. *We shall just have to wait and see, hm? Or so I told Sir Hadrian. You may imagine his alarm, and for a reason less fanciful than that his woods may be infested with liquorish beasts.*

Eh?

Marie Christophe was speaking of a gamekeeper's report, a Mayday tale of a strange creature glimpsed in the woodland, shot at, likely dealt a deathwound

to judge by the copious trail of strangely colored blood it left in its wake before
blood trail and creature both vanished utterly at the margin of the same lake of
Marie's tearful telling, but George heard only his own voice, explaining things
to Dr. Toombs:

Sir Hadrian is reason's fool, devoted to preserving the sacred name of science at all costs.
He cherishes its pristine reputation as dearly as he does his own – so Lord Edgerton tells me
– and flies into a passion at the least threat to it.

You know this to be true, Lord Edgerton reminded Dr. Toombs. You have yourself
witnessed his bloodthirsty cries for retribution against the Toftses.

The man's possessed on the subject, Dr. Toombs muttered.

He is also, alas, possessed of an equally fanatic zeal in the matter of collecting certain
– George glanced at Lord Edgerton and received the peer's reluctant nod for him
to conclude: – debts.

You've not yet repaid him that sum you owe? Dr. Toombs goggled. Good Lord, do you
know how long it's been that – ?

I know, Lord Edgerton snarled. I will not have you shame me for it any more than I
will allow that fool Hadrian the liberty.

But Sir Hadrian has his own shame to cover, George put in, and that will be Lord
Edgerton's salvation. He forbade the summoning of a midwife. Why? There can be but one
logical reason: the woman would discover that the girl's condition was too far advanced for
her misfortune to have occurred that day. Revelation would bring questioning, questioning
under which the girl might – with witnesses present – at last most artfully confess that her
tale of rampant unicorns was the product of a momentary madness brought on by her desperate secret.

To wit, that Sir Hadrian himself had long enjoyed her favors, Lord Edgerton interrupted.

Hmm, now that's the first sensible explanation I've heard in the case. Dr. Toombs
stroked his chin. It would seem that the dilemma which holds Sir Hadrian has two horns,
not one. If he presses the girl to speak the truth, his precious reputation's tarred with the
whoremaster's brush, yet if he lends even the least credence to her extraordinary tale –

– he imperils the still more precious reputation of pure science, George concluded.

Nor can he avoid the need to make that choice, Lord Edgerton said. For I was there to
hear her speak, and I will ever be there to remind him of this. Bastard or beast, what does the
girl's womb carry? There's the question! He laughed.

A question you're willing to set aside for the price of your debt. Dr. Toombs's expression was equally divided between admiration and distaste. Yet are you certain your
sheep will run the way you wish to drive them? I know how much you owe him: it would
be cheaper for Sir Hadrian to hire some servant to admit paternity than to forgive you so
great a sum.

Which is why I have built my fences sturdy and straight, all the way to the shearing shed, Lord Edgerton said. *And hired me a clever sheepdog into the bargain. Is that not so, Pengallen?*

Just so, my lord. And George reached out to open the small brown leather box on the table.

"What is that thing?" Marie exclaimed, all apprehension.

"Do not be afraid," George told her, taking the coils of wire and the polished copper paddles from the box. "You will feel nothing beyond a slight tingling, if that." He flicked back a latch sealing an inner compartment of the box and produced a thin piece of ordinary slate, then took a small brush and bottle from the leather loops securing them to the box's inner lid and proceeded to paint the slate with a reeking, viscous emulsion. "When I have finished my preparations for the imager, I will summon your mother and Sir Hadrian. All will be conducted in an atmosphere of the strictest propriety and respect, I promise you."

Overcome by some inexplicable instinct, Marie leaned forward to shield her belly. "What do you mean to do?"

"Nothing that will hurt you." George smiled persuasively. "I have already employed this invention of mine many times in the best homes in London. I call it an imager, for it uses the principles of magnetism to detect the vital emanations of the fetus and translate these into an image of the same." Seeing her bewilderment, he explained, "It makes a picture of the contents of the womb."

George had to repeat his explanation shortly later, after he had recalled Madame Christophe and Sir Hadrian for the performance. He took pleasure in the way their eyes devoured the device, curiosity warring with confusion, but he did not allow this enjoyment to distract him. There was a certain deftness of hand required to bring the plan to fruition. The blank slate must be inserted into its proper compartment in such a way as to make it seem that he opened the identical compartment when the so-called imaging was accomplished. In fact he would open an entirely different slot within the box and extract an entirely – and significantly – different slate.

I wrote to Sir Hadrian, telling him that your device is near perfection. Lord Edgerton's phantom beamed in George's memory.

A pity it's a fraud, mused Dr. Toombs. *An invention like this would be in high demand, particularly by those much-traveled men who would be assured of their wives' honesty in matters of strapping babes born a mere six months after their return home.*

Sir Hadrian, in turn, confides in me his certainty that it will reveal Mademoiselle Christophe's embarrassment was conceived at a time when he was himself abroad, and thus – how did he put it? – "unhappily unable to supervise the girl's moral comportment," Lord Edgerton went on. *In other words, he expects your "invention" to clear him of all suspicion of paternity, and has hinted that he will become your patron in marketing the device should he be impressed by the results.*

Oh, he shall be impressed by them, my lord, George replied.

"It is done. You may remove the magnets." George fiddled with the useless knobs and switches cluttering the interior of the box while Madame Christophe withdrew the copper paddles which she had, until then, been holding to the sides of her daughter's belly. Sir Hadrian came forward to undo the small leather harnesses attaching the magnets to the paddles and carefully replaced them in their separate cases, as George had previously instructed him to do. "Now!" George pretended to undo the latch of the first compartment, but in truth touched the almost invisible button securing its brother and extracted the second slate. "Now we shall see how well developed this – *Dear God in heaven!*"

It was a fine performance if he did say so himself. The shock, the horror, the helpless manner in which he groped for words and at last could do no more than surrender the previously etched slate for Sir Hadrian's inspection.

"Merciful Lord," Sir Hadrian breathed, staring at the image of a creature half human, half equine, its brow already sprouting the nub of a horn.

"It is a monster," Madame Christophe cried, casting her arms around her daughter. "Oh, my poor child!"

"Nay, *madame*, it is a miracle," George corrected her. "A miracle which must be laid before the world."

"No, no, it must not." Sir Hadrian wrung his hands. "There must be some mistake."

"How can you doubt the evidence of your eyes?" George demanded.

"The evidence of an unproved device!" Sir Hadrian's face was flushed.

"Proof will come," George said. "The incontrovertible proof of birth. In the meanwhile, I must go back to London. This is the new *stupor mundi*; it must be made known." He made a great business of packing up the box.

"Stay." Sir Hadrian's grip on George's arm was astoundingly strong for a man of his years. "I tell you, we must keep this secret. Suppose your device is accurate? Suppose the girl gives birth to such a beast as its powers foretell? What then remains impossible? What man of science will then be able to stand against the army of charlatans that will arise, each claiming that they have conceived a whole menagerie of wonders? For every truth, a thousand Toftses, and reason trampled in the dust beneath their feet!"

"And if my invention's reading is proved wrong?" George inquired.

"After you have made your great noise of it in London?" Sir Hadrian was grim. "You know without my telling you: they will call you a fraud, and they will say the same of me."

"Oh, surely not!" George feigned alarm. "Your reputation – "

"Than which there is no more fragile thing."

"Sir, I sympathize, but I am, as you yourself have said, a man of science. I cannot in good conscience conceal this potential marvel from my colleagues. If there were some way by which I might assume full responsibility for the girl until the birth, dissociate her from you completely, I would do so, but I fear I lack the means." He spoke more and more rapidly, the goal in sight. Before half a dozen breaths he intended to persuade Sir Hadrian that Lord Edgerton might be willing to accept guardianship of the girl – and the fame or infamy attending the same – if only that small matter of a certain debt might possibly be...

He never got the chance. A scream of unearthly agony tore the air of the cottage. "*Mon Dieu!*" Madame Christophe exclaimed as her daughter's fingers dug into her arms and the girl's knees drew themselves up sharply to meet the now violently heaving curve of her belly.

"It can not be!" cried Sir Hadrian, gaping in horror at the girl's sudden labor. "Now? So soon? Dear heaven, are we to birth a monster?"

There was no time to answer him, whether or not he expected any answer. Marie's back arched, bending her spine like a bow. The force of the convulsion hurled her mother halfway across the room. George threw himself forward, vainly seeking to lay hold of the girl's thrashing limbs, only to have his ears riven by a shriek that climbed the rafters of the cottage. Then it was over almost as suddenly as it had begun. The shriek was cut off as if by a sword's blow. With a final shake, her body went limp. The room was still.

George knelt upon the bed beside the dead girl, gathering her to him, rags and bones. The hideous bulge of her belly was gone. She was hardly any burden in his arms.

"Look," said Madame Christophe quietly, coming up behind him. "Look there." At first George thought she meant that he must look at the bed itself, at the inexplicable absence of any stain upon the sheets save only the dampness of sweat. Then she reached past him, past Marie's eternity-fixed eyes, and tugged aside the hem of her daughter's crumpled nightdress.

The white thing that lay curled there, velvet muzzle half veiled by silken tail, was hardly bigger than a month-grown hound pup. It seemed to sense the weight of their stares, for it lifted up its head to confront them, cheeks still damp with a fluid that smelled of linden blossom and pine. Its eyes held every possibility but fear.

I am mad, George thought as, still cradling Marie's small corpse, he watched the shimmering spot upon the creature's brow slowly grow into the certainty of the starbright horn. *Oh, I hope that I am mad!*

With a hoarse, inarticulate cry, Sir Hadrian cast his full weight across the bed, seized the newborn creature by the base of the neck, and jerked the head back suddenly. There was a snap.

"There," he said, letting the dead thing fall against the sheets. He pushed himself off the bed and brushed off his hands with the air of a man well satisfied with a good day's work. "That's an end of it." He was still smoothing down his rumpled clothes when he became aware of the looks Madame Christophe and George were giving him. "Well?" he demanded, his face reddening. "Can such monsters live and this remain a rational world?"

Madame Christophe opened her mouth as if she might desire to reply, but then she closed it and instead burst into tears. George hardly felt it when she took her daughter's body from his arms.

"You there," said Sir Hadrian. He nodded curtly at George. "When you return to London, you may tell Lord Edgerton that the poor girl died in childbed, her infant with her."

"Sir, I – "

"Moreover, in view of your services to me in a difficult time, I have elected to reward you generously, both for the use of your invention – imperfect though its properties have proved to be – as well as for your discretion. You will, I hope, likewise convey to Lord Edgerton my assurances that his own discretion will be equally appreciated. And acknowledged. To this end you will deliver to him a certain paper which I shall – "

George heard no more. Sir Hadrian's words buzzed in his ears like sun-drowsy bees. He gazed to where Madame Christophe sat rocking her child's dead body on her knees, then looked down upon the corpse of the creature to which the maiden had given life at the cost of her own. He wondered whether Sir Hadrian's chosen gods, Science and Reason, would ever yield anything half so beautiful.

Such monsters as he and I can live, he thought, watching as death filmed over the seablue eye of the unicorn, and this remain a rational world. He saw the gates of Bedlam yawn before him as he felt both the world and reason receding from him at a great rate. He laughed once, for the last time, and gladly let them go.

Sunbird

Neil Gaiman

Neil Gaiman (*www.neilgaiman.com*) lives in Menominee, Wisconsin. For over twenty years as a professional writer, Neil Gaiman has been one of the top writers in modern comics, the writer of *Sandman*. He is now a bestselling novelist, whose 2005 novel for adults is *Anansi Boys*. The film *Mirrormask*, written by Gaiman and directed by Dave McKean, a visually rich fantasy with strong appeal to the adolescent in all of us, was released in the fall of 2005, at the same time as the novel. Some of his short fiction is collected in *Angels and Visitations* (1993), *Smoke and Mirrors: Short Fictions and Illusions* (1997), and *Adventures in the Dream Trade* (2002).

"Sunbird" was published by *McSweeney's* in the original anthology (with a fifty-one-word title beginning with) *Noisy Outlaws,...* This is a story about the legend of the phoenix, told in the style of R. A. Lafferty. This is not a pale shadow of classic Lafferty, but a bright reflection. Wow!

THEY WERE A RICH AND A ROWDY BUNCH at the Epicurean Club in those days. They certainly knew how to party. There were five of them:

There was Augustus TwoFeathers McCoy, big enough for three men, who ate enough for four men and who drank enough for five. His great-grandfather had founded the Epicurean Club with the proceeds of a tontine which he had taken great pains, in the traditional manner, to ensure that he had collected in full.

There was Professor Mandalay, small and twitchy and grey as a ghost (and perhaps he was a ghost; stranger things have happened) who drank nothing but water, and who ate doll-portions from plates the size of saucers. Still, you do not need the gusto for the gastronomy, and Mandalay always got to the heart of every dish placed in front of him.

There was Virginia Boote, the food and restaurant critic, who had once been a great beauty but was now a grand and magnificent ruin, and who delighted in her ruination.

There was Jackie Newhouse, the descendant (on the left-handed route) of the great lover, gourmand, violinist and duelist Giacomo Casanova. Jackie Newhouse had, like his notorious ancestor, both broken his share of hearts and eaten his share of great dishes.

And there was Zebediah T. Crawcrustle, who was the only one of the Epicureans who was flat-out broke: he shambled in unshaven from the street when they had their meetings, with half a bottle of rotgut in a brown-paper bag, hatless and coatless and, too often, partly shirtless, but he ate with more of an appetite than any of them.

Augustus TwoFeathers McCoy was talking –

"We have eaten everything that can be eaten," said Augustus TwoFeathers McCoy, and there was regret and glancing sorrow in his voice. "We have eaten vulture, mole, and fruitbat."

Mandalay consulted his notebook. "Vulture tasted like rotten pheasant. Mole tasted like carrion slug. Fruitbat tasted remarkably like sweet guinea pig."

"We have eaten kakopo, aye-aye, and giant panda – "

"Oh, that broiled panda steak," sighed Virginia Boote, her mouth watering at the memory.

"We have eaten several long-extinct species," said Augustus TwoFeathers McCoy. "We have eaten flash-frozen mammoth and Patagonian giant sloth."

"If we had but gotten the mammoth a little faster," sighed Jackie Newhouse. "I could tell why the hairy elephants went so fast, though, once people got a taste of them. I am a man of elegant pleasures, but after but one bite, I found myself thinking only of Kansas City barbecue sauce, and what the ribs on those things would be like, if they were fresh."

"Nothing wrong with being on ice for a millennium or two," said Zebediah T. Crawcrustle. He grinned. His teeth may have been crooked, but they were sharp and strong. "But for real taste you had to go for honest-to-goodness mastodon every time. Mammoth was always what people settled for, when they couldn't get mastodon."

"We've eaten squid, and giant squid, and humongous squid," said Augustus TwoFeathers McCoy. "We've eaten lemmings and Tasmanian tigers. We've eaten bower bird and ortolan and peacock. We've eaten the dolphin fish (which is not the mammal dolphin) and the giant sea turtle and the Sumatran Rhino. We've eaten everything there is to eat."

"Nonsense. There are many hundreds of things we have not yet tasted," said Professor Mandalay. "Thousands perhaps. Think of all the species of beetle there are, still untasted."

"Oh Mandy," sighed Virginia Boote. "When you've tasted one beetle, you've tasted them all. And we all tasted several hundred species. At least the dung-beetles had a real kick to them."

"No," said Jackie Newhouse, "that was the dung-beetle balls. The beetles themselves were singularly unexceptional. Still, I take your point. We have scaled the heights of gastronomy, we have plunged down into the depths of gustation. We have become cosmonauts exploring undreamed-of worlds of delectation and gourmanderie."

"True, true, true," said Augustus TwoFeathers McCoy. "There has been a meeting of the Epicureans every month for over a hundred and fifty years, in my father's time, and my grandfather's time, and my great-grandfather's time, and now I fear that I must hang it up for there is nothing left that we, or our predecessors in the club, have not eaten."

"I wish I had been here in the Twenties," said Virginia Boote, "when they legally had Man on the menu."

"Only after it had been electrocuted," said Zebediah T. Crawcrustle. "Half-fried already it was, all char and crackling. It left none of us with a taste for long pig, save for one who was already that way inclined, and he went out pretty soon after that anyway."

"Oh, Crusty, *why* must you pretend that you were there?" asked Virginia Boote, with a yawn. "Anyone can see you aren't that old. You can't be more than sixty, even allowing for the ravages of time and the gutter."

"Oh, they ravage pretty good," said Zebediah T. Crawcrustle. "But not as good as you'd imagine. Anyway there's a host of things we've not eaten yet."

"Name one," said Mandalay, his pencil poised precisely above his notebook.

"Well, there's Suntown Sunbird," said Zebediah T. Crawcrustle. And he grinned his crookedy grin at them, with his teeth ragged but sharp.

"I've never heard of it," said Jackie Newhouse. "You're making it up."

"I've heard of it," said Professor Mandalay. "But in another context. And besides, it is imaginary."

"Unicorns are imaginary," said Virginia Boote. "But gosh, that unicorn flank tartare was tasty. A little bit horsy, a little bit goatish, and all the better for the capers and raw quail eggs."

"There's something about Sunbirds in one of the minutes of the Epicurean Club from bygone years," said Augustus TwoFeathers McCoy. "But what it was, I can no longer remember."

"Did they say how it tasted?" asked Virginia.

"I do not believe that they did," said Augustus, with a frown. "I would need to inspect the bound proceedings, of course."

"Nah," said Zebediah T. Crawcrustle. "That's only in the charred volumes. You'll never find out about it from there."

Augustus TwoFeathers McCoy scratched his head. He really did have two feathers, which went through the knot of black-hair-shot-with-silver at the back of his head, and the feathers had once been golden although by now they were looking kind of ordinary and yellow and ragged. He had been given them when he was a boy.

"Beetles," said Professor Mandalay. "I once calculated that, if a man such as myself were to eat six different species of beetle each day, it would take him more than twenty years to eat every beetle that has been identified. And over that twenty years enough new species of beetle might have been discovered to keep him eating for another five years. And in those five years enough beetles might have been discovered to keep him eating for another two and a half years, and so on, and so on. It is a paradox of inexhaustibility. I call it Mandalay's Beetle. You would have to enjoy eating beetles, though," he added, "or it would be a very bad thing indeed."

"Nothing wrong with eating beetles if they're the right kind of beetle," said Zebediah T. Crawcrustle. "Right now, I've got a hankering on me for lightning bugs. There's a kick from the glow of a lightning bug that might be just what I need."

"While the lightning bug or firefly (Photinus pyralis) is more of a beetle than it is a glow-worm," said Mandalay, "they are by no stretch of the imagination edible."

"They may not be edible," said Crawcrustle. "But they'll get you into shape for the stuff that is. I think I'll roast me some. Fireflies and habanero peppers. Yum."

Virginia Boote was an eminently practical woman. She said, "Suppose we did want to eat Suntown Sunbird. Where should we start looking for it?"

Zebediah T. Crawcrustle scratched the bristling seventh-day beard that was sprouting on his chin (it never grew any longer than that; seventh-day beards never do). "If it was me," he told them, "I'd head down to Suntown of a noon in midsummer, and I'd find somewhere comfortable to sit – Mustapha Stroheim's coffee-house, for example, and I'd wait for the Sunbird to come by. Then I'd catch him in the traditional manner, and cook him in the traditional manner as well."

"And what would the traditional manner of catching him be?" asked Jackie Newhouse.

"Why, the same way your famous ancestor poached quails and wood-grouse," said Crawcrustle.

"There's nothing in Casanova's memoirs about poaching quail," said Jackie Newhouse.

"Your ancestor was a busy man," said Crawcrustle. "He couldn't be expected to write everything down. But he poached a good quail nonetheless."

"Dried corn and dried blueberries, soaked in whisky," said Augustus TwoFeathers McCoy. "That's how my folk always did it."

"And that was how Casanova did it," said Crawcrustle, "although he used barley-grains mixed with raisins, and he soaked the raisins in brandy. He taught me himself."

Jackie Newhouse ignored this statement. It was easy to ignore much that Zebediah T. Crawcrustle said. Instead, Jackie Newhouse asked, "And where is Mustapha Stroheim's coffee-house in Suntown?"

"Why, where it always is, third lane after the old market in the Suntown district, just before you reach the old drainage ditch that was once an irrigation canal, and if you find yourself in One-eye Khayam's Carpet shop you have gone too far," began Crawcrustle. "But I see by the expressions of irritation upon your faces that you were expecting a less succinct, less accurate, description. Very well. It is in Suntown, and Suntown is in Cairo, in Egypt, where it always is, or almost always."

"And who will pay for an expedition to Suntown?" asked Augustus TwoFeathers McCoy. "And who will be on this expedition? I ask the question although I already know the answer, and I do not like it."

"Why, you will pay for it, Augustus, and we will all come," said Zebediah T. Crawcrustle. "You can deduct it from our Epicurean membership dues. And I shall bring my chef's apron and my cooking utensils."

Augustus knew that Crawcrustle had not paid his Epicurean Club membership in much too long a time, but the Epicurean Club would cover him; Crawcrustle had been a member of the Epicureans in Augustus's father's day. He simply said, "And when shall we leave?"

Crawcrustle fixed him with a mad old eye, and shook his head in disappointment. "Why, Augustus," he said. "We're going to Suntown, to catch the Sunbird. When else should we leave?"

"Sunday!" sang Virginia Boote. "Darlings, we'll leave on a Sunday!"

"There's hope for you yet, young lady," said Zebediah T. Crawcrustle. "We shall leave Sunday indeed. Three Sundays from now. And we shall travel to Egypt. We shall spend several days hunting and trapping the elusive Sunbird of Suntown, and, finally, we shall deal with it in the traditional way."

Professor Mandalay blinked a small grey blink. "But," he said. "I am teaching a class on Monday. On Mondays I teach mythology, on Tuesdays I teach tapdancing, and on Wednesdays, woodwork."

"Get a teaching assistant to take your course, Mandalay O Mandalay. On Monday you'll be hunting the Sunbird," said Zebediah T. Crawcrustle. "And how many other professors can say that?"

They went, one by one, to see Crawcrustle, in order to discuss the journey ahead of them, and to announce their misgivings.

Zebediah T. Crawcrustle was a man of no fixed abode. Still, there were places he could be found, if you were of a mind to find him. In the early mornings he slept in the bus terminal, where the benches were comfortable and the transport police were inclined to let him lie; in the heat of the afternoons he hung in the park by the statues of long-forgotten generals, with the dipsos and the winos and the hopheads, sharing their company and the contents of their bottles, and offering his opinion, which was, as that of an Epicurean, always considered and always respected, if not always welcomed.

Augustus TwoFeathers McCoy sought Crawcrustle out in the park; he had with him his daughter, Hollyberry NoFeathers McCoy. She was small, but she was sharp as a shark's tooth.

"You know," said Augustus, "there is something very familiar about this."

"About what?" asked Zebediah.

"All of this. The expedition to Egypt. The Sunbird. It seemed to me like I heard about it before."

Crawcrustle merely nodded. He was crunching something from a brown-paper bag.

Augustus said, "I went to the bound annals of the Epicurean Club, and I looked it up. And there was what I took to be a reference to the Sunbird in the index for forty years ago, but I was unable to learn anything more than that."

"And why was that?" asked Zebediah T. Crawcrustle, swallowing noisily.

Augustus TwoFeathers McCoy sighed. "I found the relevant page in the annals," he said, "but it was burned away, and afterwards there was some great confusion in the administration of the Epicurean Club."

"You're eating lightning bugs from a paper bag," said Hollyberry NoFeathers McCoy. "I seen you doing it."

"I am indeed, little lady," said Zebediah T. Crawcrustle.

"Do you remember the days of great confusion, Crawcrustle?" asked Augustus.

"I do indeed," said Crawcrustle. "And I remember you. You were only the age that young Hollyberry is now. But there is always confusion, Augustus, and then there is no confusion. It is like the rising and the setting of the sun."

Jackie Newhouse and Professor Mandalay found Crawcrustle that evening, behind the railroad tracks. He was roasting something in a tin can, over a small charcoal fire.

"What are you roasting, Crawcrustle?" asked Jackie Newhouse.

"More charcoal," said Crawcrustle. "Cleans the blood, purifies the spirit."

There was basswood and hickory, cut up into in little chunks at the bottom of the can, all black and smoking.

"And will you actually eat this charcoal, Crawcrustle?" asked Professor Mandalay.

In response, Crawcrustle licked his fingers and picked out a lump of charcoal from the can. It hissed and fizzed in his grip.

"A fine trick," said Professor Mandalay. "That's how fire-eaters do it, I believe."

Crawcrustle popped the charcoal into his mouth and crunched it between his ragged old teeth. "It is indeed," he said. "It is indeed."

Jackie Newhouse cleared his throat. "The truth of the matter is," he said, "Professor Mandalay and I have deep misgivings about the journey that lies ahead."

Zebediah merely crunched his charcoal. "Not hot enough," he said. He took a stick from the fire, and nibbled off the orange-hot tip of it. "That's good," he said.

"It's all an illusion," said Jackie Newhouse.

"Nothing of the sort," said Zebediah T. Crawcrustle primly. "It's prickly elm."

"I have extreme misgivings about all this," said Jackie Newhouse. "My ancestors and I have a finely tuned sense of personal preservation, one that has often left us shivering on roofs and hiding in rivers – one step away from the law, or from gentlemen with guns and legitimate grievances – and that sense of self-preservation is telling me not to go to Suntown with you."

"I am an academic," said Professor Mandalay, "and thus have no finely developed senses that would be comprehensible to anyone who has not ever needed to grade papers without actually reading the blessed things. Still, I find the whole thing remarkably suspicious. If this Sunbird is so tasty, why have I not heard of it?"

"You have, Mandy old fruit. You have," said Zebediah T. Crawcrustle.

"And I am, in addition, an expert on geographical features from Tulsa, Oklahoma, to Timbuktu," continued Professor Mandalay. "Yet I have never seen a mention in any books of a place called Suntown in Cairo."

"Seen it mentioned? Why, you've taught it," said Crawcrustle, and he doused a lump of smoking charcoal with hot pepper sauce before popping it in his mouth and chomping it down.

"I don't believe you're really eating that," said Jackie Newhouse. "But even being around the trick of it is making me uncomfortable. I think it is time that I was elsewhere."

And he left. Perhaps Professor Mandalay left with him: that man was so grey and so ghostie it was always a toss-up whether he was there or not.

Virginia Boote tripped over Zebediah T. Crawcrustle while he rested in her doorway, in the small hours of the morning. She was returning from a restaurant she had needed to review. She got out of a taxi, tripped over Crawcrustle and went sprawling. She landed nearby. "Whee!" she said. "That was some trip, wasn't it?"

"Indeed it was, Virginia," said Zebediah T. Crawcrustle. "You would not happen to have such a thing as a box of matches on you, would you?"

"I have a book of matches on me somewhere," she said, and she began to rummage in her purse, which was very large and very brown. "Here you are."

Zebediah T. Crawcrustle was carrying a bottle of purple methylated spirits, which he proceeded to pour into a plastic cup.

"Meths?" said Virginia Boote. "Somehow you never struck me as a meths drinker, Zebby."

"Nor am I," said Crawcrustle. "Foul stuff. It rots the guts and spoils the taste-buds. But I could not find any lighter fluid at this time of night."

He lit a match, then dipped it near the surface of the cup of spirits, which began to burn with a flickery light. He ate the match. Then he gargled with the flaming liquid, and blew a sheet of flame into the street, incinerating a sheet of newspaper as it blew by.

"Crusty," said Virginia Boote, "that's a good way to get yourself killed."

Zebediah T. Crawcrustle grinned through black teeth. "I don't actually drink it," he told her. "I just gargle and breathe it out."

"You're playing with fire," she warned him.

"That's how I know I'm alive," said Zebediah T. Crawcrustle.

Virginia said, "Oh Zeb. I *am* excited. I am so excited. What do you think the Sunbird tastes like?"

"Richer than quail and moister than turkey, fatter than ostrich and lusher than duck," said Zebediah T. Crawcrustle. "Once eaten it's never forgotten."

"We're going to Egypt," she said. "I've never been to Egypt." Then she said, "Do you have anywhere to stay the night?"

He coughed, a small cough that rattled around in his old chest. "I'm getting too old to sleep in doorways and gutters," he said. "Still, I have my pride."

"Well," she said, looking at the man, "you could sleep on my sofa."

"It is not that I am not grateful for the offer," he said. "But there is a bench in the bus station that has my name on it."

And he pushed himself away from the wall, and tottered majestically down the street.

There really *was* a bench in the bus station that had his name on it. He had donated the bench to the bus station back when he was flush, and his name was attached to the back of the bench, engraved upon a small brass plaque. Zebediah T. Crawcrustle was not always poor. Sometimes he was rich, but he had difficulty in holding onto his wealth, and whenever he had become wealthy he discovered that the world frowned on rich men eating in hobo jungles at the back of the railroad, or consorting with the winos in the park, so he would fritter his wealth away as best he could. There were always little bits of it here and there that he had forgotten about, and sometimes he would forget that he did not like being rich, and then he would set out again and seek his fortune, and find it.

He had needed a shave for a week, and the hairs of his seven-day beard were starting to come through snow white.

They left for Egypt on a Sunday, the Epicureans. There were five of them there, and Hollyberry NoFeathers McCoy waved goodbye to them at the airport. It was a very small airport, which still permitted waves goodbye.

"Goodbye, father!" called Hollyberry NoFeathers McCoy.

Augustus TwoFeathers McCoy waved back at her as they walked along the asphalt to the little prop plane, which would begin the first leg of their journey.

"It seems to me," said Augustus TwoFeathers McCoy, "that I remember, albeit dimly, a day like this long, long ago. I was a small boy, in that memory, waving goodbye. I believe it was the last time I saw my father, and I am struck once more with a sudden presentiment of doom." He waved one last time at the small child at the other end of the field, and she waved back at him.

"You waved just as enthusiastically back then," agreed Zebediah T. Crawcrustle, "but I think she waves with slightly more aplomb."

It was true. She did.

They took a small plane and then a larger plane, then a smaller plane, a blimp, a gondola, a train, a hot-air balloon, and a rented Jeep.

They rattled through Cairo in the Jeep. They passed the old market, and they turned off on the third lane they came to (if they had continued on they would have come to a drainage ditch that was once an irrigation canal). Mustapha Stroheim himself was sitting outside in the street, sitting on an elderly wicker chair. All of the tables and chairs were on the side of the street, and it was not a particularly wide street.

"Welcome, my friends, to my *Kahwa*," said Mustapha Stroheim. "Kahwa is Egyptian for café, or for coffee-house. Would you like tea? Or a game of dominoes?"

"We would like to be shown to our rooms," said Jackie Newhouse.

"Not me," said Zebediah T. Crawcrustle. "I'll sleep in the street. It's warm enough, and that doorstep over there looks mighty comfortable."

"I'll have coffee, please," said Augustus TwoFeathers McCoy.

"Of course."

"Do you have water?" asked Professor Mandalay.

"Who said that?" said Mustapha Stroheim. "Oh, it was you, little grey man. My mistake. When I first saw you I thought you were someone's shadow."

"I will have *ShaySokkar Bosta*," said Virginia Boote, which is a glass of hot tea with the sugar on the side. "And I will play backgammon with anyone who wishes to take me on. There's not a soul in Cairo I cannot beat at backgammon, if I can remember the rules."

Augustus TwoFeathers McCoy was shown to his room. Professor Mandalay was shown to his room. Jackie Newhouse was shown to his room. This was not a lengthy procedure; they were all in the same room, after all. There was another room in the back where Virginia would sleep, and a third room for Mustapha Stroheim and his family.

"What's that you're writing?" asked Jackie Newhouse.

"It's the procedures, annals and minutes of the Epicurean Club," said Professor Mandalay. He was writing in a large leather-bound book with a small black pen. "I have chronicled our journey here, and all the things that we have eaten on the way. I shall keep writing as we eat the Sunbird, to record for posterity all the tastes and textures, all the smells and the juices."

"Did Crawcrustle say how he was going to cook the Sunbird?" asked Jackie Newhouse.

"He did," said Augustus TwoFeathers McCoy. "He says that he will drain a beercan, so it is only a third full. And then he will add herbs and spices to the beercan. He will stand the bird up on the can, with the can in its inner cavity, and place it up on the barbecue to roast. He says it is the traditional way."

Jackie Newhouse sniffed. "It sounds suspiciously modern to me."

"Crawcrustle says it is the traditional method of cooking the Sunbird," repeated Augustus.

"Indeed I did," said Crawcrustle, coming up the stairs. It was a small building. The stairs weren't that far away, and the walls were not thick ones. "The oldest beer in the world is Egyptian beer, and they've been cooking the Sunbird with it for over five thousand years now."

"But the beercan is a relatively modern invention," said Professor Mandalay, as Zebediah T. Crawcrustle came through the door. Crawcrustle was holding a cup of Turkish coffee, black as tar, which steamed like a kettle and bubbled like a tarpit.

"That coffee looks pretty hot," said Augustus TwoFeathers McCoy.

Crawcrustle knocked back the cup, draining half the contents. "Nah," he said. "Not really. And the beercan isn't really that new an invention. We used to make them out of an amalgam of copper and tin in the old days, sometimes with a little silver in there, sometimes not. It depended on the smith, and what he had to hand. You need something that would stand up to the heat. I see that you are all looking at me doubtfully. Gentlemen, consider: of course the Ancient Egyptians made beercans; where else would they have kept their beer?"

From outside the window, at the tables in the street, came a wailing, in many voices. Virginia Boote had persuaded the locals to start playing backgammon for money, and she was cleaning them out. That woman was a backgammon shark.

Out back of Mustapha Stroheim's coffee-house there was a courtyard, containing a broken-down old barbecue, made of clay bricks and a half-melted metal grating, and an old wooden table. Crawcrustle spent the next day rebuilding the barbecue and cleaning it, oiling down the metal grille.

"That doesn't look like it's been used in forty years," said Virginia Boote. Nobody would play backgammon with her any longer, and her purse bulged with grubby piasters.

"Something like that," said Crawcrustle. "Maybe a little more. Here, Ginnie, make yourself useful. I've written a list of things I need from the market. It's mostly herbs and spices and wood chips. You can take one of the children of Mustapha Stroheim to translate for you."

"My pleasure, Crusty."

The other three members of the Epicurean Club were occupying themselves in their own way. Jackie Newhouse was making friends with many of the people of the area, who were attracted by his elegant suits and his skill at playing the violin. Augustus TwoFeathers McCoy went for long walks. Professor Mandalay spent time translating the hieroglyphics he had noticed were incised upon the clay bricks in the barbecue. He said that a foolish man might believe that they proved that the barbecue in Mustapha Stroheim's back yard was once sacred to the Sun. "But I, who am an intelligent man," he said, "I see immediately that what has happened is that bricks that were once, long ago, part of a temple, and have, over the millennia, been reused. I doubt that these people know the value of what they have here."

"Oh, they know all right," said Zebediah T. Crawcrustle. "And these bricks weren't part of any temple. They've been right here for five thousand years, since we built the barbecue. Before that we made do with stones."

Virginia Boote returned with a filled shopping basket. "Here," she said. "Red sandalwood and patchouli, vanilla beans, lavender twigs and sage and cinnamon leaves, whole nutmegs, garlic bulbs, cloves and rosemary: everything you wanted and more."

Zebediah T. Crawcrustle grinned with delight.

"The Sunbird will be so happy," he told her.

He spent the afternoon preparing a barbecue sauce. He said it was only respectful, and besides, the Sunbird's flesh was often slightly on the dry side.

The Epicureans spent that evening sitting at the wicker tables in the street out front, while Mustapha Stroheim and his family brought them tea and coffee and hot mint drinks. Zebediah T. Crawcrustle had told them that they would be having the Sunbird of Suntown for Sunday lunch, and that they might wish to avoid food the night before, to ensure that they had an appetite.

"I have a presentiment of doom upon me," said Augustus TwoFeathers McCoy that night, in a bed that was far too small for him, before he slept. "And I fear it shall come to us with barbecue sauce."

They were all so hungry the following morning. Zebediah T. Crawcrustle had a comedic apron on, with the words KISS THE COOK written upon it in violently green letters. He had already sprinkled the brandy-soaked raisins and grain beneath the stunted avocado tree behind the house, and he was arranging the scented woods, the herbs, and the spices on the bed of charcoal. Mustapha Stroheim and his family had gone to visit relatives on the other side of Cairo.

"Does anybody have a match?" Crawcrustle asked.

Jackie Newhouse pulled out a Zippo lighter, and passed it to Crawcrustle, who lit the dried cinnamon-leaves and dried laurel-leaves beneath the charcoal. The smoke drifted up into the noon air.

"The cinnamon and sandalwood smoke will bring the Sunbird," said Crawcrustle.

"Bring it from where?" asked Augustus TwoFeathers McCoy.

"From the Sun," said Crawcrustle. "That's where he sleeps."

Professor Mandalay coughed discreetly. He said, "The Earth is, at its closest, 91 million miles from the Sun. The fastest dive by a bird ever recorded is that of the peregrine falcon, at 273 miles per hour. Flying at that speed, from the Sun, it would take a bird a little over thirty-eight years to reach us – if it could fly through the dark and cold and vacuum of space, of course."

"Of course," agreed Zebediah T. Crawcrustle. He shaded his eyes and squinted and looked upward. "Here it comes," he said.

It looked almost as if the bird was flying out of the sun; but that could not have been the case. You could not look directly at the noonday sun, after all.

First it was a silhouette, black against the sun and against the blue sky, then the sunlight caught its feathers, and the watchers on the ground caught their breath. You have never seen anything like sunlight on the Sunbird's feathers; seeing something like that would take your breath away.

The Sunbird flapped its wide wings once, then it began to glide in ever-decreasing circles in the air above Mustapha Stroheim's coffee-house.

The bird landed in the avocado tree. Its feathers were golden, and purple, and silver. It was smaller than a turkey, larger than a rooster, and had the long legs and high head of a heron, though its head was more like the head of an eagle.

"It is very beautiful," said Virginia Boote. "Look at the two tall feathers on its head. Aren't they lovely?"

"It is indeed quite lovely," said Professor Mandalay.

"There is something familiar about that bird's headfeathers," said Augustus TwoFeathers McCoy.

"We pluck the headfeathers before we roast the bird," said Zebediah T. Crawcrustle. "It's the way it's always done."

The Sunbird perched on a branch of the avocado tree, in a patch of sun. It seemed almost as if it were glowing, gently, in the sunlight, as if its feathers were made of sunlight, iridescent with purples and greens and golds. It preened itself, extending one wing in the sunlight, then it nibbled and stroked at the wing with its beak until all the feathers were in their correct position, and oiled. Then it extended the other wing, and repeated the process. Finally, the bird emitted a contented chirrup, and flew the short distance from the branch to the ground.

It strutted across the dried mud, peering from side to side short-sightedly.

"Look!" said Jackie Newhouse. "It's found the grain."

"It seemed almost that it was looking for it," said Augustus TwoFeathers McCoy. "That it was expecting the grain to be there."

"That's where I always leave it," said Zebediah T. Crawcrustle.

"It's so lovely," said Virginia Boote. "But now I see it closer, I can see that it's much older than I thought. Its eyes are cloudy and its legs are shaking. But it's still lovely."

"The Bennu bird is the loveliest of birds," said Zebediah T. Crawcrustle.

Virginia Boote spoke good restaurant Egyptian, but beyond that she was all at sea. "What's a Bennu bird?" she asked. "Is that Egyptian for Sunbird?"

"The Bennu bird," said Professor Mandalay, "roosts in the Persea Tree. It has two feathers on its head. It is sometimes represented as being like a heron, and sometimes like an eagle. There is more, but it is too unlikely to bear repeating."

"It's eaten the grain and the raisins!" exclaimed Jackie Newhouse. "Now it's stumbling drunkenly from side to side – such majesty, even in its drunkenness!"

Zebediah T. Crawcrustle walked over to the Sunbird, which, with a great effort of will, was walking back and forth on the mud beneath the avocado tree, not tripping over its long legs. He stood directly in front of the bird, and then, very slowly, he bowed to it. He bent like a very old man, slowly and creakily, but still he bowed. And the Sunbird bowed back to him, then it toppled to the mud. Zebediah T. Crawcrustle picked it up reverently, and placed it in his arms, carrying it as if one would carry a child, and he took it back to the plot of land behind Mustapha Stroheim's coffee-house, and the others followed him.

First he plucked the two majestic headfeathers, and set them aside.

And then, without plucking the bird, he gutted it, and placed the guts on the smoking twigs. He put the half-filled beercan inside the body cavity, and placed the bird upon the barbecue.

"Sunbird cooks fast," warned Crawcrustle. "Get your plates ready."

The beers of the ancient Egyptians were flavoured with cardamom and coriander, for the Egyptians had no hops; their beers were rich and flavoursome and thirst-quenching. You could build pyramids after drinking that beer, and sometimes people did. On the barbecue the beer steamed the inside of the Sunbird, keeping it moist. As the heat of the charcoal reached them, the feathers of the bird burned off, igniting with a flash like a magnesium flare, so bright that the Epicureans were forced to avert their eyes.

The smell of roast fowl filled the air, richer than peacock, lusher than duck. The mouths of the assembled Epicureans began to water. It seemed like it had been cooking for no time at all, but Zebediah lifted the Sunbird from the charcoal bed, and put it on the table. Then, with a carving knife, he sliced it up and placed the steaming meat on the plates. He poured a little barbecue sauce over each piece of meat. He placed the carcass directly onto the flames.

Each member of the Epicurean Club sat in the back of Mustapha Stroheim's coffee-house, around an elderly wooden table, and they ate with their fingers.

"Zebby, this is amazing!" said Virginia Boote, talking as she ate. "It melts in your mouth. It tastes like heaven."

"It tastes like the Sun," said Augustus TwoFeathers McCoy, putting his food away as only a big man can. He had a leg in one hand, and some breast in the other. "It is the finest thing I have ever eaten, and I do not regret eating it, but I do believe that I shall miss my daughter."

"It is perfect," said Jackie Newhouse. "It tastes like love and fine music. It tastes like truth."

Professor Mandalay was scribbling in the bound annals of the Epicurean Club. He was recording his reaction to the meat of the bird, and recording the reactions of the other Epicureans, and trying not to drip on the page while he wrote, for with the hand that was not writing he was holding a wing, and, fastidiously, he was nibbling the meat off it.

"It is strange," said Jackie Newhouse, "for as I eat it, it gets hotter and hotter in my mouth and in my stomach."

"Yup. It'll do that. It's best to prepare for it ahead of time," said Zebediah T. Crawcrustle. "Eat coals and flames and lightning bugs to get used to it. Otherwise it can be a trifle hard on the system."

Zebediah T. Crawcrustle was eating the head of the bird, crunching its bones and beak in his mouth. As he ate, the bones sparked small lightnings against his teeth. He just grinned and chewed the more.

The bones of the Sunbird's carcass burned orange on the barbeque, and then they began to burn white. There was a thick heat-haze in the courtyard at the back of Mustapha Stroheim's coffee-house, and in it everything shimmered, as if the people around the table were seeing the world through water or a dream.

"It is so good!" said Virginia Boote as she ate. "It is the best I have ever eaten. It tastes like my youth. It tastes like forever." She licked her fingers, then picked up the last slice of meat from her plate. "The Sunbird of Suntown," she said. "Does it have another name?"

"It is the Phoenix of Heliopolis," said Zebediah T. Crawcrustle. "It is the bird that dies in ashes and flame, and is reborn, generation after generation. It is the Bennu bird, which flew across the waters when all was dark. When its time is come it is burned on the fire of rare woods and spices and herbs, and in the ashes it is reborn, time after time, world without end."

"Fire!" exclaimed Professor Mandalay. "It feels as if my insides are burning up!" He sipped his water, but seemed no happier.

"My fingers," said Virginia Boote. "Look at my fingers." She held them up. They were glowing inside, as if lit with inner flames.

Now the air was so hot you could have baked an egg in it.

There was a spark and a sputter. The two yellow feathers in Augustus TwoFeathers McCoy's hair went up like sparklers. "Crawcrustle," said Jackie Newhouse, aflame, "answer me truly. How long have you been eating the Phoenix?"

"A little over ten thousand years," said Zebediah. "Give or take a few thousand. It's not hard, once you master the trick of it; it's just mastering the trick of it that's hard. But this is the best Phoenix I've ever prepared. Or do I mean, 'this is the best I've ever cooked this Phoenix'?"

"The years!" said Virginia Boote. "They are burning off you!"

"They do that," admitted Zebediah. "You've got to get used to the heat, though, before you eat it. Otherwise you can just burn away."

"Why did I not remember this?" said Augustus TwoFeathers McCoy, through the bright flames that surrounded him. "Why did I not remember that this was how my father went, and his father before him, that each of them went to Heliopolis to eat the Phoenix? And why do I only remember it now?"

"Because the years are burning off you," said Professor Mandalay. He had closed the leather book as soon as the page he had been writing on caught fire. The edges of the book were charred, but the rest of the book would be fine. "When the years burn, the memories of those years come back." He looked more solid now, through the wavering burning air, and he was smiling. None of them had ever seen Professor Mandalay smile before.

"Shall we burn away to nothing?" asked Virginia, now incandescent. "Or shall we burn back to childhood and burn back to ghosts and angels and then come forward again? It does not matter. Oh Crusty, this is all such *fun!*"

"Perhaps," said Jackie Newhouse through the fire, "there might have been a little more vinegar in the sauce. I feel a meat like this could have dealt with something more robust." And then he was gone, leaving only an after-image.

"*Chacun à son goût*," said Zebediah T. Crawcrustle, which is French for "each to his own taste" and he licked his fingers and he shook his head. "Best it's ever been," he said, with enormous satisfaction.

"Goodbye, Crusty," said Virginia. She put her flame-white hand out, and held his dark hand tightly, for one moment, or perhaps for two.

And then there was nothing in the courtyard back of Mustapha Stroheim's *Kahwa* (or coffee-house) in Heliopolis (which was once the city of the Sun, and is now a suburb of Cairo), but white ash, which blew up in the momentary breeze, and settled like powdered sugar or like snow; and nobody there but a young man with dark, dark hair and even, ivory-coloured teeth, wearing an apron that said KISS THE COOK.

A tiny golden-purple bird stirred in the thick bed of ashes on top of the clay bricks, as if it were waking for the first time. It made a high-pitched "peep!" and it looked directly into the sun, as an infant looks at a parent. It stretched its wings as if to dry them, and, eventually, when it was quite ready, it flew upward, toward the sun, and nobody watched it leave but the young man in the courtyard.

There were two long golden feathers at the young man's feet, beneath the ash that had once been a wooden table, and he gathered them up, and brushed the white ash from them and placed them, reverently, inside his jacket. Then he removed his apron, and he went upon his way.

Hollyberry TwoFeathers McCoy is a grown woman, with children of her own. There are silver hairs on her head, in there with the black, beneath the golden feathers in the bun at the back. You can see that the feathers must once have looked pretty special, but that would have been a long time ago. She is the President of the Epicurean Club – a rich and rowdy bunch – having inherited the position, many long years ago, from her father.

I hear that the Epicureans are beginning to grumble once again. They are saying that they have eaten everything.

(For HMG – a belated birthday present)

Shard of Glass

Alaya Dawn Johnson

Alaya Dawn Johnson lives in New York City. She graduated from Columbia University in 2004 with a BA in East Asian Languages and Cultures, and has lived and traveled extensively in Japan, and once backpacked to a small island in the Keramas where she discovered a cave of human bones. At Columbia, Alaya worked as the News Editor for *The Columbia Spectator*, and interned at *The Village Voice* and *Smithsonian Magazine*. She has been published in *Internet Review of Science Fiction*, *Interzone*, *Strange Horizons*, *Chiaroscuro*, and *Arabella Magazine*. Currently, she works as an editorial assistant at QPB (the Quality Paperback Book Club).

"Shard of Glass" was published at the *Strange Horizons* website, and this is perhaps its first time in print. It is a fantasy set in the early 1960s, beginning in the American South and continuing through a variety of exotic locales. Magic shards of glass, a source of power, are distributed through a white southern family. The protagonist's mother steals one and so mother and daughter must flee.

THAT DAY, MY MOTHER picked me up from school, wearing the yellow sundress and shawl I remembered from our trip with Father the year before. She looked just like she did most days back then – a glamour queen, a movie star ("Just like Lena Horne," my friend Chloe had once said, "only darker – oh, sorry, Leah!"), but today her beauty somehow had a harder, more defiant edge to it. I could smell the expensive Dior perfume as soon as I opened the door, which surprised me, because my mom was usually fastidious about not getting perfume on her clothes. She was wearing her bug glasses – huge dark things with lenses that bulged out like fly eyes and reflected my face like a fun-house mirror. She had tied a yellow silk scarf around her hair and was taking deep pulls on a cigarette held between two immaculately manicured fingers. Only I knew about the nicotine stains she carefully covered with her special order "forest sable" cream each morning.

Tiffany, a stupid but vicious senator's daughter who I had the misfortune of sharing a classroom with, suddenly dashed from inside the school, her face flushed.

"Hello, Mrs. Wilson," she called. Before my mother could respond, she giggled and ran back to three of her friends waiting beyond the door. I could hear them laughing, but I was glad I couldn't understand their words. They were all fascinated with my mother – the black housekeeper who dressed like Katharine Hepburn and drove a Cadillac, whose daughter's "light toffee" skin indicated that she might just like her coffee with a lot of cream.

Sometimes I hated those girls.

"Get in the car, Leah," my mother said. Her already husky voice was pitched low, as though she'd been crying. That made me nervous. Why was she here?

"Ma, Chloe was going to show me her dad's new camera. Can't I go home on the bus?"

My mom pulled on the cigarette until it burned the filter, and then ground it into the car ashtray – already filled with forty or so butts. She always emptied out the ashtray each evening.

"Get in the car, Leah." My mom's voice was even huskier as she lit another cigarette and tossed the match out of the window.

I sat down and shut the door.

We rode in silence for a while. Despite her shaking hands and the rapidly dwindling box of cigarettes, she drove meticulously, even coming to a full stop at the stop signs. She *never* stopped at stop signs.

"Ma...is something wrong?" I asked hesitantly.

Her fingers tightened on the wheel until her knuckles looked even paler than my skin. "We're going on a trip, Leah," she said finally, jamming on the brakes at a stop sign.

Was that why she had chosen to wear that outfit today? "A trip? Where is it this year? Are we meeting Dad soon?" My heart sped up at just the thought of seeing him again.

"Charles," my mother corrected, deliberately. "You know you can't call him 'Dad,' Leah, I've told you a hundred times. And no, we're not going with... Charles, this time." Her voice caught on his name and for a second I thought she was going to cry.

A cop behind us leaned angrily on his horn. My mom's head jerked around so quickly I could hear the bones in her neck popping. We had been sitting in front of the stop sign for over a minute. My mom cursed and the car lurched forward. A minute later, after the cop had turned away, she seemed to relax a little.

"Did something happen to Da – Charles? And can I still go to school tomorrow? I have a geography report and, well..."

I trailed off. My mom didn't even look like she'd heard me. After checking over her shoulder again even though the cop had long since disappeared, she pulled onto the highway.

"They can't know we're gone yet," she muttered to herself. "I'm just being paranoid. They won't be looking for us for hours...." She shook her head and took off her sunglasses. The face she turned to me scared me more than anything – her mascara had run and her eyes were glazed and puffy. I knew my mom cried, of course I did, but she had always tried to hide it from me before. Now...what could have happened to make her cry so openly?

"Is he...dead?" I asked, suddenly terrified.

Her mouth twisted in a bitter half-smile. "No. No, Charles is most certainly alive. Leah..." She sighed, and handed me a thick leather-bound book.

"*Don Quixote*," I read out loud, pronouncing the second word only after careful deliberation. "What is it?"

"It's a present. One of your father's books. There's something inside.... Why don't you look, Leah, before I lose all my nerve?"

My stomach clenched, but I flipped through the pages. Somewhere in the center, I realized, part of the book had been hollowed out. Within a bed of cut-off words and ragged paper edges nestled the strangest piece of glass I had ever seen. Its beveled surface was pitch black – but unlike any other glass I had known, it didn't reflect light at all. In fact, it seemed to suck it in, so the page right beside the glass was so dark I could hardly read the print. The shard was shaped like an isosceles triangle with a chipped top – so lopsided it could only have been broken off from a larger piece. But someone had melted copper along the edges so they wouldn't cut. I looked at my mom, but she was staring doggedly at the road and wouldn't meet my gaze.

I picked up the glass and held it in front of my right eye.

"Ma!" I screamed, "Look out! You're going to hit her!"

The car swerved violently and my head knocked against the side window. Momentary pain lanced through my skull, exacerbated by screeching tires and a chorus of car horns. We pulled out of it seconds later. I looked frantically out the back window to see if she had managed to avoid hitting the woman sitting in the middle of the highway.

There was no one there.

I turned back to Mom. Her hands were trembling so badly she had dropped her cigarette, but she didn't seem angry with me. "Don't believe what you see through the glass," she said softly. "That's what he always said to me. I should have told you, but I never saw anything.... I didn't realize that you would."

"This is Dad's?" I asked.

"It's yours now, Leah, but...promise me you'll never show it to anyone else. It's our secret, okay?"

I stared at my mother. The worn copper on the outside of the shard was biting into my sweat-slicked palm. I didn't know what else to do but agree.

"I promise. Ma...are we going on the trip now?"

She nodded.

"When are we coming back?" I was almost too afraid to ask the question.

"I don't know. Not for a very long time."

Very carefully, I put the shard back inside the book and shut the cover.

"Where are we going?"

"I bought tickets to Rome this morning," she said, "but that was just to lead them off. Is there anywhere in the world you want to go, Leah?"

I thought about the geography presentation I would never have the chance to give. We were each supposed to do it on a different country. I didn't really know much about mine – I had only picked it because it was cute and small.

"Luxembourg," I said.

My mom just nodded. She never asked me where it was. To this day, I still don't know if she had ever heard of it, but she nodded just the same.

At the airport, she went into the bathroom alone. When she came out, she was no longer an anomaly, a black movie queen in a white woman's clothes. The woman who left that bathroom was not my mother – she was one of the invisible thousands, a black woman in gray, serviceable housekeeping clothes and a scuffed but sturdy pair of white tennis shoes. She had pulled her nappy hair back in a bun, washed her makeup off of her face. Now, her bloodshot eyes just looked like part of the uniform.

"Your dress..." I said, struggling to keep myself from panicking, breaking down. I had always known my mother used to be a housekeeper, but I had never understood what it meant until now. "Charles...gave it to you, didn't he? Where...?"

My mom's eyes were hard, but I knew she wanted to cry too. "I threw it out," she said.

And when I followed behind her, carrying along the bit of luggage she had dared to bring, I was no longer the daughter of a woman who looked like a dark Lena Horne, I was just a nappy-headed brat of uncertain paternity, whose possessions had suddenly been reduced to three sets of clothing, a book, and a shard of glass.

I was twelve years old.

We were careless in Luxembourg – too obviously secretive or suspiciously casual. We hadn't yet learned that fundamental lesson of disappearing: it's not enough to just vanish, even to a place thousands of miles away; to truly disappear, you must blend in.

My mother cried each night and I knew she kept a picture of my father in her bag, but the face she turned to me every morning was as hard as my piece of glass. She never asked me if I wanted our fugitive existence, but the idea of letting them catch us didn't occur to me until much later. She never really told me what had happened that day she wore the yellow dress, but I knew my father and his family were chasing us because of something she had done. Somehow, it didn't matter. I loved my father, but he had been like a smiling shadow my whole life – not a real person, just a grainy four-color facsimile. A man who sent me fancy clothes and jewelry on my birthday under fake names, visited me and my mother at strange times of night and then vanished for months on end. No, I loved my father, but my mother owned my soul. How could it have been otherwise?

Three weeks after we arrived in Luxembourg, my mother and I huddled together for warmth in a reeking alley behind an expensive French restaurant. The window on the side of the building was a bit too high for either of us, but I could see through a gap in the curtains when she hoisted me up. Inside, a man who looked sort of like my father, only with less hair and a bigger belly, was slowly sipping a glass of fifty-franc wine as he watched the front door with lidded eyes.

"Is he still there?" she whispered.

"On his third glass of wine," I said, softly as I could. "The waiter keeps coming back, but he won't order any food. I think he's waiting for someone."

"Us, probably. Just like that damned family to spend a small fortune feeding us before they throw us in jail."

"Who is he?" I asked.

I could practically hear my mother's frown. "Your uncle," she said, finally. "Henry. He's part of the family business."

"What's the family business?"

"Money. Politics. Mostly money." She sounded bitter, but I didn't quite understand why. Despite the confusion of the last few weeks, the glow of adventure somehow still hadn't worn off for me. I guess that I couldn't imagine my father actually hurting us. The danger was something only my mother understood – she knew what she had taken, and how much they would risk to take it back.

She had spied him around the corner when we were walking back from the market. We had cowered behind the gigantic loaves in a baker's window as he walked past and into a restaurant. Luckily, Mom had insisted we take our bags with us wherever we went – if they had traced us all the way to Luxembourg City, then surely they would have found our tiny second-floor apartment by now. They would expect us to flee the city, and were probably watching every possible method of transportation for just that eventuality. So, we hid in the safest place we could think of – behind the restaurant where my uncle waited for us, sipping his expensive wine.

"Leah," my mom whispered, "my shoulders are getting tired. I'm going to put you down, okay?"

The door in the front of the restaurant opened. "No, wait!" I said. Two men who didn't look anything like my father brushed straight past the maitre d'

and sat down in front of my uncle. The two newcomers spoke quietly for a few
moments, but whatever they said made my uncle livid. He slammed his glass on
the table, and some wine sloshed over the rim. He stood up, tossed a few francs
on the red-stained table cloth, and stalked out of the restaurant.

"Dammit!" he cursed as he stepped out onto the sidewalk. "I always told
Charles that pet bitch of his would get him in trouble. You're sure there was no
sign of them? Or the glass? Did you check the rooms?"

They had stopped in front of the alleyway, the three of them making long
shadows in the flickering streetlights. My mother and I pressed ourselves against
the wall.

"I turned the rooms upside down," one of the other men said. "Had to pay the
landlady for two nights just so she wouldn't call the cops. I mean, somebody'd
obviously been there, but they didn't leave anything behind. Not even a tooth-
brush."

"Did you show the landlady their pictures?" my uncle asked.

The second man nodded. "She wasn't sure about the woman, but she said it
looked like the same girl."

My hands slid to my jacket pocket. The coat my mom had bought for me in
Luxembourg was made for someone much bigger, and its pockets were deep
enough for even the fat book to fit inside comfortably. I don't know why I took it
out – I hadn't dared look through the glass since that near-disaster on the highway. But curiosity gripped me. Why did my uncle care so much about this glass?
What would it show me if I used it to look at him?

"They can't have left yet," my uncle was saying as I pulled out the glass, hands
shaking with every heartbeat. "I have to get back to Richmond for a fund-raiser,
but I want you to stay here."

I held it up to my eye. My mom's face was drawn with panic, but she didn't
tell me to stop. "Comb the whole damn country if you have to, but find them.
And the glass."

Something seemed to shudder in the lamplight. A tall, thin white man
wearing a bowler hat and a pea coat held the limp form of a little girl in his arms.
My uncle was leaning against the side of a blue car, sweat running from his
forehead into his eyes. He had hair, I realized after a moment, and his stomach
didn't hang over the edge of his belt. This younger version of my uncle swayed
unsteadily, but his face was a mask of contempt. The two men were yelling at
each other, but I could only hear oddly warped snatches of sounds, as though
they were at the other end of a long, twisted corridor. Suddenly, my uncle lurched
from the car and shoved the other man backwards. He stumbled and dropped
the girl. When she fell limply to the ground, I realized that she wasn't breathing.

Rage flared in the other man's eyes and he leapt onto my uncle, wrestling him to the ground. Even drunk, my uncle was much stronger. He wrapped his hands around the other man's throat, his face contorted with fury.

I had the curious sensation of leaning closer, even though the glass was flush against my eye.

"...money..." I heard the other man say, and then some more words that were too distant and garbled to make out. "...papers, you killed my daughter! Why... money...I swear..."

My uncle slammed the man's head viciously on the ground once, and stood up. "I'll give you..." He walked around the car while the man rolled on his side and retched in the grass on the edge of the road. The man gently wiped some of the vomit off the girl's arm, which was beginning to stiffen.

I glanced back at my uncle and bit back a gasp; he was holding a gun. The other man barely had time to bleat before the bullet caught him in the neck. Blood pulsed in a macabre spray as he convulsed. My uncle tossed the gun in the car and drove away. When I tried to turn and follow him, the scene dissolved into a thousand smaller images, so loud and clamoring that it hurt just to look at them. I put down the glass.

My uncle was looking into the alley. For a terrified second, I thought that he had found us, but he seemed to be staring out blindly, lost in thought.

"Um...Senator Richards? Are you okay?"

My uncle shuddered and began walking away. The two other men hurried to keep up with him.

My mother looked at me. "Where...do you want to go, Leah?"

I thought for a minute.

"Japan," I said, finally.

After four months of grueling, terrifying overland travel, which nearly exhausted our modest supply of money, we took a ferry to Osaka. On the way, my mother dared to purchase a small Japanese learner's dictionary, although she bought ones for German, Dutch, and Korean as well, just in case my father's family caught our trail. Once, on a crowded local train in northern China, I thoughtlessly opened my father's book. I was about to pull out the glass when my mom slapped my hand away. The look she gave me made me want to melt into the seat. It was hard to always remember who we were and what we were hiding from.

My mother and I had mastered some rudimentary Japanese phrases by the time we arrived, although we soon discovered that most of the locals were too busy staring at us to bother wading through our mangled Japanese. Mostly, we got by with hand signals. Once, I remember, young girls walking to the trains after school crowded around my mother, shyly asking if they could touch her hair.

Even in that large city, we were anomalies, walking circus exhibits who couldn't even speak properly. My mother felt profoundly uncomfortable there, I think. We left after just a few weeks, traveling by ferry and local train to one of the most remote areas in Japan: the Kerama islands, just to the west of Okinawa's main island. The war had ravaged this place, you could see it in the faces of the women in hitched kimonos who hacked at the sugar cane or in the occasional mortar that washed up on the rocky beaches. My mom found a job as a housekeeper in the only hotel on the islands – not a hotel, really, just a modest two-floor inn with Japanese-style furnishings and a window where the locals liked to pick up their lunches. Almost despite ourselves, we began to settle into a routine, reassemble our lives from the pieces my mom had scattered that day she picked me up from school. The line between my mom's eyebrows never entirely disappeared, but as the weeks passed and she began to hope that we were finally safe, I saw her begin to smile again. Once in a while, I would catch her staring out at one of the magnificent island sunsets, her nappy hair ruffling in the wind, and I would be reminded once again of how beautiful she was. Even here, in this island in the middle of nowhere, she stood like a woman who wouldn't quite forget that she had once been a glamour queen.

The main school was on our island, but my mother thought it was too dangerous for the other kids to get to know me, even here. So I stayed behind, often helping Sato-san, the owner's wife, batter and fry the fish and vegetables for lunch. In the mornings, I would wake up early and go with her husband (also Sato-san, which sometimes got confusing) to the docks, where we would wade in the water up to our thighs with buckets to catch the crabs as they ran in from the tide. On our way back we bought the first catch from the fishermen and then hauled it all back to the inn on a rickety wheelbarrow. My mom didn't speak more than she had to, but I had been starved for conversation for months and my Japanese soon became fluent.

The Satos had two boys, one six and the other about my age. On weekends, their father would take us out on his small rowboat and we would sit for hours, catching fish. The boys had been afraid of me at first, but after a few weeks it seemed that they had forgotten I was a foreigner, let alone an American. Koichi and I would run around the island together, with Yuki tagging along behind when we let him. We found all of the island's secrets – the grottos with the best crabs, the beach with the deepest water, the cliff where you could sometimes see the humps of huge whales arcing above the waves at sunset and dawn. And then, one day, Koichi and I found the island's greatest secret of all.

It was sunset. Koichi and I scrambled in bare feet over the top of an unfamiliar cliff on the western side of the island.

"Sun," I said in English, pointing to the rapidly sinking red ball.

Koichi grimaced. "Do we have to do this?" he asked.

"I told Sato-san I would teach you English. What's she going to say if you don't know any new words?"

So I taught him a few more: *stone, cliff, beach, crab, adventure.* He repeated them good-naturedly, and I tried to correct some of his pronunciation as we walked along the rock.

"We have crab adventure on stone beach," he said slowly.

I clapped my hands and laughed. "That's good!" I said. "Say that to your mom and she might let us share one of the *manju* she got from your aunt."

"Never. She saves all of those for Yuki, the spoiled brat." He paused before a small outcropping and put his arm on my left side, so I couldn't get past.

"You know," I said, "we should really get back before the sun goes all the way down. I have to do your math homework, remember?" Koichi hated homework and my mom wanted me to get an education, so I had ended up practically being his tutor.

Koichi nodded, but he didn't move. His broad face had a curious look to it, as though he were staring at me through a tank of water. I shifted uncomfortably.

He kissed me. Out of sheer surprise, I staggered backwards. Instead of hitting the rock, however, I fell through a hole. Koichi tumbled down on top of me.

We untangled ourselves and looked around. The cave was fairly large, considering its small, hidden opening. For a few moments the descending sun shone directly into the crevice, illuminating the back wall of the cave.

Koichi and I saw them at the same time.

The cave was littered with human bones.

It looked as though these people – whoever they were – had not been disturbed since they died. In one corner I saw a heap of pathetically tiny bones nestled near the ribcage of someone I could only assume had been its mother. My breath began sticking in my throat.

"Where are we?" I asked.

Koichi looked at me. That strange fish-aquarium look had left his eyes. Now, inexplicably, I only saw anger.

"These are *your* bones!" he shouted.

Before I could even ask him what he meant, he picked up a jawbone and tossed it at my head. I caught the grisly token and watched him rush out of the cave. I should have followed him – I knew how dangerous it was to be stuck on the rocks after the sun had gone down – but I was angry and confused. I brooded for nearly an hour, until the sun had disappeared and the moon had come up to replace it. I could smell the encroaching storm clouds, but still I didn't move. Who were these dead people that surrounded me?

And then, when I heard the first distant rumble of thunder, I finally remembered how I could find out.

I pulled the glass from the book and held it to my eyes.

For a long moment, nothing happened. Then, with an almost physical lurch, I was in a different world.

A tall man stood in the mouth of the cave, carrying a paper lantern in one hand and a knife in the other. Three others huddled inside: a woman clutching a baby to her chest, and a little boy just about Yuki's age.

The man looked out of the crevice, as though he was searching for something, and then turned back, shaking his head. "They'll be here by dawn, they said. We can't...we can't let ourselves be taken." Their voices still sounded distant, but not so garbled as when I had looked through the glass before.

"Did you see them?" the woman asked. She looked dazed with terror. "Are you sure they're coming? They could miss us, couldn't they? We could just hide up here until they're gone, no one will find us – "

"Quiet!" the man said, his voice hard as a slap. The baby began to cry and the little boy held onto his mother's skirts, quietly snuffling.

The man walked closer to the woman. "We have no choice, Eriko. What do you think the Americans will do to us when they get here? It's better for us to end it now, with dignity."

Slowly, she nodded. He bent down to kiss her, and as he did so I saw him move the knife just above her heart. She leaned forward.

So did I.

It felt as though I were moving through a mountain of sand, but desperation and terror pushed me through. "No," I shouted, in both Japanese and English. "Don't do this!"

And somehow, the woman heard me.

As the blood blossomed around the hilt of the blade and ran down the front of her kimono, she turned her head and met my eyes.

"What are you doing here?" she asked. Her voice was sad, but so calm it was incongruent with the blood and her screaming children. "You don't belong here. Why wake this up?" She slid off the end of the blade and collapsed on the floor. The high-pitched screams of her children seemed to have receded – I could only hear the woman. Her husband sliced the neck of the boy first, and then the infant.

"Why not let it fade?" she said as she cradled her dying infant on the floor. "Why won't you let it fade?"

"I'm sorry," I whispered. I couldn't feel my throat, but my voice was hoarse. Was I crying?

I had gone so far that time, it took a while to pull back out. Just before I lowered the glass, I had the strange impression that I glimpsed my father. He seemed sad and worn, but in some strange way, it made him look even more handsome. I realized that I had nearly forgotten his face.

After I put away the shard, I crawled out of the cave and tried to shelter myself from the pelting rain under a small overhang nearby. I fell asleep clutching the book to my chest, crying for the woman in the cave and wishing I could see my father again.

Sato-san and the others found me the next morning, after the rains had stopped. I tried to climb down, but my legs wouldn't stop shaking and I felt light-headed. I rode home on Sato-san's back. My father used to carry me around like that, I remembered, but he had always smelled of red wine and expensive cologne. Sato-san smelled like saltwater and sweat and crabs, but it was still somehow reassuring.

"What...happened? She okay?" I heard my mother ask in her broken Japanese.

"I'm fine," I said in English.

They helped me to our small room on the second floor. My mom had rolled out my futon already and started undressing me like a baby. I would have objected to the treatment if I hadn't already been shivering uncontrollably. I couldn't tell if it was from residual fear or actual illness.

"Ma," I said that night as I shivered under extra covers. "What is that glass? What do I see when I look through it?"

My mom was silent for so long that I nearly fell asleep again.

"Memories," she said finally. "I asked Charles once, and that's what he said. 'There's nothing more powerful than a memory,' he said. But there you go, that's the Richardses for you. There's no such thing as beauty without power."

"You don't have any power and Dad thinks you're beautiful," I said.

My mom laughed. "But he had power *over* me. That was almost as good. Then I took all that away, and now I'm just a fly for him to crush. Flies aren't beautiful, Leah."

The next day Koichi apologized to me awkwardly over breakfast. I accepted it solemnly, and I never asked him what he had meant when he said they were my bones. I had looked at the memory and I knew – I just wished I didn't feel guilty every time I thought of it.

That weekend Sato-san took us with him to Naha, the major city in Okinawa. The inn needed certain supplies and Sato-san decided to take the two of us along as a treat. My mother begged me with her eyes not to go, but I ignored her and boarded the ferry with Koichi while Yuki stayed behind with his mother. At first talking to Koichi felt horribly awkward, but by the time the ferry landed we were friends again. We wandered around the arcaded shops while his father haggled over a crate of dried bonito and some Satsuma miso paste, which was the kind his wife liked the most. We passed a bank, where someone had left an American newspaper on a bench by the door. I picked it up and flipped through the headlines. There were stories of demonstrations and police violence, school segregation and growing American concerns about Vietnam. I was a little shocked – it had been over a year since I had heard anything about my home country. Koichi wandered away from me while I scoured the rest of the paper. An item toward the bottom of the second-to-last page caught my attention:

> *Three weeks away from the election, popular Florida senatorial candidate Charles Richards (brother of staunch anti-integration Virginia senator Henry Richards) and his wife, Linda, have suffered the tragic death of their premature child, Mary. The infant died of respiratory failure last night following a series of unsuccessful surgeries. Richards says that he will be back on the campaign trail next week, but that he must "have some time to grieve for the loss of my child." Analysts wonder if his week-long leave of absence will give Dale Hearn, the Democratic contender, a chance to pick up more votes.*

His wife, it said. My hands were shaking so badly I could hear the paper rattling. Why was I so surprised, anyway? He might have paid for our apartment and my school, but all the time he and my mom had been together, he had never offered to marry her. When I was younger, I had always wondered why. Now, I realized, I knew. His brother, the "staunch anti-integration Virginia senator," would hardly have approved, let alone the rest of his political family.

Should I tell my mother how enormously the man she loved had betrayed her?

And then, the strangest thought occurred to me: Did she already know?

Could that possibly be why we left?

We stayed there for another year. Koichi never tried to kiss me again, even though there were some days when I wished he would, when I wished that we had never fallen into that stupid cave. One evening, I sat with my legs dangling over the harbor wall, thinking about how nice it would be just to live on this island forever. I liked it better than America – here I was foreign before I was black, and even before that I was part of the Satos' family. I pulled the shard from my pocket – it was too hot in the summer to lug around the book, even though my mom got angry when I left it at home.

There were many memories on this island, I had learned, some much older than others. Sometimes they noticed me, and sometimes they seemed oblivious – but I never told anyone what I learned from them. I felt like a voyeur whenever I looked through the glass; I was spying on the innermost thoughts of people long dead.

The shard's beveled surface drank in even today's bright noon sun, remaining opaque until I held it in front of my eyes. Down below me, on one of the algae-slicked rocks, I saw a woman, her belly swollen with pregnancy, laughing as her little son struggled to catch the crabs that were scuttling away from him.

"Don't run so fast," she said. "You might slip and hurt yourself."

Surprise nearly made me put down the glass. I knew that voice. When I looked closer, I recognized her face, too, although terror had done much to hide her natural beauty. I began to push forward, struggling through the strange sand that separated us. It was easier this time than it had been in the cave, but I didn't stop to wonder why. I pushed until it seemed I was sitting next to her, even though I was still vaguely aware of my body perched on the wall.

She turned to me. "Hello," she said. "I've never had someone visit before."

Somehow I had expected more venom. "You don't recognize me?" I asked.

She looked at me more closely and then shook her head. "No, should I?"

Of course she didn't recognize me, I realized. This was a different memory.

"Do you know how you're going to die?" I asked.

She looked sad. "I'm dead, then? I thought I might be, but it's so happy here...." She looked away. "My son," she said quietly, "is he...also..."

I put a phantom hand over hers and felt a jolt. "Not here," I said, "not for you."

She turned to smile at me, but as she did so her image wavered and I felt a sickening lurch. Suddenly, I was back in the sand again, but I had no orientation – where was that woman's memory? Where was the glass? I felt as though the sand was sucking me in one direction, and so I struggled the other way. Then, before me, I saw my uncle's thinning brown hair and wide-set brown eyes, indistinct and wavering like a television getting a bad signal. He smiled.

"What are you doing here, Leah?" he asked. His words sounded mangled and slurred, as though they had been repeated in a game of Telephone. "Have you mastered the glass already, then? Or are you just lost and unlucky?"

"Leave us alone!" I said in Japanese.

Then I realized my mistake.

Koichi pulled me off the ledge and I skinned my elbow on the road. I lay blinking uncomprehendingly at the sky for a few moments before I realized that I had escaped.

"Leah," Koichi said, kneeling beside me, "are you all right? What were you doing?"

"Talking to a memory," I said.

*

I didn't tell my mother. For months afterwards, I tried to convince myself that he wouldn't have recognized the Japanese, that there was no way I could have destroyed our perfect haven with a stupid slip of the tongue.

I should have known better.

They found us five months later, on a clear evening in what passed for autumn here. Koichi came running into the kitchen where I was helping his mother make dinner.

"Foreigners," he said, gasping, "they came in on the ferry. Said they were looking for a little black girl and her mother."

I dropped the knife I was using to gut a fish.

"What did you tell them, Koichi?" his mother asked.

"I told them to look on the other side of the island," he said. "They might just go away, right?"

Sato-san and I exchanged a glance. We both knew what this meant. "We have to leave, Koichi," I said. "Tonight we hide, and then when it's safe, we have to take the ferry."

My mother packed our meager belongings silently. She was ready for this, I realized as I watched her. I had relaxed and fooled myself into believing that we could live here forever, but wariness had never entirely left her. She had never forgotten we were fugitives. I said goodbye to the Sato-sans and Yuki, who cried even though we told him that we were only going on a short trip.

"Where are you going to hide?" Koichi asked, just before we left.

"The cave. The cave with my bones."

He looked down, embarrassed. "Before...I didn't mean that," he said softly.

"Yes, you did," I said.

Then I kissed him.

My mother and I huddled in the cave of bones that night, praying that my uncle's men would take the morning ferry back when they realized we weren't there. It was a chilly night, and my mother was so quiet that sometimes I thought the bones made for better company.

"When did he get married?" I asked, breaking hours of sleepless silence.

She didn't ask me who I meant. "Just after we left," she said. "Henry picked her. She's some kind of an heiress."

"Is that why we disappeared?" I asked.

"No." And then, more quietly, "Maybe that was part of it."

"Do you know whose bones these are?" I asked, minutes later.

My mother shook her head.

"That man," I said, pointing to the shapeless huddle of bones beside the entrance, "killed his whole family, and then himself. They were afraid of being captured alive by the Americans, and so they killed themselves."

"We won't get captured alive," my mother said.

Years passed, and countries turned into a blur: Korea, Thailand, Ceylon, Papua New Guinea, Ethiopia. Our pursuers started getting more persistent, deadlier. I bought a gun on the Ceylon black market and kept it in my pocket next to the book. I was careful when I looked through the glass now, and eventually I realized that I could change the way I waded through the sand. I discovered that if I moved silently enough, I could spy on my uncle, and sometimes my father, as they looked though their own glass. Whatever they were using, it was far inferior to mine – most memories stayed hidden from them, and they could not find me very easily. We stayed a half step ahead of them – as soon as I learned that they had found us, we would move. We never stayed anywhere longer than six months, though, and for that I was grateful. I missed our island and Koichi so much sometimes – I didn't want to come to love any other place that much and then lose it in another afternoon. My mother grew old on those trips; gray hair began to pepper the brown, and worry lines seemed as though they had been etched into her face with a chisel.

And then, when we were walking through a crowded market in New Delhi, they shot my mother. It hit her in the shoulder, and she went down amid sudden pandemonium. It was a stupid place to shoot us – I hauled her up and dragged her out of the plaza, hiding within the milling crowd. I didn't dare take her to a hospital in the city – my uncle's men would surely be watching every one. So I bound her shoulder as best I could and we took the next train out of the country. We traveled all night and part of the next day until we crossed the border to Nepal. There, I felt safe enough to take her to a hospital. The bullet had apparently passed through cleanly, but the doctor gave us some penicillin to ward off infection. We found a small room in a back alley tenement in Katmandu. She slept there for practically three days straight while I went out to find work. I was eventually hired as a dishwasher in the kitchens of one of the Western hotels. It paid barely enough for the rent, but my mother was too weak to get a job herself.

Sometimes I wonder why I didn't notice how tired she seemed, how just getting out of bed in the morning was becoming a daily struggle for her. Why did I just assume it was exhaustion, and not something more serious? But my mother was a woman in her forties who had spent the last five years in nearly constant terror. The grueling pace of our lives would exhaust anyone, I thought.

I began to wear a plain orange sari and cover my hair – my lips and nose were a little large, but my skin color was perfect, and in the right clothes I looked like a local. No one would associate my schoolgirl picture with the Nepalese kitchen worker I had become.

And then one day, a few months after we arrived, I saw my father. I was in the market, haggling over a fish for dinner (the one thing I could convince my mother to eat, these days), when I heard his voice.

"She should be about this tall," he said, "brown skin. Living with her mother. Their names are Leah and Carol."

The man he was talking to snorted. "You're just looking for a teenage girl living with her mother. Oh, well, there's only one of those in this city. But perhaps you can buy this vase – very cheap, only thirty American dollars and I'll see what I can do."

I snorted – the vase vendor was robbing my father blind. I looked at him surreptitiously from under my scarf. He was thinner than I remembered, which made his face look harder and more vulnerable at the same time. His hair had turned silver at the temples, but it was as thick as I remembered it. For a moment, I allowed myself to be happy to see him. Then I acknowledged what this meant: they had found us. I took my bag of fish and calmly paid the vendor, glancing around to see if there were other Westerners in the market. It looked like he was alone. I walked the few feet to where my father was standing. He had pulled out his wallet and looked like he was actually shelling out the thirty dollars.

"If you want to find the woman, I can take you to her," I said in my best Nepali accent.

My father paused and turned to me. He gave me a searching look, but after a few moments I realized that he didn't recognize me. It made me feel lonely.

"What about the girl?" he asked.

I shook my head. "I don't know about a girl, but I can take you to the woman."

"How much do you want?"

"Sixty American dollars. Thirty here, thirty after you meet her." I figured I could rob my own father just as well as a vase vendor.

My father nodded and handed me the money. I took him the wrong way down the street, to confuse the vendors who knew where I lived. I walked the most circuitous route I knew back home, to disguise the fact that we lived just a few blocks away. I could see him trying to memorize the street corners and I knew that he would never be able to find his way back. The lack of street signs in the back alleys of Katmandu would help me here.

I led him up the rickety staircase to our second-floor apartment.

"Wait here," I said, before I opened the door. My mom was sitting by the window, flipping the pages of a book with her left hand. She looked up when I came in, but I put my finger over my lips and she didn't say anything. She looked afraid and wary, but most of all, I thought, she looked tired. I bit my lip. What was I doing, bringing my father here? He was probably the last person she wanted to see. What had possessed me to put both of us in so much danger?

"He doesn't know me," I whispered. And then, much louder, my voice accented, "You can come in."

He stood in the threshold for a long time, staring at my mother. My back was to him, but I could see my mother's face. There was shock there, and anger, of course, but most of all I saw longing. Deep, bone-aching longing.

My father broke first. "What happened to your arm?" he asked. His voice was hoarse.

I shut the door behind him. We didn't need to draw attention to ourselves.

"One of Henry's people shot me. Or was it one of yours?" As tired as she was, with one arm in a sling and wearing a shapeless house dress, when she said that, my mom became beautiful again.

"Carol, I would never...I had no idea...." He crossed the room in three long strides and embraced her.

My mother didn't exactly resist him, but she didn't return the gesture. She just lay there, stiff in his arms.

"Please come back with me," he said. "Come back with me and you won't have to live in this hellhole. I'll take care of you and Leah...where is Leah, though? Is she okay?"

My mother ignored his question. "You'll take me back...will you marry me, then? Or will I just go back to being your weekend whore?"

My father pulled back a little. He looked almost like he wanted to cry. "Do you know how much I've missed you, Carol? I'm married, you know that, but you've always been the only one I wanted."

"Then why wouldn't you marry me?" It was the first time I had heard my mother yell in a very long time. "Why would you keep me hidden like I was some dirty secret?"

"They won't accept us, Carol. Maybe if we lived in a more...accepting world, but now – isn't it enough just to be together?"

Her mouth twisted bitterly. "So tell me, this new law. The Civil Rights Act. Tell me, Mr. Senator, how are you going to vote?"

He seemed confused. "Against it, of course. What does that have to do – "

She laughed. I wondered if I had ever heard a laugh sound so painful. "It has everything to do with everything, Charles. You never understood that, did you? You say the world won't accept us – what you mean is your brother won't accept us, your parents won't accept us. You have a chance to change all that, but you don't seem to care. I'm one of those niggers, your daughter is one of those niggers that you want to make sure drinks from a separate water fountain. If I lived with you again, it would be like spitting on myself, my parents, my daughter every day. I did that for twelve years, Charles. I'm not going to do it again. Now go. I'm tired."

For a moment I thought he was going to try to embrace her again, but instead he stood up and walked to the door.

"I loved you, Carol," he said.

"I still love you, Charles." She turned to the window. She wouldn't want him to see her tears.

I opened the door. "Come," I said. He followed me blindly outside, and didn't seem to notice how suspiciously husky my voice was.

I led us back to the market a different way, through back alleys bordered by foul-smelling sewage ditches and a few crowded thoroughfares.

I stopped in front of the vase seller, who was packing up his wares.

"Here," my father said, pulling a hundred-dollar bill out of his wallet. "Keep it."

I nodded, and tucked it in the top of my sari.

"Tell her...that they know she's here. They'll find her soon. She should leave."

"I will," I said, without the accent. His head snapped up. "I'm glad I got to see you again, Father."

And before he could say anything, I ducked back into an alley and ran.

When people die, their memories explode. No matter how peaceful the death, its aftermath is violence. Sometimes people's lives explode in a thousand tiny fragments, most of which will wither and fade with time. Once in a rare while, a person's memories hardly fragment at all, and those are the ones most people call spirits.

I saw a lot of death in the Ghanaian hospital where I took my mother after we left Nepal. Stomach cancer, the doctors told me. It was very advanced; she must have been living with it for long time. I thought of her exhaustion, her bad appetite, and wished that I hadn't been so stupid. It was only a matter of time, they said. When my mother broached the subject of me going back to the States, I realized that she knew she was going to die.

"What about the glass?" I asked.

"Give it back to them. I must have been crazy to take it...what kind of mother was I, dooming you to this kind of life...." She sighed. "I didn't want them to have it. That glass makes them powerful, and I thought that if I stole it...well, it doesn't matter what I thought. You should just give it back, Leah."

But I didn't want to give it back. The more I thought about it, the angrier I got. I followed the news out of the States: the Civil Rights Act had passed the

House and was about to go to the Senate. My uncle, Henry Richards, was one of the strongest voices of opposition, and his behind-the-scenes power was making things difficult.

My mom was getting weaker by the day. She never said it, but I knew that she wanted to see my father. Somehow, I had to end this for her.

One evening a week later, I was helping take down patients' names and information in the emergency room. A man walked in, carrying a young girl who was coughing feebly in his arms. I was overwhelmed with a sensation of déjà vu, even though I had never seen either of them before. Why did they seem so familiar?

A nurse wheeled an empty gurney past me. Its sheet was stained with splotches of fresh blood that suddenly seemed to be the color of expensive red wine, carelessly spilled on a tablecloth. For a moment I was twelve years old again, huddled in an alley behind a restaurant, clutching a shard of glass whose power I didn't understand.

Of course. How had the Richardses become so powerful? Because with the glass they could see memories. And what were memories, fundamentally, but secrets?

And I knew my uncle's darkest secret of all.

The scandal broke just before the Senate was scheduled to vote on the bill. My uncle recused himself and resigned a week later, when the bill passed. By then the spotlight was firmly focused on the suddenly rejuvenated investigation of the murder of Jim Yarrow, a shop owner near Dartmouth, where my uncle went to college. Apparently, my uncle had bought the upstairs apartment from him but then refused to pay for it, even when the man told him that he needed the money to take his daughter to the hospital. That argument that I had seen had taken place after the girl died. I wrote a letter to my father, knowing full well that he would not come alone, and not really caring.

I met him in the lobby of the hospital. The people behind him looked like bodyguards, but they didn't touch me. I wondered if they would save that until after my mother died.

"How is she?" he asked when he saw me.

I shrugged, as though just thinking about it didn't make me want to weep. "Any day now, they say."

"We should take her back to the States. I have a plane, I'm sure the doctors there could – "

"It's too late, Charles," I said. It made me feel stronger, somehow, to say his first name.

He looked so lost when he nodded that I felt sorry for him. He was weak and he was a bigot, but he had been raised on those twin pillars since he was a baby, and I knew it was too much for me to expect him to change, even for love of my mother.

"Have you come to take the glass?" she asked, when he came into the room.

My father shook his head, but one of the men behind him nodded. "We're ending it here. You'll give it back, one way or another."

My father stayed with her until the end. I touched the glass, sometimes, for comfort, but I never looked through it. I didn't want to know what memories were sharing our misery with us. My mom slipped into a coma during a thunderstorm just like the one from all those years ago in Japan, when I discovered the cave of bones.

Just before, she gripped my hand. She didn't say a thing, she only looked at me, with eyes so fierce in that gaunt face I almost thought they were glowing. I knew what she was asking me, what she couldn't bring herself to say.

"I won't give it back, Ma," I whispered. "I won't let them take me alive."

They were all in the room the morning she died. My father was crying silently beside the bed, but I was finished with my tears. I didn't look at her wasted, lifeless body – I thought of her eyes, dug my nails into my palm, and waited.

"You'll give us back the glass now," one of the men said. He stepped forward. His arms were motionless at his sides, but so tense with energy it was more frightening than a bared fist. I knew that he would not hesitate to hurt me.

"Please, just come back with us, Leah. This running...it killed Carol. Just come back."

I turned toward my father. "The Civil Rights Act...how did you vote?" I asked.

"I didn't," he said. "I didn't cast a ballot."

I smiled. "An invisible vote," I said, "for an invisible daughter."

I pulled the shard out of my pocket. The men glanced at each other warily, but my father only looked miserable.

My mother was standing by his side, wearing her yellow sundress and bug glasses.

"Leah," I heard her say, as though she saw me. "Get in the car."

I stepped through the glass.

The Farmer's Cat

Jeff VanderMeer

Jeff VanderMeer (*www.oivas.com/vanderworld/main.html*) lives in Tallahassee, Florida, with his wife, Ann. VanderMeer is the author of several surreal/magic realist novels and story collections, including *City of Saints & Madmen*, *Veniss Underground*, and *Shriek: An Afterword*. His fiction has appeared in several year's best anthologies as well as in *Asimov's* and *Polyphony*, among many others. For years he was the publisher/editor of Ministry of Whimsy, a small press that produced a number of excellent books, and co-editor of *Leviathan*, an original anthology of speculative fiction and the fantastic. He has been a leading figure in the field in favor of transgressing genre boundaries for at least a decade.

"The Farmer's Cat," a tale of migrating trolls, and a farmer who is oppressed by them, appeared in *Polyphony* 5, the latest in that distinguished series of original speculative fiction anthologies edited by Deborah Layne and Jay Lake. It's a masterful, short bit of classic story retelling in the art-folktale mode.

A LONG TIME AGO, in Norway, a farmer found he had a big problem with trolls. Every winter, the trolls would smash down the door to his house and make themselves at home for a month. Short or tall, fat or thin, hairy or hairless, it didn't matter – every last one of these trolls was a disaster for the farmer. They ate all of his food, drank all of the water from his well, guzzled down all of his milk (often right from the cow!), broke his furniture, and farted whenever they felt like it.

The farmer could do nothing about this – there were too many trolls. Besides, the leader of the trolls, who went by the name of Mobhead, was a big brute of a troll with enormous claws who emitted a foul smell from all of the creatures he'd eaten raw over the years. Mobhead had a huge, gnarled head that seemed green in one kind of light and purple in another. Next to his head, his body looked shrunken and thin, but despite the way they looked his legs were strong as steel; they had to be or his head would have long since fallen off of his neck.

"Don't you think you'd be more comfortable somewhere else?" the farmer asked Mobhead during the second winter. His wife and children had left him for less troll-infested climes. He had lost a lot of his hair from stress.

"Oh, I don't think so," Mobhead said, cleaning his fangs with a toothpick made from a sharpened chair leg. The chair in question had been made by the farmer's father many years before.

"No," Mobhead said. "We like it here just fine." And farted to punctuate his point.

Behind him, one of the other trolls devoured the family cat, and belched.

The farmer sighed. It was getting hard to keep help, even in the summers, when the trolls kept to their lairs and caves far to the north. The farm's reputation had begun to suffer. A few more years of this and he would have to sell the farm, if any of it was left to sell.

Behind him, one of the trolls attacked a smaller troll. There was a splatter of blood against the far wall, a smell oddly like violets, and then the severed head of the smaller troll rolled to a stop at the farmer's feet. The look on the dead troll's face revealed no hint of surprise.

Nor was there a look of surprise on the farmer's face.

All spring and summer, the farmer thought about what he should do. Whether fairly or unfairly, he was known in those parts for thinking or tricking his way out of every problem that had arisen during twenty years of running the farm. But he couldn't fight off the trolls by himself. He couldn't bribe them to leave. It worried him almost as much as the lack of rain in July.

Then, in late summer, a traveling merchant came by the farm. He stopped by twice a year, once with pots, pans, and dried goods and once with livestock and pets. This time, he brought a big, lurching wooden wagon full of animals, pulled by ten of the biggest, strongest horses the farmer had ever seen.

Usually, the farmer bought chickens from the tall, mute merchant, and maybe a goat or two. But this time, the merchant pointed to a cage that held seven squirming, chirping balls of fur. The farmer looked at them for a second, looked away, then looked again, more closely, raising his eyebrows.

"Do you mean to say..." the farmer said, looking at the tall, mute merchant. "Are you telling me..."

The mute man nodded. The frown of his mouth became, for a moment, a mischievous smile.

The farmer smiled. "I'll take one. One should be enough."

The mute man's smile grew wide and deep.

That winter, the trolls came again, in strength – rowdy, smelly, raucous, and looking for trouble. They pulled out a barrel of his best beer and drank it all down in a matter of minutes. They set fire to his attic and snuffed it only when Mobhead bawled them out for "crapping where you eat, you idiots!"

They noticed the little ball of fur curled up in a basket about an hour after they had smashed down the front door.

"'Ere now," said one of the trolls, a foreign troll from England. "Wot's this, wot?"

One of the other trolls – a deformed troll, with a third eye protruding like a tube from its forehead – prodded the ball of fur with one of its big clawed toes. "It's a cat, I think. Just like the last one. Another juicy, lovely cat."

A third troll said, "Save it for later. We've got plenty of time."

The farmer, who had been watching all of this, said to the trolls, "Yes, this is our new cat. But I'd ask that you not eat him. I need him around to catch mice in the summer or when you come back next time, I won't have any grain, and no grain means no beer. It also means lots of other things won't be around for you to eat, like that homemade bread you seem to enjoy so much. In fact, I might not even be around, then, for without grain this farm cannot survive."

The misshapen troll sneered. "A pretty speech, farmer. But don't worry about the mice. We'll eat them all before we leave."

So the farmer went to Mobhead and made Mobhead promise that he and his trolls would leave the cat alone.

"Remember what you said to the trolls who tried to set my attic on fire, O Mighty Mobhead," the farmer said, in the best tradition of flatterers everywhere.

Mobhead thought about it for a second, then said, "Hmmm. I must admit I've grown fond of you, farmer, in the way a wolf is fond of a lamb. And I do want our winter resort to be in good order next time we come charging down out of the frozen north. Therefore, although I have this nagging feeling I might regret this, I will let you keep the cat. But everything else we're going to eat, drink, ruin, or fart on. I just want to make that clear."

The farmer said, "That's fine, so long as I get to keep the cat."

Mobhead said he promised on his dead mothers' eyeteeth, and then he called the other trolls around and told them that the cat was off limits. "You are not to eat the cat. You are not to taunt the cat. You must leave the cat alone."

The farmer smiled a deep and mysterious smile. It was the first smile for him in quite some time. A troll who swore on the eyeteeth of his mothers could never break that promise, no matter what.

And so the farmer got to keep his cat. The next year, when the trolls came barging in, they were well into their rampage before they even saw the cat. When they did, they were a little surprised at how big it had grown. Why, it was almost as big as a dog. And it had such big teeth, too.

"It's one of those Northern cats," the farmer told them. "They grow them big up there. You must know that, since you come from up there. Surely you know that much?"

"Yes, yes," Mobhead said, nodding absent-mindedly, "we know that, farmer," and promptly dove face-first into a large bucket of offal.

But the farmer noticed that the cat made the other trolls nervous. For one thing, it met their gaze and held it, almost as if it weren't an animal, or thought itself their equal. And it didn't really look like a cat, even a Northern cat, to them.

Still, the farmer could tell that the other trolls didn't want to say anything to their leader. Mobhead liked to eat the smaller trolls because they were, under all the hair, so succulent, and none of them wanted to give him an excuse for a hasty dinner.

Another year went by. Spring gave on to the long days of summer, and the farmer found some solace in the growth of not only his crops but also the growth of his cat. The farmer and his cat would take long walks through the fields, the farmer teaching the cat as much about the farm as possible. And he believed that the cat even appreciated some of it.

Once more, too, fall froze into winter, and once more the trolls came tumbling into the farmer's house, led by Mobhead. Once again, they trashed the place as thoroughly as if they were roadies for some drunken band of Scandinavian lute players.

They had begun their second trashing of the house, pulling down the cabinets, splintering the chairs, when suddenly they heard a growl that turned their blood to ice and set them to gibbering, and at their rear there came the sound of bones being crunched, and as they turned to look and see what was happening, they were met by the sight of some of their friends being hurled at them with great force.

The farmer just stood off to the side, smoking his pipe and chuckling from time to time as his cat took care of the trolls. Sharp were his fangs! Long were his claws! Huge was his frame!

Finally, Mobhead walked up alongside the farmer. He was so shaken, he could hardly hold up his enormous head.

"I could eat you right now, farmer," Mobhead snarled. "That is the largest cat I have ever seen – and it is trying to kill my trolls! Only I get to kill my trolls!"

"Nonsense," the farmer said. "My cat only eats mice. Your trolls aren't mice, are they?"

"I eat farmers sometimes," Mobhead said. "How would you like that?"

The farmer took the pipe out of his mouth and frowned. "It really isn't up to me. I don't think Mob-Eater would like that, though."

"Mob-Eater?"

"Yes – that's my name for my cat."

As much as a hairy troll can blanch, Mobhead blanched exactly that much and no more.

"Very well, I won't eat you. But I will eat your hideous cat," Mobhead said, although not in a very convincing tone.

The farmer smiled. "Remember your promise."

Mobhead scowled. The farmer knew the creature was thinking about breaking his promise. But if he did, Mobhead would be tormented by nightmares in which his mothers tortured him with words and with deeds. He would lose all taste for food. He would starve. Even his mighty head would shrivel up. Within a month, Mobhead would be dead...

Mobhead snarled in frustration. "We'll be back when your cat is gone, farmer," he said. "And then you'll pay!"

If he'd had a cape instead of a dirty pelt of fur-hair, Mobhead would have whirled it around him as he left, trailing the remains of his thoroughly beaten and half-digested trolls behind him.

"You haven't heard the last of me!" Mobhead yowled as he disappeared into the snow, now red with the pearling of troll blood.

The next winter, Mobhead and his troll band stopped a few feet from the farmer's front door.

"Hey, farmer, are you there?!" Mobhead shouted.

After a moment, the door opened wide and there stood the farmer, a smile on his face.

"Why, Mobhead. How nice to see you. What can I do for you?"

"You can tell me if you still have that damn cat. I've been looking forward to our winter get-away."

The farmer smiled even more, and behind him rose a huge shadow with large, yellow eyes and rippling muscles under a thick brown pelt. The claws on the shadow were big as carving knives, and the fangs almost as large.

"Why, yes," the farmer said, "as it so happens I still have Mob-Eater. He's a very good mouser."

Mobhead's shoulders slumped.

It would be a long hard slog back to the frozen north, and only troll to eat along the way. As he turned to go, he kicked a small troll out of his way.

"We'll be back next year," he said over his shoulder. "We'll be back every year until that damn cat is gone."

"Suit yourself," the farmer said, and closed the door.

Once inside, the farmer and the bear laughed.

"Thanks, Mob-Eater," the farmer said. "You looked really fierce."

The bear huffed a deep bear belly laugh, sitting back on its haunches in a huge comfy chair the farmer had made for him.

"I am really fierce, father," the bear said. "But you should have let me chase them. I don't like the taste of troll all that much, but, oh, I do love to chase them."

"Maybe next year," the farmer said. "Maybe next year. But for now, we have chores to do. I need to teach you to milk the cows, for one thing."

"But I hate to milk the cows," the bear said. "You know that."

"Yes, but you still need to know how to do it, son."

"Very well. If you say so."

They waited for a few minutes until the trolls were out of sight, and then they went outside and started doing the farm chores for the day.

Soon, the farmer thought, his wife and children would come home, and everything would be as it was before. Except that now they had a huge talking bear living in their house.

Sometimes folktales didn't end quite the way you thought they would. But they did end.

Crab Apple

Patrick Samphire

Patrick Samphire (*www.patrick.samphire.btinternet.co.uk/*) lives in Leeds, UK. He says, "I am a British speculative fiction writer who has lived in Africa, South America and Europe. I now live in Leeds, UK with my wife, Stephanie Burgis, and our border collie, Nika." He attended the 2001 Clarion West Writers' Workshop. "At the moment," he says, "I work for the University of Leeds as an administrator and webmaster." He has published fantasy and science fiction stories, as well as stories for children and young adults. He published several stories in 2005 that were candidates for this volume.

"Crab Apple" was published in *Realms of Fantasy*, which is now equal in quality to *The Magazine of Fantasy & Science Fiction*, at the top of the genre. Samphire says, "This story is set in the Somerset Levels, near where the author grew up, an area of Britain inhabited since before Roman times." It is a Theodore Sturgeonesque fantasy, romantic and disturbing, about a teenage girl who seems to be some sort of dryad.

I SAW HER FIRST the day I found Dad on the kitchen floor. The new girl. The wild girl.

At first I thought Dad had been drinking again. There were beer cans scattered across the floor. But the cans were still full, and I couldn't smell alcohol.

There was something strange about the way Dad was lying. He was too still. His stick-thin arms and legs were sprawled loosely across the tiles. I thought for a moment he was dead.

He was still breathing, though, a wheezy, tight sound, as though a plastic whistle was stuck in his throat. He didn't wake when I shook him.

I'd begun taking first aid classes at school when Dad started losing weight and coughing. There was no one else at home to help. But they had never shown us how to deal with this. I put him in the recovery position and called an ambulance.

The girl was there when I went outside to wait for the ambulance. She was squatting on our garden wall like a wild-haired monkey. She had on a dirty white T-shirt and shorts that showed scratched legs. I guessed she was about fourteen, the same age as me. Her eyes were as brown as oak and her cheeks were freckled and sunburned. There were leaves in her tangled hair.

"What's your name?" she said. "You, what's your name?"

"Josh," I said.

"Joshua," she laughed. "Stupid name."

She winked down at me. Her grin was as wide as her face.

Then she leapt from the wall and dashed away up the hill, her wild hair streaming behind her like a comet's tail. I watched her disappear.

In the distance I heard the ambulance siren approaching.

"You want to see something?"

The wild girl leaned against the school lockers. She was wearing a school uniform, without the tie, but she'd got mud on her blouse already, and her hair was the same mess.

I'd spent most the night at the hospital, by Dad's bed, waiting for him to wake up. He hadn't.

"No," I said.

"You want to know my name?"

"No."

She shoved her sunburned face close to mine. Her brown eyes glittered. "I don't care. Stupid boy."

She laughed and spun down the corridor, arms outstretched. "Stupid, stupid, stupid, stupid, stupid," she shouted as she spun. My face turned red.

The door to the staff room burst open, and Mrs. Wilson strode out, her thick skirt slapping like a whip against her legs.

"What is going on? Come back here."

The wild girl looked back.

"Screw you."

Then she ran again.

Mrs. Wilson pushed back her glasses. Her lips were tight. "Little madam," she said. She glared at me as though I was to blame. "She's got the devil in her, that one. She'll be nothing but trouble, you mark my words, Josh. Nothing but trouble."

"He's awake," the nurse said. She let me into Dad's room.

He was sunk into the stiff white sheets like a balloon with half its air let out. There was a tube running up his nose and another leading to his arm from a bag of clear liquid hooked up on a stand.

He turned his head, blinking.

"Josh." His voice was hoarse, like he'd been shouting.

"How are you doing, Dad?" I tried to stop my voice shaking. I didn't want to seem like a kid.

"Been better, been worse." He worked his lips, as though his mouth was dry. "See, the old devil's put his hand into my chest, lad. Left a bit of a gift for me."

He coughed. His thin chest shuddered. He turned and spat into a metal bowl by his bed. The spit was thick and threaded with blood. He gave me a painful grin.

"Want to hear a name for the devil they never taught you in that Sunday school, lad? Forty-a-day. Good, hey?" He laughed. It was a painful, breathless sound. "Old forty-a-day'll get you every time."

I tried to smile, but couldn't. He looked shriveled away, eaten from the inside. His cheeks were caved in, his skin almost yellow and sagging against his bones, his eyes bloodshot and too big in his face. This wasn't my dad. It was his reflection in a dead mirror, a body from the desert.

"Want to see my X-rays?" he said.

"Okay," I said.

"End of the bed. The blue folder."

I pulled them out and held them up to the window. I could see his ribs and spine as clear white. Two large gray shapes behind the ribs must have been his lungs.

"What's this?"

I pointed at a black lump almost as large as one of Dad's fists in the bottom of the right lung.

"Apple. Swallowed an apple. Hey? Hey?" He coughed again. "I'm tired, lad. Bloody tired. You wouldn't think so after all that sleep." His eyes fluttered shut. He sighed, and his body relaxed on the bed.

I stood over him, staring down at that exhausted face. I wondered how long he'd been so tired. I hadn't noticed. Too busy rushing around. I swallowed to stop a sob. He looked twenty years older than I remembered.

For a moment his eyelids popped open again. "Don't let your mum worry, hey?" he croaked.

"No, Dad," I said.

Mum had been dead since I was five.

Aunt Chris came to stay, to look after me she said. She was waiting on the porch when I got home. She bundled Dad's beer cans into a bin bag and left it outside for the trash collectors. She emptied his ashtrays and put them in the cupboard, right on the top shelf. She threw away all the old magazines and newspapers. Then she started scrubbing, as though she wanted to scrub away every trace of Dad. I went up to my room.

Something woke me in the night. The moon was heavy through the trees at the end of the garden. Somewhere in the dark, an owl hooted, a forlorn, lost sound. I wondered if that had been what had woken me. Then I heard a scratching just below the window. My heart started to thump. A bird, maybe, or even a mouse. That would be it. My hands bunched into fists around the sheets. I closed my eyes. I wasn't a kid anymore, to be frightened by my imagination.

When I opened my eyes, there was a face at the window. I nearly screamed. It was pressed up close, pale but shadowed with the moon behind it. I took a deep breath. The face moved, and I saw the mass of tangled hair.

The wild girl pulled herself up onto my windowsill, and crouched there, staring in. "Open the window," she mouthed.

Wrapping my sheet around me, I stood and hurried over.

"What do you want?"

"Open the window."

I pulled it up, letting in the cool night air. The girl hopped inside.

"Jeez, you're hard to wake."

"It's the middle of the night."

She gave me a wide grin. "You want to see something?"

"What?"

"You have to come and see."

I glanced at the clock. It was two o'clock. I'd have to be up for school in five hours.

"Good," she said, before I could answer. "I'll meet you downstairs. Get dressed." She giggled. "You look stupid with that sheet." Then she clambered back out onto the windowsill. She lowered herself so she was dangling by her hands then looked up at me with that wild face.

"You want to know my name?"

"No," I said.

"It's Emma. Do you like it?"

"It's okay."

"Good."

She dropped, and I heard a soft thud from the ground below. I saw her dart around the side of the house.

I thought about going back to bed, but I just had this feeling that she'd climb back up to my window if I did. I didn't even think she would care if she woke Aunt Chris. She didn't seem to care about anything.

"You should cry, you know. Or scream. Or throw something." She picked up a rock and flung it toward the rooftops below. "Like that. Let yourself go."

We were climbing Braddock Hill, which rose sharply between the scattered houses on my side of the hill and the sprawling, dirty town on the other. It was cold out, and the sky was clear.

"Why?" I said.

"Because of your dad. You can't deal with anything while you're all sewn up like a pillow. You need to escape, let all your feathers fly around the room. Then you can handle anything."

"You can handle anything, can you?" I said.

She jumped in the air, twirling as she did so. "Anything." She laughed. It was a feral sound, like a fox barking in the darkness.

We topped the hill and began to descend. The ground flattened to the left. Emma led me that way, into the trees. I hung back for a moment. It was dark in there. I wasn't so sure this was a good idea anymore. Emma looked back.

"Scared, Josh? You a stupid, scared little boy?"

"No," I said, and followed her in.

There had been an orchard here once, but it had been long abandoned. Hawthorn and ash had sprung up between the apple trees, and tangles of brambles rose in hillocks between the trunks. Right in the center, larger than any of the other trees, stood a spreading crab apple tree. Nothing grew beneath its branches save a layer of thick moss.

Emma stopped beneath it.

"It's a tree," I said. "Big deal."

She leaned back against the bark. "Come closer." She crooked a finger and stared up at me through her eyelashes. Her sweater was tight against her chest. She winked. My heart trembled. My pulse fluttered loudly in my ears. My lips were dry.

She pushed herself away again with a squawk of laughter.

"Just wait," she said, "and watch."

"What?"

"There." She pointed to halfway up the trunk of the massive tree. For a moment I couldn't see what she was pointing at. Then I saw it. The bark of the tree was pulsing, as though there was a slow heart beneath it, or a giant insect trapped in syrup.

The pulses grew. The branches shuddered.

Slowly, something pulled itself from the tree. The bark stretched like toffee, clinging to the creature that was emerging, and then finally snapping back. I thought of a butterfly emerging from its cocoon, but this was no butterfly.

It was shaped almost like a man, but it wasn't a man. It was wrong. Its fingers were as long as my forearm. From its head and its elbows and its knees grew twisted twigs. Its skin was as rutted as bark, but as silver as the moon. Its teeth, when it spread its wide mouth open, were as sharp as pins. Its eyes were bright yellow. I saw claws curling from its fingers and toes. It clung to the tree, and then slowly turned, so that its head was pointing downward, and began to descend.

It moved with the reaching slowness of a stick insect. It would take forever to reach the ground, I thought, but even as I thought that, it moved in a rush I could hardly follow, and it was standing beneath the crab apple tree, not a dozen steps away from us. My breath turned to tar in my throat.

The creature was male, I could see that now. He wore no clothes. Moonlight gathered around him like cold mist. He was tall, towering above me. I wanted to reach out and touch him. He was beautiful. He was the way I thought an angel should look, glorious, alien, and terrible.

I was cold. My legs shook. The hairs on my arms and neck stood painfully on end. I thought he would drown me with his radiant, ugly beauty. I was dark and insignificant before him. He sucked at my thoughts, leaving my head empty. I was inadequate, pathetic, scared.

Through a dry mouth I said, "Who...who are you?"

He was right in front of me. He reached a long, twisted hand toward me, brushed sharp fingers that could slice skin across my face. Suddenly, all I wanted to do was run.

"Crab," he said. "They call me Crab."

He stepped back, and Emma was beside him, grinning her wild grin at me.

"Isn't he beautiful?"

His cruel hand smoothed over her hair, her face, her neck, her shoulders. I backed away. She leaned against him, a little scrap of wildness against his terrible form.

I turned and ran. Behind me, I heard her cry out: "Josh. Come back." But I didn't. I just kept on running.

Dad was asleep when I visited during the next two days.

"You mustn't disturb him," the nurse said. "He needs all the strength he can get."

So I sat beside him, holding his hand, gazing at his wasted body and his face that was so tired it looked bruised.

We used to play football in the park. If I scored a goal he would throw me over my shoulder like a fireman and go whooping down the pitch and dump me through the other goal. I reckoned I could pick him up with one hand now he looked so frail. His breathing was a thin wheeze, in and out, in and out, each breath creasing his face. Once I broke down and sobbed on his chest, but he just kept wheezing in, wheezing out. His skin was as dry as a winter leaf.

On the third day, he was awake, propped up on his pillows. He smiled at me when I came in.

"Been waiting up for you, lad," he said. "Well past my bedtime." He gasped a chuckle. The effort exhausted him. His eyelids fluttered almost shut, but he forced them open again. "Don't let me fall asleep."

"How are you feeling, Dad?"

"Been better, been worse."

I sat beside him. "Brought you some cards." I set them out on the table.

"Nice," he said. "Lad, I got my biopsy results today."

"What's a biopsy?"

He screwed up his old face. "They stuck this tube up my nose, all the way down into my lungs and scooped out a bit of that apple I swallowed." He coughed. "Tested it." He reached out to me with a frail hand and laid it over mine. His fingers curled around mine. "No surprise," he said, looking at me. "It's cancer."

My hand tightened, and he winced.

"Sorry," I said, but I croaked so much it hardly came out.

"They're going to operate," Dad said. "Take out that whole side of the lung. Probably do some other stuff too. Chemotherapy or radiation therapy. We haven't decided yet."

I couldn't move. My whole body was shaking.

"I'm sorry," he said. And as he did, I started to cry, big, painful sobs that shook the chair and his bed.

He waited until I'd finished, and then pulled my hand closer. "Listen, lad, I've been wanting to say this. The drink, see, it took away the pain. Just thought I was getting old. Didn't want to think it was this. So I got drunk and tried to ignore it. I'm sorry."

His breath had become gasps. He was sweating from his forehead. His eyes were bloodshot and tinted yellow with exhaustion.

"Go to sleep, Dad," I said, and he did.

I hadn't seen Emma at school during those three days, but the day after, she was there, leaning against the lockers again, grinning at me.

"Where you going?" she said.

Her hair was more of a mess than ever. It was full of leaves. I shuddered when I thought about where they might have come from. That tree. That creature in it. I had tried to tell myself it was a nightmare, but I knew it wasn't. My shoes had been muddy when I'd got back, and there had been dried leaves on my bedroom floor, near the window.

"First aid class," I said. But I didn't move, just stood there and stared at her.

"Skip it," she said.

I shrugged. "Okay." There didn't seem much point in it anymore. Not unless they could teach me a cure for cancer. I had no time for bandages and mouth-to-mouth.

It was lunchtime. The corridors were heaving, but no one was taking any notice of us. I grabbed Emma's arm as we let ourselves be swept along toward the lunch hall.

"What is he?" I whispered. "Crab. What is he?"

"He's a Dane," she said.

"What, like from Denmark?"

She rolled her eyes, and her mouth turned down. She almost hissed in my face. "No, not like from Denmark. Stupid, ugly, stupid boy. No. The Danes, like in the Fates, the People of Peace, the Fane, the Pharisees." She lowered her voice. "The Fay."

"You mean fai – "

She yanked my arm. "Don't say it! It's bad luck to say that name." She hunched her thin shoulders. "Bad luck."

"That's ridiculous," I said, but my skin wanted to shiver.

"Oh yeah," she said. "So what is he then?"

I shook my head.

"He likes you," she said. "He wants you."

I squinted at her. "What does that mean?"

She bit her lip. For an instant I thought she looked scared. "I don't know," she said. Then she stared defiantly at me again. "I don't care."

We came out into the dining room. Mr. Miller and Mrs. Wilson were on duty. Mrs. Wilson glared at us. I turned away, but Emma stuck out her tongue. Mrs. Wilson went stiff, and her neck reddened.

"Why did you do that?" I whispered.

Emma shrugged. "Why not? Did you see the look she gave us? She can't stand me."

"Let's get something to eat," I said.

Emma touched my hand. I glanced at her. She looked nervous. There was a line of sweat above her lip, and her hand was trembling. She licked her lip.

"I brought you something to eat." She held out her hand. "It's an apple," she said.

It was tiny and too green. I took it from her hand.

"It's okay," she said. "It tastes fine. Eat it."

She didn't meet my eyes.

Slowly, watching her all the time, I brought it up to my mouth.

Someone put a hand on my arm. "Don't eat that."

I looked up. Mr. Miller was standing in front of me.

"That's not a real apple," he said. "It's a crab apple. It's a nasty, bitter, sour thing."

I looked at Emma. She just stared at her shoes.

"Why did you give him that, Emma?" Mr. Miller said softly.

"Because she's an evil little cow," Mrs. Wilson said from behind us.

Emma's head jerked up. "You're the evil cow," she shouted at Mrs. Wilson. "You're the evil, fat, ugly, stupid cow. You."

Emma shoved past us, out into the middle of the hall. Her body was shaking

like a branch in a storm. Her arms windmilled madly around her, sending plates
and trays cascading onto the floor. All the while she kept up an inhuman shriek.
In the middle of it all, her eyes fixed on mine, and I could have sworn that they
were no longer wood-brown, but yellow. Burning yellow.

I found her later in the schoolyard, back pressed up against the concrete wall
of the science block. She was staring up at the thick woods that cloaked Braddock Hill. She had been crying.

"I'm sorry," she said. "I'm so sorry. I didn't mean to do any of that. It's just...
it's just..."

"Just what?" I said.

She turned on me, her eyes narrowed to slits.

"Nothing. It's nothing. Dull, stupid, ugly boy. Go away, go away." She leaped
to her feet and ran.

"Mrs. Tully from school says you've got a new friend," Dad said. "What's her
name?"

"Emma."

"What's she like, hey?" He winked.

"Wild," I said, sighing.

"Wild, hey?" He laughed his breathless laugh.

Sunday afternoon, and dying summer had decided to throw up one final, wonderful, hot day. The air was still and clean, the sky a ferocious blue.

Emma was waiting at the garden gate. She wore jeans and a light, long-
sleeved T-shirt.

"Want to walk?" she said.

"Not to the orchard," I said.

"No." She shivered as though a spider was crawling up her back. "Not to the
orchard."

We climbed the path that led around the other side of Braddock Hill. The
Somerset levels were laid out before us, lush green and gently rumpled. Hundreds of irregularly sized fields, divided by head-high hawthorn and blackthorn
hedges studded with ash, oak, and hazel, stretched to the rise of the Mendip
Hills in the distance. Sunlight glittered from the streams and drainage ditches,
like trails of mercury laid on green felt. Gray stone farmhouses were dotted here
and there. Once every one of them would have had an orchard. Not any more.

We walked close, almost touching, arms brushing once or twice.

"Is your dad going to die?" Emma said.

My throat turned to miserable stone. "Maybe. I guess."

"Oh."

She stared into my eyes. Hers were wide and that deep, swallowing brown. "I don't think I'll die," she said. I could hardly hear her voice. "But...but I think it might be worse."

I touched her shoulder.

"I want to help you," I said. "If I can."

She shook her head. "You can't," she whispered. "He's inside me."

"I could try. If you told me how."

I thought she might cry.

"Let's get out the sun. It's too bright." She pointed to a stand of trees.

We sat in the shade, our backs against a tall oak, sharing the Pepsi and Mars Bar she'd brought with her. I could hear insects buzzing, but they left us alone. The air was so clear it might not even have been there.

I glanced over at Emma. She was staring far out over the levels, watching something I couldn't see. Her face was peaceful, relaxed. She had a twig sticking out her hair. I reached up and pulled it to get it out. It snapped off. Her head jerked forward and she screamed. Sap – and a single drop of blood – welled up in the broken twig.

She turned on me, jumping to her feet. Her brown eyes had turned yellow. Her face was twisted. I scrambled to my feet too. I grabbed her arm and pulled up the sleeve. The skin below was wrinkled, hard, and silvery. I felt sweat under my collar, on my hands.

"You're becoming like him, like Crab," I shouted. "Aren't you? Aren't you?"

She swung for me. Fingernails like claws scraped along my arm. I jumped back.

"Keep away from me, Josh. Keep away."

She turned and was gone, into the trees.

I didn't see her again until the end of the month. Dad came home for a couple of weeks. His operation wasn't scheduled for three months, and the hospital said he was strong enough to be discharged. He didn't look it. His skin was pallid and unhealthy. I could see his veins through it. He couldn't walk more than about four steps without panting.

Aunt Chris cut her way through the jungle that was the back garden, uprooting weeds, cutting back plants, while Dad sat and glowered from the window.

Thursday evening, at the end of his second week home, and Dad had to go back in for tests. Aunt Chris went with him. I sat at home, by the phone, waiting for one of them to call. At ten, the phone rang. It was Aunt Chris.

"Listen, Joshua," she said. "We're staying here overnight." I heard her voice tremble. "They...they say the cancer has begun to metastasize. It's begun to spread. They're going to operate tomorrow at two."

"I want to come in," I said.

"Tomorrow," she said. "He's got to sleep now."

I stood and went to the window and stared out across the moonlit garden.

It took me several minutes to notice the shape at the end of the garden, because it didn't move, but then I saw it for what it was. A person, standing rigid, half-hidden by shadows.

I went to the door and opened it, stepped out.

Her head snapped around. It was Emma. I'd known it would be.

"Stay away from me, Josh," she hissed, then turned and ran.

This time I wasn't going to let her get away. I followed her. She ran fast, keeping to the shadows at the side of the road, but I knew where she was going. To the orchard. To Crab. I dashed after her.

I was out of breath by the time I reached the orchard. My lungs were raw and my throat painful. I saw her standing beneath the crab apple tree, staring up.

She turned, and in the moonlight I saw her clearly. Her fingers were too long. Twisted sticks poked from her head and elbows and knees. Her skin was silver and creased like the bark of a tree. Her eyes were burning yellow, bright in the darkness. Her teeth were pointed and sharp.

"Josh..."

Above her, the bark of the tree began to pulse and bulge.

I ran toward her. She hissed, and her razor-sharp claws darted at my throat. I threw myself back, and she followed. There was nothing of Emma in those eyes.

She swung again, and I ducked, feeling the claws slice through my hair. I punched. My fist caught her jaw. She stumbled back.

She blinked. For a moment her eyes were brown again. I saw panic and fear in them.

"Let me help you," I shouted.

Crab had freed one of his twisted limbs from the bark of the tree. His head was turning to peer down at us.

"Get it out of me, Josh," Emma whispered, her voice cracking. "Get him out of me."

She started to cough, great choking coughs that shook her whole body. Then her eyes turned yellow again.

Before she could move, I darted behind her and grabbed her, my arms circling her body. Above us, Crab freed his last limb and began to descend.

Emma's claws raked my arms. Blood trickled over my skin. I bunched one hand into a fist, crossed the other over it. Emma was struggling, lashing her twisted body to and fro, screaming. But still she was coughing, and still I held her tight.

A thud, and Crab landed in front of us. He rose, his radiance growing. For a moment I felt weak, scared, pathetic. His magnificence was like a ton of sand, pushing down on me, burying me. My arms weakened, and I almost let go. But then I remembered Emma's frightened brown eyes, and I knew I wouldn't let him take her.

Ignoring the pain and fear and weakness, I pushed my fist below her ribs, the way they'd shown us in first aid class, and jerked it upward in time with her cough.

Her body convulsed and she choked, gasped. Something flew from her mouth. We collapsed forward together.

Lying on the moss, still damp from her saliva, was a small green crab apple.

I looked up. Crab was standing there above us. But he no longer looked fearsome or terrible. He looked lonely. He looked like an old, old branch of a tree that had broken off and fallen. His yellow eyes gazed down at us. Then he turned, and climbed back into his crab apple tree.

"I'll be honest with you," the doctor said, looking down at me over his little glasses. "Your dad's got a twenty percent chance, at most. We've got to get the whole cancer out in one go."

Emma and I sat side by side. We had just seen Dad's trolley being pushed into the operating theater. They had wheeled him away like they'd wheeled Mum away when I'd been five. She never came back.

The doctor gave us a nod and then disappeared through the door.

My throat was hard. My teeth were clamped tight shut. I had to close my eyes to stop tears coming.

"Twenty percent," I whispered. "That's no chance at all. He's going to die."

I felt Emma reach for me and take my hand. She pushed something solid and round into it. I opened my eyes. It was the crab apple, whole, undamaged, out of her. She was smiling a wild, free smile. I smiled back, and clasped her hand.

We sat, the crab apple held pressed between our palms, and waited for the doctors to come back out.

Comber

Gene Wolfe

Gene Wolfe (tribute sites include: www.ultan.org.uk and www.urth.net) lives in Barrington, Illinois. He is one of the finest living writers of fantasy. His four volume Book of the New Sun is an acknowledged masterpiece. His most recent book is *The Wizard Knight*. *Soldier of Sidon*, a fantasy novel in the world of *Latro, the Soldier of the Mist*, is out in fall 2006. Collections of his short fiction include *The Island of Dr Death and Other Stories and Other Stories*, *Storeys from the Old Hotel*, *Endangered Species*, *Strange Travelers*, *Innocents Aboard*, and *Starwater Strains*.

"Comber" was published in *Postscripts*, the fine new genre quarterly from the UK. The setting is a city floating on a huge wave. Perhaps it is a fantasy about continental drift – if continental drift went much faster and worked with smaller chunks.

THE NEWS WHISPERED BY HIS RADIO this morning was the same as the news when he and Mona had gone to bed: the city had topped the crest, and everything was flat and wonderful – if only for a day or two. "You're flat yourselves," he told it softly, and switched it off.

Mona was still asleep when he had shaved and dressed, her swollen belly at rest on the mattress, her face full of peace, and her slow inhalations loud to his acute hearing. He grabbed a breakfast bar on his way through the kitchen and wondered how the hell he could start the car without waking her up.

There was a ball on the driveway, a chewed-up rubber ball some dog had stopped chasing when it had stopped running. He picked it up and bounced it off the concrete. It bounced a few more times and settled down to rest again, as round as Mona, though not quite as happy. He tossed it into the car and followed it.

Press the accelerator, let it up, twist the key. The little engine purred to life as if it knew its work would be easy today. The suburb passed in a familiar blur.

From the tollway, he eyed the tall buildings that marked the center of the city. The last crest had come before he was born (the crest of a wholly different wave, something he found hard to imagine) but he knew that not one of those spumecatchers had been built then. Now the city might have to pay for its pride and the convenience of having so many offices close together. Pay with its very existence, perhaps.

The brass inclinometer he had bought when he had foreseen the danger the year before was waiting for him when he reached his desk, solidly screwed to the desktop, its long axis coinciding exactly with the direction of motion of the plate. He squinted at the needle, and at last got out a magnifying glass. Zero. It seemed supernatural: a portent.

A memo taped to his monitor warned him that the new angle "which will soon grow steep" would be the reverse of what it called "the accustomed angle." Everything was to be secured a second time with that new angle in mind. Workmen would make the rounds of all offices. He was asked to cooperate for the good of the company. He tossed the memo, woke his processor, and opened Mona's private dream house instead. His design was waiting there to be tinkered with, as it would not have been if anyone in authority had found it.

"Okay if I look at your gadget?" It was Phil, and Phil looked without waiting for his permission. "Flat," Phil said happily, and laughed. "The plate's flat. First time in my life."

"The last time, too." He closed Mona's dreamhouse. "For either one of us."

Phil rubbed his hands. "It will all be different. Entirely different. A new slant on everything. Want to go up to the roof, ol' buddy? Should be a great view."

He shook his head.

It would be very different indeed, he reflected when Phil had left, if the plate overturned. As it very well might. If the building did not break up when it hit the water, it would point down and would be submerged. Water would short out the electrical equipment, probably at once; and in any event, the elevators would no longer operate. Rooms and corridors might (or might not) hold some air for a few hours – most of it down on what were now the lower floors. He might, perhaps, break a window and so escape; if he lived long enough to rise to street level, the edge of the plate, and air, would be what? Thirty miles away? Forty?

Back home, Mona would have drowned. If the plate were going to turn over, he decided, it would be better if it did it while he was at home with her. Better if they died together with their unborn child.

Next day the inclinometer was no longer on zero, and the chewed ball he had left on his desk had rolled to one side; as he wrote letters and called contacts, as he began to sketch the outline of his next project, he watched the space between the end of the needle and the hair-thin zero line grow.

By Friday the needle was no longer near zero, and there were intervening marks which he did not trouble to read. Because on Friday, at not-quite eleven o'clock of that bright and still almost-level morning, Edith Benson called to say that Mona had gone into labor while they chatted across the fence, and that she had driven Mona to the hospital.

He took some time off. By the time he returned to his desk, the needle was no more than a pencil's width from the peg. It seemed to him to tremble there, and he was reminded of his conversation with the proprietor of the little shop in which he had bought the inclinometer. He had asked why the scale went no further; and the proprietor had grinned, showing beautifully regular teeth that had certainly been false. "Because you won't be there to look at it if she goes farther than that," the proprietor had told him.

A note taped to his desk informed him that he had neglected to set the brake on his swivel chair. It had pushed open the door of his office and crashed into Mrs. Patterson's desk. He apologized to her in person.

At quitting time, the space between the point of the needle and the peg would admit three of his business cards, but not four.

That evening he and Mona sat up until their son's next feeding, talking about colleges and professions. It would be up to Adrian to choose, they agreed on that. But would not their own attitudes, the training they gave him, and their very table-talk, influence Adrian's choices? At ten they kissed, looked in on Adrian, and kissed again.

"Goodnight, honey," Mona said; and he, knowing that she did not want him to watch, "Goodnight, darling."

As he combed his hair the next morning, he found that his thoughts, which should have been focused on work, were full of Adrian – and the plate. More and taller buildings would go up when this was over. More and taller buildings would be built, that was to say, if there was anyone left alive to plan and build them. His firm would have a part of that, and would profit by it. Those profits would contribute to his profit-sharing plan.

He shrugged, rinsed his comb, and put it away. The new and wonderful house that he himself had designed – with a den and a sewing room, and enough bedrooms for five children – would not be quite so far off then.

At work, he found the needle not quite so near the peg as it had been. Three business cards slipped into the opening easily. Four would just clear.

Up on the roof, a little knot of his coworkers were marveling at the vastness of the tossing green waters that stretched to the horizon in every direction. The secretary with the gold pince-nez gripped his arm. "I come up here every morning. We'll never be able to see anything like this again, and today will be the last day we're this high up."

He nodded, trying to look serious and pleased. The secretary with the gold pince-nez was the CEO's, and although he had seen her often he had never spoken to her – much less been spoken to.

An executive vice president laid large soft hands on his shoulders. "Take a good long look, young man. If it sticks with you, you'll think big. We always need people who think big."

He said, "I will, sir."

Yet he found himself looking at the people who looked, and not at the boundless ocean. There was the freckled kid from the mailroom who whistled, and over there the pretty blonde who never smiled.

All alone, at the very edge of the gently slanting roof, was old Parsons. Hadn't Parsons retired? Clearly Parsons had not; and Parsons had set up a tarnished brass telescope on a tripod – a telescope through which he peered down into the watery abyss that had opened before the city, not out at the grandeur of the horizon.

"Something in the water?"

Parsons straightened up. "Sure is."

"What is it?"

Gnarled fingers stroked bristling, almost invisible white whiskers. "That," Parsons said slowly, "is what I'm trying to figure, young feller."

"A whale?" he asked.

Parsons shook his head. "Nope. 'Tain't that. You might think it'd be easy to figure, with a good glass. But 'tain't." Parsons stepped aside. "You want to look?"

He bent as Parsons had and made a slight adjustment to the focus.

It was a city, or a town at least, nestled now in the trough. Narrow streets, roofs that seemed to be largely of red tiles. A white spire rose above its houses and shops, and for an instant – only an instant, it seemed to him that he had caught the gleam of the gold cross atop the spire.

He straightened up, swallowed as though his throat and stomach had some part in absorbing what he had just seen, and bent to look again.

Something white fluttered and vanished above one red roof. A pigeon, he felt certain. There were pigeons as well as gulls there, circling above the houses and shops; pigeons that no doubt nested in the eaves and scavenged the town's streets, whatever food might be found in them.

"Been lookin' on my old computer at home," Parsons said. "There's views of various places on there, if you know where to look. My guess is Les Sables-d'Olonne. Mind now, I'm not sayin' I'm right. Just my guess, I said. You got one?"

He shook his head. "If – It'll be out of the way, won't it? By the time we get there? The next wave will pick it up first, won't it?" As he spoke, he discovered that he did not believe a word of it.

"Can't say." Parsons scratched his bristling jaw. "Pretty slow, generally, goin' up. Slidin' down's faster 'n blazes, and you go a long way." Turning his head, he spat. "We're heading right at it."

"If it wasn't, if it was still in the way... And we hit – "

"Might bust our plate. I dunno. I phoned up one of them geologists. They're s'posed to know all about all that. He said he didn't know neither. Depend on how fast each was goin'. Only you ought to think 'bout this, young feller – ain't a buildin' on ours that could stand it if we bump with much speed a-tall. Knock 'em flat, ever' last one of 'em."

Reluctantly he nodded. "You're right, it will. May I ask who you called, sir?"

"Doctor Lantz, his name was. Said don't talk about it, only he don't have any right to give *me* orders." Old Parsons appeared to hesitate. "Won't matter to me. I'll be gone long before. You might still be around, though, a healthy young feller like you."

"Yes," he said. Images of the baby, of Adrian, filled his mind; he continued to talk almost by reflex. "I asked about the geologist because I know a geologist. Slightly. I've gotten to know him slightly. His name isn't Lantz, though. It's Sutton. Martin Sutton. He lives one street over from us."

He debated the matter with himself for more than an hour before telephoning Sutton. "You know some things I need to know, Marty," he said when the preliminaries were complete, "and I'm going to pick your brain, if you'll let me. This city or town or whatever it is in the trough – are we going to hit it?"

There was a lengthy silence before Sutton said, "You know about it, too."

"Correct."

"They've kept it off TV. They'll keep it out of the papers, if they can. I wonder how many people know."

"I have no idea. Are we, Marty?"

"That's not my field. I'm a geologist, okay? I study the plate."

"But you know. Are we?"

Sutton sighed. "Probably. How'd you find out?"

"I looked though a telescope, that's all. There's a town down there. Or a small city – take your pick. It's got fields and gardens around it. What are the odds?"

Sutton's shrug was almost audible. "One in ten, maybe."

"One in ten of hitting?"

"No. One in ten of missing. They were calling it one in five yesterday. You mustn't tell anybody I've told you, okay?"

"I won't. But they told you. So you could tell them whether our plate would break?"

Another silence, this one nearly as long as the first. Then: "Yeah."

"They did, but that wasn't the main reason. What's the other thing? It might help if you'd tell me."

"For God's sake keep it under your hat." Even over the phone, Sutton sounded desperate.

"I will, I swear. What is it?"

"They wanted to talk about the feasibility of breaking up the other plate in advance. You know – the one we're going to hit."

"I understand. Go on."

"Suppose we could do it. Suppose we could break it into three pieces. They'd drift apart, and we might not hit all three."

He nodded slowly to himself. "And even if we did, three small shocks wouldn't be as damaging as one big one."

"Right." Sutton seemed a little less nervous now.

"They'll try to prepare for them too, of course. We've got a crew going through our offices double-bolting everything. Steel boots to hold the legs of the desks, and they're screwing our file cabinets to the walls as well as the floor. I was watching it a few minutes ago."

"I suppose we'll get that here too," Sutton said, "but it hasn't started yet."

"Your superiors don't know."

"I guess not."

"I see. I suppose mine have been asked whether it would be practical to reinforce certain buildings. One more question, please, Marty, and it may be the last one. Would what they asked you about be feasible? Breaking up the plate we're going to hit like that?"

"I think so. Probably.... Listen, I'm not supposed to talk about this, but I'd like to get it off my chest. First, I've had to assume that their plate's pretty much like ours. Ours is the only one we're familiar with."

"Sure."

"Assuming that it is, we'd have to drill into it and plant charges about a hundred feet down. I said the people there aren't going to stand still for that, and they said they'd take them by surprise. It's not very big, okay? A thousand men, well trained and heavily armed. Hydrofoils that will launch when we're close. I'll probably be one of the men on the boats. Everyone else here is older, they'll be old men by the time it happens. I'm not much older than you are. I'll still be active."

"What about somebody younger? Somebody who hasn't graduated yet?"

"There won't be anybody like that." Sutton's voice went flat, stripped of all emotion. "I might as well tell you this, too – it's the kind of thing that can't be kept secret. The university's dropped geology. They've closed the whole department, effective immediately."

That night, over wieners and sauerkraut, he told Mona. "I promised a person who trusted me that I wouldn't talk about this, but you're going to have to know."

When he had finished outlining the situation, she said, "But won't it work? This man you talked to said it would."

"Probably not." He paused, listening to the trees murmur in the wind that would soon become a years-long gale: the wind of the city's swift descent. "They must surely see us coming at them, just as we see them in our path. They'll start preparing, and both sides have ten or fifteen years to prepare in. They can arm everyone who's willing to fight, and put up obstacles to keep our people from landing. I think we can count on both those."

"They could break up their plate for us."

He nodded. "Yes, they could. We could break up ours, too. Do you think the government will?"

For a long moment Mona stared at him. At last she said, "How horrible! No. Of course they won't."

"But we could do it ourselves." The idea had come to full flower during his long call to Sutton; he had seized it eagerly, and hoped now to inspire her to an equal acceptance. "We could plant charges that would exploit known weaknesses in our plate. The force of the explosions would start our piece moving away from the city, and out of the collision path the city's on now."

"But, darling – "

"Adrian would have a future. Don't you see, Mona? We wouldn't take just this residential neighborhood, but a piece of the infrastructure big enough to be economically viable. We could make things for ourselves then, make things to trade, grow gardens, and fish. That town the city's going to hit – French or Belgian or whatever it is – people survive there. They even prosper. I've bounced this off of a man over on the next street, a geologist. He agrees it might be possible, and he's coming over to talk about it."

"Bumpers! We could build bumpers, things with springs in them. Or – or big sacks full of air."

He shook his head. "Nothing we could build would have much effect on a mass as great as the plate's, and if we succeeded in slowing it down much – we wouldn't – the wave would break over us and drown everybody."

"But..." Mona looked desperate. "But, Honey – "

He glanced at his watch. "Sutton's coming at eight. You won't have to feed him, but coffee and cookies might be nice. Or cake. Something like that."

"Okay." Mona's voice was scarcely audible.

An hour later she said, "Won't you please stop combing your hair with your fingers like that? And pacing up and down and up and down?"

For the twentieth time he looked at his watch. "Sutton could be here right now."

"He could," Mona conceded, "if he'd come at least ten minutes early. Honestly, I'm going to get hysterical. Sit down and relax. Or – or go outside where you can see his headlights as soon as he turns onto the street. Please? If I start screaming I'll wake Adrian. Won't you, pretty please, Honey, for me?"

He nodded, suddenly grateful, and discovered that he had been on the point of running his fingers through his hair again. "Okay. I'll do that. I won't come back in until he gets here."

The wind had turned the night cold. He walked out to the street. *How many charges would they need, and how big would each have to be? Would they have to enlist a chemist to make the explosives? Dynamite, or whatever?* To his right, looming white above the treetops though far more distant, he could only just glimpse the boiling crest of the wave. Those trees were wrongly slanted now. Come morning, they would find themselves pointed away from the sun. He chuckled softly. It could not be often that smug suburban trees received such an unpleasant surprise.

When he returned to the house to sit on the stoop, Mona had drawn the blinds. She was being overly cautious, he decided, but he could not find it in his heart to blame her.

Out at the curb again and still nervous, he held his breath as headlights turned off Miller Road. They crept up the sloping street as though the driver were checking house numbers, and then – incredibly, miraculously – swung into the driveway.

Sutton climbed out, and they shook hands. "I hadn't forgotten where you live," Sutton said, "but this new angle has me a little disoriented."

He nodded. "All of us are. I think that may work in our favor."

"Maybe you're right." The wind snatched away Sutton's baseball cap. Sutton grabbed for it, missing by a foot or more. "Help me find that, will you? I'd hate to lose it."

They had searched the bushes for a minute or more when Sutton straightened up and said, "Something wrong? What's the matter with you?"

He had straightened up already. "Sirens." He pointed east, northeast, and after a momentary hesitation, north. "Don't you hear them?"

Sutton shook his head. "No, I don't."

"Well, I do. Three or four cars, and they're getting closer."

One by one, the sirens grew louder – and abruptly fell silent. For almost the last time, he ran nervous fingers through his hair.

"What's up?" Sutton began. "If you – "

Before the third word, he had turned and sprinted for the door. It was locked. His key turned the lock and the bolt clicked back, but the night bolt was in place. Once only, his shoulder struck the unyielding wood.

By that time the first police car had turned the corner on two screaming wheels, and it was too late to hide.

Walpurgis Afternoon

Delia Sherman

Delia Sherman (*www.sff.net/people/kushnerSherman/Sherman/*) lives in Somerville, Massachusetts. Her website bio says, "She spent much of her early life at one end of a classroom or another, first at Vassar and Brown University, where she earned a Ph.D. in Renaissance Studies in 1981," and later taught at Boston University and Northeastern. She was nominated for the Campbell Award for Best New SF Writer in 1990, and is a member of the Motherboard of the James Tiptree, Jr. Award Council. In 1995, she became a contributing editor for Tor Books. She is working with others in organizing the Interstitial Arts movement, "dedicated to the proposition that the boundaries between artistic genres exist to be crossed." Her novel *The Porcelain Dove* is a classic of contemporary fantasy. Her short fiction has appeared in *The Magazine of Fantasy & Science Fiction*, *Xanadu II*, *The Armless Maiden*, *Ruby Slippers*, *Golden Tears*, *A Wolf at the Door*, and *The Green Man*, among others. She is married to Ellen Kushner and collaborated with her on the novel, *The Fall of Kings*. Sherman's new novel out in 2006 is *Changeling*.

"Walpurgis Afternoon" was published in *The Magazine of Fantasy & Science Fiction*. It is the story of a huge Victorian house that arrives in a snooty New England Brahmin neighborhood overnight. The scalpel of satire has never been more precisely wielded than in this terrific story. And it is an interesting contrast to the Heather Shaw story later in this book.

THE BIG THING about the new people moving into the old Pratt place at Number 400 was that they got away with it at all. Our neighborhood is big on historical integrity. The newest house on the block was built in 1910, and you can't even change the paint-scheme on your house without recourse to preservation committee studies and zoning board hearings.

The old Pratt place had generated a tedious number of such hearings over the years – I'd even been to some of the more recent ones. Old Mrs. Pratt had let it go pretty much to seed, and when she passed away, there was trouble about clearing the title so it could be sold, and then it burned down.

Naturally a bunch of developers went after the land – a three-acre property in a professional neighborhood twenty minutes from downtown is something like a Holy Grail to developers. But their lawyers couldn't get the title cleared either, and the end of it was that the old Pratt place never did get built on. By the time Geoff and I moved next door, the place was an empty lot. The neighborhood kids played Bad Guys and Good Guys there after school and the neighborhood cats preyed on its endless supply of mice and voles. I'm not talking eyesore, here; just a big shady plot of land overgrown with bamboo, rhododendrons, wildly rambling roses, and some nice old trees, most notably an immensely ancient copper beech big enough to dwarf any normal-sized house.

It certainly dwarfs ours.

Last spring all that changed overnight. Literally. When Geoff and I turned in, we lived next door to an empty lot. When we got up, we didn't. I have to tell you, it came as quite a shock first thing on a Monday morning, and I wasn't even the one who discovered it. Geoff was.

Geoff's the designated keeper of the window because he insists on sleeping with it open and I hate getting up into a draft. Actually, I hate getting up, period. It's a blessing, really, that Geoff can't boil water without burning it, or I'd never be up before ten. As it is, I eke out every second of warm unconsciousness I can while Geoff shuffles across the floor and thunks down the sash and takes his shower. On that particular morning, his shuffle ended not with a thunk, but with a gasp.

"Holy shit," he said.

I sat up in bed and groped for my robe. When we were in grad school, Geoff had quite a mouth on him, but fatherhood and two decades of college teaching have toned him down a lot. These days, he usually keeps his swearing for Supreme Court decisions and departmental politics.

"Get up, Evie. You gotta see this."

So I got up and went to the window, and there it was, big as life and twice as natural, a real *Victorian Homes* centerfold, set back from the street and just the right size to balance the copper beech. Red tile roof, golden brown clapboards, miles of scarlet-and-gold gingerbread draped over dozens of eaves, balconies, and dormers. A witch's hat tower, a wrap-around porch, and a massive carriage house. With a cupola on it. Nothing succeeds like excess, I always say.

"Holy shit."

"Watch your mouth, Evie," said Geoff automatically.

I like to think of myself as a fairly sensible woman. I don't imagine things, I face facts, I hadn't gotten hysterical when my fourteen-year-old daughter asked me about birth control. Surely there was some perfectly rational explanation for this phenomenon. All I had to do was think of it.

"It's an hallucination," I said. "Victorian houses don't go up overnight. People do have hallucinations. We're having an hallucination. Q.E.D."

"It's not a hallucination," Geoff said.

Geoff teaches intellectual history at the University and tends to disagree, on principle, with everything everyone says. Someone says the sky is blue, he says it isn't. And then he explains why. "This has none of the earmarks of a hallucination," he went on. "We aren't in a heightened emotional state, not expecting a miracle, not drugged, not part of a mob, not starving, not sense-deprived. Besides, there's a clothesline in the yard with laundry hanging on it. Nobody hallucinates long underwear."

I looked where he was pointing, and sure enough, a pair of scarlet long johns was kicking and waving from an umbrella-shaped drying-rack, along with a couple pairs of women's panties, two oxford-cloth shirts hung up by their collars, and a gold-and-black print caftan. There was also what was arguably the most beautifully designed perennial bed I'd ever seen basking in the early morning sun. As I was squinting at the delphiniums, a side door opened and a woman came out with a wicker clothes basket propped on her hip. She was wearing shorts and a T-shirt, had fairish hair pulled back in a bushy tail, and struck me as being a little long in the tooth to be going barefoot and braless.

"Nice legs," said Geoff.

I snapped down the window. "Pull the shades before you get in the shower," I said. "It looks to me like our new neighbors get a nice, clear shot of our bathroom from their third floor."

In our neighborhood, we pride ourselves on minding our own business and not each others' – live and let live, as long as you keep your dog, your kids, and your lawn under control. If you don't, someone calls you or drops you a note, and if that doesn't make you straighten up and fly right, well, you're likely to get a call from the town council about that extension you neglected to get a variance for. Needless to say, the house at Number 400 fell way outside all our usual coping mechanisms. If some contractor had shown up at dawn with bulldozers and two-by-fours, I could have called the police or our councilwoman or someone and got an injunction. How do you get an injunction against a physical impossibility?

The first phone call came at about eight-thirty: Susan Morrison, whose back yard abuts the Pratt place.

"Reality check time," said Susan. "Do we have new neighbors or do we not?"

"Looks like it to me," I said.

Silence. Then she sighed. "Yeah. So. Can Kimmy sit for Jason Friday night?"

Typical. If you can't deal with it, pretend it doesn't exist, like when one couple down the street got the bright idea of turning their front lawn into a wildflower meadow. The trouble is, a Victorian mansion is a lot harder to ignore than even the wildest meadow. The phone rang all morning with hysterical calls from women who hadn't spoken to us since Geoff's brief tenure as president of the neighborhood association.

After several fruitless sessions of what's-the-world-coming-to, I turned on the machine and went out to the garden to put in the beans. Planting them in May was pushing it, but I needed the therapy. For me, gardening's the most soothing activity on Earth. When you plant a bean, you get a bean, not an azalea or a cabbage. When you see that bean covered with icky little orange things, you know they're Mexican bean beetle larvae and go for the pyrethrum. Or you do if you're paying attention. It always astonishes me how oblivious even the garden club ladies can be to a plant's needs and preferences.

Sure, there are nasty surprises, like the winter that the mice ate all the Apricot Beauty tulip bulbs. But mostly you know where you are with a garden. If you put the work in, you'll get satisfaction out, which is more than can be said of marriages or careers.

This time though, digging and raking and planting failed to work their usual magic. Every time I glanced up, there was Number 400, serene and comfortable, the shrubs established and the paint chipping just a little around the windows, exactly as if it had been there forever instead of less than twelve hours.

I'm not big on the inexplicable. Fantasy makes me nervous. In fact, fiction makes me nervous. I like facts and plenty of them. That's why I wanted to be a botanist. I wanted to know everything there was to know about how plants worked, why azaleas like acid soil and peonies like wood ash and how you might be able to get them to grow next to each other. I even went to graduate school and took organic chemistry. Then I met Geoff, fell in love, and traded in my Ph.D. for an M-R-S, with a minor in Mommy. None of these events (except possibly falling in love with Geoff) fundamentally shook my allegiance to provable, palpable facts. The house next door was palpable, all right, but it shouldn't have been. By the time Kim got home from school that afternoon, I had a headache from trying to figure out how it got to be there.

Kim is my daughter. She reads fantasy, likes animals a lot more than she likes people, and is a big fan of *Buffy the Vampire Slayer*. Because of Kim, we have two dogs (Spike and Willow), a cockatiel (Frodo), and a lop-eared Belgian rabbit (Big Bad), plus the overflow of semi-wild cats (Balin, Dwalin, Bifur, and Bombur) from the Pratt place, all of which she feeds and looks after with truly astonishing dedication.

Three-thirty on the nose, the screen door slammed and Kim careened into the kitchen with Spike and Willow bouncing ecstatically around her feet.

"Whaddya think of the new house, Mom? Who do you think lives there? Do they have pets?"

I laid out her after-school sliced apple and cheese and answered the question I could answer. "There's at least one woman – she was hanging out laundry this morning. No sign of children or pets, but it's early days yet."

"Isn't it just the coolest thing in the universe, Mom? Real magic, right next door. Just like *Buffy*."

"Without the vampires, I hope. Kim, there's no such thing as magic. There's probably a perfectly simple explanation."

"But, *Mom!*"

"But nothing. You need to call Mrs. Morrison. She wants to know if you can sit for Jason on Friday night. And Big Bad's looking shaggy. He needs to be brushed."

That was Monday.

Tuesday morning, our street looked like the Expressway at rush hour. It's a miracle there wasn't an accident. Everybody in town must have driven by, slowing down as they passed Number 400 and craning out the car window. Things quieted down in the middle of the day when everyone was at work, but come 4:30 or so, the joggers started and the walkers and more cars. About 6:00, the police pulled up in front of the house, at which point everyone stopped pretending to be nonchalant and held their breath. Two cops disappeared into the house, came out again a few minutes later, and left without talking to anybody. They were holding cookies and looking bewildered.

The traffic let up on Wednesday. Kim found a kitten (Hermione) in the wild-flower garden and Geoff came home full of the latest in a series of personality conflicts with his department head, which gave everyone something other than Number 400 to talk about over dinner.

Thursday, Lucille Flint baked one of her coffee cakes and went over to do the Welcome Wagon thing.

Lucille's our local Good Neighbor. Someone moves in, has a baby, marries, dies, and there's Lucille, Johnny-on-the-spot with a coffee cake in her hands and the proper Hallmark sentiment on her lips. Lucille has the time for this kind of thing because she doesn't have a regular job. All right, neither do I, but I write a gardener's advice column for the local paper, so I'm not exactly idle. There's the garden, too. Besides, I'm not the kind of person who likes sitting around in other people's kitchens drinking watery instant and hearing the stories of their lives. Lucille is.

Anyway. Thursday morning, I researched the diseases of roses for my column. I'm lucky with roses. Mine never come down with black spot, and the Japanese beetles prefer Susan Morrison's yard to mine. Weeds, however, are not so obliging. When I'd finished Googling "powdery mildew," I went out to tackle the rosebed.

Usually, I don't mind weeding. My mind wanders, my hands get dirty. I can almost feel my plants settling deeper into the soil as I root out the competition. But my rosebed is on the property line between us and the Pratt place. What if the house disappeared again, or someone came out and wanted to chat? I'm not big into chatting. On the other hand, there was shepherd's purse in the rosebed, and shepherd's purse can be a real wild Indian once you let it get established, so I gritted my teeth, grabbed my Cape Cod weeder, and got down to it.

Just as I was starting to relax, I heard footsteps passing on the walk and pushed the rose canes aside just in time to see Lucille Flint climbing the stone steps to Number 400. I watched her ring the doorbell, but I didn't see who answered because I ducked down behind a bushy Gloire de Dijon. If Lucille doesn't care who knows she's a busybody, that's her business.

After twenty-five minutes, I'd weeded and cultivated those roses to a fare-thee-well, and was backing out when I heard the screen door, followed by Lucille telling someone how *lovely* their home was, and thanks again for the *scrumptious* pie.

I caught her up under the copper beech.

"Evie dear, you're all out of breath," she said. "My, that's a nasty tear in your shirt."

"Come in, Lucille," I said. "Have a cup of coffee."

She followed me inside without comment, and accepted a cup of microwaved coffee and a slice of date-and-nut cake.

She took a bite, coughed a little, and grabbed for the coffee.

"It is pretty awful, isn't it?" I said apologetically. "I baked it last week for some PTA thing at Kim's school and forgot to take it."

"Never mind. I'm full of cherry pie from next door. " She leaned over the stale cake and lowered her voice. "The cherries were *fresh*, Evie."

My mouth dropped open. "Fresh cherries? In May? You're kidding."

Lucille nodded, satisfied at my reaction. "Nope. There was a bowl of them on the table, leaves and all. What's more, there was corn on the draining-board. Fresh corn. In the husk. With the silk still on it."

"No!"

"Yes." Lucille sat back and took another sip of coffee. "Mind you, there could be a perfectly ordinary explanation. Ophelia's a horticulturist, after all. Maybe she's got greenhouses out back. Heaven knows there's enough room for several."

I shook my head. "I've never heard of corn growing in a greenhouse."

"And I've never heard of a house appearing in an empty lot overnight," Lucille said tartly. "About that, there's nothing I can tell you. They're not exactly forthcoming, if you know what I mean."

I was impressed. I knew how hard it was to avoid answering Lucille's questions, even about the most personal things. She just kind of picked at you, in the nicest possible way, until you unraveled. It's one of the reasons I didn't hang out with her much.

"So, who are they?"

"Rachel Abrams and Ophelia Canderel. I think they're lesbians. They feel like family together, and you can take it from me, they're not sisters."

Fine. We're a liberal suburb, we can cope with lesbians. "Children?"

Lucille shrugged. "I don't know. There were drawings on the fridge, but no toys."

"Inconclusive evidence," I agreed. "What did you talk about?"

She made a face. "Pie crust. The Perkins's wildflower meadow. They like it. Burney." Burney was Lucille's husband, an unpleasant old fart who disapproved of everything in the world except his equally unpleasant terrier, Homer. "Electricians. They want a fixture put up in the front hall. Then Rachel tried to tell me about her work in artificial intelligence, but I couldn't understand a word she said."

From where I was sitting, I had an excellent view of Number 400's wisteria-covered carriage house with its double doors ajar on an awe-inspiring array of garden tackle. "Artificial intelligence must pay well," I said.

Lucille shrugged. "There has to be family money somewhere. You ought to see the front hall, not to mention the kitchen. It looks like something out of a magazine."

"What are they doing here?"

"That's the forty-thousand-dollar question, isn't it?"

We drained the cold dregs of our coffee, contemplating the mystery of why a horticulturist and an artificial intelligence wonk would choose our quiet, tree-lined suburb to park their house in. It seemed a more solvable mystery than how they'd transported it there in the first place.

Lucille took off to make Burney his noontime franks and beans and I tried to get my column roughed out. But I couldn't settle to my computer, not with that Victorian enigma sitting on the other side of my rosebed. Every once in a while, I'd see a shadow passing behind a window or hear a door bang. I gave up trying to make the disposal of diseased foliage interesting and went out to poke around in the garden. I was elbow-deep in the viburnum, pruning out deadwood, when I heard someone calling.

It was a woman, standing on the other side of my roses. She was big, solidly curved, and dressed in bright flowered overalls. Her hair was braided with shiny gold ribbon into dozens of tiny plaits tied off with little metal beads. Her skin was a deep matte brown, like antique mahogany. Despite the overalls, she was astonishingly beautiful.

I dropped the pruning shears. "Damn," I said. "Sorry," I said. "You surprised me." I felt my cheeks heat. The woman smiled at me serenely and beckoned.

I don't like new people and I don't like being put on the spot, but I've got my pride. I picked up my pruning shears, untangled myself from the viburnum, and marched across the lawn to met my new neighbor.

She said her name was Ophelia Canderel, and she'd been admiring my garden. Would I like to see hers?

I certainly would.

If I'd met Ophelia at a party, I'd have been totally tongue-tied. She was beautiful, she was big, and frankly, there just aren't enough people of color in our neighborhood for me to have gotten over my Liberal nervousness around them. This particular woman of color, however, spoke fluent Universal Gardener and her garden was a gardener's garden, full of horticultural experiments and puzzles and stuff to talk about. Within about three minutes, she was asking my advice about the gnarly brown larvae infesting her bee balm, and I was filling her in on the peculiarities of our local microclimate. By the time we'd inspected every flower and shrub in the front yard, I was more comfortable with her than I was with the local garden club ladies. We were alike, Ophelia and I.

We were discussing the care and feeding of peonies in an acid soil when Ophelia said, "Would you like to see my shrubbery?"

Usually when I hear the word "shrubbery," I think of a semi-formal arrangement of rhodies and azaleas, lilacs and viburnum, with a potentilla perhaps, or a butterfly bush for late summer color. The bed should be deep enough to give everything room to spread and there should be a statue in it, or maybe a sundial. Neat, but not anal – that's what you should aim for in a shrubbery.

Ophelia sure had the not-anal part down pat. The shrubs didn't merely spread, they rioted. And what with the trees and the orchids and the ferns and the vines, I couldn't begin to judge the border's depth. The hibiscus and the bamboo were okay, although I wouldn't have risked them myself. But to plant bougainvillea and poinsettias, coconut palms and frangipani this far north was simply tempting fate. And the statue! I'd never seen anything remotely like it, not outside of a museum, anyway. No head to speak of, breasts like footballs, a belly like a watermelon, and a phallus like an overgrown zucchini, the whole thing weathered with the rains of a thousand years or more.

I glanced at Ophelia. "Impressive," I said.

She turned a critical eye on it. "You don't think it's too much? Rachel says it is, but she's a minimalist. This is my little bit of home, and I love it."

"It's a lot," I admitted. Accuracy prompted me to add, "It suits you."

I still didn't understand how Ophelia had gotten a tropical rainforest to flourish in a temperate climate.

I was trying to find a nice way to ask her about it when she said, "You're a real find, Evie. Rachel's working, or I'd call her to come down. She really wants to meet you."

"Next time," I said, wondering what on Earth I'd find to talk about with a specialist on artificial intelligence. "Um. Does Rachel garden?"

Ophelia laughed. "No way – her talent is not for living things. But I made a garden for her. Would you like to see it?"

I was only dying to, although I couldn't help wondering what kind of exotica I was letting myself in for. A desertscape? Tundra? Curiosity won. "Sure," I said. "Lead on."

We stopped on the way to visit the vegetable garden. It looked fairly ordinary, although the tomatoes were more August than May, and the beans more late June. I didn't see any corn and I didn't see any greenhouses. After a brief side-bar on insecticidal soaps, Ophelia led me behind the carriage house. The unmistakable sound of quacking fell on my ears.

"We aren't zoned for ducks," I said, startled.

"We are," said Ophelia. "Now. How do you like Rachel's garden?"

A prospect of brown reeds with a silvery river meandering through it stretched through where the Morrison's back yard ought to be, all the way to a boundless expanse of ocean. In the marsh it was April, with a crisp salt wind blowing back from the water and ruffling the brown reeds and the white-flowering shad and the pale green unfurling sweetfern. Mallards splashed and dabbled along the meander. A solitary great egret stood among the reeds, the fringes of its white courting shawl blowing around one black and knobbly leg. As I watched, open-mouthed, the egret unfurled its other leg from its breast feathers, trod at the reeds, and lowered its golden bill to feed.

I got home late. Kim was in the basement with the animals, and the chicken I was planning to make for dinner was still in the freezer. Thanking heaven for modern technology, I defrosted the chicken in the microwave, chopped veggies, seasoned, mixed, and got the whole mess in the oven just as Geoff walked in the door. He wasn't happy about eating forty-five minutes late, but he was mostly over it by bedtime.

That was Thursday.

Friday, I saw Ophelia and Rachel pulling out of their driveway in one of those old cars that has huge fenders and a running board. They returned after lunch, the back seat full of groceries. They and the groceries disappeared through the kitchen door, and there was no further sign of them until late afternoon, when Rachel opened one of the quarter-round windows in the attic and energetically shook the dust out of a small, patterned carpet.

On Saturday, the invitation came.

It stood out among the flyers, book orders, bills, and requests for money that usually came through our mail-slot, a five-by-eight silvery-blue envelope that smelled faintly of sandalwood. It was addressed to The Gordon Family in a precise italic hand. I opened it and read:

Rachel Esther Abrams and Ophelia Desirée Canderel
Request the Honor of your Presence
At the
Celebration of their Marriage.
Sunday, May 24 at 3 P.M.
There will be refreshments before and after the Ceremony.

I was still staring at it when the doorbell rang. It was Lucille, looking fit to burst, holding an invitation just like mine.

"Come in, Lucille. There's plenty of coffee left."

I don't think I'd ever seen Lucille in such a state. You'd think someone had invited her to parade naked down Main Street at noon.

"Well, write and tell them you can't come," I said. "They're just being neighborly, for Pete's sake. It's not like they can't get married if you're not there."

"I know. It's just.... It puts me in a funny position, that's all. Burney's a founding member of Normal Marriage for Normal People. He wouldn't like it at all if he knew I'd been invited to a lesbian wedding."

"So don't tell him. If you want to go, just tell him the new neighbors have invited you to an open house on Sunday, and you know for a fact that we're going to be there."

Lucille smiled. Burney hated Geoff almost as much as Geoff hated Burney. "It's a thought," she said. "Are you going?"

"I don't see why not. Who knows? I might learn something."

The Sunday of the wedding, I took forever to dress. Kim thought it was funny, but Geoff threatened to bail if I didn't quit fussing. "It's a lesbian wedding, for pity's sake. It's going to be full of middle-aged dykes with ugly haircuts. Nobody's going to care what you look like."

"I care," said Kim. "And I think that jacket is wicked cool."

I'd bought the jacket at a little Indian store in the Square and not worn it since. When I got it away from the Square's atmosphere of collegiate funk it looked, I don't know, too sixties, too artsy, too bright for a fortysomething suburban matron. It was basically purple, with teal blue and gold and fuchsia flowers all over it and brass buttons shaped like parrots. Shaking my head, I started to unfasten the parrots.

Geoff exploded. "I swear to God, Evie, if you change again, that's it. It's not like I want to go. I've got papers to correct; I don't have time for this" – he glanced at Kim – "nonsense. Either we go or we stay. But we do it now."

Kim touched my arm. "It's *you*, Mom. Come *on*."

So I came on, my jacket flashing neon in the sunlight. By the time we hit the sidewalk, I felt like a tropical floral display; I was ready to bolt home and hide under the bed.

"Great," said Geoff. "Not a car in sight. If we're the only ones here, I'm leaving."

"I don't think that's going to be a problem," I said.

Beyond the copper beech, I saw a colorful crowd milling around as purposefully as bees, bearing chairs and flowers and ribbons. As we came closer, it became clear that Geoff couldn't have been more wrong about the wedding guests. There wasn't an ugly haircut in sight, although there were some pretty startling dye-jobs. The dress-code could best be described as eclectic, with a slight bias toward floating fabrics and rich, bright colors. My jacket felt right at home.

Geoff was muttering about not knowing anybody when Lucille appeared, looking festive in Laura Ashley chintz.

"Isn't this fun?" she said, with every sign of sincerity. "I've never met such interesting people. And friendly! They make me feel right at home. Come over here and join the gang."

She dragged us toward the long side-yard, which sloped down to a lavishly blooming double-flowering cherry underplanted with peonies. Which shouldn't have been in bloom at the same time as the cherry, but I was getting used to the vagaries of Ophelia's garden. A willowy young person in chartreuse lace claimed Lucille's attention, and they went off together. The three of us stood in a slightly awkward knot at the edge of the crowd, which occasionally threw out a few guests who eddied around us briefly before retreating.

"How are those spells of yours, dear? Any better?" inquired a solicitous voice in my ear, and, "Oh!" when I jumped. "You're not Elvira, are you? Sorry."

Geoff's grip was cutting off the circulation above my elbow. "This was not one of your better ideas, Evie. We're surrounded by weirdoes. Did you see that guy in the skirt? I think we should take Kimmy home."

A tall black man with a flattop and a diamond in his left ear appeared, pried Geoff's hand from my arm, and shook it warmly. "Dr. Gordon? Ophelia told me to be looking out for you. I've read *The Anarchists*, you see, and I can't tell you how much I admired it."

Geoff actually blushed. Before the subject got too painful to talk about, he used to say that for a history of anarchism, his one book had had a remarkably elite readership: three members of the tenure review committee, two reviewers for scholarly journals, and his wife. "Thanks," he said.

Geoff's fan grinned, clearly delighted. "Maybe we can talk at the reception," he said. "Right now, I need to find you a place to sit. They look like they're just about ready to roll."

It was a lovely wedding.

I don't know exactly what I was expecting, but I was mildly surprised to see a rabbi and a wedding canopy. Ophelia was an enormous rose in crimson draperies. Rachel was a calla lily in cream linen. Their heads were tastefully wreathed in oak and ivy leaves. There were the usual prayers and promises and tears; when the rabbi pronounced them married, they kissed and horns sounded a triumphant fanfare.

Kim poked me in the side. "Mom? Who's playing those horns?"

"I don't know. Maybe it's a recording."

"I don't think so," Kim said. "I think it's the tree. Isn't this just about the coolest thing ever?"

We were on our feet again. The chairs had disappeared and people were dancing. A cheerful bearded man grabbed Kim's hand to pull her into the line. Geoff grabbed her and pulled her back.

"Dad!" Kim wailed. "I want to dance!"

"I've got a pile of papers to correct before class tomorrow," Geoff said. "And if I know you, there's some homework you've put off until tonight. We have to go home now."

"We can't leave yet," I objected. "We haven't congratulated the brides."

Geoff's jaw tensed. "So go congratulate them," he said. "Kim and I will wait for you here."

Kim looked mutinous. I gave her the eye. This wasn't the time or the place to object. Like Geoff, Kim had no inhibitions about airing the family linen in public, but I had enough for all three of us.

"Dr. Gordon. There you are." The *Anarchists* fan popped up between us. "I've been looking all over for you. Come have a drink and let me tell you how brilliant you are."

Geoff smiled modestly. "You're being way too generous," he said. "Did you read Peterson's piece in *The Review*?"

"Asshole," said the man dismissively. Geoff slapped him on the back, and a minute later, they were halfway to the house, laughing as if they'd known each other for years. Thank heaven for the male ego.

"Dance?" said Kim.

"Go for it," I said. "I'm going to get some champagne and kiss the brides."

The brides were nowhere to be found. The champagne, a young girl informed me, was in the kitchen. So I entered Number 400 for the first time, coming through the mudroom into a large, oak-paneled hall. To my left a staircase with an ornately carved oak banister rose to an art-glass window. Ahead was a semicircular fireplace with a carved bench on one side and a door that probably led to the kitchen on the other. Between me and the door was an assortment of brightly dressed strangers, talking and laughing.

I edged around them, passing two curtained doors and a bronze statue of Alice and the Red Queen. Puzzle fragments of conversation rose out of the general buzz:

"My pearls? Thank you, my dear, but you know they're only stimulated."

"And then it just went 'poof'! A perfectly good frog, and it just went poof!"

" ...and then Tallulah says to the bishop, she says, 'Love your drag, darling, but your *purse* is on fire.' Don't you love it? 'Your *purse* is on fire!'"

The kitchen itself was blessedly empty except for a stout gentleman in a tuxedo, and a striking woman in a peach silk pantsuit, who was tending an array of champagne bottles and a cut-glass bowl full of bright blue punch. Curious, I picked up a cup of punch and sniffed at it. The woman smiled up at me through a caterpillary fringe of false lashes.

"Pure witch's brew," she said in one of those Lauren Bacall come-hither voices I've always envied. "But what can you do? It's the *spécialité de la maison*."

The tuxedoed man laughed. "Don't mind Silver, Mrs. Gordon. He just likes to tease. Ophelia's punch is wonderful."

"Only if you like Ty-dee Bowl," said Silver, tipping a sapphire stream into another cup. "You know, honey, you shouldn't stand around with your mouth open like that. Think of the flies."

Several guests entered in plenty of time to catch this exchange. Determined to preserve my cool, I took a gulp of the punch. It tasted fruity and made my mouth prickle, and then it hit my stomach like a firecracker. So much for cool. I choked and gasped.

"I tried to warn you," Silver said. "You'd better switch to champagne." Now I knew Silver was a man, I could see that his hands and wrists were big for the rest of her – him. I could feel my face burning with punch and mortification.

"No, thank you," I said faintly. "Maybe some water?"

The stout man handed me a glass. I sipped gratefully. "You're Ophelia and Rachel's neighbor, aren't you?" he said. "Lovely garden. You must be proud of that asparagus bed."

"I was, until I saw Ophelia's."

"Ooh, listen to the green-eyed monster," Silver cooed. "Don't be jealous, honey. Ophelia's the best. Nobody understands plants like Ophelia."

"I'm not jealous," I said with dignity. "I'm wistful. There's a difference."

Then, just when I thought it couldn't possibly get any worse, Geoff appeared, looking stunningly unprofessorial, with one side of his shirt collar turned up and his dark hair flopped over his eyes.

"Hey, Evie. Who knew a couple of dykes would know how to throw a wedding?"

You'd think after sixteen years of living with Geoff, I'd know whether or not he was an alcoholic. But I don't. He doesn't go on binges, he doesn't get drunk at every party we go to, and I'm pretty sure he doesn't drink on the sly. What I do know is that drinking doesn't make him more fun to be around.

I took his arm. "I'm glad you're enjoying yourself," I said brightly. "Too bad we have to leave."

"Leave? Who said anything about leaving? We just got here."

"Your papers," I said. "Remember?"

"Screw my papers," said Geoff and held out his empty cup to Silver. "This punch is dy-no-mite."

"What about your students?"

"I'll tell 'em I didn't feel like reading their stupid essays. That'll fix their little red wagons. Boring as hell anyway. Fill 'er up, beautiful," he told Silver.

Silver considered him gravely. "Geoff, darling," he said. "A little bird tells me that there's an absolutely delicious argument going on in the smoking room. They'll never forgive you if you don't come play."

Geoff favored Silver with a leer that made me wish I were somewhere else. "Only if you play too," he said. "What's it about?"

Silver waved a pink-tipped hand. "Something about theoretical versus practical anarchy. Right, Rodney?"

"I believe so," said the stout gentleman agreeably.

A martial gleam rose in Geoff's eye. "Let me at 'em."

Silver's pale eyes turned to me, solemn and concerned. "You don't mind, do you, honey?"

I shrugged. With luck, the smoking-room crowd would be drunk too, and nobody would remember who said what. I just hoped none of the anarchists had a violent temper.

"We'll return him intact," Silver said. "I promise." And they were gone, Silver trailing fragrantly from Geoff's arm.

While I was wondering whether I'd said that thing about the anarchists or only thought it, I felt a tap on my shoulder – the stout gentleman, Rodney.

"Mrs. Gordon, Rachel and Ophelia would like to see you and young Kimberly in the study. If you'll please step this way?"

His manner had shifted from wedding guest to old-fashioned butler. Properly intimidated, I trailed him to the front hall. It was empty now, except for Lucille and the young person in chartreuse lace, who were huddled together on the bench by the fireplace. The young person was talking earnestly and Lucille was listening and nodding and sipping punch. Neither of them paid any attention to us or to the music coming from behind one of the curtained doors. I saw Kim at the foot of the stairs, examining the newel post.

It was well worth examining: a screaming griffin with every feather and every curl beautifully articulated and its head polished smooth and black as ebony. Rodney gave it a brief, seemingly unconscious caress as he started up the steps. When Kim followed suit, I thought I saw the carved eye blink.

I must have made a noise, because Rodney halted his slow ascent and gazed down at me, standing open-mouthed below. "Lovely piece of work, isn't it? We call it the house guardian. A joke, of course."

"Of course," I echoed. "Cute."

It seemed to me that the house had more rooms than it ought to. Through open doors, I glimpsed libraries, salons, parlors, bedrooms. We passed through a stone cloister where discouraged-looking ficuses in tubs shed their leaves on the cracked pavement and into a green-scummed pool. I don't know what shocked me more: the cloister or the state of its plants. Maybe Ophelia's green thumb didn't extend to houseplants.

As far as I could tell, Kim took all this completely in stride. She bounded along like a dog in the woods, peeking in an open door here, pausing to look at a picture there, and pelting Rodney with questions I wouldn't have dreamed of asking, like "Are there kids here?"; "What about pets?"; "How many people live here, anyway?"

"It depends," was Rodney's unvarying answer. "Step this way, please."

Our trek ended in a wall covered by a huge South American tapestry of three women making pots. Rodney pulled the tapestry aside, revealing an iron-banded oak door that would have done a medieval castle proud. "The study," he said, and opened the door on a flight of ladder-like steps rising steeply into the shadows.

His voice and gesture reminded me irresistibly of one of those horror movies in which a laconic butler leads the hapless heroine to a forbidding door and invites her to step inside. I didn't know which of three impulses was stronger: to laugh, to run, or, like the heroine, to forge on and see what happened next.

It's some indication of the state I was in that Kim got by me and through the door before I could stop her.

I don't like feeling helpless and I don't like feeling pressured. I really don't like being tricked, manipulated, and herded. Left to myself, I'd have turned around and taken my chances on finding my way out of the maze of corridors. But I wasn't going to leave without my daughter, so I hitched up my wedding-appropriate long skirt and started up the steps.

The stairs were every bit as steep as they looked. I floundered up gracelessly, emerging into a huge space sparsely furnished with a beat-up rolltop desk, a wingback chair and a swan-neck rocker on a threadbare Oriental rug at one end, and some cluttered door-on-sawhorse tables on the other. Ophelia and Rachel, still dressed in their bridal finery, were sitting in the chair and the rocker respectively, holding steaming mugs and talking to Kim, who was incandescent with excitement.

"Oh, there you are," said Ophelia as I stumbled up the last step. "Would you like some tea?"

"No, thank you," I said stiffly. "Kim, I think it's time to go home now."

Kim protested, vigorously. Rachel cast Ophelia an unreadable look.

"It'll be fine, love," Ophelia said soothingly. "Mrs. Gordon's upset, and who could blame her? Evie, I don't believe you've actually met Rachel."

Where I come from, social niceties trump everything. Without actually meaning to, I found I was shaking Rachel's hand and congratulating her on her marriage. Close up, she was a handsome woman, with a decided nose, deep lines around her mouth, and the measuring gaze of a gardener examining an unfamiliar insect on her tomato leaves. I didn't ask her to call me Evie.

Ophelia touched my hand. "Never mind," she said soothingly. "Have some tea. You'll feel better."

Next thing I knew, I was sitting on a chair that hadn't been there a moment before, eating a lemon cookie from a plate I didn't see arrive, and drinking Lapsang Souchong from a cup that appeared when Ophelia reached for it. Just for the record, I didn't feel better at all. I felt as if I'd taken a step that wasn't there, or perhaps failed to take one that was: out of balance, out of place, out of control.

Kim, restless as a cat, was snooping around among the long tables.

"What's with the flying fish?" she asked.

"They're for Rachel's new experiment," said Ophelia. "She thinks she can bring the dead to life again."

"You better let me tell it, Ophie," Rachel said. "I don't want Mrs. Gordon thinking I'm some kind of mad scientist."

In fact, I wasn't thinking at all, except that I was in way over my head.

"I'm working on animating extinct species," Rachel said. "I'm particularly interested in dodos and passenger pigeons, but eventually, I'd like to work up to bison and maybe woolly mammoths."

"Won't that create ecological problems?" Kim objected. "I mean, they're way big, and we don't know much about their habits or what they ate or anything."

There was a silence while Rachel and Ophelia traded family-joke smiles. "That's why we need you," Rachel said.

Kim looked as though she'd been given the pony she'd been agitating for since fourth grade. Her jaw dropped. Her eyes sparkled. And I lost it.

"Will somebody please tell me what the hell you're talking about?" I said. "I've been patient. I followed your pal Rodney through more rooms than Versailles and I didn't run screaming, and believe me when I tell you I wanted to. I've drunk your tea and listened to your so-called explanations, and I still don't know what's going on."

Kim turned to me with a look of blank astonishment. "Come on, Mom. I can't believe you don't know that Ophelia and Rachel are witches. It's perfectly obvious."

"We prefer not to use the W word," Rachel said. "Like most labels, it's misleading and inaccurate. We're just people with natural scientific ability who have been trained to ask the right questions."

Ophelia nodded. "We learn to ask the things themselves. They always know. Do you see?"

"No," I said. "All I see is a roomful of junk and a garden that doesn't care what season it is."

"Very well," said Rachel, and rose from her chair. "If you'll just come over here, Mrs. Gordon, I'll try to clear everything up."

At the table of the flying fish, Ophelia arranged us in a semi-circle, with Rachel in a teacherly position beside the exhibits. These seemed to be A) the fish; and B) one of those Japanese good-luck cats with one paw curled up by its ear and a bright enameled bib.

"As you know," Rachel said, "my field is artificial intelligence. What that means, essentially, is that I can animate the inanimate. Observe." She caressed the porcelain cat between its ears. For two breaths, nothing happened. Then the cat lowered its paw and stretched itself luxuriously. The light glinted off its bulging sides; its curly red mouth and wide painted eyes were expressionless.

"Sweet," Kim breathed.

"It's not really alive," Rachel said, stroking the cat's shiny back. "It's still porcelain. If it jumps off the table, it'll break."

"Can I pet it?" Kim asked.

"No!" Rachel and I said in firm and perfect unison.

"Why not?"

"Because I'd like you to help me with an experiment." Rachel looked me straight in the eye. "I'm not really comfortable with words," she said. "I prefer demonstrations. What I'm going to do is hold Kim's hand and touch the fish. That's all."

"And what happens then?" Kim asked eagerly.

Rachel smiled at her. "Well, we'll see, won't we? Are you okay with this, Mrs. Gordon?"

It sounded harmless enough, and Kim was already reaching for Rachel's hand. "Go ahead," I said.

Their hands met, palm to palm. Rachel closed her eyes. She frowned in concentration and the atmosphere tightened around us. I yawned to unblock my ears.

Rachel laid her free hand on one of the fish.

It twitched, head jerking galvanically; its wings fanned open and shut.

Kim gave a little grunt, which snapped my attention away from the fish. She was pale and sweating a little.

I started to go to her, but I couldn't. Someone was holding me back.

"It's okay, Evie," Ophelia said soothingly. "Kim's fine, really. Rachel knows what she's doing."

"Kim's pale," I said, calm as the eye of a storm. "She looks like she's going to throw up. She's not fine. Let me go to my daughter, Ophelia, or I swear you'll regret it."

"Believe me, it's not safe for you to touch them right now. You have to trust us."

My Great-Aunt Fanny I'll trust you, I thought, and willed myself to relax in her grip. "Okay," I said shakily. "I believe you. It's just, I wish you'd warned me."

"We wanted to tell you," Ophelia said. "But we were afraid you wouldn't believe us. We were afraid you would think we were a couple of nuts. You see, Kim has the potential to be an important zoologist – if she has the proper training. Rachel's a wonderful teacher, and you can see for yourself how complementary their disciplines are. Working together, they...."

I don't know what she thought Kim and Rachel could accomplish, because the second she was more interested in what she was saying than in holding onto me, I was out of her hands and pulling Kim away from the witch who, as far as I could tell, was draining her dry.

That was the plan, anyway.

As soon as I touched Kim, the room came alive.

It started with the flying fish leaping off the table and buzzing past us on Saran Wrap wings. The porcelain cat thumped down from the table and, far from breaking, twined itself around Kim's ankles, purring hollowly. An iron plied itself over a pile of papers, smoothing out the creases. The teddy bear growled at it and ran to hide behind a toaster.

If that wasn't enough, my jacket burst into bloom.

It's kind of hard to describe what it's like to wear a tropical forest. Damp, for one thing. Bright. Loud. Uncomfortable. Very, very uncomfortable. Overstimulating. There were flowers and parrots screeching (yes, the flowers, too – or maybe that was me). It seemed to go on for a long time, kind of like giving birth. At first, I was overwhelmed by the chaos of growth and sound, unsure whether I was the forest or the forest was me. Slowly I realized that it didn't have to be a chaos, and that if I just pulled myself together, I could make sense of it. That flower went there, for instance, and the teal one went there. That parrot belonged on that vine and everything needed to be smaller and stiller and less extravagantly colored. Like that.

Gradually, the forest receded. I was still holding Kim, who promptly bent over and threw up on the floor.

"There," I said hoarsely. "I told you she was going to be sick."

Ophelia picked up Rachel and carried her back to her wingchair. "You be quiet, you," she said over her shoulder. "Heaven knows what you've done to Rachel. I told you not to touch them."

Ignoring my own nausea, I supported Kim over to the rocker and deposited her in it. "You might have told me why," I snapped. "I don't know why people can't just explain things instead of making me guess. It's not like I can read minds, you know. Now, are you going to conjure us up a glass of water, or do I have to go find the kitchen?"

Rachel had recovered herself enough to give a shaky laugh. "Hell, you could conjure it yourself, with a little practice. Ophie, darling, calm down. I'm fine."

Ophelia stopped fussing over her wife long enough to snatch a glass of cool mint tea from the air and hand it to me. She wouldn't meet my eyes, and she was scowling. "I told you she was going to be difficult. Of all the damn-fool, pig-headed...."

"Hush, love," Rachel said. "There's no harm done, and now we know just where we stand. I'd rather have a nice cup of tea than listen to you cursing out Mrs. Gordon for just trying to be a good mother." She turned her head to look at me. "Very impressive, by the way. We knew you had to be like Ophie, because of the garden, but we didn't know the half of it. You've got a kick like a mule, Mrs. Gordon."

I must have been staring at her like one of the flying fish. Here I thought I'd half-killed her, and she was giving me a smile that looked perfectly genuine.

I smiled cautiously in return. "Thank you," I said.

Kim pulled at the sleeve of my jacket. "Hey, Mom, that was awesome. I guess you're a witch, huh?"

I wanted to deny it, but I couldn't. The fact was that the pattern of flowers on my jacket was different and the colors were muted, the flowers more English garden than tropical paradise. There were only three buttons, and they were larks, not parrots. And I felt different. Clearer? More whole? I don't know – different. Even though I didn't know how the magic worked or how to control it, I couldn't ignore the fact – the palpable, provable fact – that it was there.

"Yeah," I said. "I guess I am."

"Me, too," my daughter said. "What's Dad going to say?"

I thought for a minute. "Nothing, honey. Because we're not going to tell him."

We didn't, either. And we're not going to. There's no useful purpose served by telling people truths they aren't equipped to accept. Geoff's pretty oblivious, anyway. It's true that in the hungover aftermath of Ophelia's blue punch, he announced that he thought the new neighbors might be a bad influence, but he couldn't actually forbid Kim and me to hang out with them because it would look homophobic.

Kim's over at Number 400 most Saturday afternoons, learning how to be a zoologist. She's making good progress. There was an episode with zombie mice I don't like to think about, and a crisis when the porcelain cat broke falling out of a tree. But she's learning patience, control, and discipline, which are all excellent things for a girl of fourteen to learn. She and Rachel have reanimated a pair of passenger pigeons, but they haven't had any luck in breeding them yet.

Lucille's the biggest surprise. It turns out that all her nosy-parkerism was a case of ingrown witchiness. Now she's studying with Silver, of all people, to be a psychologist. But that's not the surprise. The surprise is that she left Burney and moved into Number 400, where she has a room draped with chintz and a gray cat named Jezebel and is as happy as a clam at high tide.

I'm over there a lot, too, learning to be a horticulturist. Ophelia says I'm a quick study, but I have to learn to trust my instincts. Who knew I had instincts? I thought I was just good at looking things up.

I'm working on my own garden now. I'm the only one who can find it without being invited in. It's an English kind of garden, like the gardens in books I loved as a child. It has a stone wall with a low door in it, a little central lawn, and a perennial border full of foxgloves and Sweet William and Michaelmas daisies. Veronica blooms in the cracks of the wall, and periwinkle carpets the beds where old-fashioned fragrant roses nod heavily to every passing breeze. There's a small wilderness of rowan trees, and a neat shrubbery embracing a pond stocked with fish as bright as copper pennies. Among the dusty-smelling boxwood, I've put a statue of a woman holding a basket planted with stonecrop. She's dressed in a jacket incised with flowers and vines and closed with three buttons shaped like parrots. The fourth button sits on her shoulder, clacking its beak companionably and preening its brazen feathers. I'm thinking of adding a duck pond next, or maybe a wilderness for Kim's menagerie.

Witches don't have to worry about zoning laws.

Monster

Kelly Link

Kelly Link (*www.kellylink.net*) lives in Northampton, Massachusetts. She and her husband, Gavin Grant, are the founders and proprietors of Small Beer Press, and the publishers of *Lady Churchill's Rosebud Wristlet*, a 'zine of high quality (*www.lcrw.net*). They also co-edit, with Ellen Datlow, one of our competitors, *The Year's Best Fantasy and Horror*. She is the editor of *Trampoline*, an anthology of cutting-edge fiction, and is the author of two distinguished collections of stories, *Stranger Things Happen* and *Magic For Beginners*, which was called one of the five best books of fiction published in the US in 2005 by *Time*, quite a triumph.

"Monster" appeared in *McSweeney's*, in the special issue *Noisy Outlaws...* It is a children's story for adults, which seems to have been the point of that issue. It is a monster story about children at summer camp, with Daniel Pinkwateresque irony and wit, and disturbing implications, all done with a delicate touch.

NO ONE IN BUNGALOW 6 wanted to go camping. It was raining, which meant that you had to wear garbage bags over your backpacks and around the sleeping bags, and even that wouldn't help. The sleeping bags would still get wet. Some of the wet sleeping bags would then smell like pee, and the tents already smelled like mildew, and even if they got the tents up, water would collect on the ground cloths. There would be three boys to a tent, and only the boy in the middle would stay dry. The other two would inevitably end up squashed against the sides of the tent, and wherever you touched the nylon, water would come through from the outside.

Besides, someone in Bungalow 4 had seen a monster in the woods. Bungalow 4 had been telling stories ever since they got back. It was a no-win situation for Bungalow 6. If Bungalow 6 didn't see the monster, Bungalow 4 would keep the upper hand that fate had dealt them. If Bungalow 6 did see a monster – but who wanted to see a monster, even if it meant that you got to tell everyone about it? Not anyone in Bungalow 6, except for James Lorbick, who thought that monsters were awesome. But James Lorbick was a geek and from Chicago and he had a condition that made his feet smell terrible. That was another thing about camping. Someone would have to share a tent with James Lorbick and his smelly feet.

And even if Bungalow 6 did see the monster, well, Bungalow 4 had seen it first, so there was nothing special about that, seeing a monster after Bungalow 4 went and saw it first. And maybe Bungalow 4 had pissed off that monster. Maybe that monster was just waiting for more kids to show up at the Honor Lookout where all the pine trees leaned backwards in a circle around the bald hump of the hill in a way that made you feel dizzy when you lay around the fire at night and looked up at them.

"There wasn't any monster," Bryan Jones said, "and anyway if there was a monster, I bet it ran away when it saw Bungalow 4." Everybody nodded. What Bryan Jones said made sense. Everybody knew that the kids in Bungalow 4 were so mean that they had made their counselor cry like a girl. The Bungalow 4 counselor was a twenty-year-old college student named Eric who had terrible acne and wrote poems about the local girls who worked in the kitchen and how their breasts looked lonely but also beautiful, like melted ice cream. The kids in Bungalow 4 had found the poetry and read it out loud at morning assembly in front of everybody, including some of the kitchen girls.

Bungalow 4 had sprayed a bat with insect spray and then set fire to it and almost burned down the whole bungalow.

And there were worse stories about Bungalow 4.

Everyone said that the kids in Bungalow 4 were so mean that their parents sent them off to camp just so they wouldn't have to see them for a few weeks.

"I heard that the monster had big black wings," Colin Simpson said. "Like a vampire. It flapped around and it had these long fingernails."

"I heard it had lots of teeth."

"I heard it bit Barnhard."

"I heard he tasted so bad that the monster puked after it bit him."

"I saw Barnhard last night at dinner," Colin Simpson's twin brother said. Or maybe it was Colin Simpson who said that and the kid who was talking about flapping and fingernails was the other twin. Everybody had a hard time telling them apart. "He had a Band-Aid on the inside of his arm. He looked kind of weird. Kind of pale."

"Guys," their counselor said. "Hey guys. Enough talk. Let's pack up and get going." The Bungalow 6 counselor was named Terence, but he was pretty cool. All of the kitchen girls hung around Bungalow 6 to talk to Terence, even though he was already going out with a girl from Ohio who was six-feet-two and played basketball. Sometimes before he turned out the lights, Terence would read them letters that the girl from Ohio had written. There was a picture over Terence's camp bed of this girl sitting on an elephant in Thailand. The girl's name was Darlene. Nobody knew the elephant's name.

"We can't just sit here all day," Terence said. "Chop chop."

Everyone started complaining.

"I know it's raining," Terence said. "But there are only three more days of camp left and if we want our overnight badges, this is our last chance. Besides it could stop raining. And not that you should care, but everyone in Bungalow 4 will say that you got scared and that's why you didn't want to go. And I don't want everyone to think that Bungalow 6 is afraid of some stupid Bungalow 4 story about some stupid monster."

It didn't stop raining. Bungalow 6 didn't exactly hike; they waded. They splashed. They slid down hills. The rain came down in clammy, cold, sticky sheets. One of the Simpson twins put his foot down at the bottom of a trail and the mud went up all the way to his knee and pulled his tennis shoe right off with a loud sucking noise. So they had to stop while Terence lay down in the mud and stuck his arm down, fishing for the Simpson twin's shoe.

Bryan Jones stood next to Terence and held out his shirt so the rain wouldn't fall in Terence's ear. Bryan Jones was from North Carolina. He was a big tall kid with a friendly face, who liked paint guns and BB guns and laser guns and pulling down his pants and mooning people and putting hot sauce on toothbrushes.

Sometimes he'd sit on top of James Lorbick's head and fart, but everybody knew it was just Bryan being funny, except for James Lorbick. James Lorbick was from Chicago. James Lorbick hated Bryan even more than he hated the kids in Bungalow 4. Sometimes James pretended that Bryan Jones's parents died in some weird accident while camp was still going on and that no one knew what to say to Bryan and so they avoided him until James came up to Bryan and said exactly the right thing and made Bryan feel better, although of course he wouldn't really feel better, he'd just appreciate what James had said to him, whatever it was that James had said. And of course then Bryan would feel bad about sitting on James's head all those times. And then they'd be friends. Everybody wanted to be friends with Bryan Jones, even James Lorbick.

The first thing that Terence pulled up out of the mud wasn't the Simpson twin's shoe. It was long and round and knobby. When Terence knocked it against the ground, some of the mud slid off.

"Hey. Wow," James Lorbick said. "That looks like a bone."

Everybody stood in the rain and looked at the bone.

"What is that?"

"Is it human?"

"Maybe it's a dinosaur," James Lorbick said. "Like a fossil."

"Probably a cow bone," Terence said. He poked the bone back in the mud and fished around until it got stuck in something that turned out to be the lost shoe. The Simpson twin took the shoe as if he didn't really want it back. He turned it upside down and mud oozed out like lonely, melting soft-squeeze ice cream.

Half of Terence was now covered in mud, although at least, thanks to Bryan Jones, he didn't have water in his ear. He held the dubious bone as if he was going to toss it off in the bushes, but then he stopped and looked at it again. He put it in the pocket of his rain jacket instead. Half of it stuck out. It didn't look like a cow bone.

By the time they got to Honor Lookout, the rain had stopped. "See?" Terence said. "I told you." He said it as if now they were fine. Now everything would be fine. Water plopped off the needles of the pitiful pine trees that leaned eternally away from the campground on Honor Lookout.

Bungalow 6 gathered wood that would be too wet to use for a fire. They unpacked their tents and tent poles, and tent pegs, which descended into the sucking mud and disappeared forever. They laid out their tents on top of ground cloths on top of the sucking, quivering, nearly-animate mud. It was like putting a tent up over chocolate pudding. The floor of the tents sank below the level of the mud when they crawled inside. It was hard to imagine sleeping in the tents. You might just keep on sinking.

"Hey," Bryan Jones said, "look out! Snowball fight!" He lobbed a brown mud-ball which hit James Lorbick just under the chin and splashed up on James's glasses. Then everyone was throwing mudballs, even Terence. James Lorbick even threw one. There was nothing else to do.

When they got hungry, they ate cold hot dogs for lunch while the mud dried and cracked and fell off their arms and legs and faces. They ate graham crackers with marshmallows and chocolate squares and Terence even toasted the marsh-mallows with a cigarette lighter for anyone who wanted. Since they couldn't make a fire, they made mud sculptures instead. Terence sculpted an elephant and a girl on top. The elephant even looked like an elephant. But then one of the Simpson twins sculpted an atom bomb and dropped it on Terence's elephant and Terence's girlfriend.

"That's okay," Terence said. "That's cool." But it wasn't cool. He went and sat on a muddy rock and looked at his bone.

The twins had made a whole stockpile of atom bombs out of mud. They decided to make a whole city with walls and buildings and everything. Some of the other kids from Bungalow 6 helped with the city so that the twins could bomb the city before it got too dark.

Bryan Jones had put mud in his hair and twisted it up in muddy spikes. There was mud in his eyebrows. He looked like an idiot, but that didn't matter, because he was Bryan Jones and anything that Bryan Jones did wasn't stupid. It was cool. "Hey man," he said to James. "Come and see what I stole off the clothes line at camp."

James Lorbick was muddy and tired and maybe his feet did smell bad, but he was smarter than most of the kids in Bungalow 6. "Why?" he said.

"Just come on," Bryan said. "I don't want anyone else to see this yet."

"Okay," James said.

It was a dress. It had big blue flowers on it and James Lorbick got a bad feeling.

"Why did you steal a dress?" he said.

Bryan shrugged. He was smiling as if the whole idea of a dress made him happy. It was a big, happy, contagious smile, but James Lorbick didn't smile back. "Because it will be funny," Bryan said. "Put it on and we'll go show everybody."

"No way," James said. He folded his muddy arms over his muddy chest to show he was serious.

"I dare you," Bryan said. "Come on, James, before everybody comes over here and sees it. Everybody will laugh."

"I know they will," James said. "No."

"Look, I'd put it on, I swear, but it wouldn't fit me. No way would it fit. So you've got to do it. Just do it, James."

"No," James said.

James Lorbick wasn't sure why his parents had sent him off to a camp in North Carolina. He hadn't wanted to go. It wasn't as if there weren't trees in Chicago. It wasn't as if James didn't have friends in Chicago. Camp just seemed to be one of those things parents could make you do, like violin lessons, or karate, except that camp lasted a whole month. Plus, he was supposed to be thankful about it, like his parents had done him a big favor. Camp cost money.

So he made leather wallets in arts and crafts, and went swimming every other day, even though the lake smelled funny and the swim instructor was kind of weird and liked to make the campers stand on the high diving board with their eyes closed. Then he'd creep up and push them into the water. Not that you didn't know he was creeping up. You could feel the board wobbling.

He didn't make friends. But that wasn't true, exactly. He was friendly, but nobody in Bungalow 6 was friendly back. Sometimes right after Terence turned out the lights, someone would say, "James, oh, James, your hair looked really excellent today" or "James, James Lorbick, I wish I were as good at archery as you" or "James, will you let me borrow your water canteen tomorrow?" and then everyone would laugh while James pretended to be asleep, until Terence would flick on the lights and say, "Leave James alone – go to sleep or I'll give everyone five demerits."

James Lorbick knew it could have been worse. He could have been in Bungalow 4 instead of Bungalow 6.

At least the dress wasn't muddy. Bryan let him keep his jeans and T-shirt on. "Let me do your hair," Bryan said. He picked up a handful of mud pushed it around on James's head until James had sticky mud hair just like Bryan's.

"Come on," Bryan said.

"Why do I have to do this?" James said. He held his hands out to the side so that he wouldn't have to touch the dress. He looked ridiculous. He felt worse than ridiculous. He felt terrible. He felt so terrible that he didn't even care anymore that he was wearing a dress.

"You didn't have to do this," Bryan said. He sounded like he thought it was a big joke, which it was. "I didn't make you do it, James."

One of the Simpson twins was running around, dropping atom bombs on the sagging, wrinkled tents. He skidded to a stop in front of Bryan and James. "Why are you wearing a dress?" the Simpson twin said. "Hey, James is wearing a dress!"

Bryan gave James a shove. Not hard, but he left a muddy handprint on the dress. "Come on," he said. "Pretend that you're a zombie. Like you're a kitchen girl zombie who's come back to eat the brains of everybody from Bungalow 6, because you're still angry about that time we had the rice pudding fight with Bungalow 4 out on the porch of the dining room. Like you just crawled out of the mud. I'll be a zombie too. Let's go chase people."

"Okay," James Lorbick said. The terrible feeling went away at the thought of being a zombie and suddenly the flowered dress seemed magical to him. It gave him the strength of a zombie, only faster. He staggered with Bryan along toward the rest of Bungalow 6, holding out his arms. Kids said things like, "Hey, look at James! James is wearing a DRESS!" as if they were making fun of him, but then they got the idea. They realized that James and Bryan were zombies and they ran away. Even Terence.

After a while, everybody had become a zombie. So they went for a swim. Everybody except for James Lorbick, because when he started to take off the dress, Bryan Jones stopped him. Bryan said, "No, wait. Keep it on. I dare you to wear that dress until we get back to camp tomorrow. I dare you. We'll show up at breakfast and say that we saw a monster and it's chasing us, and then you come in the dining room and it will be awesome. You look completely spooky with that dress and all the mud."

"I'll get my sleeping bag all muddy," James said. "I don't want to sleep in a dress. It's dumb."

Everybody in the lake began to yell things.

"Come on, James, wear the dress, okay?"

"Keep the dress on! Do it, James!"

"I dare you," said Bryan.

"I dare you," James said.

"What?" Bryan said. "What do you dare me to do?"

James thought for a moment. Nothing came to him. "I don't know."

Terence was floating on his back. He lifted his head. "You tell him, James. Don't let Bryan talk you into anything you don't want to do."

"Come on," Bryan said. "It will be so cool. Come on."

So everybody in Bungalow 6 went swimming except for James Lorbick. They splashed around and washed off all the mud and came out of the pond and James Lorbick was the only kid in Bungalow 6 who was still covered in crusty mud. James Lorbick was the only one who still had mud spikes in his hair. James Lorbick was the only one wearing a dress.

The sun was going down. They sat on the ground around the campfire that wouldn't catch. They ate the rest of the hotdogs and the peanut butter sandwiches that the kitchen girls always made up when bungalows went on overnight hikes. They talked about how cool it would be in the morning, when James Lorbick came running into the dining room back at camp, pretending to be a monster.

It got darker. They talked about the monster.

"Maybe it's a werewolf."

"Or a were-skunk."

"Maybe it's from outer space."

"Maybe it's just really lonely," James Lorbick said. He was sitting between Bryan Jones and one of the Simpson twins, and he felt really good, like he was really part of Bungalow 6 at last, and also kind of itchy, because of the mud.

"So how come nobody's ever seen it before?"

"Maybe some people have, but they died and so they couldn't tell anybody."

"No way. They wouldn't let us camp here if somebody died."

"Maybe the camp doesn't want anybody to know about the monster, so they don't say anything."

"You're so paranoid. The monster didn't do anything to Bungalow 4. Besides, Bungalow 4 is a bunch of liars."

"Wait a minute, do you hear that?"

They were quiet, listening. Bryan Jones farted. It was a sinister, brassy fart.

"Oh, man. That's disgusting, Bryan."

"What? It wasn't me."

"If the monster comes, we'll just aim Bryan at it."

"Wait, what's that?"

Something was ringing. "No way," Terence said. "That's my cell phone. No way does it get reception out here. Hello? Hey, Darlene. What's up?" He turned on his flashlight and shone it at Bungalow 6. "Guys. I've gotta go down the hill for a sec. She sounds upset. Something about her car and a Chihuahua."

"That's cool."

"Be careful. Don't let the monster sneak up on you."

"Tell Darlene she's too good for you."

They watched Terence pick his way down the muddy path in a little circle of light. The light got smaller and smaller, farther and farther away, until they couldn't see it anymore.

"What if it isn't really Darlene?" a kid named Timothy Ferber said.

"What?"

"Like what if it's the monster?"

"No way. That's stupid. How would the monster know Terence's cell phone number?"

"Are there any marshmallows left?"

"No. Just graham crackers."

They ate the graham crackers. Terence didn't come back. They couldn't even hear his voice. They told ghost stories.

"And she puts her hand down and her dog licks it and she thinks everything is okay. Except that then, in the morning, when she looks in the bathtub, her dog is in there and he's dead and there's lots of blood and somebody has written HA HA I REALLY FOOLED YOU with the blood."

"One time my sister was babysitting and this weird guy called and wanted to know if Satan was there and she got really freaked out."

"One time my grandfather was riding on a train and he saw a naked woman standing out in a field."

"Was she a ghost?"

"I don't know. He used to like to tell that story a lot."

"Were there cows in the field?"

"I don't know, how should I know if there were cows?"

"Do you think Terence is going to come back soon?"

"Why? Are you scared?"

"What time is it?"

"It's not even 10:30. Maybe we could try lighting the fire again."

"It's still too wet. It's not going to catch. Besides, if there was a monster and if the monster was out there and we got the fire lit, then the monster could see us."

"We don't have any marshmallows anyway."

"Wait, I think I know how to get it started. Like Bungalow 4 did with the bat. If I spray it with insecticide, and then – "

Bungalow 6 fell reverently silent.

"Wow. That's awesome, Bryan. They should have a special merit badge for that."

"Yeah, to go with the badge for toxic farts."

"It smells funny," James Lorbick said. But it was nice to have a fire going. It made the darkness seem less dark. Which is what fires are supposed to do, of course.

"You look really weird in the firelight, James. That dress and all the mud. It's kind of funny and kind of creepy."

"Thanks."

"Yeah, James Lorbick should always wear dresses. He's so hot."

"James Lorbick, I think you are so hot. Not."

"Leave James alone," Bryan Jones said.

"I had this weird dream last year," Danny Anderson said. Danny Anderson was from Terre Haute, Indiana. He was taller than anyone else in Bungalow 6 except for Terence. "I dreamed that I came home from school one day and nobody was there except this man. He was sitting in the living room watching TV and so I said, 'Who are you? What are you doing here?' And he looked up and smiled this creepy smile at me and he said, 'Hey, Danny, I'm Angelina Jolie. I'm your new dad.'"

"No way. You dreamed your dad was Angelina Jolie?"

"No," Danny Anderson said. "Shut up. My parents aren't divorced or anything. My dad's got the same name as me. This guy said he was my *new* dad. He *said* he was Angelina Jolie. But he was just some guy."

"That's a dumb dream."

"I know it is," Danny Anderson said. "But I kept having it, like, every night. This guy is always hanging out in the kitchen and talking to me about what we're going to do now that I'm his kid. He's really creepy. And the thing is, I just got a phone call from my mom, and she says that she and my dad are getting divorced and I think maybe she's got a new boyfriend."

"Hey, man. That's tough."

Danny Anderson looked as if he might be about to cry. He said, "So what if this boyfriend turns out to be my new dad? Like in the dream?"

"My stepdad's pretty cool. Sometimes I get along with him better than I get along with my mom."

"One time I had a dream James Lorbick was wearing a dress."

"What's that noise?"

"I didn't hear anything."

"Terence has been gone a long time."

"Maybe he went back to camp. Maybe he left us out here."

"The fire smells really bad."

"It reeks."

"Isn't insect stuff poisonous?"

"Of course not. Otherwise they wouldn't be able to sell it. Because you put it on your skin. They wouldn't let you put poison on your skin."

"Hey, look up. I think I saw a shooting star."

"Maybe it was a spaceship."

They all looked up at the sky. The sky was black and clear and full of bright stars. It was like that for a moment and then they noticed how clouds were racing across the blackness, spilling across the sky. The stars disappeared. Maybe if they hadn't looked, the sky would have stayed clear. But they did look. Then snow started to fall, lightly at first, just dusting the muddy ground and the campfire and Bungalow 6 and then there was more snow falling. It fell quietly and thickly. It was going to be the thirteenth of June tomorrow, the next-to-last day of camp, the day that James Lorbick wearing a dress and a lot of mud was going to show up and scare everyone in the dining room.

The snow was the weirdest thing that had ever happened to Bungalow 6.

One of the Simpson twins said, "Hey, it's snowing!"

Bryan Jones started laughing. "This is awesome," he said. "Awesome!"

James Lorbick looked up at the sky, which had been so clear a minute ago. Fat snowflakes fell on his upturned face. He wrapped his crumbly mud-covered arms around himself. "*Awesome*," he repeated.

"Terence! Hey Terence! It's snowing!"

"Nobody is going to believe us."

"Maybe we should go get in our sleeping bags."

"We could build a snow fort."

"No, seriously. What if it gets really cold and we freeze to death? All I brought is my windbreaker."

"No way. It's going to melt right away. It's summer. This is just some kind of weather event. We should take a picture so we can show everybody."

So far they had taken pictures of mud, of people pretending to be mud-covered zombies, of James Lorbick pretending to be a mud-haired, dress-wearing monster. Terence had taken a picture of the bone that wasn't a cow bone. One of the Simpson twins had put a dozen marshmallows in his mouth and someone took a picture of that. Someone had a digital photo of Bryan Jones's big naked butt.

"So why didn't anyone from Bungalow 4 take a picture of the monster?"

"They did. But you couldn't see anything."

"Snow is cooler anyway."

"No way. A monster is way better."

"I think it's weird that Terence hasn't come back up yet."

"Hey, Terence! Terence!"

They all yelled for Terence for a few minutes. The snow kept falling. They did little dances in the snow to keep warm. The fire got thinner and thinner and started to go out. But before it went out, the monster came up the muddy, snowy path. It smiled at them and it came up the path and Danny Anderson shone his flashlight at it and they could all see it was a monster and not Terence pretending to be a monster. No one in Bungalow 6 had ever seen a monster before, but they all knew that a monster was what it was. It had a white face and its hands were red and dripping. It moved very fast.

You can learn a lot of stuff at camp. You learn how to wiggle an arrow so that it comes out of a straw target without the metal tip coming off. You learn how to make something out of yarn and twigs called a skycatcher, because there's a lot of extra yarn and twigs in the world, and someone had to come up with something to do with it. You learn how to jam your feet up into the mattress of the bunk above you, while someone is leaning out of it, so that they fall out of bed. You learn that if you are riding a horse and the horse sees a snake on the trail, the horse will stand on its hind legs. Horses don't like snakes. You find out that tennis rackets are good for chasing bats. You find out what happens if you leave your wet clothes in your trunk for a few days. You learn how to make rockets and you learn how to pretend not to care when someone takes your rocket and stomps on it. You learn to pretend to be asleep when people make fun of you. You learn how to be lonely.

The snow came down and people ran around Honor Lookout. They screamed and waved their arms around and fell down. The monster chased them. It moved so quickly that sometimes it seemed to fly. It was laughing like this was an excellent fun game. The snow was still coming down and it was dark, which made it hard to see what the monster did when it caught people. James Lorbick sat still. He pretended that he was asleep or not there. He pretended that he was writing a letter to his best friend in Chicago who was spending the summer playing video games and hanging out at the library and writing and illustrating his own comic book. *Dear Alec, how are you? Camp is almost over, and I am so glad. This has been the worst summer ever. We went on a hike and it rained and my counselor found a bone. This kid made me put on a dress. There was a monster which ate everybody. How is your comic book coming? Did you put in the part I wrote about the superhero who can only fly when he's asleep?*

The monster had one Simpson twin under each arm. The twins were screaming. The monster threw them down the path. Then it bent over Bryan Jones, who was lying half inside one of the tents, half in the snow. There were slurping noises. After a minute it stood up again. It looked back and saw James Lorbick. It waved.

James Lorbick shut his eyes. When he opened them again, the monster was standing over him. It had red eyes. It smelled like rotting fish and kerosene. It wasn't actually all that tall, the way you'd expect a monster to be tall. Except for that, it was even worse than Bungalow 4 had said.

The monster stood and looked down and grinned. "You," it said. It had a voice like a dead tree full of bees: sweet and dripping and buzzing. It poked James on the shoulder with a long black nail. "What are you?"

"I'm James Lorbick," James said. "From Chicago."

The monster laughed. Its teeth were pointed and terrible. There was a smear of red on the dress where it had touched James. "You're the craziest thing I've ever seen. Look at that dress. Look at your hair. It's standing straight up. Is that mud? Why are you covered in mud?"

"I was going to be a monster," James said. He swallowed. "No offense."

"None taken," the monster said. "Wow, maybe I should go visit Chicago. I've never seen anything as funny as you. I could look at you for hours and hours. Whenever I needed a laugh. You've really made my day, James Lorbick."

The snow was still falling. James shivered and shivered. His teeth were clicking together so loudly he thought they might break. "What are you doing here?" he said. "Where's Terence? Did you do something to him?"

"Was he the guy who was down at the bottom of the hill? Talking on a cell phone?"

"Yeah," James said. "Is he okay?"

"He was talking to some girl named Darlene," the monster said. I tried to talk to her, but she started screaming and it hurt my ears so I hung up. Do you happen to know where she lives?

"Somewhere in Ohio," James said.

"Thanks," the monster said. He took out a little black notebook and wrote something down.

"What are you?" James said. "Who are you?"

"I'm Angelina Jolie," the monster said. It blinked.

James's heart almost stopped beating. "Really?" he said. "Like in Danny Anderson's dream?"

"No," the monster said. "Just kidding."

"Oh," James said. They sat in silence. The monster used one long fingernail to dig something out between its teeth. It belched a foul, greasy belch. James thought of Bryan. Bryan probably would have belched right back, if he still had a head.

"Are you the monster that Bungalow 4 saw?" James said.

"Were those the kids who were here a few days ago?"

"Yeah," James said.

"We hung out for a while," the monster said. "Were they friends of yours?"

"No," James said. "Those kids are real jerks. Nobody likes them."

"That's a shame," the monster said. Even when it wasn't belching, it smelled worse than anything James had ever smelled before. Fish and kerosene and rotting maple syrup poured over him in waves. He tried not to breathe.

The monster said, "I'm sorry about the rest of your bungalow. Your friends. Your friends who made you wear a dress."

"Are you going to eat me?" James said.

"I don't know," the monster said. "Probably not. There were a lot of you. I'm not actually that hungry anymore. Besides, I would feel silly eating a kid in a dress. And you're really filthy."

"Why didn't you eat Bungalow 4?" James said. He felt sick to his stomach. If he looked at the monster he felt sick, and if he looked away, there was Danny Anderson, lying facedown under a pine tree with snow on his back and if he looked somewhere else, there were Bryan Jones's legs poking out of the tent. There was Bryan Jones's head. One of Bryan's shoes had come off and that made James think of the hike, the way Terence lay down in the mud to fish for the Simpson twin's shoe. "Why didn't you eat them? They're mean. They do terrible things and nobody likes them."

"Wow," the monster said. "I didn't know that. I would have eaten them if I'd known, maybe. Although most of the time I can't worry about things like that."

"Maybe you should," James said. "I think you should."

The monster scratched its head. "You think so? I saw you guys eating hotdogs earlier. So do you worry about whether those were good dogs or bad dogs when you're eating them? Do you only eat dogs that were mean? Do you only eat bad dogs?"

"Hot dogs aren't really made from dogs," James said. "People don't eat dogs."

"I never knew that," the monster said. "But see if I worried about that kind of thing, whether the person I was eating was a nice guy or a jerk, I'd never eat anyone. And I get hungry a lot. So to be honest, I don't worry. All I really notice is whether the person I'm chasing is big or small or fast or slow. Or if they have a sense of humor. That's important, you know. A sense of humor. You have to laugh about things. When I was hanging out with Bungalow 4, I was just having some fun. I was just playing around. Bungalow 4 mentioned that you guys were going to show up. I was joking about how I was going to eat them and they said I should eat you guys instead. They said it would be really funny. I have a good sense of humor. I like a good joke."

It reached out and touched James Lorbick's head.

"Don't do that!" James said.

"Sorry," said the monster. "I just wanted to see what the mud spikes felt like. Do you think it would be funny if I wore a dress and put a lot of mud on my head?"

James shook his head. He tried to picture the monster wearing a dress, but all he could picture was somebody climbing up to Honor Lookout. Somebody finding pieces of James scattered everywhere like pink and red confetti. That somebody would wonder what had happened and be glad that it hadn't happened to them. Maybe someday people would tell scary stories about what had happened to Bungalow 6 when they went camping. Nobody would believe the stories. Nobody would understand why one kid had been wearing a dress.

"Are you shivering because you're cold or because you're afraid of me?" the monster said.

"I don't know," James said. "Both. Sorry."

"Maybe we should get up and run around," the monster said. "I could chase you. It might warm you up. Weird weather, isn't it? But it's pretty, too. I love how snow makes everything look nice and clean."

"I want to go home," James said.

"That's Chicago, right?" the monster said. "That's what I wrote down."

"You wrote down where I live?" James said.

"All those guys from the other bungalow," the monster said. "Bungalow 4. I made them write down their addresses. I like to travel. I like to visit people. Besides, if you say that they're jerks, then I should go visit them? Right? It would serve them right."

"Yeah," James said. "It would serve them right. That would be really funny. Ha ha ha."

"Excellent," the monster said. It stood up. "It was great meeting you, James. Are you crying? It looks like you're crying."

"I'm not crying. It's just snow. There's snow on my face. Are you leaving?" James said. "You're going to leave me here? You aren't going to eat me?"

"I don't know," the monster said. It did a little twirl, like it was going to go running off in one direction, and then as if it had changed its mind, as if it was going to come rushing back at James. James whimpered. "I just can't decide. Maybe I should flip a coin. Do you have a coin I can flip?"

James shook his head.

"Okay," the monster said. "How about this. I'm thinking of a number between one and ten. You say a number and if it's the same number, I won't eat you."

"No," James said.

"Then how about if I only eat you if you say the number that I'm thinking of? I promise I won't cheat. I probably won't cheat."

"No," James said, although he couldn't help thinking of a number. He thought of the number four. It floated there in his head like a big neon sign, blinking on and off and back on. Four, four, four. Bungalow 4. Or six. Bungalow 6. Or was that too obvious? Don't think of a number. He would have bet anything that the monster could read minds. Maybe the monster had put the number four in James's head. Six. James changed the number to six hundred so it wouldn't be a number between one and ten. Don't read my mind, he thought. Don't eat me.

"I'll count to six hundred," the monster said. "And then I'll chase you. That would be funny. If you get back to camp before I catch you, you're safe. Okay? If you get back to camp first, I'll go eat Bungalow 4. Okay? I tell you what. I'll go eat them even if you don't make it back. Okay?"

"But it's dark," James said. "It's snowing. I'm wearing a dress."

The monster looked down at its fingernails. It smiled like James had just told an excellent joke. "One," it said. "Two, three, four. Run, James! Pretend I'm chasing you. Pretend that I'm going to eat you if I catch you. Five, six. Come on, James, run!"

James ran.

Robots and Falling Hearts

Tim Pratt and Greg van Eekhout

Tim Pratt (*www.sff.net/people/timpratt*) lives in Oakland, California, with his wife, Heather Shaw, and co-edits a 'zine with her, *Flytrap*. His fiction and poetry have appeared in publications like *The Best American Short Stories: 2005*, *The Year's Best Fantasy and Horror*, *Strange Horizons*, *Realms of Fantasy*, *Asimov's*, *Lady Churchill's Rosebud Wristlet*, and *Year's Best Fantasy*. His first novel, *The Strange Adventures of Rangergirl*, was published in 2005; his first collection is *Little Gods* (2003). His second collection is *Hart & Boot & Other Stories* (2006).

Greg van Eekhout (*www.sff.net/people/greg/*) lives in Tempe, Arizona. He is an Instructional Designer and Multimedia Developer for Arizona State University. His stories have appeared in *The Magazine of Fantasy and Science Fiction*, *Asimov's*, *Year's Best Fantasy and Horror*, *Starlight 3*, and other places. He maintains a blog at *writingandsnacks.com/blog*.

"Robots and Falling Hearts" was published in *Realms of Fantasy*. It is a fine Philip K. Dickian fantasy about the shifting nature of reality. It's a love story, too, and full of surprises.

DOWN IN THEIR INNERMOST HEARTS, people expect the occasional rain of frogs or blood, people bursting into spontaneous flames, animals speaking in human tongues. Such things are part of our shared heritage, the mysteries of human history, and while they might confound and frighten us, deep down, they don't feel *wrong*.

But no one knew quite how to react to the recent plague of robots.

I went to Los Angeles, because it was supposed to be the worst there, maybe even the place where the plague started, robots going unnoticed for a long time because of Hollywood. For a while people assumed the robots were props or publicity stunts or refugees from public-access television junkyard wars, until it became obvious that they were something more.

My first day in the city I sat at a table outside Peet's in Brentwood, sipping a caramel apple cider, watching the beautiful people walk by. This was much nicer than crouching on an exposed, frozen mountainside, sipping barley tea flavored with rancid yak butter – though that experience had its charms, too.

Half an hour after I sat down I saw my first L.A. robot, crouched on top of a passing BMW. The robot was like a starfish made of articulated metal, all chrome except for brass joints, and it clung to the car's roof rack, a whip antenna rising up from the center of its body. I wondered if the driver knew about his robotic passenger. I threw away my cup and went walking, ostensibly window-shopping, but really keeping my eyes open for more robotic manifestations.

I paused to tie a loose shoelace and a squat robot, like a dirty white trashcan on tank-treads, trundled out of an alley toward me. A red light on top of its domelike top blinked erratically. It said, in a high-pitched voice, "Klaatu barada nikto." A small panel slid open in its front, and a pole with a cup on the end telescoped out. There were a few coins in the cup, mostly pennies and nickels, and the robot jingled the cup significantly.

"Take me to your leader," I said, wishing it could be that simple, knowing that these things are never that simple.

The robot beeped at me and jingled its cup harder, the coins rattling.

"It won't go away unless you give it some change," said a woman standing on the corner. "It followed me all the way to work one day, and hung around outside the door like a dog for hours."

"Yeah?" I said, taking a good look at her. She wasn't uncommonly pretty, but I'd been on assignment in the Himalayas for several months previous, and she was the first woman who'd spoken to me in seasons. "Has it been around here long?"

She shrugged. "I guess. Even a penny will get rid of it."

I looked down at the robot. "Piss off," I said, enunciating clearly, just to see what it would do.

A low grinding noise came from deep inside the robot's squat body, and I took a step back, expecting something nasty to happen. Instead it just said "Danger! Danger!" and flailed its single arm around wildly for a moment, coming dangerously close to spilling its coins.

I gave in and dropped a quarter into its cup. The robot beeped contentedly and rolled away.

"See?" the woman said.

"Can I ask you a question?" I said. "Do you remember the first time you saw a robot here in the city?"

"Sure," she said. "Everybody remembers that." But then the light changed, and she started to cross the street.

"Um," I said, going after her. "If I could have just a moment..."

She continued walking, and with a half-glance over her shoulder, she reached into her purse and came out with a jangling cluster of keys attached to a matte black cylinder. Pepper spray, I figured. Or maybe a TASER.

"I'm a student," I said, pulling up even with her. "I mean, sort of, I'm a student. And I'm doing research on the robot plague, and if I could interview you, it would only take a few minutes – "

Her thumb moved over a little red button on the top of her keychain, and when we reached the curb, she turned and looked me up and down. As she performed a threat-assessment on me, I decided that, in her own way, she really was rather attractive. I liked the freckles sprinkling her round cheeks, and despite the hard set to her jaw, her pale lips formed pleasing, sensuous curves. Her hands were slender but strong: thick-veined, with blunt, unpainted fingernails, hands built for more than office work. The sun caught coppery highlights in her brown hair, which she wore pulled back into a tight pony tail, leaving just a few free strands that floated with liquid grace in the slight breeze.

After a moment, her shoulders relaxed a little, and she started holding the keychain the way one holds a keychain instead of the way one holds an anti-creep weapon. "If you want to know about the robots," she said, "you should be talking to City Hall or the cops or the brainiacs at Caltech. I don't even subscribe to the newspaper. I just live here."

I was about to tell her that I didn't want so-called expert opinions, that I'd read all the official reports and already knew what the politicians and pundits and consultants had to say, that what I really needed, if I were going to get to the bottom of this thing, was the word on the street, and that she smelled of oranges and shampoo and that after spending weeks on the edge of a frozen rock in a tent that smelled of sweat and farts and men, I really wanted to buy her lunch. But a mechanical voice cut me off before I could even get two or three words out.

"Whizmo!"

"Oh, great," the woman said. "Now it's Whizmo." She grabbed my wrist and started tugging me down the sidewalk.

"Whizmo!"

She dragged me beneath an overpass, behind a broad concrete support pillar, as the vast clattering grew louder. I started to speak, and she covered my mouth with her hand – it was all I could do not to kiss her palm.

From behind the pillar, we watched as Whizmo zoomed by. His original shape was wholly obscured by the spoilers, stick-on rearview mirrors, handlebars, small plastic Buddhas, and other assorted junk bristling from his frame, all of it banging together, reminding me of certain mountain ceremonies useful in dispelling ghosts and unfriendly wildlife. When Whizmo was out of sight, she took her hand from my mouth. "He used to be a pretty boring robot," she said. "He looked like a gas-powered generator on wheels. But then the neighborhood kids started sticking bumper stickers on him, and someone else attached a bicycle horn and some reflectors, and it went on from there. Now he chases people until they add something to his chassis. Whizmo knocked down a guy once, but he wasn't hurt too badly."

I thought of Master Tenzin's temple, which he encouraged visitors to embellish with carvings and drawings and the occasional glob of chewing gum, and his story of the group of explorers who visited his first temple forty years before. When asked to add their own touches to that temple, the drunken explorers burned the building down. After the flames died, Master Tenzin stood in the midst of the ashes, turning slowly around, then knelt and drew a single jagged line in the soot. The explorers, who'd expected to break the Master's preternatural calm, jeered at him, but then went on their way. They died in an avalanche that afternoon, but when I drew the obvious conclusion that Master Tenzin's drawing had somehow contributed to that snowy death, he merely shook his head, sadly, as if I'd missed the point.

"You were going to tell me about the first time you saw the robots," I said. We were still standing very close together. Getting back to the business at hand seemed the wisest course.

She stepped away, out of arm's reach. "No, you asked me to. I told you to ask people who actually *know* something."

I nodded. I sighed. "See," I said. "See. The thing is. And this isn't something that just anyone knows. But. Well. Look, where do *you* think the robots come from?"

She shrugged. "I guess it's just a bunch of people building them for fun, setting them loose all over the world. Or maybe it's like a government experiment in artificial intelligence, they build a bunch of robots and release them to see if they can learn. Who knows?"

"Nobody knows," I said. "But everyone began from the assumption that the robots were *built*, just like you did. The thing is, the scientists have broken a lot of these robots open, they've checked out the mechanisms...and these robots shouldn't work *at all*. There's machinery inside them, circuit boards and wires and even the occasional vacuum tube, but none of it's connected in a way that makes sense. These things...they're more like *sculptures* of robots than real robots. But there it is, inarguably, they work! They move, they interact, they learn. Some of them steal! Some of them harass! Some of them save children from burning buildings! Some of them gouge potholes in the roadways, and some of them repair broken traffic lights! They do all these things, when they shouldn't be able to do anything at *all*!"

She blinked. I realized I'd been shouting. I get excited.

"I haven't heard about anything like that," she said. "About how they shouldn't work."

"Yeah, well," I said. "It's not something the officials are spreading around. I'm only telling you because I want your help. You were here when it started. The first time the robots showed up, in the first place."

"We thought it was a publicity thing for some sci-fi movie," she said.

"So tell me about it."

She shook her head. "Who *are* you? How do you know that the scientists are keeping secrets? What exactly are you trying to find out? You said you're a student?"

"Sort of a student." I thought about how to explain my job – my calling – and what I hoped to find out about the plague of robots. Random words and images appeared in my mind. A childhood fascination with the Fiji mermaid. That disastrous internship with the Society for Fortean Studies. Cryptophenom-enology. The corporate-sponsored codification of transcendental experiences. How I'd gone to the Himalayas to investigate a levitating monk and, instead, met Master Tenzin.

Ah, but Master Tenzin had taught me how to respond in such situations, when the very complex needed to be communicated in a succinct and interest-ing way.

"I'd better tell you a parable," I said.

"You know, no offense, but I'm not really one of those yoga, tofu people..."

"Yoga's good for your back," I said absently, sorting through my days spent at the feet of Master Tenzin. Should I tell her of the ram and the shepherd? Of the king and the bamboo sliver? Of the fat man and the paper chair?

No.

Of all the lessons I took from the cold mountains, there seemed only one that might help her understand why I had come here, to this vast puzzle box of a city, to learn about the robots and thus peel back the secrets of the world.

So I told her this:

There was a man who sat at the edge of the market, surrounded by frogs of all manner: frogs blue as sapphire, frogs red as blood, frogs the size of a pea, frogs large as dogs, frogs bewinged, frogs with teeth, frogs with as many legs as a spi-der. Each day he squatted in the dust amidst a chorus of croaks, and wrote in tiny script on a crowded piece of parchment. It was said that the parchment listed and described every kind of frog on Earth, and that when the last frog was prop-erly catalogued, the old man would die.

One morning a boy came to the man, offering for sale a frog he had found by the river with eyes on stalks, like a snail. After some negotiation, the frog man gave the boy some few coins – a very fair trade – and yet the boy remained.

"Why do you linger?" asked the frog man of the boy. "Is there something more you wanted?"

"Are you not going to list my frog?" the boy asked.

The frog man showed the boy a corner near the upper edge of the parch-ment, where the ink was old and faded. The writing described a frog with eyes like a snail's, and also a little boy who found a frog by a stagnant green river and brought the frog to an old man who spent his days scribbling in the market, surrounded by baskets and bamboo cages containing frogs. "But of course I have already written of this," the old man said. "Long ago. Otherwise, how would there have been a frog for you to find?"

And he told the boy to go home, and to write of his own frogs, so that when he became an old man there would still be frogs awaiting young boys by the river.

The woman smirked and cocked her head, and I entertained the notion that there was a remote possibility she found me cute. "Okay," she said, "I'll be your Grasshopper. So, the little boy is you, and the frogs are the robots, and the old man expresses the indistinguishable natures of cause and effect. Yeah? Did I get it right?"

Her eyes were the color of iced tea in the sun.

"No, you did not get it right."

We both spun toward the voice at our backs. A six-foot-tall robot like a barber poll mounted on a single bicycle wheel rolled toward us, spinning a ribbon of silver and gold and bronze. Here and there it was decked out with chrome and leather trim, like the backseat of a car in *American Graffiti*, and it exuded the smells of clean oil and menthol. Its head, a polished globe as brilliant as a shaving mirror, extended toward us on a scissors-arm, and when I looked into it, I felt the sidewalk go a little sideways beneath my feet.

For it wasn't my face I saw reflected in the robot's head.

A battered face, with a bulbous nose, red eyes, and a split lip peered out at me, distorted by the curved nature of the sphere. Upon closer inspection, I realized that it *was* my face, but a horribly damaged, nearly unrecognizable version of it, beaten to pulp. Excitement gathered in the pit of my stomach. There was something here, something about the flesh as grass, something about the futility of desire and Earthly things. It had occurred to me – more than once, many times, in fact it was the closest thing I had to a hypothesis at this point – that the robots were bodhisattvas for a new age, alien saints, holy fools. And this strange, bright, sleek thing before me was a –

"Fucking doombot," the woman said wearily.

The robot swung its sphere toward her, and I caught a glimpse of the shifting face in the sphere – now it was her face, hideously disfigured, and I looked away, far more disturbed by the thought of her flesh ravaged than I'd been at the sight of my own.

"You got it wrong," the doombot said, and made a snorting noise, mechanical but still full of disdain. It mimicked her viciously, perfectly: "'The little boy is you, and the frogs are the robots, and the old man expresses the indistinguishable natures of cause and effect.' Bah! Parables aren't *metaphors*. They don't map exactly to a given situation – they provide insight. If that's what you got out of a parable, I despair to think of what you'd do with a koan!"

"It's no use talking to this doombot," she said. "All it ever does is bitch and belittle."

"But it seems to be conscious," I said. "It's speaking in complete sentences. I bet I could learn a lot from it. It's not like the others I've seen."

"You'd be wasting your time. The doombot was one of the first robots to show up here. It came the first day, and since it talked, everyone thought it was the spokesman, or the king, or something. The mayor's task force spent hours and hours interviewing it, and never got it to talk sense, or talk about its origins, or anything – it just complained and insulted them. Eventually they gave up and let it go. Now it's a free-range doomsayer."

The doombot extended its sphere toward her, and she swung at it irritably with her purse. "Thirty pounds of flax," the doombot muttered, jerking its head back. The sphere retracted, the face in its glass pixellating into nonsense. The barber-pole swirl started turning more quickly, and I began thinking about the endless spiral of life, a stairway to the infinite.

Then I cocked my head and frowned at the woman. "How do you know what the mayor's task force thought? I thought you didn't even read the papers?"

She sighed and looked away. "Because. I used to be part of the task force. My part didn't last long. I don't like to talk about it."

This was unreal – she'd had close, intimate contact with the first robots, had at the very least been fully briefed on the events of the day of their arrival. What a resource! I was, for a moment, ashamed for thinking of her in such utilitarian terms, but I *did* have a mission to fulfill. "What was your position on the task force?" I asked. Her face was still turned away from me, and the absence of her gaze made me feel like winter.

The doombot thrust its sphere between our heads. "Stupid stupids," it said, voice flat with disgust. "I'll tell you what her position was."

The woman lashed out at the sphere, striking it with the flat of her hand, making it swing away on the end of its scissors-arm and slam into the concrete pillar, where the glass shattered, little slivers of prismatic glass raining down. Half-demolished, the remaining part of the sphere looked like a cup with jagged edges. I leaned over, suddenly sure there was something inside the sphere, some revelation, some –

There was a small green frog inside. I think it looked back at me when I looked at it. It was hard to tell, because its eyes were on stalks, moving independently, like a snail's.

"Shit," the woman said. She hadn't seen the frog yet. "I didn't mean to do that. The sphere was always unbreakable before! Believe me, people try to break it all the time!"

The woman poked the gleaming shards of the doombot's head with her toe. While she was preoccupied, I bent down and enclosed the frog in my cupped hands. Its skin was cool and soothing against my palms.

"Tell me," I said. "What did you do on the investigatory commission? What was your job?"

Her mouth formed a bitter smirk. "My job? I wouldn't call it a job. I answered questions. Every day for more than a month, I sat in various stuffy little rooms, or drafty offices, and I answered their questions. There were also some examinations – blood work, CT-scans, that kind of thing." Her eyes shone, and a tremor had crept into her voice. "But mostly, it was just questions."

I had caused her discomfort, as surely as a gunshot causes an avalanche. Though the mountainside may have been unstable before I fired the shot, the responsibility was still mine. I didn't want to cause her more distress. But I had to know. "What was it the commission hoped to learn from you?" My voice failed to express the regret I felt in pursuing this course.

"Think of a robot," she said, not looking at me.

"A robot? I don't know what you – "

"What color is it?" she snapped. "Silver? Bronze? Matte black? Green, like copper patina? Gray, like primer paint? Envision a color. Quickly."

"White," I said, and only after I said it did I realize that I had still been thinking about ice-capped mountains. The frog shifted in my hands. Loathe to hurt it, I loosened my grip.

"Don't tell me about the robot," she said. "Just think it."

She instructed me to think of the robot's size, its shape, its texture. She told me not to dwell on these features, but to lock onto the first coherent thing that entered my head. It was the sort of thought exercise that Master Tenzin might have led me through.

Finally, she asked me how it moved, and I knew the answer immediately.

The frog was still cold and smooth. But it was a different kind of cold. A different kind of smooth.

I released it on the ground. White as ice, it took a hop, and then another, its servos whirring as it made quick leaps toward the gutter. When it leaped again, the woman rushed forward and caught it in her purse.

"I made a robot," I said, astonished.

"Did you? Are you sure?"

"You made the robot?"

"Who made the robot is a question best left for philosophers." She made a dismissive gesture with her hand, and I tried not to feel insulted. "The question is: How do we stop it?"

From within her purse, the robot frog croaked. There was a bit of low-fidelity 8-bit compression hiss behind the sound. "Why is it necessary to stop it? You said yourself that the robots are more an annoyance than a danger. I think they're beautiful in a way. Cryptophenomena, the secret weather of the world...it's the song changing key. It's how nature turns the page on the book we've all been reading too long. It's the Tower of Babylon collapsing, forcing us to learn new languages, to adapt to new patterns, to *better* ourselves. When nature gives us something strange to deal with, we're forced to evolve." I'd grown excited again. Breathless. "I'm thankful for the robots," I concluded lamely. "I think they're going to transform us."

"Listen," she said, waving her hands as if dispelling a foul stink. "That's fine. That's fine as long as the robots are just funny jalopies, or toy frogs, or even insulting barber poles. But I'm starting to think of bad robots." Her shoulders fell in extreme fatigue. Perhaps even despair. She took both my hands in hers. "I'm starting to think of robots that scare me."

"Ah," I said, staring down at her hands. "I can see how that might be a problem. Some people are panicking, especially as the robots spread throughout the country. I guess, if enough people start to think about scary robots – "

"It doesn't take 'enough people,'" she said. "It just takes me."

"But *my* thoughts changed the frog, just then – "

"Did they?" she said quietly. "Did I? I don't know. But the robots don't change ...they don't *appear*...when I'm not around. I know that. They aren't born from nothing, from, I don't know, a-robo-genesis. It has something to do with me."

I recalled Master Tenzin's warning that madness and enlightenment were separated by a membrane as thin as an ox's hair, and his caution that discovering one impossible thing did not automatically prove that all impossible things were true. Someone living every day in the company of robots might come to believe herself the center of the new metallic universe, even if it wasn't true.

But then, just a moment ago, I'd felt a tiny frog transform into a machine in my very hands. I should treat her statement as truth, and see what I could learn. Even the wrong path can lead to a place of beauty, after all. And she did smell quite marvelous. "If you are somehow related to the robots," I said slowly, "then I understand why you were on the mayor's commission, and why they might want to ask you a lot of questions. Probably very difficult questions."

"Even harder than 'what's the sound of one hand clapping,'" she said wryly.

"But what I don't understand is why they let you quit." And why I hadn't heard of her, when I'd had access to every piece of intelligence about the robots. But there was no reason to scare her with that kind of spook talk.

She let go of my hands and folded them in her lap. Her bag croaked, then made a sound like whirring servos. The frogbot was growing restless. She looked down at the shards of glass from the broken doombot. "I don't know why I trust you," she said. "Maybe because somebody who talks in parables and koans wouldn't bother to lie, when they can be confusing enough just telling the truth. They didn't let me off the commission – I *escaped*. They looked for me, but they couldn't find me. Then they stopped looking, because they forgot about me. They forgot about me *retroactively*. Everyone did. My presence on the commission was edited out of existence. Even the videotapes of our sessions changed. Consensual reality underwent a statutory rape."

I nodded, but I was thinking: Paranoia. Conspiracy theory. Delusions of grandeur.

She sighed. "You don't believe me. Listen. You asked me to tell you about the first day the robots came. I said you should ask someone else, because *every-one* remembers that. And everyone does. But I don't remember what everyone *else* remembers. What *they* remember is something like a golden mushroom growing up from the ground in the middle of Hollywood Boulevard, something like a closed bulb that opened up into a flower with fractal edges, and then the first robots came out, trundling, flapping, hopping, rolling. Some of the robots opened up their own little hatches or chutes or tubes, and other, smaller robots came out of their bodies, and skittered into the alleys and side streets, and then other robots began dismantling the mushroom-thing and running off, carrying the pieces with them. There was nothing left behind in the street except a big pothole. People clapped. They thought it was publicity for a movie, some sci-fi spectacular. But then there were more robots, and more, and we all realized... you know all this, right?"

"Sure." I'd read the same story, with countless variations, in the Pentagon's files.

"Of course. Everyone knows it. Except it's not what *happened*. The golden mushroom opened, and there was only one robot inside it, eight-feet-tall, shaped almost like a person, her body shining white as ice, with fingers of transparent crystal and eyes of cobalt glass. She spoke to the crowd – she told *them* why she'd come, and what she wanted to do, and what *they* all had to do. And then she opened a hinged door in her chest – where the heart would be, on a person – and tiny robots poured out, carrying pieces of bigger robots, and assembling them. They had tools, too, and they passed them out to people in the crowd. Everyone helped build the robots. Everyone understood why they were doing it." She was crying now, her head bent, tears dripping onto her hands and her purse in her lap.

"What did they understand?" I asked, and in a way, it was the same question

I'd been asking myself for years. I wanted to understand, too.

"I don't remember," she said, voice hollow, almost mechanical. "That's one of the things that changed, when I ran away from the commission. When I changed."

"Changed...how?"

"You like parables, but I'm not good at those, I don't think. Maybe I used to be. I used to be...different. I think I should just show you. You see what I am. You should see something of what I used to be."

She lifted her head and looked at me.

Her eyes were made of cobalt glass. And her fingers, when she touched my hand, were heavy crystal, transparent.

Nothing else about her had changed.

Everything about everything else had changed.

The ground beneath my feet: Black glass threaded with silver wires.

The shops and office buildings around me: Big blocks that looked like gutted radios, hung with jungles of striped cables, capacitors the size of hot water heaters, blobs of solder you'd have to carry with both hands.

The sky over my head: The dull silver of a well-spent coin.

On the sidewalk, there were no people. At least not people I'd come to recognize as people. There were figures of glass and figures of bronze and figures of cobbled-together cell phones and computer peripherals and sprung audio tapes and pistons and hydraulic limbs. The people moved about with their shopping bags and purses and brief cases, oblivious to the miracles they'd just become.

I held my own hand before my face. The hairs on my knuckles glinted silver. Tiny lights blinked beneath my translucent plastic fingernails.

And now I believed. I believed this woman was what I'd hoped, and my heart soared with joy, my mission so close to completion. Mixed with those feelings, though, was a spiraling sense of panic. I had prepared all my life for a moment like this, but I was still a man of a world in which the rules of gravity and electromagnetism and temporal mechanics could be counted on to apply. Hardwired into my brain was the notion that reality ought not be excessively elastic.

"Can you change things back?" I asked.

On the verge of hyperventilation, her chest rose and fell heavily. "I don't know."

"It's okay if you can't," I assured her, trying to assure myself at the same time. "But if you can, it would be very interesting to me."

She gathered herself, eyes closed. Her glass hand was cold in my grip. I shut my eyes, too.

"Okay," she said after a moment. "Okay. How's that?"

Something smashed on the ground near my feet. It was an oblong blob, red with rust, about the size of two joined fists. Impact had cracked it open, revealing gears and wires and tubes. Seconds later, another hit the ground a few yards away, and then another closer by. They were coming down more steadily now, one every several seconds. Around us, people – and they *were* people again – ran for the cover of doorways.

It was raining mechanical hearts, but given the presence of the Los Angeles robots, it didn't seem like an impossible situation.

The girl once more looked like herself, flesh and freckles and brown eyes. Or, I should say, she looked like herself in this aspect of the world.

Gently, I drew her to me, held her close, the clean citrus smell of her hair filling my mind with unproductive thoughts. "You are so, so beautiful," I murmured in her ear. "You are, perhaps, the most beautiful woman I have ever known. You are an incredibly beautiful re-weaver."

Abruptly, she pulled back from me. It felt as though someone had yanked my own heart out without anesthesia. "I'm a *what?*" she said. "And no parables or koans or any of that Bhodi Tree crap. Just tell me."

Hearts continued to fall about us.

I winced, for what better way to let her know what she was, and how I had come to be with her today, now, on this street, ready to claim possession of this miracle, than the tale of the sea cow and the concubine? But maybe she was right. Perhaps now was not the time. I cleared my throat.

"I told you of the man in the market who created the kingdom of frogs. A man who shaped the world with only the tools of his thoughts. Such people have always existed, and always will. They bring the impossible into the world. Some are only slightly gifted, and they bring down rains of blood and whirlwinds of fish. In their wake, bulls speak with human tongues. People burst into flames. These re-weavers of the world are often oblivious to the influence they have on things around them. But then there are men like my teacher, Master Tenzin. He knew what he was, what he could do, and he understood the nightmares he could unleash upon the world if he didn't discipline his mind and learn to calm his own heart. So, near the high ceiling of the world, he created a small refuge for himself. A place to meditate. A place to sequester himself from the temptation to re-weave the world as he willed. When Westerners came and burned down his temple, he killed them. In a moment of weakness, he drew a line in the ash and brought the mountain down upon them.

"There were witnesses, of course – Sherpa guides from the village below. One of them understood the potential in what he'd just seen. He understood its worth, and he knew there were people who would pay well for the information. So he contacted the United States government and told them of the incredible weapon living amidst charred rubble on the side of the mountain.

"The Americans sent some of their best men, but they never found Master Tenzin. But decades later, they finally did catch up with his apprentice. They caught up with me."

The girl stared. "And you're...one of us?" she asked. "Like your Master Tenzin? Like me?"

I barked a laugh. Does one confuse an apostle with Jesus? Does one credit an elf with being Santa Claus? "Oh, no, nothing like that," I said. "I'm a mere student. A researcher. An observer. I have studied the secret weather of the world, as well as those who craft it. I came to Los Angeles to learn about the robots, and I have found so much more." I dared to touch her cheek, just brushing it with my fingertips. "Instead, I have found you."

Her expression grew hard. Hostile. Those warm brown eyes darkened, and I felt a pang of fear. Only a fool would wish to make a re-weaver angry. I withdrew my hand.

"And now that you've discovered me," she said. "What's your plan?"

"My plan?

"I assume once the Americans found you, they decided to exploit your expertise."

Reluctantly, I nodded.

"What am I to you, then? A weapon? Something to transform the arsenals of the government's rivals to sea cucumbers?"

"No, no, nothing like that – "

"Or will you keep me for yourself, like a genie in a bottle, a magical woman who grants your fondest wishes and wears a halter-top? Will you use me like an engine and ride to power on my back? What am I to you?"

"You are the truth," I said. "You are a new truth, and you drive actuality. By coming to understand you, I will come to understand everything. I am a student. You are the master I have always wanted. And I think I love you."

My voice broke as I said these things.

She looked away for several long moments, as if going into a completely internal world, which was possible, for her, in more than one sense. When she turned back to me, I couldn't read her expression. Then, suddenly, she pulled my face close to hers and kissed me in a way that reversed the Earth's rotation. It was like falling, and the sensation was beautiful and strange and impossible, and no matter what else happens to me or to the world around me, I will never forget that feeling. It was as close to enlightenment as I have ever gotten. I am almost certain it is as close as I ever will get. I kept my eyes closed, holding on to the sensation.

"I have nothing to teach you," she said, gently, but with finality. "And I won't be studied."

When I opened my eyes, she was gone. I caught a glimpse of motion in my peripheral vision, something small hopping into the gutter, but what it was, I never knew.

I stood alone in the street.

All around me hundreds of hearts fell, crashing and shattering, to the ground.

On a late afternoon, I sat at an outdoor café in Santa Monica, sipping a caramel macchiatto and dwelling on the thoughts that tangled in the back of my mind, trying to tease out the essential from the mess of the peripheral. I remembered a world transformed, occupied by robots and frogs and a beautiful, strange girl or goddess whose name I never learned. Lately my dreams were like a memory from earliest childhood, flashes of an alien world more than half-hidden, something longed-for that dances outside the reach of one's grasp, a golden butterfly, beautiful and coveted, but perhaps best left uncaptured.

Yes, things happened the way I remembered them. But, yes, they also had happened differently. The world contained robots that shouldn't function. It contained hearts that fall from the sky, and frogs with wings, and buildings bedecked with living circuitry. And yet it was also true that the world contained none of those things.

Out on the boulevard, mermen poled an opalescent whale through traffic, their scaled muscles catching the gold of the sinking sun. Pygmy dolphins rode the whale's wake, occasionally leaping into the air and singing snatches of a Doors tune ("Love Her Madly," I think). It was a perfect Los Angeles postcard moment, but on this day its charms were wasted on me. Somewhere, somehow, I had touched a world much more interesting than the pretty but prosaic scene visible from my sidewalk bistro chair. I wondered if I'd ever find it again.

Draining the last of my drink, I stood and set out to wave down a passenger squid. It was time to start looking and learning again.

That was my job.

Still Life with Boobs

Anne Harris

Anne Harris (*www.inventingmemory.com*) lives in Royal Oak, Michigan. Harris has lived in the metro Detroit area all her life, and her first two novels (*The Nature of Smoke* and *Accidental Creatures*) are set in near-future Detroit industrial dystopias. Harris has been a long-term advocate of women's rights, reproductive freedom, and GLBT rights. Her website says, "Common themes in her work are chaos theory, biotechnology, personal freedom and transformation." Harris has also published short fiction in *Realms of Fantasy*, *Nova Express* and *Bristlecone*. Her blog is *annesible.livejournal.com*.

"Still Life with Boobs" was published in *Talebones*, a good small press magazine that has been around for a decade or more. It is an outrageous fantasy about a woman with the blues, whose breasts (George and Gracie) begin to leave her occasionally to have adventures. This is excellent humor, psychology, fantasy. "Over the top" is the phrase that comes to mind to describe the slapstick surrealism of this story.

SHE COULD NO LONGER ignore the fact that her breasts were going out at night without her. Gwen stood in front of the bathroom mirror and gave George and Gracie a long hard stare. They bore marks she knew they had not acquired in her presence; scratches, smears of dirt and other, less identifiable substances.

"Shit," she swore under her breath. "What do you want from me?" But George and Gracie just stared back at her innocently with their cold-puckering nipples, like two children caught making mud pies in their Sunday clothes.

They hadn't looked so innocent when she'd caught up with them last night in the back room of Menzer's Art Supply.

She'd fallen asleep in front of the television again. That was her routine these days, plop on the couch with a carton of peppermint stick ice cream and let prime time rob her of the capacity for coherent thought.

When she and David were still together they'd have stimulating conversations about art and politics. She'd watch him paint or they'd go to art openings. She hadn't minded her job back then, because she was working to foster something she believed in: David's art.

It was David who named her breasts George and Gracie. He had a regular puppet show he'd do. "Say goodnight, Gracie," he'd say in a deep voice, jiggling the left one. In a high-pitched voice he'd answer, "Goodnight Gracie," as he jiggled the right one. And then he'd kiss them, his mouth soft and open, with a flicker of his tongue that still sent shivers down her spine, just thinking about it. Gwen sighed and stepped into the shower.

She'd nodded off last night sometime between *Law & Order* and *Conan*

O'Brien, awakening again around two-thirty in the morning. An old black-and-white movie painted the room in flickering shades of noir and the ice cream had melted and leaked out the bottom of the carton, forming a pink lake in the middle of the coffee table.

When she got up to clean the mess she realized her breasts were gone. She ran her hands over the blank, flat place where George and Gracie should be, and felt a tremor of panic deep inside. She'd had this dream before, she thought, and pinched the featureless flesh hard. It hurt. The ice cream dripped off the edge of the table. She wasn't dreaming.

She threw on a sweater, sweatpants, and a pair of slippers and ventured out into the hallway of the apartment building just in time to see the elevator doors closing. Without stopping to consider if breasts even know how to use an elevator, Gwen plunged down the stairs.

But the lobby was deserted. She ran out onto the street and fancied she saw two small round objects rolling around the corner. She hurried after them and found herself in an alley behind a row of shops. The night was windy and damp. She shivered and wondered how her breasts could stand it. Up ahead, a door was just closing. Gwen ran to it, pulled on the handle and found it unlocked.

There was a small step up into a short hallway. Light leaked out from a doorway up ahead and she moved toward it. The muted thump of an insistent disco beat grew louder with every step she took. Gwen peeked around the edge of the doorway into a storeroom lit with Christmas lights. A disco ball made out of foil candy wrappers hung from the ceiling. Somewhere a stereo pounded out "Do You Wanna Touch Me?" by Rod Stewart.

Dozens of detached body parts cavorted about the room. There were penises, pussies, breasts, mouths, and even a couple of asses. She spotted George and Gracie off in one corner, wobbling lustily up and down the shaft of some rampant dick.

Shocked, Gwen started toward them, wading ankle-deep through bundles of bobbing flesh. George and Gracie froze in their cavorting, their nipples swiveling to face her like dark brown bull's eyes. They made a little squeal she didn't know breasts were capable of and darted for the doorway.

She ran after them. George and Gracie were remarkably swift for having no feet. They were out the back door before she could catch up with them. Gwen burst through the doorway and completely forgot about the step. She pitched forward, landing hard on the concrete. Groaning she lifted her head and saw a pair of men's brown oxford shoes. She gasped, staggering to her feet. "Hey, careful now. You okay?" said the guy, and she got a vague impression of light brown hair and a white shirt. He put his hands out to steady her, but just grazed her sleeve as she fled down the alley.

She never did catch up with George and Gracie, but they came home sometime before dawn and when she awoke, there they were, looking pretty much as she would have expected. Grimacing, Gwen got a good lather going on her body puff, closed her eyes and scrubbed.

Late for work again, Gwen charged into her bedroom and grabbed panties and pantyhose from the clean pile by the bed. But couldn't find a bra. She definitely needed a bra. She rummaged around in the bottom of the closet where she generally threw everything she didn't want to deal with. She really had to clean this mess up, she thought as she tossed aside a butterfly net she'd had since she was six.

Finally she found a black lace bra she'd bought back when she was still with David. It was far from ideal. Under the circumstances, she'd prefer full coverage and reinforced straps, but there was no time to worry about that. She sniffed the bra to determine if it was clean enough, decided it was, and put it on.

After work that day Gwen and her friend Tammi browsed through racks of bras at Target. They both worked at J. Thomas Design, Tammi in sales, Gwen in accounts receivable.

"I can't believe you put up with that crap from Charlie Axel, Gwen," said Tammi, tilting her curly brown head to one side and flashing her a glistening lip-gloss grimace. "I don't care how great a designer he is, he wouldn't call me a lower life form and walk away from it."

"I believe his exact words were, 'I won't put up with this constant badgering from some low-level bean counter,'" Gwen corrected her.

"Yeah, after he dumped a foot-high stack of memos and specs on your desk and told you to sort through them yourself. And you probably will. Why does that guy have you so whipped? Don't tell me it's the artist thing."

Gwen shrugged. "He is talented," she admitted. "His multi-media piece, 'Bart Simpson's Guernica,' won first prize in a juried show at the Pierce Gallery."

Tammi gave her a sour look and changed the subject. "So, what's the occasion for new lingerie? Could it be the ice age has ended at last? Do you have a date? Who is it?" Tammi grinned and elbowed Gwen in the ribs. "Is it the new guy in accounting? He's got a cute butt."

Gwen shook her head. "It's not for a date. It's for my breasts."

"Well, duh!" Tammi held up a leopard print underwire with black lace trim and eyed it critically.

"No." Gwen shoved aside a frothy lavender concoction and pulled out a white cotton sports bra. "I mean I need something more substantial, something... architectural, if possible."

Tammi cast a doubtful eye at Gwen's bust line. "I don't know if they make those kind in your size. You usually don't see those 'foundation garment' grandma bras in anything less than a 40C. Besides, you don't need it. All you need is a little underwire, a little shaping." She took the sports bra from Gwen and hung it back up again. Twisting her bangle bracelets she shrugged and said, "Maybe a little padding?"

Gwen rolled her eyes. "I need a lot more than that."

Tammi frowned. "Oh come on! What are you complaining about? You're beautiful." Her mouth quirked in irritation. "You wouldn't have any trouble finding guys if you'd just get out a little more. Which reminds me, Buzz wants to go to Moosejaw's next Friday for dinner and drinks. He's got this friend Tom, and I was thinking, he could bring Tom, and you could join us." She wiggled her eyebrows.

Gwen sighed and turned to the Playtex stand, rifling through the cardboard boxes, trying to find something in her size. "I don't think so, Tammi. I'm not much in the mood for dating right now."

Tammi rolled her eyes. Her chewing gum gleamed pink between her whitened teeth. "Gwenny, I love you, but you have got to get out of this rut."

She was in a rut, Gwen admitted to herself. She'd thought it was a comfortable rut, but now that had changed. You could hardly describe a rut in which your breasts were detaching from your body and getting into God knows what as being comfortable. "All right," she said. "I'll go."

That night Gwen sat cross-legged on the floor of her closet, rooting through old clothes and boxes still packed from when she'd moved here after her breakup with David.

In a far corner of the closet, beneath a red sequined dress Tammi had talked her into buying, she unearthed a carefully sealed cardboard box about the size of a bowling ball. For a split second she had no recollection of it, and then, like the sinking of an unsinkable ship, her mind capsized, plunging into remembrance and giving her a good long look at the rest of the iceberg.

She was seventeen, and she was going to be a famous sculptor.

Unbidden, Gwen's hands peeled back the tape on the box.

She loved the smooth, slippery feeling of wet clay, the act of molding it in her hands, the damp earth smell and the rich golden-red color.

The flaps of the box squeaked against each other as she pulled them open. The newspaper rustled and fell away like shed scales as she lifted the statue out.

Sitting in her room at night, naked in front of the mirror, seeing herself...touching herself...as a woman for the first time. In art class the next day molding the clay with her memory as a model. Forming her face, her body, with her hands, exploring herself as she sculpted the figure. And when she was finished, her art teacher, Mr. Teslop, standing over her, tell-

ing her that it was "exquisite" and "very advanced." Her body rushing with pleasure at his words. She quickly agreed to his suggestion to enter it in the district art competition.

And she won. Oh, how sweet it had felt, standing there in the Menominee County Convention Center as the judge tied the blue ribbon around her statue and she smiled into popping flashbulbs and they ran her picture in the paper. Her statue went on display back at the high school, right in there with the football and wrestling trophies. She got a little jolt every time she passed it.

Gwen sat cross-legged on the floor of her closet and held herself in her lap, running her fingertips over her tiny clay face, her shoulders, her breasts. Trapped in their new, full coverage bra, George and Gracie tingled. What pleasure it had been to feel the clay taking form in her hands, to see a thing of beauty and to think, I made that.

And then came the next day. The last day of her sculpting career. Walking to civics class with her "friend" Charlene Ryans.

"Oh, is that your statue?" asked Charlene as the display case came into view. And Gwen's own prideful, foolish, "Yes."

They paused before the statue as Charlene peered at it, and Gwen's heart swelled with more pride, more idiotic self-satisfaction.

"Oh my God, Gwen," said Charlene, and Gwen prepared to receive her admiration for this great work of art. Then Charlene turned to her and said, "Is that you?"

Gwen's big, swollen prideful heart was ripped right out of her. Her face went red. Charlene laughed, and very loudly in the crowded hallway cried, "Oh my God, Gwen, you sculpted yourself naked. It's a self-portrait!"

Soon after that her sculpture was removed from the case of honor and returned to her in a square cardboard box. But long after it was gone, the statue haunted her. She was "Boobs" Bramble after that, all the way through high school.

Gwen sighed and put the statue back in its box. She was about to close it when she hesitated, and then all at once, not giving herself time to consider it, she took it back out, ran into the living room and set it down on the coffee table. She stood back, waiting for what she didn't know, an explosion, or Charlene Ryans pounding on her door. But nothing happened.

Moosejaw's was a new wilderness-themed restaurant next to Costco. The menu was sprinkled indiscriminately with game in much the same manner as the walls were festooned with every kind of backwoods paraphernalia imaginable. There was even a stuffed bear standing just inside the door, a box of menus wedged between its paws. Gwen had to admire the logic. There was something about sitting beneath an owl rowing a birch bark canoe that made eating boar empanadas seem normal.

"So I said, the best way to maximize your potential is to proactively pursue advantageous opportunities and contacts," said Tom. He was in his mid-forties with wavy chestnut-brown hair and freckles. "Be an evangelist of your product. People can't resist a prophet, or a profit. Hey, I like that! Be a prophet of profit." He whipped a Palm Pilot out of his breast pocket and jotted his bon mot down. "I'm collecting all these inspirational sayings for my book, 101 *Things To Do When There's Nothing You Can Do.* See, the first lesson is, there's always something you can do." Tom took a drink of his Rusty Nail and leaned closer to her. "Look at me. Two years ago I was at rock bottom. My second marriage had just fallen apart, I owed the IRS $75,000 in back taxes, and I hated my job. Now thanks to Maxway, I'm living proof that no dream is out of reach if you can identify it." He fixed her with a manic stare. "Do you have a dream, Gwen?"

George and Gracie stirred inside her bra, and Gwen crossed her arms to quell them. "I – I don't know," she stammered, but obviously her breasts were of a different opinion. They quivered and surged. She tightened her arms.

"It's okay," said Tom, "I was afraid at first too, but realizing what you really want is the hardest part. Once you do that, the rest is easy."

George and Gracie wiggled beneath her entrapping arms. "No, really, I'm very happy."

Tammi snorted. "Yeah, right."

Gwen's breasts gave up trying to pry free from her arms and started sliding down instead. George made a break for it and Gwen grabbed at her, elbowing her wine glass in the process. The glass twirled on its base and Gwen reached for it, her fingers glancing off the rim and knocking it off orbit. The glass tumbled to the table, spilling Chardonnay across the nachos with venison and sage sausage.

"Oh!" cried Gwen as George and Gracie squeezed through the bottom of her bra and rolled out from beneath the hem of her blouse. She thrust her hands into her lap, grasping for their warm, pliable flesh, but they tumbled free. Gwen ducked her head beneath the polyurethaned raw oak table, but it was dark down there, and the pale mound beside Buzz's shoe was only a crumpled paper napkin.

The rest of the evening was agony. Gwen kept spotting her breasts everywhere; in the bric-a-brac on the walls, on people's plates. She nearly had a heart attack when Buzz uncovered the rolls, and her quail and wild asparagus croquettes were a trial to her.

Finally they were down to coffee and Gwen thought she might get out of this with only minor humiliation. Buzz and Tammi were discussing their plans for Labor Day, and Tom was calculating the tip on his Palm.

"We're either going to Four Bears Water Park or Six Flags," said Tammi. "Six Flags has better roller coasters, but Four Bears has all the water slides and stuff

– Oh!" Something over Gwen's left shoulder caught Tammi's eye. "Oh look! I hadn't noticed that before. That's really funny!"

"Geez," said Buzz. "I'm surprised they can get away with that. This is supposed to be a family place."

"Wow," said Tom. "I guess it's a girl bear."

Before she even turned around, Gwen knew what they were looking at. George and Gracie had been found. She craned her neck around to look, and there they were, each nestled in a crook of the bear's arms. By now other people were pointing and murmuring. Laughter ran through the restaurant as more and more people noticed that the bear was wearing Gwen's breasts.

Gwen's head felt light and the restaurant swayed around her. "Excuse me," she said, fumbling money out of her wallet and standing up. "I have to go now. I forgot I – I have to do something. It was nice meeting you, Tom."

Gwen fled the restaurant, glaring at George and Gracie as she passed them, but they didn't seem to notice. Caught up, no doubt, in being the center of attention. She managed to make it all the way to her car before losing her croquettes on the blacktop.

Gwen lay on the couch eating peppermint stick ice cream and brooding over her fate. George and Gracie were back again, but she knew it didn't mean anything. They could leave again at any moment and no bra could stop them. She wondered if she really needed them anyway. Maybe they were more trouble than they were worth.

She put down the ice cream and lifted up her shirt, looking down through the neck hole. They were pretty breasts, she had to admit. Gracie a little more so than George, who was larger and kind of droopy, but they both had a soft roundness to them which was very appealing. She snaked her arms beneath her shirt and ran her hands under them, hefting them in her palms, enjoying their watery weight and warmth. A thought occurred to her. If they could detach...

She cradled George in her hands, raised the jiggling lump of flesh to her mouth and rolled the nipple over her tongue. A jolt of pleasure shot down her body, making her toes tingle. Restless, Gracie rolled into her lap and burrowed at her crotch. Gwen relaxed her legs even as she continued sucking on George's nipple. It felt good. It felt so good it was almost certainly wrong, but so what? Her life was already ruined, why not wallow in whatever debased pleasures the situation offered? Stuffing as much of George into her mouth as she could, she unfastened her jeans and reached for the ice cream.

Gwen lay in a sticky stupor on the couch, the ice cream carton tucked into the crook of her arm. Inside George and Gracie lolled indolently in the melted pink froth. They really loved that stuff. Gwen sighed and gazed at the ceiling with blissful satisfaction, not caring, at least for the moment, why and how she felt that way.

Someone knocked on the door. "Gwenny?" came her mother's voice from the other side.

Gwen shot up off the couch, grabbing the lid to the ice cream and shoving it over George and Gracie. She refastened her jeans and wiped away the worst of the ice cream film with a paper napkin. "Just a second, Ma!" she yelled, racing into the bedroom to throw on a bulky sweater.

She answered the door and her mother swept in dressed in a powder blue micro-fiber jogging suit, her bleached curls sticking out from around a coordinating headband. "Sweetheart, I was just over at Kohl's and they have the cutest little sweater sets that'd be just perfect for you." She leaned forward to give Gwen a kiss.

Gwen quickly pecked her mother's cheek and backed away before she could get a hug in.

"They're on sale," her mother continued. "I thought maybe we could go back together – maybe have a little lunch while we're out."

Gwen took a deep breath to steady herself. "Oh, no thanks, Mom. I'm uh, kind of busy right now."

"Hmm. I can see that." Her mother glanced around the disordered apartment and then turned to eye Gwen closely. "Are you okay?"

"Oh yeah! Yeah, I'm fine." Desperately Gwen searched for something to distract her mother. "H-hey, look what I found," she said, pointing at the statue on the coffee table.

"Oh, isn't that pretty!"

Gwen flushed. "Thanks, mom."

"Where did you buy it? Was it on sale?"

Gwen stared at her. "Mom, I made it. In high school, remember?"

Her mother shook her head. "I don't remember you ever sculpting, Sweetie. You've always been such a good, practical girl." She looked around the apartment again in disapproval. "I just wish you weren't so messy. I mean look," she picked the ice cream carton up from where Gwen had left it on the floor, "how can you just leave this sitting out like this?"

"Mom, please..."

But her mother ignored her. "I bet it's all melted now," she said, opening the lid.

Her eyes widened briefly and then she froze, staring into the carton. It wobbled slightly as her hand shook. She shot a glance at Gwen, taking in her bulky sweater, and then looked back into the carton. She replaced the lid carefully and set it down on the coffee table next to Gwen's statue. She sat down on the couch. "They are yours?"

Open mouthed, Gwen nodded.

"Well, that's something, at least." Her mother sighed. "Dotty Greenfield's boy wound up with somebody else's testicles and he got his girlfriend pregnant with them. It was a mess."

Gwen couldn't contain the laughter that burst inappropriately from her lips.

Her mother scowled, frown lines standing out around her mouth. "Oh, you think that's funny, do you?"

Helplessly, Gwen nodded her head and sank to the couch, weeping with laughter. She laid her head on her mother's shoulder and suddenly her giggles became sobs.

"Oh, now. There, there, Honey," said her mother, wrapping her arms around Gwen and rocking her, just like when she was a little girl. "Come on now, don't cry. It's not so bad."

Gwen sat back up, rubbing her eyes. "Not so bad? How can you say that? You're not the one whose breasts are gallivanting all over town!"

"No, but I was, once."

"What?" Shock made Gwen's hands and feet tingle.

Her mother sighed again. "Oh yes. I was a little older than you, but they say every generation matures earlier, so..."

Gwen shook her head. "So you're saying this happens to everyone? How come I've never heard about it before?"

"Well, it doesn't happen to everyone, dear. Just an unlucky few. And of course no one talks about it. I mean, it's just too embarrassing, isn't it?"

She nodded in agreement, and for a while they sat in silence, staring at the ice cream carton. At last Gwen said, "But it happened to you?"

"Mmm-hmm."

"B-but it doesn't anymore?"

"No. Thank God."

Gwen turned and looked at her mother. "So what happened?"

She shrugged. "One day, they just didn't come back."

"Oh my God! How horrible!"

"No." Her mother shook her head and took Gwen's hands in hers, gripping them tightly. "No. It was the best thing that ever happened to me. And the best thing for you to do is tape that ice cream carton shut, pop it in the freezer and never take it out again. Take it from me, Gwenny, you'll be better off without them."

Gwen stared at her mother in horror. "How can you say that?"

"Because they'll destroy your life if you let them. Unless you give them exactly what they want, they will publicly humiliate you over and over again, until you lose your friends, your job, everything." She released Gwen's hands and folded her arms.

"What they want?"

"Mmm-hmm." Gwen's mother gave her a sinister look.

Running a hand over her sticky jeans, Gwen thought she had a pretty good idea what George and Gracie wanted.

Gwen's mother patted her knee and stood up. "Now you need to get your mind off all of this, Gwenny. Focus on something else." She smiled brightly and clasped her hands together. "I know, why don't you put the ice cream away and come shopping with me? Mervyns has some lovely oversized knits you might like."

Gwen shook her head. "No thanks, Mom. I think I'd like to be alone for a little while."

Her mother sighed and pursed her lips. "Suit yourself," she said as she headed for the door, "but believe me, you'll feel a lot better once you take matters into your own hands."

"I'm sure you're right, Mom," said Gwen, following her. "And thanks." She gave her a big hug. "Thanks for stopping by."

Armed with a cost-estimate form and the bulging Pottery Barn file, Gwen approached Charlie Axel. Charlie was on the phone, so Gwen stood in front of his desk waiting. Her arms ached from holding the huge file, but with the enormous graphics monitor, the scanner, and countless printouts and CDs, there wasn't a square inch of space open on his desk.

"Okay, I'll email you a thumbnail this afternoon, and as soon as you approve it, I'll go ahead with the final layout... Great. Bye." Charlie hung up and immediately dialed another number. "Hey Baby, how you doing?... Ha!... Me? Not much... Hey, you want to go to the Icebox tonight? DJ Jah Love is spinning."

"Um. Excuse me," said Gwen.

Charlie glanced at her and put his hand over the receiver. "Just a sec," he said.

Gwen stood there for fifteen minutes while Charlie and his girlfriend made plans for the evening, discussed the local music scene and critiqued their friends' fashion sense.

"Dean should have stuck with black work. His new Elvis tattoo clashes with his hair... Oh, you gotta go?... Catch you later then, Baby, bye."

"Excuse me Charlie," said Gwen, edging closer to the desk as he hung up and returned his gaze to the monitor. "I need to talk to you about the Pottery Barn account."

"Sure, what do you need to know?" he asked, fingers briskly tapping at the keyboard. He never took his eyes off the monitor.

"Well – " Gwen shifted her weight and adjusted her grip on the file as a blush crept over her face. Suddenly she was furious with this smart, smarmy, hotshot young "artist," sitting there, not even looking at her, barely acknowledging her as a human being.

What gave him the right? What made him better than her? That he had talent? Well everybody has talent, just not everybody gets to use theirs. He was lucky. He was lucky and that meant he could treat her like a moderately bright stapler? "There's a few things," she said sweetly as she very gently shoved half the crap on his desk onto the floor and made room for the Pottery Barn file.

"What the hell are you doing?" She had Charlie's undivided attention at last. He gaped at her as she walked around his desk toward him.

"I have to file an invoice for this job tomorrow," she said, brandishing the cost-estimate form. "And I don't have one useful piece of information in this whole stack!" She smacked the Pottery Barn file with her other hand.

The noise made Charlie jump. "Geez, chill out! It's just an invoice. That's valuable work you just threw on the floor, dude!"

"Not if we can't bill for it," she said, resting one hand on his desk and leaning in toward him. "It may be 'just an invoice' to you, but it's my freaking job, *dude*. For weeks now, you haven't been letting me do my job."

Charlie blinked. "Okay, okay. Relax. Just leave the form with me and I'll fill it out and get it back to you tomorrow."

"Oh no," she said as she hauled a chair over beside his. "We're going to fill in the information on the form right now. And then I'll have what I need, and I can leave you alone, which is what we both want. And next time, you can avoid all this by filling out the form yourself." She looked Charlie in his bratty, talented, dumbstruck face, and she smiled.

When Gwen got to the elevator the new guy in accounting was just stepping inside. He held the door for her. He had sandy brown hair and an earnest, slightly perplexed expression. "Thanks," she said, and then wondered if he'd witnessed her little freak out with Charlie. She blushed and stood very still, staring at the brushed stainless steel of the elevator doors.

"I hate that guy," he said conversationally. "My first day here he kept me waiting at his desk for half an hour while he negotiated a new deal with his cellular provider. All I needed was his signoff on a Fed-Ex receipt. What a jerk."

Gwen smiled and glanced at him, and found him smiling back.

"That needed to be done," he said, and his smile became a grin. He swept one arm out in front of him, "Swoosh!"

*

Though her social life was in ruins and her job hung by a thread, Gwen's relationship with her breasts had improved considerably. They seemed to appreciate the attention she gave them. They didn't go out quite as much, and when they did they always came back in the manner of excited children eager to share their adventures. Gwen would wake up around four or five in the morning, her breasts bouncing on top of her chest. She'd fondle them for a little while, until they got sleepy and nudged away the covers so they could reattach themselves.

One night she awoke to find three blobs of flesh wiggling on her. She fumbled for the bedside lamp and beheld in the amber glow George and Gracie perching proudly on either side of a semi-flaccid penis. It was a testament to her reconciliation with her situation that she didn't scream and fling the thing across the room. Clearly, her breasts had meant well, but there was no telling where this little cock had been, and no way she was going to let it join their nocturnal games.

Groaning, Gwen sat up and stared at the penis, which regarded her with cycloptic innocence. She took a slip from the floor by the bed, draped it over the wayward penis and scooped it up, padding across the room to her dresser. She placed the penis gently in her underwear drawer, shut it, and went back to sleep.

The following afternoon was J. Thomas Design's annual office party. They'd taken over the lobby of the Hilton for the event. Towering posters of award-winning advertising images stood about, guests mingling among them. Gwen almost didn't mind being there. Since she'd been pleasuring her breasts there'd been no more public incidents and she felt more in control of her life than she had in weeks.

"...so I figured, at least with accounting I could always find a job," said the new guy in accounting. "All in all, I think I did the right thing, switching majors."

Gwen, who'd been taking full advantage of the open bar, smiled pleasantly and allowed herself to focus on his nicely formed shoulders.

He smiled back at her, but at the same time his eyes darted nervously over her shoulder, like he was looking for someone. He seemed to catch himself and refocus on her. "So what about you, how do you like working here?" he asked her.

"Oh, it's great," she said, feeling her smile calcify into a rigid grin. "J. Thomas is a great company to be with and I love working around creative people." As she paused to drain her third whisky sour, she distinctly felt something warm and soft roll free from under her bra and drop down the front of her dress.

She looked down in time to see George scampering beneath the hors d'oeuvres table.

No. Oh God no, not now. Swearing under her breath, Gwen ran after her left breast. She pulled up the tablecloth and stuck her head under the hors d'oeuvres table. George was nowhere in sight.

A pair of men's brown oxfords appeared beside the table. "Did you lose something?" asked the new guy in accounting.

She straightened, slamming the back of her head against the underside of the table, creating a minor shower of pigs in blankets. The new guy in accounting helped extricate her from the tablecloth. "Careful now. Are you okay?"

"Oh! Oh yeah." She folded her arms across her chest, as much to imprison Gracie as to hide George's absence. "I – I, um, lost my earring."

He wrinkled his brow. "But you have two now."

"Oh, oh yeah."

At the far end of the room stood an enormous poster of a model in a dress comprised entirely of pink balloons. The crowd before it parted momentarily, and she thought she saw George rolling behind it. "Excuse me," she said, and dashed off to investigate.

The poster stood in an alcove, one side pushed up against the wall, forming a little cul-de-sac behind it. And there in the shadows was her breast. Gwen got to her hands and knees and squeezed behind the poster. George rolled to the far corner, but could not escape. With a cry of exultation, Gwen grabbed her.

Awkwardly she managed to unbutton the top of her dress and push her bra down, but as she tried to put George back in her rightful place, the breast bucked, causing her to bump the poster with her elbow. The foam-board wobbled, and then, with a whooshing sound, toppled over. Gasps erupted and everyone turned to stare, and then silence fell as they saw Gwen, on her knees, naked from the waist up, clutching her left breast in her hands.

Still shaking with humiliation, Gwen rummaged in her bedroom closet until she found the box she'd kept her statue in. She got a roll of duct tape out of the junk drawer and put them both on the coffee table next to her high school masterpiece. Now maybe she'd be able to keep her job, she thought, steeling herself. Now maybe she'd meet someone and settle down to a nice, ordinary life. She stripped to the waist, and took George and Gracie lovingly in her hands. "I don't want to do this, but you've left me no other option," she told them.

As she grasped them more firmly, George and Gracie wiggled free from her hands. They rolled under the couch and she shoved it over onto its back. They fled to the bedroom and tried to hide in the bed covers. Gwen fished the butterfly net out of the closet and pulled the covers back in a whoosh. She swiped at them with the net, missed and dashed across the bed after them as they rolled into the bathroom.

Twenty minutes later she had them trapped behind the refrigerator. She rousted them out with the handle of the net and almost got them as they slipped out between the refrigerator and the stove. As they raced back into the living room, Gwen was right behind them. They sprinted across the carpet, heading for the television, but the overturned couch was in their way.

They thought they were being clever; George went one way around, Gracie the other, but Gwen leapt onto the couch and caught them on the other side. Unable to stop themselves, they rolled into her waiting net and she swung it up with a shout of triumph.

Her breasts hung heavy and limp in the swaying net, and Gwen reached forward to grab it and trap them inside. She overbalanced and the next thing she knew she was flying forward off the couch, right into her sculpture sitting on the coffee table. As she slid across the table, clutching the net in one hand, she reached for the sculpture, but it sailed free of her grasp and crashed to the floor, smashing into hundreds of pieces.

Gwen lay across the coffee table on her stomach, panting, her breasts struggling feebly in the net. She stared at her sculpture, her beautiful sculpture, destroyed, and then glanced at the box lying on its side nearby and suddenly great wracking sobs welled up inside her and shook her body. Hot tears streamed down her face and she couldn't stop crying.

The net slipped from her hand as she crawled off the coffee table and knelt beside the shattered remains of her sculpture. Sobbing, she sifted through the fragments, but much of the clay had turned to powder when it hit the floor. There was no repairing it. The one thing she'd ever done that she was really proud of was gone. It wasn't worth it, she thought. It just wasn't worth it. George and Gracie rolled into her lap and nuzzled against her as if to comfort her. She held them to her and cried until she was empty, and then she got the broom.

She struggled through the doorway with the block of clay and took it into the living room. With one foot she cleared the coffee table of dirty dishes and magazines and dropped the clay on top of it with a slam. She got a bowl of water from the kitchen, sat down on the couch and sank her fingers into the soft moist clay. It was smooth and cool, receptive to her every thought, every twitch of her fingers.

She didn't think about what she was doing, what form she wanted to wrest from the blank block, she just did it, molding and smoothing, feeling all her sadness, fear and self-doubt ebb away as she gave herself up to the task at hand. With wonder she watched the forms take shape as if of their own volition, emerging whole and perfect from between her fingers.

When she was finished, her arms, face, pants and blouse were streaked with red-brown clay. She sat back with satisfaction and looked at what she had created. An assemblage of fruit – apples, pears, bananas and peaches, and among them two round, disembodied breasts, almost indistinguishable from the fruit until you looked at it awhile. And then you began to wonder about that banana. She decided instantly on a name, "Still Life with Boobs."

Gwen smiled, more pleased with herself than she'd been in years. She didn't care if the piece was good or not, she didn't care if anyone laughed at it, or her. She was through living for appearances. It wasn't worth it. It made you miss out on the really good stuff. It made you forget why you were alive in the first place.

Someone knocked on her door. Startled, Gwen wiped her hands on her jeans and opened it.

The new guy from accounting stood there, shifting restlessly from foot to foot. "Um. Hi. I – uh, I'm sorry to bother you but... Geez, this is embarrassing. I – uh, I lost my – I lost something and I was wondering if..." His blue eyes wandered past her to peer into the apartment, desperation and dread warring on his face.

Gwen suddenly remembered the penis in her dresser drawer. Good Lord. "Why don't you come in?" she said.

He looked relieved.

"Sit down," she said, gesturing to the couch. "I'll be right back."

She went to the bedroom and rummaged through her underwear drawer until she found the penis. But she couldn't just go out there with it in her hand. It seemed too...personal. She emptied the basket where she kept her scrunchies and placed the penis inside, then took a scarf and arranged it on top, as if it were a loaf of bread she wanted to keep warm.

She went back out. He was still sitting on the couch, hands clenched on his knees, his head tilted down, peering at his crotch. Bingo.

"Is this yours?" she asked.

He took the basket, tentatively lifting up one corner of the scarf. He heaved a sigh of relief. "Oh my God. Thank you...I – Could you excuse me a moment?"

She smiled. "Sure, bathroom's down that way, second door on the left."

When he came back he looked a lot more relaxed. She offered him a beer and they sat on the couch, drinking together in companionable silence for a few minutes. At last she said, "It was my breasts. They brought...him here. It wasn't me."

He laughed. "Oh, I know. Anyway, knowing him, he probably talked them into it."

She smiled. "How did you know he came here?"

"It's Frank, by the way." He stuck out a hand.

"How did you know Frank came here?"

"No, I'm Frank, he's Clyde. As in Bonnie and Clyde? It was a thing my old girlfriend would always say, back before we broke up."

"Oh, I'm sorry."

"Not your fault." He looked away. "Anyway, to answer your question, I followed him. I saw them all come in here, only at the time, I didn't have the guts to knock on the door. I was hoping he'd just come back, he usually does, but he's never been gone this long before and I was pretty desperate."

"I can imagine."

"So, has this been happening to you for long?" he asked.

She shrugged, caught up in the square line of his jaw, the compact sturdiness of his shoulders. She'd like to sculpt him. "About six weeks."

"Heh, me too. It's insane isn't it? I mean, I thought I was, until...until now." He leaned closer to her, his face intent, as if he were discovering something.

"Yes," she said, her voice a husky whisper. "Maybe we are crazy, but I don't care anymore, do you?"

He shook his head ever so slightly. "No."

"Me neither," she said, and she kissed him.

Their lips, soft and crushable, locked onto one another with sudden urgency. He ran his hands down her arms, across her back, holding her tight, and she brought her own arms around and up, to play with the hair at the back of his neck, to clutch his shoulders and crumple the starchy whiteness of his shirt between her fingers.

They parted, and his gaze focused on the sculpture. "Hey, that's beautiful. Did you do that?"

In her blouse George and Gracie tingled, and Gwen smiled broadly. "Yeah."

"Wow. That's great that you do something creative like that. I wish I could be creative. I used to love to draw, but I haven't done it for years."

"You should pick it back up again."

He looked pleased. "Really, you think?"

"Oh, definitely."

Heads Down, Thumbs Up

Gavin J. Grant

Gavin J. Grant (*www.lcrw.net*) lives in Northampton, Massachusetts, with his wife, Kelly Link, and is trying to balance freelancing, Small Beer Press, and renovating an old farmhouse. He is the publisher of Small Beer Press and, since 1996, editor and publisher of *Lady Churchill's Rosebud Wristlet*, a twice-yearly small press 'zine. Originally from Scotland, he moved to the USA in 1991. He worked in bookshops in Los Angeles and Boston, and while in Brooklyn, worked for BookSense.com, a Web site for independent bookshops. He also runs the KGB Fantastic Fiction Reading Series in New York City with Ellen Datlow, with whom he and Link also co-edit (see the Kelly Link story note, above).

"Heads Down, Thumbs Up" was published at *SciFiction.com*, the excellent website edited by Ellen Datlow that featured much distinguished original fantasy and SF. This is perhaps its first time in print. It presents a world in which, when boundaries move during war, there are sudden transformations and people immediately speak a different language and remember different stories, and sing different songs. This transformation is much easier for the children than for the grownups, and the protagonist is a child. It's a provocative story about war, politics, and memory and an interesting comparison to Gene Wolfe's story, earlier in this book.

MRS. BLACK REPEATED HER QUESTION, but then the border wobbled over us again. She sighed. There was a knock at the door, and the school secretary came in.

"Yes, yes," said Mrs. Black before the secretary could say anything. "I know, I know."

She turned to us. "Boys and girls. Two minutes of heads down, thumbs up."

She went to the sink at the back of the classroom and wet her handkerchief. She touched the tops of our heads as she passed, a diagonal line of us whose hair stood up on the backs of our necks. I wanted to be touched. She took her hankie to the blackboard and stretched up to the top corner and wiped her name away. Her name was Ms. Sterling now. I sneaked a look at Jeanine. She'd never learned to sculpt the letter r out from the other sounds. She had her head down, but her eyes were open. She was staring at her math book (we'd have to use the other set now) and her face was slowly turning red. She hated it, too, the change.

Ms. Sterling said something, and everyone sat up. She said it again, and now she was looking at me but I hadn't been listening, and now she was using a different language.

"Ardgrur-; rjinnsfller?" she asked.

And then I knew what she meant, the other language coming over me like the dirty water spreading across the painting table when I knocked over my paint cup. I hoped it wouldn't last. I liked our other country; the stories were better. In this one the witch always escapes and sometimes she even marries the children's father. Ms. Sterling cried sometimes in the art supply cupboard after reading these stories. But she won't be allowed to tell the other ones anymore. That's what happened to Ms. Frobisher, our teacher when we were last this country. She was ancient, and she always forgot who we were.

After school, Dad was late and I told myself the story where the witch got put in the oven. I liked singing the song the brother and sister sang when they gathered apples and herbs to bake with her. Once, when I was in the first class, we got a story where the witch ate all the children. We all cried.

Dad was late because he waited for Mum to come home before coming to get me. Neither of them ask about school. I didn't want to tell them anything anyway. I heard my Dad tell Edward's dad I'm a chatterbox. I curl up in my seat and watch the men out on the road painting the white lines light blue.

Dad drove even slower than usual. Mum started talking about how hard it was to sign in for her new job at the library. She wants him to speed up, but I know she'll never actually ask him. Dad jumps when she puts her hand on his leg. Dad's rubbish in this country. I wish the border would go back.

Next day Jeanine doesn't come in. But neither does Bobbie or Bobby or Brian. Someone at the back sends a note forward, but I don't take it. Alison digs her nails into my leg and I jump like my dad in the car. Ms. Sterling notices, and I have to stand in the corner. Alison should be laughing, but she's not. There's something wrong with her eyes, they're too big or something. Her dad's in the other country's army. I wonder if he's dead yet.

Last time the border came over we saw dead people everywhere. They said they'd been Pee Oh Double Yous, but we knew they were dead. They appeared after school. They were gray and cold and wanted to hold us. Edward said they were zombies. We all knew zombies wanted to crack our heads open and suck our brains out. We ran and ran. I didn't know where I was when I stopped. I'd run up a hill, and all the dead people ("Wait. It's me. Your Uncle Billy.") couldn't follow because they were too tired. There were lots of houses up there, and they all looked the same. I thought I knew someone from school who lived there, Caroline, but I didn't know which house she lived in. I don't remember getting home. Sometimes I think I went back to the wrong house. "Where's Sarah?" I asked when I got home. I remember Mum and Dad looking at each other. They thought I couldn't understand the look, but I did. I always understand adults. I wonder if they were ever children: if they don't remember how easy they are to understand.

When we get home I ask Dad why adults don't know children understand. But he says, "Don't, shh. Just ...just pretend, okay?"

"I don't want to," I say.

"When I was young," he says, and he picks me up, sits me on his knees. "When I was young, we didn't have adults."

I know this game. He used to do this a lot when I was younger. But I still scream when he opens his knees to drop me. He holds my arms, and I hang there for a second, pulling my legs up so that my feet don't touch the ground.

"We all lived together. Boys and girls. There were hundreds and hundreds of us," and he pulls me back onto his knees. "You wouldn't have liked it," he says.

I know this story. There are birds nailed to a barn. Cats and squirrels for dinner. There are scary adults who try to get into the children's big house, and sometimes they do and they take some of the children away. Sometimes the adults disappear and Dad gets a look in his eye. I don't like him then. Then there's his friend Ranald who went away (like Bobby and Bobbie? I wonder), and something Dad said once made me wonder if actually he got eaten.

When Dad tells stories, he changes. He likes to play and roll about and then later he makes dinner. I like that and try and get him to tell more stories. For dinner he usually makes scrambled eggs in rolls, and he can't stop smiling when he uses lots and lots of butter and cheese. Mum would make sausages to go with eggs, but after story time Dad won't eat meat until the next day; or maybe the next week.

He drops me through his knees again, and this time I spring back up immediately. He lets go my hands, catches my waist, throws me in the air; I can feel his smile on my back. He stands up really fast and catches me and throws me still further up. Suddenly I realize who he is and what he's done. In this country he's sad because in this country he was cruel and he isn't going to catch me. I start screaming.

He plucks me from the air. "What's wrong?" he asks, and there are ugly lines all over his face. He's breathing fast, "Are you okay? Did I hurt you?"

I catch my breath, but I can't look at him. Mum comes running in. Dad shrugs his shoulders at her, and even as I cling to him, she peels me off and carries me over to her chair. She's colder than he is and has harder edges.

Dad usually finishes stories by saying, "I had many friends then. I met your mother there. We were very lucky."

*

Ms. Sterling is replaced. "Just for two weeks, class," says the headmistress. Once we had a man for headmistress – he wanted to be called headmaster. We didn't like him, and when the border passed over again he ran away. We were so happy. It was like Saturday, and summer, and that holiday they have in autumn on that side, all in one.

Our new teacher says, "My name is Ms. Matchless. However," and she bends her cracking knees, and then her gray hair and heavy glasses are right down in front of us, "you," and she tickles under Berenice's chin, "*you* can call me Joanna."

Listening to her, I realize the cake, the apple, the hard black and white liquorice mints, any and all of these will be enough to make me climb into the oven. Ms. Matchless stands, smiles at us.

"Now," she says, beaming, "let's go out to the garden. Who can tell me what we've been growing in the school garden?"

I have always stayed away from the garden. I like drawing. I was going to be an artist, and whenever the border changed I was going to paint new murals in the school halls, but now I throw my hand in the air and tomatoes and cabbages are all I ever want to grow.

Dad's got a beard and he goes to sleep earlier than me now. He makes me laugh, and sometimes I go in to kiss him and tuck him in. He is half-asleep and calls me Ranald, but I'm used to that here. He hopes the border will move back soon. I hope so, too, but I don't want Ms. Matchless to leave.

Ms. Matchless has been our teacher for five weeks. The headmistress stopped visiting our class in the second week, when she saw we weren't upset about Ms. Sterling. But then she started coming again, and now she helps Ms. Matchless every afternoon. She never did that before. She laughs when Ms. Matchless laughs. I wish she wouldn't come.

Ms. Matchless tells us all about our country. Some of us remember our anthem. I don't. We never sing it at home, except when people come over for dinner. I don't like this anthem. The other song is better, but I know not to say that. Ms. Matchless – I don't call her Joanna, no one does – has a very sharp ear and can tell who's singing. I'm learning the words, and I sing very loud. I have a good, high voice although I know it won't last. Dad has a deep voice and likes to sing with me when we walk. We hold hands, and sometimes he swings me around, even though we both know I'm too big.

Ms. Matchless says that our country has one of the biggest forests in the world. She points to it on the map and says she grew up there. We are quiet.

There is no forest near us, and we are imagining what it would be like to grow up in a cottage deep in the woods.

"There is nothing as beautiful as the Long Forest," Ms. Matchless says softly.

"Miss, please, miss." I am standing and waving my hand, and she smiles at me.

"Yes?"

I fall back in my chair. "Please, miss, can we go there? Can we see the forest?"

She looks surprised and pleased. Maybe I'll get a green circle on my report card.

"Well, that is an interesting idea! Who else wants to visit the forest?"

Everyone waves their hands in the air. Something hits me in the back of the head, hard enough to sting. I glance back, but all I can see are waving hands and smiling faces.

I am going away for a whole week, and we still haven't told Dad. I've never gone anywhere for a week. Once we drove for hours and then went on a ferry to visit my grandparents, my mum's mum and dad. It smelled of bitter mint and moth-balls, and I hated it. There was a lot of shouting at night. I didn't like sleeping in-between my parents. Mum wanted to leave the next day, and Dad wanted to stay forever. I wish I wasn't going on this trip.

I'd waited until Dad went to bed before giving Mum the release form and asking for the trip money.

When she read the form, I didn't like the way she looked at me. "You suggested this?" she'd asked, and I saw Ms. Matchless had put in an extra note just for Mum.

I didn't have anything to say. Mum signed the form and said not to tell Dad just yet.

Now, when I am brushing my teeth, she says, "We'll just tell him tomorrow." But in the morning, Dad has left for work before I get up.

In front of the school there is a big white luxury coach with its engine running with a handwritten sign in the driver's window, MS. MATCHLESS, THE LONG FOREST, and I forget about Dad until lunchtime, when the bus stops and we eat our packed lunches. Mum made mine last night, and my sandwiches are hard around the edges. But I swap my apple for Alison's orange and then we sit next to each other and I think maybe I have a girlfriend.

We don't reach the forest until the next day. We stop for the night at a youth hostel and sleep in two big, dark rooms. The driver sleeps in the boys' room in the bed nearest the door. I lie awake until after he comes in and goes to sleep. I am too frightened to go to the toilet in the night, but I don't wet myself. Early in the morning there is a knock on the door. The driver is still asleep, so I run over and open it. Ms. Matchless smiles at me and kisses me on the cheek. I rush past her to the toilet. When I get back, I find that Lucas needed the toilet, too, but couldn't hold it. I listen to the other boys and I'm very, very happy I held it.

This morning we can see the dark line of the forest, but it is still very far away. I tell Alison ghost stories, and even though it's daytime lots of people get scared because of me. Ms. Matchless walks up the bus and tells me to stop or tonight the witch of the forest will take me away. I can't help but grin, and she does, too. She has false teeth, and they are very white. I've seen her move them around during quiet time at school when we put our heads down on our desks and she marks our homework. The others are still scared from my stories, and I am happy. Maybe I will stay at Ms. Matchless's house in the forest and never go home.

She sits down next to me, and I have to squeeze over beside Alison. No one else can see, so I hold Alison's hand.

When everyone is quiet, Ms. Matchless tells us that there are trees in the Long Forest that are not found anywhere else in the world. They go straight up for hundreds of feet then weave their branches together so that it is very dark below. She says that lots of people live in the forest – some in houses far above the ground – but there is no way to count them all. She says there are more ways into the forest than out. Alison shivers, and I squeeze her hand.

"It's because there's a big city," I burst out. "The capital." Ms. Matchless nods at me but watches the others. I have read far ahead in my textbook, and I know all about the capital and how all the people left the forest towns.

"There are two million people. It has two airports, two big stadiums and lots of small ones, and the parliament buildings, which are very beautiful on the inside because they are made from wood from the Long Forest."

Alison nods her head, and other people do, too. I am smarter in this country. If we stay here, maybe I will be a teacher when I grow up.

Then the bus goes into the forest and it is almost as dark as night because we are driving under the tallest trees we have ever seen. Everyone is quiet. We drive for two hours under the trees, and all the time we are going up.

The forest is like another country. Even the cars are different. Alison gets bored, so there is some seat swapping and me and Edward sit together and count cars. He knows more of them than me, but I have a girlfriend, so I don't care.

The capital is huge. The day after we arrive, we go to the parliament, which is boring on the outside – the walls are gray and very, very thick and the windows all have bars. Inside it's like a church. There are glass walls in front of the wooden walls, and I can see where the old wooden walls look thin where lots of people have touched them. Parliament is in session, and a man is speaking when we go to the visitors' balcony. He is not very interesting, but I like his clothes: they have bright buttons and sharp creases I'd like to touch. We all clap when Ms. Matchless claps, and the man waves up at us. We all wave back, and lots of people laugh. Then we have lunch outside in the gardens. There are huge concrete flowerpots and concrete picnic tables all around the parliament.

The rest of the week we walk everywhere. My feet hurt, but I like the city. We stay in another youth hostel but now I know not to drink anything before bed. I am very thirsty in the morning and I drink lots of milk.

One morning Ms. Matchless tells us to bring our bags down after breakfast. We take them outside and find that the bus is waiting for us. We all protest it isn't time to go back yet, but we are shooed onto the bus. Ms. Matchless says we are going farther into the Long Forest, and we are all quiet. Alison sneaks over and makes Edward swap seats. Berenice is unhappy, and Edward will say he has a girlfriend but he doesn't really.

Leaving, it is hard to tell where the city ends and the forest begins, but then we slow down and turn off the expressway onto a narrow, dark road. We are silent and watch the forest, which is different now that we see it up close. The trees grow far apart, but they go back a long, long way. Their trunks are smooth and silvery and look difficult to climb. The forest is hard, dark, frightening, but Ms. Matchless is smiling.

The driver goes even slower, the front of the bus swings almost into the trees when it goes around corners. Occasionally we see empty cars parked beside the road, but we never see houses or people walking.

We stop at a parking lot and I see there is a path up to a big hall or castle. We walk in twos, holding hands. Edward is now very happy. I am, too, but I know where we are and he doesn't. This is where we will live with Ms. Matchless from now on. We will cook and clean, some of us will be gardeners, some of us will be children, and the noisy ones will be dinner.

This house is not like the youth hostels: we do not sleep in big rooms. Us boys are on the second floor and the girls are somewhere up above. Edward, John, Richard, and me are in a room together. There is a window seat, a fireplace, and four small beds. We each have our own bedside cabinet carved with a forest of trees with lots of apples. Little cottages are hidden among the trees, there are mountains in the distance, and everywhere there are tiny, running wolves. I run my fingers over the carving, pretending I am in the forest. I run away from the hall where Ms. Matchless is showing the class how to bake the cakes she loved as a child. I come upon the wolves, and they chase me, but I find it is not so hard to scramble up one of the silver trees. I throw the apples down at the wolves, trying to drive them away. The wolves are very hungry. For years they have wanted the beautiful golden apples but have not been able to reach them. I throw one apple to each wolf, and the wolves gobble them up. Their smiles get bigger and bigger, and then they all howl. I put my hands over my ears and close my eyes. Suddenly there is a lot of laughing. I am surrounded by boys and by girls, too. The girls should not be here. We had been planning to raid the girls' rooms as soon as the lights are out. I think that when I gave the wolves apples, they changed into these children. I am still on my knees, my fingers tracing the carvings.

At dinner we sit on benches at two long tables. They are round underneath, and Ms. Matchless says they are two halves of one huge birchlike tree from the forest. It's not very comfortable, until I sit on one foot: then I can swing my other foot underneath me. We eat and eat and eat. When I am at home, Mum and Dad don't cook like this. I don't know what I'm eating! There is meat and potatoes and mushy orange and green vegetables, but I don't know what type of meat it is. I imagine it's the wolves: that's why it's dark and chewy. Or maybe I am a wolf like the others. I growl as I eat. Even though they are horrid, I eat the vegetables. I like the bread. It's black and crunchy on the outside and chewy on the inside. I see Ms. Matchless put lots and lots of butter and then salt on it, and I do the same.

After dinner Ms. Matchless says she is going to give us a tour of the house.

I put my hand up. "Is this your house?" I ask.

She is already leading us out of the dining room and she only shakes her head.

There are dusty old paintings on each side of the hallway. Pointing up to the first one, Ms. Matchless says, "This is Edward Doubleaxe."

Edward is grinning so much I wonder if his head will fall off. Ms. Matchless is smiling at him in a way I don't recognize. Later, at home, whenever I think of Edward, I remember this smile.

"Doubleaxe was the first man to rule the whole forest. He burned down a village to build his castle here by the river. Later, during the coup in which he killed his father, Doubleaxe's son burned the castle to the ground and built another – but that was much later. There have been many castles here, but Doubleaxe's was the first.

"Doubleaxe was handsome, but his nose was so large he only allowed painters to paint him from the front. Once, a painter tried to paint a portrait of Doubleaxe and his wife with the light coming from the side so that there would be the slightest hint of a shadow of his nose." She smiled at us. "Doubleaxe was not a man who enjoyed being laughed at. This is not that painting."

Behind Ms. Matchless the others are laughing at Edward and using their hands to make pointy beaks. "Beaky, Beaky," Berenice whispers.

The way home was much harder. We did not have the bus. We had to walk. The Long Forest was dark and, at the end, when the trees grew farther apart, the bushes were hard to push through. There were gray wolves, black bears. I was glad I was not the oldest boy, the second brother, or the youngest girl, who would get the prince but had to do all the dirty work first. I thought of my father and his friend, Ranald, and after the mushrooms, acorns, and the leaves that made me sick were gone, I ate what I had to eat. We walked and we walked and Ms. Matchless always walked behind us.

During the day, we couldn't see the sun. I saw Beaky once, but he did not see me. He was a scout, he said, and tried to keep in front of us. We could all smell him, and we tried to stay away from him.

Alison stayed away from me at first. The boys were weaker, the girls stronger. Ms. Matchless was the strongest of all. Once, when we met two soldiers, she took them out of our sight. She made them scream. She limped when she came back, but her eyes were bright. She had tied a khaki shirt around her calf, and as we walked it slowly turned red, brown, black. We liked the soldiers' rations.

She sang songs we'd never heard. She said they were forest songs that didn't belong to any country. This was the first thing I did not understand. I would have hated her for this, but she was my everything: my bare foot stepping in front of my other bare foot; my waking up in the morning, my sidling behind trees to watch her finding food. I learned the songs inside, but I did not sing anymore. I knew now that only girls sang. I will ask my father if Ranald sang. Maybe that was his mistake. I don't want to make any more mistakes.

We got into the forest so easily, but that road is far behind now. My shoes are broken and gone, my trousers torn. I smell like nothing I have ever smelled. I do not like it. I think about Edward Doubleaxe ruling the whole forest and the houses built on top of the first village. Bigger and bigger houses, but always made of wood, and always so easy to burn.

Before we left the big house, after the television stopped, we listened to what the radio said about the border. Ms. Matchless (we never learned her new name; she said she did not have one in this country) said that this border had never crossed the house before, that was why everyone there was so upset.

I spat. I was eleven and I knew what borders did. I could have told them, but no one wanted to listen. I knew they didn't have to go around digging ditches and shouting about parents and blood and our party, their party. They could have changed the flag, washed the windows, and gotten ready for the army's visit.

They made me angry. I'm just a boy, I thought. I understand. Why don't they?

Ms. Matchless punches me in the side of the head. It is night, and I have been on guard. Even with her limp I did not notice her. I deserve to be punched harder. I salute, and she walks away. All the soldiers' guns make her walk slower, but she won't let me carry one until much later.

We reach the last border back to our country and find that it has stopped moving. There are guards with guns, big silver and black dogs that look like wolves, and spike-topped fences that run from the road into the forest. We slip back into the forest, and Ms. Matchless leads us along the wire. No one can keep up the borders in the forest, she says.

We wait and cross at night. It is more like swimming. The words buzz and crawl in my mouth, fighting each other. I realize Ms. Matchless is not following us. We have gone back to holding hands, walking in twos, pulling each other along. I am lucky: Alison has left the girls and walks with me. She is very strong. The border makes me want to sing the forest songs, the songs that don't belong to anyone, but I am a boy. I am a boy.

We look back and see Ms. Matchless waving. She points her gun at us, and I point the other one at her. Then she salutes, waves, walks tall and strong and limping back into the forest.

Mother and Father are happy to see me. Once I stop eating I will tell them that I am happy to see them, too. Or maybe after I sleep. I do not know when I will sleep. Who will stand guard? I hid the gun in the garden before I knocked on the door. Later, when Mother and Father are asleep, I will get it. Mother and Father think I *am* just a boy. I am a boy. I understand.

One day, soon after, I climb high up Unionist Bridge and I see Ms. Sterling's little car coming into town. Beaky's voice says, "It's a Silver Satellite," in the forest language, but I ignore it. A man in a dark suit is driving, and I know he is Police Army. Ms. Sterling sits in the back and does not see me.

The headmistress brings Ms. Sterling to class the next morning and we all stand and say we are happy to see her. We thank the blurry-faced secretary who has been trying to teach us. Ms. Sterling limps, but on the other leg from Ms. Matchless, and everyone says she has a wooden leg now, to go with her new glass eye. Last year I wouldn't have liked her glass eye because it never moves, but I do now. Sometimes I think it works like a real eye. I wave at it when her real eye is looking the other way, but she never says anything to me. The headmistress nods at her in the hall. We all nod, too. We're children, we know what to do.

*

Then one day during multiplication tables the border crosses over us again. For a long moment (such a long moment inside), I think it will be something new, some place we've never been before. I am excited and I stop reciting even stop watching for problems.

We'll learn new songs, always wear bright shirts on this day, eat sweet red cakes on a special Wednesday in spring, sour white dumplings on the opposite Wednesday in autumn. The girls will wear their hair long (or maybe I will), and I will grow up tall and blond – my hair has been growing back, but darker than it was before.

Then I feel the old words trying to sink into my teeth, my tongue.

Ms. Sterling says, "Sit down. Heads down until I say," and makes her slow way to the sink to get something to clean the board. Ms. Sterling will be Mrs. Black again, and now we know Ms. Matchless is not coming back. I think of Ms. Matchless limping and hunting and eating in the Long Forest. I wonder if she will go back to where she grew up. Would she stay there in the place with no country, singing the songs from before there were borders? I do not think so. She is too strong. She will leave the forest to fight for the capital. Alison is looking out the window, seeing something I can't. I do not think I am the only one that misses Ms. Matchless.

I am still standing. "Rjihnsfjil; – ardrruwer," I say.

"Shut up," says Mrs. Black. She doesn't touch anyone as she shuffles back from the sink. A thought settles inside me: she is not Ms. Matchless, but she is a girl: she is strong.

She limps by me and punches me on the side of the head just like Ms. Matchless. It is night in my head, and I have let down my guard.

"Foolish boy," she says. She limps to the blackboard, erases her name.

Mom and Mother Teresa

Candas Jane Dorsey

Candas Jane Dorsey (*www.sfcanada.ca/members/dorsey.html*) lives in Edmonton, Alberta. She is a founder of SF Canada, an editor and reviewer, and was for ten years the publisher of Tesseracts Books. Her novel *Black Wine* won the 1997 Crawford Award for best first fantasy novel, the 1998 James Tiptree, Jr. Memorial Award, and the 1998 Aurora Award for Best Long-Form Work in English. In addition to her SF novel, *A Paradigm of Earth*, her award-winning body of work includes her collection *Machine Sex and Other Stories* (speculative fiction), *Leaving Marks* (poetry), *Vanilla and Other Stories* (short fiction). She is currently working on *The Adventures of Isabel* (a postmodern mystery). She was once, in her first career, a social worker and child care worker, which is particularly relevant to this story.

"Mom and Mother Teresa" was published in *Tesseracts Nine*, which we consider one of the best anthologies of the year. It is a pleasantly disturbing, low-key fantasy story about saving humanity. Mother Teresa, a saint, comes to Edmonton, moves in and takes over the house and life of the protagonist's controlling mother.

MOTHER TERESA came to live with my mother in the fall of 2001. The famous nun had been touring around the war zones of the world, but she was much frailer since her nearly-fatal heart attack a few years before and perhaps she felt it was time to tackle problems of a different nature – no less serious difficulties of the human condition, but in a more peaceful milieu.

My mother was a healthy eighty-two at the time, a healthy, fat, sedentary, angry widow who looked fifteen years younger than her age and charmed strangers with her clear thoughts, her delightful conversation, her grasp of world events, and her vigour. I found her less charming as I extracted her from her agoraphobic denial patterns and drove her to her doctor's appointments, grocery shopping, and visits with friends, listening non-stop to her fears, her complaints about how difficult my mild father had been really, her catalogue of how little help she got from anyone or how alone she was. She often telephoned me to just run her out to – somewhere – in my lunch hour, and the resulting trip usually took three hours or more. My boss had had me in for two little talks already.

My mother's adult years of desultory attendance at the nearest United Church had not served to erase her Scots Presbyterian childhood with its message of duty, sacrifice, and unhappiness, but the reality these reflexes were based on was a long time ago. When she opened the door that day and found a little, spry, sari-clad Catholic nun on her doorstep with a suitcase, I must credit my mother for reacting according to the training of her parents and grandparents. She invited the little woman in and offered her tea and the second-most-comfortable bed in the house.

"I don't drink tea," said Mother Teresa. "Thank you for your hospitality. Thank you, God, for providing this plenty. Nice house. Does anyone else live here?"

"No," said my mother. "My husband died a year ago. I miss him so much, though it was a terrible struggle taking care of him for the last few years. I just couldn't do anything. It was a nightmare time..."

"Plenty of room," said Mother Teresa. "I think I'll just sleep here in the front verandah. It's cooler anyway, and I don't like a lot of clutter around."

"Would you like some lunch?" said my mother. She had just been starting to make egg salad sandwiches.

"Lovely," said Mother Teresa. "How about if you make a lot more of those?" She was already on the telephone. Before the sandwiches were finished, there was a knock on the door, and two young nuns ushered in about two dozen orphans. You could tell they were orphans, my mother told me later, because they were all dressed alike and their last names were alphabetical by age: Anderson, Ben-Adhem, Carnegie, Daillard, Endicott, Feinberg, Griffon and so on, to Singh, Taillenen, Underwood, Versailles, Wooster, Xander, Yung...there was no Zed orphan.

The orphans stayed for lunch. My mother opened several cans of Campbell's cream of celery soup and used up the last of her milk making it wholesome. She thawed out another couple of loaves of white bread from the downstairs fridge and opened cans of sardines for sardine salad. The older orphans helped her chop onions very fine and one spooned in the mayonnaise, licking the spoon afterward with frightening eagerness. By adding water to the four litre jug of orange juice in the refrigerator my mother was able to give them all orange punch. Mother Teresa said grace, then doled the punch out in the Royal Doulton cups that the grandfather and grandmother that I never met had rescued from the forest fire by burying them (the cups, not the grandparents) in the North Ontario woods and digging them up after the fire had gone through.

The orphans were all pretty careful, and the young nuns washed the dishes and put them back exactly where they came from. My mom appreciated that.

"Now," said Mother Teresa briskly, looking at the orphans, "where shall we put you all?"

It was at that point that my mother left the first message on my voice mail.

It was a hot, "Indian-summer" day, and Mother Teresa decided that the cool basement would make the best dormitory. She hobbled down the stairs step by step, my mother following her anxiously. "Be careful on those steep stairs," my mother said. The young nuns followed unobtrusively, then all the twenty-five orphans in single file alphabetically.

"This will do when we get these things out of here," said Mother Teresa. She began to pull boxes of papers and family antiques out of the corners, and organised the orphans into a kind of bucket brigade carrying the useless stuff outside to the yard. After they discovered that one of the windows hinged up the work went a lot faster, with a few orphans in the yard to receive the boxes and stack them by the garage.

Any box that held anything useable Mother Teresa waved aside and the nuns unpacked it. The old set of dishes my parents hadn't used in the ten years since they moved into that house, the family silver plate, various linens and laces emerged from their newspaper or old-sheet wrappings and were stacked in corners or taken upstairs. After the basement floor was washed down and the soapy water swept into the drain, linens from my mother's upstairs closet were carried down. The orphans, who had been joined by a couple of men in olive green outfits driving a three-ton cube van, started handing in through the window, in pieces, bunk-bed frames of a faintly military nature, and thin sturdy mattresses with striped ticking. Mother Teresa was deft at putting these together, and orphans and nuns followed her lead. Mother Teresa had to resort to her nitro pills at one point, but she didn't make a big deal of it. Soon the basement was transformed into quite a capable dormitory, with bunks stacked three up and clean white sheets hung as curtains to separate the age groups and genders of children. Each orphan had a towel and washcloth and the first shift were taking their baths.

At this point my mother, having left several increasingly frantic messages for me at home and at work, was out in the yard trying to cover the stack of trunks and boxes containing her family history and photographs with a large sheet of six mill plastic my father had used for a paint dropcloth in 1973 and which had been stored in and moved with the garage contents ever since. That's why she was the one to see the bus draw up to the curb, and two other nuns, both older and a little wearier, more street-savvy looking than the two inside, start unloading the families and homeless single men and women.

My mother went in and found Mother Teresa on the telephone. "Excuse me," she said, " but I really think..."

"Good, there you are," said Mother Teresa. "I'm glad you are so capable, and have this many resources here. It makes my job much easier. Now that you've finished outside, perhaps you would help Sister Sophia and Sister Rosario settle the new families in? One family in the back bedroom, one in the middle bedroom. I've had them move your things into the study, because I'm sure you'll want to keep on with your work in your spare time. Really, you have all you need in there – it's a lovely little set-up. Very cozy. I've moved the little desk out to the porch for my office. Once we get everything going, we'll need places to do the administrative work. Right now, though, we should put the men in the living room, don't you think? They're used to sleeping rough. The women – we'll have to figure something else for the women. Especially the ones with children."

"I have to use the phone," said my mother.

"I'll be done soon," said Mother Teresa. "Oh, your doctor phoned. He said to tell you your EEG tracing was normal, all the tests were normal. Your blood pressure was upper normal but he said he thought that was white coat syndrome. He advised you to keep taking the Atavan, and to try to eat less cream and butter. Lose a little weight. The bone density scan was remarkably good, especially for a woman your age. Good. I recognised that you are a woman blessed by God. Is there a car here?"

"Yes," said my mother. "I haven't been able to bear to sell my husband's car yet. He put so much money into that damned old thing when we needed – I mean, he loved that car so much. I'm sure it's a valuable antique, or at least a classic. I don't know how on earth I can get what it's worth. When they see your hair is white, they think they can take advantage of that. I just don't know how I can – with my arthritis, and my vision – it's a nightmare time..."

"Yes, the vision is a problem," said Mother Teresa, "I'm taking into account that you can't drive, so I think it will work best if you give the keys to one of the soldiers. Sergeant Fortunato perhaps. He drove the half-track we used in Palestine to get the disabled children out of the hospital there. By the grace of God, he knows his way around old vehicles. Someone has to pick up the tents and arrange for delivery of groceries. Do you have one of those bank card things? Perhaps you'd better go with him."

It was at this point that my mother barricaded herself in the study and began to phone me on the speed dial, one number after another, until finally someone at the office told her I had gone to the Minister's Office. She actually phoned me there again, despite the fact that after what happened last time I had begged her not to endanger my job that way. The message wasn't clear, but the panic-stricken tone was both familiar and demanding. I had to explain to the Assistant Deputy Minister that if Mother called there after all that they had said last time, this must be an emergency. She said that the last four calls from my mother hadn't been much of an emergency, and that working out this Action Request for the Minister was an emergency too, especially given his problems with bad publicity lately, but I told her that the Minister already had everything in his briefing book that the office needed to answer the letter, and I was sure it was serious. I wasn't convinced myself, but I presented my case firmly, then left while they were still looking for the briefing book. That was actually the last I saw of my job, but by the time I heard that my boss had fired me, I had figured out that I wouldn't starve if I – what do they say? – pursued other options. I learned a lot from Mother Teresa, even if I am more interested doctrinally in Buddhism.

When I arrived at my mother's house I almost didn't recognise the place. The marquee was already up on the back lawn, joined to the porch of the house on one side and the garage on the other by striped awnings, and the tent city was being erected on the large, long front lawn. The ramshackle picket fence that the landlord wouldn't fix was already half-dismantled so that the provisions could be unloaded into the marquee where a sort of summer kitchen had been set up with half-oil-drum barbecue stoves borrowed from the local Lions and Shriners Clubs. The pieces of the fence were going in on top of the briquettes to make a roaring fire in each stove, and people were wrapping potatoes in tinfoil, filling huge pots with water from the hose and putting them on to boil, and cutting up carrots and celery.

A troupe of neat-as-a-pin orphans worked alongside a few soldiers, several young sari-clad nuns, and two homeless men. One of them, I found out later, had been bottle-collecting in the alley (it was the day before the recycling pickup) when Mother Teresa engaged him in conversation, and discovering that he had been in a residential school, suggested that his experience could help the orphans avoid pitfalls in the system and protect themselves from the unscrupulous among their caregivers. As he carried cases of canned goods and sacks of potatoes out of the truck, he was giving the orphans laconic advice: "Take a friend along when you go to confession," was the one phrase I heard, and only heard the context later, so as I walked by I had the odd impression he was repeating some Martha Stewart homily he'd seen in a woman's magazine at the supermarket from which the groceries had come.

"Where shall I put all this day-old fruit we got for free?" one of the orphans said to a small woman standing at the top of the back-porch steps.

"Take it inside; the girls are making fruit salad for everyone and then canning the rest," she said, and I realised with shock that I was seeing the famous Mother Teresa.

My shock had a guilty element. Okay, I can confess it now, but if you ever tell my mother, I'll deny I said it: I actually was the one that told a friend of mine that if she needed to billet anyone for this ecumenical conference she was organising, I was sure my mom had space. After all, when my mother was a kid, her family housed the student ministers for the little rural church they'd helped build. Also, I thought it would bring her out of herself, and, I confess, distract her from her attempt to get the same level of service from me as she had had from my father. When my pal said, "What about Mother Teresa?" I thought she was kidding, and

I said, "Sure, that would be perfect!" I had no idea Mother Teresa really was coming to our little city and I certainly figured if she did she'd stay somewhere else, somewhere holy and Catholic and conventy. I have never told my mother about this, and I am really not kidding when I say I never want her to know. I figure having to work with her every day is karmic punishment enough.

Anyway, it's too late to change things. It was already too late when I showed up on the lawn, though my mother has never let me forget that she called me for help and instead I immediately got drafted into helping make the fruit salad and Mother didn't find out I was there until two hours later when she finally gave in and came out of her room to take a painkiller and an Atavan.

"But, Mom," I say to her over and over, every time she brings it up. "I knew where all the knives and stuff were. It made perfect sense. I just couldn't say no to a greater need."

From under the folds of the sari covering her abundant white hair, my mother looks at me reproachfully. Luckily, usually, before we get any further, one of the younger nuns comes in and says, "Excuse me, ma'am, there are some new women here; do you have any more clothes?" or "Excuse me, missus, but I'm wondering if you would mind if we gave these talking books you've finished with to that blind woman who's running the tent city?" and she has to bustle off and help with something. Anyway, by the time our day is over I'm ready to leave for my apartment with the other nuns I've got staying there with me, we're both too tired to argue after a hard day's work helping Mother Teresa.

My mother doesn't much like the sari, but since she's become so much more active, she's lost so much weight that none of her clothes fit anymore. Besides, the homeless women, the formerly homeless women I mean, are getting a lot more wear out of all those outfits than she ever did.

Newbie Wrangler

Timothy J. Anderson

Timothy J. Anderson (*www.geocities.com/canadian_SF/pages/authors/anderson.htm*) lives in Edmonton, Alberta. His background is impressive: "A graduate of the Carleton School of Journalism specializing in economic reporting and the petroleum economies of Southeast Asia, Mr. Anderson's education also includes Combined Honours in Political Science, a Bachelor of Music (University of Ottawa), and graduate studies in music theatre (Banff School of Fine Arts) and arts administration (York University)... Mr. Anderson is an accomplished classical singer, a professional actor, and a composer. He has performed in opera, oratorio and musicals across Canada, in Singapore, Hong Kong, and at Carnegie Hall in New York." His writing includes two books (the poetry collection *Neurotic Erotica* and the erotic science fiction thriller *Resisting Adonis*), and published short fiction and non-fiction. Two novels related to *Resisting Adonis* are forthcoming: *Echoing Narcissus* and *Invoking Venus*.

"Newbie Wrangler" appeared in the distinguished Canadian original anthology, *Tesseracts Nine*, edited by Nalo Hopkinson and Geoff Ryman. The afterlife is a strange and desperate place. A man in a war zone whose legs have been amputated wakes. Hungry children come to his tent wanting oranges. Contradictory details emerge. He has died, but this is not what he had anticipated.

AT FIRST IT SEEMED the silence had woken me, ominous and heavy outside the tent. A slip of grey light slid under the canvas when a slight breeze stirred, just enough light to bring to life the serious black eyes peering at me from the other side of the brass rail at the foot of the bed. I pretended to sleep.

A grubby hand at the end of a thin grey arm nudged my foot through the glimmering sheet. A waif of the desert, I thought.

"Can I have an orange?"

Cheeky beggar, coming into the tent. At least the kid asked instead of robbing me blind in my sleep. I grunted a little and stretched, and I could hear the kid open my pack. I kept my eyes closed so I wouldn't have to look on disappointment.

"Thanks," the urchin said. "I like 'em fresh."

A pulse of light as the tent flap flashed open, and then the dim grey once more. The sound of a child's voice piping high in a language I didn't recognize, answered by several others. I burrowed my head under the pillow, enjoying the peace, the relative cool of the morning, the solitude.

A small hand shook my foot.

"Mister, can I have an orange too?"

"Yeah, sure," I mumbled. "If you can find one, go right ahead."

The last oranges had come at least a month ago. They had been a miracle, tumbling out of the supply truck and into the bright desert sun. We'd devoured them. We even ate the rinds, we were so hungry for anything that didn't come from a pouch. We'd cleared away the rotting body parts and planted the seeds in the sand and we all agreed to set aside a ration of water toward the future orange grove. For two weeks we allowed ourselves to think of a future. Then the hostilities broke out again, and our carefully tended plot of sand was cratered by shells and littered with pieces of our friends and we used our water to clean wounds.

I stretched under the thermal sheet, breathing in the citrus-scented acrid air filtered through the sheets, my tongue feeling like a foreign substance in my mouth, dry enough to click, I thought. This would be a good day to learn the local language.

A whisper of tent flap and tiny hands jiggling both my heels. "Hey! Hey!"

"Take your bloody oranges and let me sleep."

Treble giggles and the sound of sand scuffed into the legs of the bed by tiny sandals. There must have been a cease-fire, I figured. So many children wandering through the camp in the morning, looking for anything to eat after the destruction of the night before. By now they would be halfway to the rubble of their homes, taking their oranges back to anxious mothers moaning in the rubble.

The images flooded in: imploding buildings, dust, the spray of concrete, of blood, the litter of papers and lives torn apart, the noise and stench and numbness.

Another hand touched my heel and I started, drawing it up and away.

"I told you it was too late," the voice of the first beggar said. "They're all gone."

"Is there anything else?" a second voice asked.

"Nothing we want. Maybe later. Let's go!"

I stayed on the bed, lying on my stomach, and watched the patch of light where the tent didn't quite meet the sand. I waited for it to brighten, for the line of shade to move as the sun moved across the sky. I waited to feel another small hand on my foot, to see another pinched face on the other side of the brass footboard. While I waited, the memories of war played themselves out in a series of lucid dreams which I knew I could stop at any time if I got out of bed.

The children didn't come and the light got no brighter, and my memories filled my brain with a clattering montage that didn't stop when the tent flap opened and the interior brightened for a moment.

"Time to get up, newbie," a man's voice said. "Bring your guitar. We've got work to do."

The sound of canvas flapping back into place.

The kids took the oranges but not the guitar? Hunger will do that to you.

There it was, at least I thought it must be the guitar, a vague shape lying against the side of the tent. I reached out from my prone position, but the guitar was out of reach. Odd that it was out of the case. Not great to have it in this dryness. I shouldn't have brought it, not to the desert.

I hadn't. I'd left the guitar at home. The brass bed – I hadn't slept in the brass bed since I visited my grandparents after the second year of college. The oranges came weeks ago and we devoured them and planted the seeds. My feet had been taken off by a blast three days ago. Well, mostly by a blast and the rest was done by a surgeon.

The flap opened again, and in the light I could see there was no guitar, only absurdly green camouflage canvas.

"Hurry up!" the guitar voice said. "Oh...um, you stay right there and I'll be back, okay? Just hang on."

It didn't sound like anyone I knew. One of the young guys, maybe, the new recruits whose voices were changing as they grew up.

I could hear voices outside the tent, this time in English.

"An orange? And you...what did you get? Geez, the lot of you. We need instruments, things we can play."

"He could go back to sleep." It was one of the small piping voices. "We could try again."

"It's too late. The guitar's gone and it won't be back."

"He's got lots of sand," another voice said.

"And what are we going to do with more sand?" asked guitar man. "There's no end of sand and rock and earth. We need music."

There was a tense silence broken only by the shuffling sound of sandals on sand. Then a huge sigh and the voice of guitar man:

"Go. Gogogogogo. Always ask for the instrument first, and if you can't see one, ask for a tuba or a pipe organ. Or a piccolo. We need to round up a thousand piccolos. Now go!"

Off they ran, screaming shrilly.

He came into the tent, leaving the flap slightly open to the light. I squinted and rolled over so I could see him better. He looked like a boy I'd met once, on summer vacation in the middle of high school. His clothes were things my brother wore when he was a teenager: low-rise denim bellbottoms, a plaid shirt unbuttoned halfway to the navel, water buffalo sandals. Retro hippy chic. His face was still indistinct in the gloom of the tent.

"Hi," he said. I didn't answer.

"Sorry about the confusion. The kids hadn't had a decent orange in a while. They're just kids, you know? I was kinda hoping you'd have brought your guitar." He looked toward the spot where I could have sworn the guitar had been, only I knew it wasn't.

"Anyway," he went on, "not having the guitar isn't the end of the universe or anything. You remember how to sing, right?" He stood at the end of the cot, and there was no brass anything between us. I could see that the bedclothes were flat below my knees, no sign of legs or feet.

"What's going on?" I asked.

Guitar man sighed, and the sound made him more concrete somehow. "I'm a talent scout. I need to put together a huge band to make an amazing noise, but no one seems to be travelling with their instruments these days. I sent the kids for your guitar but they took the oranges instead. Oranges," he said with a chuckle in his voice, "make lousy instruments."

"You look like someone," I ventured.

"Yeah, I know. You got drunk and tried to have sex with me in your first semester at college."

Suddenly his features pulled into focus. He'd been a Jim Morrison clone: soft pouting lips, sexually charged, dangerous. I'd been the good kid: clean cut, law-abiding, and ripe for experience. The details of the party were hazy, but I remembered him coming on to me, pressing against me, and me wanting to know.

Guitar man smiled. "Can't remember my name, but you remember the rest of me quite well. Careful – I'm horny and it's been a long time."

"What are you doing here?"

He grinned. "Don't worry, newbie. I'm not expecting a rematch. Not," he quickly added, "that it wouldn't be fun. As I said, I'm here to put together a mighty shout. And I'm hoping you'll help. Come on."

There's a nasty kind of dream you have when you come out of the anaesthetic on the field. It's a dream that combines the memories of home with the reality of the battle. After they took the dangling bits of my legs off, the dreams were of the locker room at high school. All of us changing, laughing, running. And then huge explosions rocking the lockers, making them fall like dominoes. Dreams of the soccer field. Dreams of kicking the ball against the garage door forever.

"They fixed your legs," the guitar man said. "That's why you're feeling so woozy. They did another operation and fixed your legs. So let's go!"

I threw back the sheet, now a heavy grey striped wool like the ones we had in training, and there were my legs, just as I remembered them.

"Let's go let's go let's go!" he barked, a hippy parody of a drill sergeant. "Time is of the essence here. We have to get you singing."

I have no memory of getting dressed or of what I saw when we left the tent. My impression is that the day was hazy but not too hot. There wasn't another soul in sight, and we were in the desert or the brown grassy fields closer to home. And we were walking and laughing as if we really knew each other. I expected at any moment for someone I knew to come around the corner or over the next rise: a buddy from my outfit, a dead relative, a spirit guide. But guitar man, all electricity and promise, propelled me along with his ease, his fitness for the new and changing world.

"What'll you sing?" he asked. "You'd better think of it now or everyone else will be singing and you'll be mouthing the words."

It had been so long since I sang anything. Then, like a mirage slinking over the field, I could smell salt air and the sand was slippery and studded with bits of driftwood and broken shells. "'Stairway to Heaven,'" I whispered. "That's what I'll sing."

"I had hoped for something by Jim Morrison," the man said, "but 'Stairway' will do fine. It's a strong memory."

I was sixteen and at the beach with a boombox and a bag of marshmallows, and a girl I had never seen before loaned me her lighter to start the fire. By 10:30 I had imagined our whole life together and was ready to propose, and "Stairway to Heaven" played and we danced in the sand.

"Whoa, whoa, whoa newbie!" guitar man called out. "You're losing me! Stay with the program, okay?"

He was ahead of me, running through the beach grass toward me, and the dunes were lit by bonfires and trash cans and burning buildings.

"Sing! Let's go! Singsingsing!"

He put his arm around me and I could smell him the way I had smelled him that night, like every secret I would ever have was encrypted in his sweat. And we sang until the burning stopped and we collapsed on the sand, giddy with pleasure at being alive.

I looked at him then, the memorized pores of his face, the huge hazel eyes, and I had the courage to ask:

"Why didn't the others come?"

The face slackened, and with effort he spoke the words I could not. "I'm a wrangler. I am your purest memory of a person. Not the most important person," he said quickly, "but the simplest, most direct memory. I will be clear longer than the rest, but not for long."

He got up, brushed off the sand and held out a hand. It was true. I could remember that hand, the surprise at finding his arms to be smooth and strong, the breathtaking energy and electricity of our drunken exploration.

"Why did you want the guitar?" I asked, taking his hand and allowing him to pull me up.

"We need a big noise, lots of harmonics. People remember how to play, remember their skills, but they forget their instruments early. Once in a while we get a techhead who remembers every bit of an amp system, but we can't count on it." He strode away, across the desert and toward the mountains.

"Wait up," I called. I ran after him, and we continued in near silence. He was humming snatches of "Stairway," and I knew it was to keep it fresh in my mind.

"So why did the guitar disappear?" I asked. "It was there, right?"

"The oranges," he sighed. "Those kids, the ones you remember from the peacekeeping mission, they sensed that you had a very strong fresh memory of oranges, and that's what they wanted. Memories don't last long once you're dead. They have to be corralled quickly. Do you remember the kids?"

They'd been there, in my tent. I tried to remember them, but nothing would come. The tent flap opening, a pressure on my heel, but nothing else.

"That's why I came. They were supposed to bring you and the guitar, but they got distracted. I'm the memory strong enough to get us to the meeting."

"Where I will sing 'Stairway to Heaven'?"

"Where everyone will sing, and anyone who brought their instruments will play, and we will raise a mighty noise..." Guitar man stopped. "A mighty noise, and we hope it is enough."

"Enough for what?"

He looked toward the mountains and took a deep breath. "Enough to wake God," he said.

I looked toward the mountains too, half expecting a shaft of white light and a booming voice to welcome me into heaven.

"This isn't getting us anywhere," guitar man said. "Where did you last meet God? Can you remember the place well enough to get us there?"

The desert landscape shimmered and shook as I went through the various possibilities, memories dissolving as soon as I touched them. I had not met God on a golf course, as many claim to do. I had certainly called the name at moments when it seemed appropriate – often in my bedroom or the bedrooms of relative strangers – but namedropping isn't the same as meeting. There were the children at play in the hot rubble. Yes, in a way I suppose I had glimpsed God from the top of a tank patrolling a war zone. I had met God in narrow laneways full of debris and splintered pieces of wood, God looking out from unglazed windows and scraping up a life from nothing, out of chaos.

Then we were there. The two of us, the guitar man looking as relaxed and easy as he always had, and me in my fatigues, and there was a steeply rising curved pebbly passageway between the buildings, narrow enough to be slightly shaded from the near-noon sun.

"Up there," I whispered. "God is up there."

We walked up the path, the debris shifting in and out of focus. I remembered that dented can. I remembered a bleached chicken bone, a rusty bottlecap, a crushed cigarette pack. I knew with certainty that when we got to the top of the curve, we would come out into a plaza with an improbably intact fountain, not working but in one piece, and lines of white washing, like huge truce flags, hung out in the sun. In the fragile peace and the brilliant sun, the face of God would be shining.

"It's been harder and harder to keep God awake," said the guitar man. "It's a strain, paying attention all the time. Tiring. It takes more and more noise just to register. And when God falls asleep, the universe runs amok. It's our job," he said. I could hear his breath shallowing out as we ascended the path.

"There are lots of newbies," he continued. "No shortage, not these days. But they're dumbstruck, so busy looking ahead for the damned light they've been told about that we can't harness their memories, can't ride 'em to a meet. It's hard enough to keep God interested twenty-four seven without surrounding the Deity with slack-jawed sightseers."

Then, slowing down a bit to catch his breath, he sang.

I joined in, still walking forward and up, seeing the sharp shadows of the sun on the battered buildings. I felt lighter, my legs felt stronger than they had been on the sands. Faces looked out of the windows, smiling faces, tired faces. There was a little girl with serious black eyes and a half-eaten orange in her grimy hands.

The young man fell behind, but I heard him call out: "Thanks for the ride. Sing. Loud! And when you're done, come ride the newbies!"

I strode into the plaza, playing my guitar and singing at the top of my lungs, the sound bouncing off the walls and through the flapping white sheets and the young man faded into the stones. The wind brought the smell of oranges from the desert grove and the sound of singing, of a world singing and playing, and pulsing into the ear of God until we lost the memory of music, of language, of voice.

Being Here

Claude Lalumière

Claude Lalumière (lostpages.net) lives in Montreal, Quebec. He used to own and operate two independent bookstores in Montreal, one a literary hangout, the other the Montreal SF & fantasy bookshop Nebula, until 1998. But he gave it up and sold them, to be a writer, a reviewer, and an editor. He writes the Montreal Gazette's Fantastic Fiction column (archived online at InfinityPlus). His fiction began appearing in 2002 (in Interzone). He's since published in On Spec, Tesseracts, SciFiction, and others.

He has edited several non-genre anthologies, and three fantasy and SF, all of high quality: Witpunk, an anthology of Sardonic Fiction; Open Space: New Canadian Fantastic Fiction; and Island Dreams: Montreal Writers of the Fantastic.

"Being Here" was published in Tesseracts Nine. It is a well-done ambiguous supernatural tale, with a sort of post–Robert Aickman strange atmosphere. A man becomes invisible to his girlfriend, who misses him. He is the protagonist and is still present, but completely isolated. And it just gets stranger.

THE NIGHT BEFORE, you and I had fought, and it had taken me forever to fall asleep. We didn't make up then, and I still regret that. We'd argued about nothing and everything – the dishes, the vacuuming, the cat litter. A stupid fight. One in which none of the important things got said, in which all the real reasons for the tension between us were carefully avoided.

Exasperated, you had turned your back to me; a snore interrupted me mid-sentence. Waking you up would only have made a bad situation worse. There was nothing I could have said at that moment that would have brought us closer. I let you sleep and tried to calm myself.

It was useless. I lay awake for hours, unable even to keep my eyes closed, until I fell from sheer exhaustion into an unrestful sleep.

I woke up at dawn, as I always did. The clock on my bedside dresser told me it was not quite six yet. I usually took advantage of the time before I woke you up at eight to go running in the park. That morning, thinking I had a choice, I decided to be lazy and stay in bed. I knew the exercise would help snap me out of my funk, but I just couldn't gather the energy to get up and start my day.

After a few minutes, it occurred to me that in the morning I always needed to pee urgently. And yet there I was, feeling absolutely no pressure on my bladder.

I wanted to enjoy a drowsy morning in bed, just rest and relax. But I couldn't get comfortable. The blankets were so heavy.

*

The clock read 7:12. The feeling of being trapped by the blankets was unbearable. I was getting tenser and angrier by the second. I couldn't muster the strength to get up. I liked mornings, but already I was hating this one.

The digital readout on the clock became my lifeline to sanity. That every minute a numeral changed filled me with a strange and pathetic reassurance.

Still irritated from the previous night, I wanted to shout at you to stop snoring, but, with our fight still so fresh, I knew waking you up this early would only make things worse.

Lying there, I was hypersensitive to noises I usually blanked out. The morning traffic, the creaking building, the shrill wind outside. I could make out what the neighbours were saying through the walls; they were calmly reading each other snippets from the morning paper. Everything was so loud.

And the smell! The cat litter stank like we hadn't changed it in months. Were we really that bad? The whole apartment reeked: the unwashed laundry, the sinkful of dirty dishes, the garbage. How could we have let things slide so much, I thought.

Finally, it was eight o'clock; time to wake you.

No matter how hard I tried, I couldn't push the blankets off me, I couldn't reach over and touch you. I wasn't paralyzed, though. I could move my neck, my face, and the top of my right shoulder – everything that wasn't caught under the blankets. I tried to say your name over and over again, but no sound came out of my mouth. I thought: you'll be late for work; you'll be furious with me.

And then the fact that I couldn't speak hit me, hit me much harder than being trapped in bed. I panicked, losing track of time, unable even to think, until I heard you roar my name.

But that was no roar, not really, only a mumble amplified by my hypersensitive hearing. You were finally waking up. The clock told me it was 10:34. You always mumbled my name when you were in that dozy state, rising from sleep to wakefulness. I loved that.

You turned toward me – I'd never noticed before how pungent your morning breath was – and your eyes popped open. You were looking past me at the clock. You flung out of bed, screaming my name without looking at me, shouting abuse and insults because I hadn't woken you up in time. The noise and stress combined to give me the god of all headaches.

When you got out of bed, the blankets moved enough so that my other shoulder was freed. But no more than that. I could move that shoulder again. Such frustrating relief.

Ten minutes later, you stomped back into the bedroom – your skin moist from the shower – and, still angry, shouted, "Where the fuck are you?" You turned on the light, and it was too much for my eyes. I squeezed them shut to block out the searing brightness. I mean, I tried to. My face wasn't paralyzed. I could feel my facial muscles react when I moved them – even my eyelids. But closing them didn't stop the light. While putting your clothes on, you kept shouting at me like I wasn't there.

Before slamming the front door on your way out, you had let George in from the backyard. He jumped on the bed and walked all over me. His paws were like steel girders; the bed under me gave with his every step. After a minute or so of this, he zeroed in on my crotch and kneaded it mercilessly. Purring. My life was pain. At least you had turned off the lights.

George stayed nestled on my crotch until you came back home after work. How much did he weigh? Eight pounds? Ten? Something like that. It felt like a bowling ball was crushing my pelvis.

As soon as he heard you unlock the front door, he leapt off me. He meowed to be let out. You cooed at him and opened the back door. These noises were still too loud, but by this time, having had to cope with it for a whole day, I'd become somewhat used to my newfound sensitivity. Even the light and smells, while still harsh, didn't bother me as much. In general, the pain was getting duller – an irritation instead of an assault.

After shutting the back door, you called my name. I tried to answer, but I still couldn't manage to make any sound.

I heard you pick up the phone, no doubt checking for messages. The phone hadn't rung all day. I was thankful for that bit of silence.

You swore and slammed the phone down. You turned on the TV and set the volume high. I braced myself for the pain, but I was adapting well – too well – to my condition. There was no discernible increase in my pain level.

I heard you wander through the apartment, shuffling papers, opening doors. You returned to the living room and plunked yourself down on the couch. Over the sounds of a car advertisement, I could hear you sniffle and sob. Already, I missed you so much.

You watched TV all evening, not bothering to eat. At 1:04 in the morning, you finally turned off the TV and walked into the bedroom. You looked miserable. You stared at me. In a tearful whine, you said, "Where are you?"

Desperate, I tried to channel all my strength, all my energy into screaming that I was right there, but I still failed. Couldn't you see me? It's not like I was dead. If I were, there'd be a corpse, a body.

And that's when I couldn't ignore it anymore.

I craned my neck to look down at myself, at where I felt my body squeezed into immobility by the blankets, and...and there was nothing there.

I stayed awake that whole night.

You fell asleep on your stomach, without taking your clothes off. You didn't move all night, but you snored – of course, you snored. Your left arm fell across me and crushed my chest – the part of me that still felt like a chest – until you woke up at 10:42 the next morning.

It was only after your arm had been separating my upper self from my lower for several hours that I noticed that I was no longer breathing. When I thought about it, I was pretty sure that I hadn't breathed since I'd woken up in this condition.

Whatever that was.

I listed the symptoms: I was invisible, even to myself; I didn't get hungry; I didn't need to pee or shit; I didn't get tired, but I felt a constant, numbing weakness; my senses were too acute for comfort; I wasn't breathing; blankets were too heavy for me to lift.

Like a list was going to explain everything, or anything.

And where was my body? How could I feel so much physical pain if I didn't have a body?

You rolled on your back, away from me. I felt my rib cage pop back up. Did I still have a rib cage? I looked at where I felt my body to be, and there still wasn't even the slightest hint of a shape. Was I even in there with you? Or was that sensation an illusion of some kind?

I told you, silently, that I was sorry for everything, for being so distant, for so often only pretending to listen to you, for so often having some stupid thing to do when all you wanted was to enjoy spending time with me – and in the middle of my futile apology George sat on my face.

You called in sick for the next two days. Minutes crawled by like weeks, sleepless days and nights like lifetimes.

You called my office and a few of my friends, but I could tell from your voice the emotional price you were paying for doing this. You gave that up quickly.

Couldn't you see that all my clothes were still there? My keys by the bed? Couldn't you feel that I was still there, longing for you?

Your orbit consisted of the bed, the fridge, the couch, and the toilet. The centre of your universe was the TV.

You stopped calling in sick. You just stayed home. When the phone rang, you ignored it.

*

A week later, your sister used her spare key to come in when you failed to respond to the doorbell. At first she was furious, yelling at you to snap out of it. Eventually, you broke down and started crying. That mollified her.

You told her that I'd vanished on you with no warning. She said she was surprised at that; she'd always thought of me as good for you.

You were an odd combination of fragile and tough, and I'd fallen in love with the intensity that accompanied that mix. You needed undivided attention to feel loved. You didn't give your trust easily, but, once you did, you trusted without question. Being with you was a heady experience that left little time or energy for anything else. I indulged like an addict: your intensity was a powerful narcotic. You had tended to attract lovers who abused your fragility, who took pleasure in shattering someone so strong who could nevertheless be so easily broken. Your sister had liked that I made you laugh, had seen how it thrilled me to have you permeate my whole world.

Eventually, life outside our bubble intruded. Friends, work, whatever. And I drifted away. I let you suffer, even though I knew you were suffering; I let my growing indifference chip away at you. And, like a coward, instead of talking to you and trying to mend the rift, I just ignored it. I ignored you.

Sex with you was so beautiful, such a complete escape, sad and hard, silly and serious, in all the best ways. How could I let anything get in the way of that? Of being close to you?

I've never wanted to comfort you as much as when I heard you tell your sister how much you'd been hurt by my disappearance. But I'd started to disappear much earlier than you were telling her, and I hated myself for that. For betraying you. For betraying myself.

Do you remember when, the week before we moved in together, you stopped by my office and took me out to lunch? Warming your hands on my cup of tea, a fleck of something green stuck between your teeth, you asked me what I needed, and we bonded because of our common goal: your happiness. When did that stop being important?

Your sister couldn't see me either. She cleaned the bathroom. After she put you in a hot bath, she turned off the TV and put on the radio instead. Classical. Worse: opera. Then, she attacked the embarrassing mess of our apartment. I'd like to say that most of it was due to your recent binge, but our place was always a disaster area.

And then she changed the bed.

The weakness disappeared when the weight of the blankets was lifted off me.

And, just like that, I was free. I was free! I danced and leapt and twirled and ran and –

And then I caught the words "missing" and "disappeared" on the radio news report.

There was, all around the world, an alarming increase in missing-person reports. The prime minister of Canada. The CEO of Toshiba. The US ambassador to the UN. The populations of whole villages in Africa. Hundreds of Afghan women. And so on. From the most disenfranchised to the most powerful, people everywhere were vanishing.

The news that I probably was not the only victim of this peculiar condition did not reassure me, but rather filled me with overwhelming dread. I walked into the bathroom, needing the security of your presence, and sat on the edge of the tub. You had no reaction when I reached out and stroked your face. Was I that insubstantial?

I could no longer take comfort in the slight plumpness of your cheek. To my touch, your flesh was as hard and unyielding as concrete.

When your sister left the apartment, I took advantage of the open door – all physical objects now being immovable, impassable obstacles – and left with her. I didn't follow her. I had been cooped up inside for so long. I needed the open air. I just wandered around. And I mulled over what I had heard on the news. I was already so used to the pain from the sensory overload that it was no longer even a distracting irritant.

Were all the vanished in the same situation I was? If I met another vanished person, would we see each other?

Outside I discovered that rain, even the mildest precipitation, knocked the strange substance of my nearly insubstantial body to the ground, raindrops hammering into me like nails. Yet, for all that I had some, if almost negligible, physical presence, I cast no shadow. I was truly invisible.

There were fewer and fewer people about every day. Obviously, we vanished could not perceive each other. What people were left acquired a haunted or persecuted look. They knew that their time would soon come.

Less than a week after I escaped from the apartment, civil order broke down. Vandalized and overturned police cars burned on street corners. All the stores I passed had their windows broken, their stock looted or destroyed.

The city grew quiet, as traffic dwindled away and industry stopped dead.

The silence was occasionally punctuated by bursts of gunshots and quickly silenced screams. Those sounds filled me with more dread than my inexplicable vanishing ever did. I was always careful to walk away from such noises and never discovered exactly what was happening.

Dogs wailed and wandered everywhere, searching for their vanished human companions, scavenging through garbage for food.

I saw stray cats hunt some of the smaller wildlife that was reclaiming the city. They gave the bears a wide berth, though. Often, I thought I saw George, but the cat was always gone before I could be sure.

During that time, I returned to the apartment only once. The door had been torn off. Everything had been trashed. A raccoon family was living in our bedroom. By then you must have vanished, like me. I wanted to find you, hold you. But you were beyond my reach.

I was following a bear around, excited by what would have been in normal circumstances suicidal behaviour, when a giant shadow fell over me. I looked up. Swift grey clouds covered the afternoon sky. Scraps of old newspapers were being blown every which way. There was so much wind – wild, chaotic wind. Before I could think to take cover, I was hit on all sides – by a ragged shirt, a torn magazine, a broken beer bottle, cigarette butts, gum wrappers. I was jabbed and crushed and flattened and stabbed and twisted. It hadn't hurt this much since that first morning.

The storm erupted; the sharp, heavy rain felled me, knifed through my prone body.

The storm ended; the clouds parted and revealed the moonlit sky, glittering with stars. I lay there on the ground, recovering from the storm, and gazed at the sky. There were more stars visible than before: when people had vanished, so had the city lights that had made the nighttime too bright for starlight.

I stayed like that until dawn, and then someone stepped on me.

I looked around; the streets were filled with people. Naked as newborns, they walked calmly but with a sense of purpose, murmuring softly to each other, casually touching each other, sharing complicit glances.

I recognized a few faces – no one I knew well, but people I'd seen in shops or cafés.

Still wobbly, I stood up. Was this ordeal finally over? Was I back, too? A quick test – trying in vain to see my hands or any part of my body – told me I wasn't. I tried to call out to the people around me, but I was still mute.

What about you? Could you have returned? I ran to our apartment.

When I neared home, I saw them. They were also heading there: hand in hand, smiling and laughing, so obviously deeply in love with each other.

It was you and me. More beautiful, more in love, more confident, more at peace than we'd ever been. Serene.

But it wasn't you, was it? No more than it was me. You must still be vanished like me. Neither dead nor alive. And so it must be for everyone.

Do you, like me, spend your time watching our doppelgangers? Are frustrated at being unable to understand their language? Are you jealous at how much better they are at being us – at loving each other – than we ever were? At how much even George seems happier with them? Are you envious that all these new people have made the world a better place?

I want to end my life, but I don't think I can. I've tried jumping off roofs, but all I get out of it is more pain – never death.

Are you here with me, my love?

I long to die with you.

To be really dead. Together. Forever oblivious.

The Imago Sequence

Laird Barron

Laird Barron (*www.benjamindesign.com/lairdbarron/index.html*) lives in Olympia, Washington. Barron was born in Alaska, where he raised and trained huskies for many years. He completed the Iditarod in 1991, '93, and '94 – a twelve-hundred-mile dog-team race beginning in Anchorage and ending in Nome, Alaska. He moved to Seattle in the mid '90s and began to concentrate on writing poetry and fiction. He has published a handful of stories since 2000, characteristically horrific, in *SciFiction* and *The Magazine of Fantasy & Science Fiction*, and he has been reprinted in *The Year's Best Fantasy and Horror*. The three stories he published in 2005 show a mature and exceptionally talented writer at work.

"The Imago Sequence" was published in *The Magazine of Fantasy & Science Fiction*. It is a first class piece of supernatural horror fantasy, perhaps the best horror story of the year, a year in which there was very strong competition. Unusually for horror, it has a tough-guy protagonist.

Imago. Imago. Imago.

— WALLACE STEVENS

I.

LIKE THE SHROUD OF TURIN, the disfigured shape in the photograph was a face waiting to be born. An inhuman face, in this instance – the Devil, abstracted, or a black-mouthed sunflower arrested mid-bloom. Definitely an object to be regarded with morbid appreciation, and then followed by a double scotch to quash the heebie-jeebies.

I went to Jacob Wilson's Christmas party to see his uncle's last acquisition, one that old man Theodore hadn't stuck around to enjoy. A *natural Rorschach*, Jacob said of the photo. It had been hanging in the Seattle Art Museum for months, pending release at the end of its show. Jacob was feeling enigmatic when he called about the invitation three days before Christmas and would say no more. No need – the hook was set.

I hadn't talked to Jacob since the funeral. I almost skipped his party despite that guilt, aware of the kind of people who would attend. Whip-thin socialites with quick, sharp tongues, iron-haired lawyers from colonial families, and sardonic literati dredged from resident theater groups. Sleek, wealthy, and voracious; they inhabited spheres far removed from mine. As per custom, I would occupy the post of the educated savage in Jacob's court. An orangutan dressed for a calendar shoot, propped in the corner to brood artfully. Perhaps I could entertain them with my rough charm, my lowbrow anecdotes. It wasn't appealing. Nonetheless, I went because I always went, and because Carol gave me her

sweetest frown when I hesitated; the one that hinted of typhoons and earth-
quakes.

The ride from my loft in downtown Olympia served to prepare my game
face. I took the 101 north, turned onto Delphi Road and followed it through the
deep, dark Capitol Forest and up into the Black Hills. Carol chattered on her cell,
ignoring me, so I drove too fast. I always drove too fast these days.

The party was at full steam as I rolled along the mansion's circle drive and
angled my rusty, four-door Chrysler into a slot among the acres of Porsches,
Jaguars, and Mercedes. Teddy Wilson might've only been a couple of months
in his grave, but Jacob was no neophyte host of galas. He attracted the cream,
all right.

Bing Crosby and a big band were hitting their stride when the front doors
gave way. A teenage hood in a spiffy white suit grabbed our coats. I automatically
kept one hand over my wallet. The bluebloods congregated in a parlor domi-
nated by a fiery synthetic tree. A slew of the doorman's white-tuxedoed breth-
ren circulated with trays of champagne and hors d'oeuvres. The atmosphere was
that of a cast party on the set of *Casablanca*. Jarring the illusion was Wayne Newton's body double slumped on the bench of the baby grand, his pinky ring winking against the keys. I didn't think he was playing; a haphazard pyramid of shot
glasses teetered near his leg and he looked more or less dead.

Guests milled, mixing gleeful ennui with bad martinis. Many were suffi-
ciently drunk to sand down the veneer of civility and start getting nasty. Jacob
presided, half seas over, as the Cockney used to say, lolling before his subjects
and sycophants in Byzantine splendor. I thought, *Good god, he's wearing a cape!* His
attire was a silken clash of maroon and mustard, complete with ruffles, a V-neck
shirt ripped from the back of a Portuguese corsair, billowing pantaloons, and
wooden sandals that hooked at the toe. A white and gold cape spread beneath
his bulk, and he fanned himself with a tricorner hat. Fortunately, he wasn't wearing the hat.

Carol glided off to mingle, stranding me without a backward glance. I tried
not to take it personally. If not for a misfortune of birth, this could have been
her tribe.

Meanwhile, I spotted the poster-sized photograph upon its easel, fixed in the
center of the parlor. Heavy as a black hole, the photograph dragged me forward
on wires. Shot on black and white, it detailed a slab of rock, which I assumed was
subterranean. Lacking a broader frame of reference, it was impossible to know.
The finer aspects of geology escaped me, but I was fascinated by the surreal
quality of this glazed wall, its calcified ridges, webbed spirals and bubbles.
The inkblot at its heart was humanoid, head twisted to regard the viewer. The
ambient light had created a blur not unlike a halo, or horns, depending on

the angle. This apish thing possessed a broad mouth slackened as an unequal ellipse. A horrible silhouette; lumpy, misshapen, and dead for epochs. Hopefully dead. Other pockets of half-realized darkness orbited the formation; fragments splintered from the core. More cavemen, devils, or dragons.

Hosts occurred to me.

A chunky kid in a turtleneck said it actually resembled a monstrous jellyfish snared in flowstone, but was undoubtedly simple discoloration. Certainly not any figure – human or otherwise. He asked Jacob his opinion. Jacob squinted and declared he saw only the warp and woof of amber shaved bare and burned by a pop flash. Supposedly another guest had witnessed an image of Jesus on Golgotha. This might have been a joke; Jacob had demolished the contents of his late uncle's liquor cabinet and was acting surly.

I seldom drank at Jacob's cocktail socials, preferring to undertake such solemn duty in the privacy of my home. But I made a Christmas exception, and I paid. Tumblers began clicking in my head. A queasy jolt nearly loosened my grip on my drink, bringing sharper focus to the photograph and its spectral face in stone. The crowd shrank, shivered as dying leaves, became pictographs carved into a smoky cave wall.

A dung fire sputtered against the encroaching well of night, and farther along the cave wall, scored with its Paleolithic characters, a cleft sank into the humid earth. Flies buzzed, roaches scuttled. A reed pipe wheedled an almost familiar tune –

My gorge tasted alkaline; my knees buckled.

This moment of dislocation expanded and burst, revealing the parlor still full of low lamplight and cigarette smog, its mob of sullen revelers intact. Jacob sprawled on his leather sofa, regarding me. His expression instantly subsided into a mask of flabby diffidence. It happened so smoothly and I was so shaken I let it go. Carol didn't notice; she was curled up by the fireplace laughing too loudly with a guy in a Norwegian sweater. The roses in their cheeks were brick-red and the sweater guy kept slopping liquor on the rug when he gestured.

Jacob waved. "You look shitty, Marvin. Come on, I've got medicine in the study."

"And you look like the Sun King."

He laughed. "Seriously, there's some grass left. Or some vicodin, if you prefer."

No way I was going to risk Jacob's weed if it had in any way influenced his fashion sense. On the other hand, vicodin sounded too good to be true. "Thanks. My bones are giving me hell." The dull ache in my spine had sharpened to a railroad spike as it always did during the rainy season. After we had retreated to the library and poured fresh drinks, I leaned against a bookcase to support my back. "What's it called?"

He sloshed whiskey over yellow teeth. "*Parallax Alpha*. Part one of a trio enti-
tled the *Imago Sequence* – if I could lay my hands on *Parallax Beta* and *Imago*, I'd
throw a *real* party." His voice reverberated in the rich, slurred tones of a professional speaker who'd shrugged off the worst body blows a bottle of malt scotch
could offer.

"There are two others!"

"You like."

"Nope, I'm repulsed." I had gathered my nerves into one jangling bundle;
sufficient to emote a semblance of calm.

"Yet fascinated." His left eyelid drooped in a wink. "Me too. I'd kill to see the
rest. Each is a sister of this piece – subtle perspective variances, different fields
of depth, but quite approximate."

"Who's got them – anybody I know?"

"*Parallax Beta* is on loan to a San Francisco gallery by the munificence of a collector named Anselm Thornton. A trust fund brat turned recluse. It's presumed
he has *Imago*. Nobody is sure about that one, though. We'll get back to it in a
minute."

"Jake – what do you see in that photo?"

"I'm not sure. A tech acquaintance of mine at UW analyzed it. 'Inconclusive,'
she said. *Something's* there."

"Spill the tale."

"Heard of Maurice Ammon?"

I shook my head.

"He's obscure. The fellow was a photographer attached to the Royal University of London back in the '40s and '50s. He served as chief shutterbug for pis-
sant expeditions in the West Indies and Africa. Competent work, though not
Sotheby material. The old boy was a craftsman. He didn't pretend to be an artist."

"Except for the *Imago* series."

"Bingo. *Parallax Alpha*, for example, transcends journeyman photography,
which is why Uncle Teddy was so, dare I say, obsessed." Jacob chortled, pressed
the glass to his cheek. His giant, red-rimmed eye leered at me. "Cecil Eaton was
the first to recognize what Ammon had accomplished. Eaton was a Texas oil
baron and devoted chum of Ammon's. Like a few others, he suspected the photos were of a hominid. He purchased the series in '55. Apparently, misfortune
befell him and his estate was auctioned. Since then the series has changed hands
several times and gotten scattered from Hades to breakfast. Teddy located this
piece last year at an exhibit in Seattle. The owner got committed to Grable and
the family was eager to sell. Teddy caught it on the hop."

"Define obsession for me." I must've sounded hurt, being kept in the dark about one of Teddy's eccentric passions, of which he'd possessed legion, because Jacob looked slightly abashed.

"Sorry, Marvo. It wasn't a big deal – I never thought it was important, anyway. But ...Teddy was on the hunt since 1987. He blew maybe a quarter mill traveling around following rumors and whatnot. The pieces moved way too often. He said it was like trying to grab water."

"Anybody ever try to buy the whole enchilada?"

"The series has been fragmented since Ammon originally sold two to Eaton and kept the last for himself – incidentally, no one knows much about the final photograph, Imago. Ammon never showed it around and it didn't turn up in his effects."

"Where'd they come from?"

"There's the weird part. Ammon kept the photos' origin a secret. He refused to say where he took them, or what they represented."

"Okay. Maybe he was pumping up interest by working the element of mystery." I'd watched enough artists in action to harbor my share of cynicism.

Jacob let it go. "Our man Maurice was an odd duck. Consorted with shady folks, had peculiar habits. There's no telling where his mind was."

"Peculiar habits? Do tell."

"I don't know the details. He was smitten with primitive culture, especially obscure primitive religions – and most especially the holy pharmaceuticals that accompany certain rites." He feigned taking a deep drag from a nonexistent pipe.

"Sounds like a funky dude. He lived happily ever after?"

"Alas, he died in a plane crash in '57. Well, his plane disappeared over Nairobi. Same difference. Bigwigs from the University examined his journals, but the journals didn't shed any light." Jacob knocked back his drink and lowered his voice for dramatic effect. "Indeed, some of those scholars hinted that the journals were extremely cryptic. Gave them the willies, as the campfire tales go. I gather Ammon was doubtful of humanity's long-term survival; didn't believe we were equipped to adapt with technological and sociological changes looming on the horizon. He admired reptiles and insects – had a real fixation on them.

"The series went into private-collector limbo before it was subjected to much scrutiny. Experts debunked the hominid notion. Ammon's contemporaries suggested he was a misanthropic kook, that he created the illusion to perpetrate an intricate hoax."

Something in the way Jacob said this last part caused my ears to prick up. "The experts only satisfy four out of five customers," I said.

He studied his drink, smiled his dark smile. "Doubtless. However, several reputable anthropologists gave credence to its possible authenticity. They maintained official silence for fear of being ostracized by their peers, of being labeled crackpots. But if someone proved them correct...."

"The photos' value would soar. Their owner would be a celebrity, too, I suppose." Finally, Jacob's motives crystallized.

"Good god, yes! Imagine the scavenger hunt. Every swinging dick with a passport and a shovel would descend upon all the remote sites where Ammon ever set foot. And let me say, he got around."

I sat back, calculating the angles through a thickening alcoholic haze. "Are the anthropologists alive; the guys who bought this theory?"

"I can beat that. Ammon kept an assistant, an American grad student. After Ammon died, the student faded into the woodwork. Guess who it turns out to be? – The hermit art collector in California. Anselm Thornton ditched the graduate program, jumped the counterculture wave in Cali – drove his upper-crust, Dixie-loving family nuts, too. If anybody knows the truth about the series, I'm betting it's him."

"Thornton's a southern gentleman."

"He's of southern stock, anyhow. Texas Panhandle. His daddy was a cattle rancher."

"Longhorns?"

"Charbray."

"Ooh, classy." I crunched ice to distract myself from mounting tension in my back. "Think papa Thornton was thick with that Eaton guy? An oil baron and a cattle baron – real live American royalty. The wildcatter, a pal to the mysterious British photographer; the Duke, with a son as the photographer's protégé. Next we'll discover they're all Masons conspiring to hide the missing link. They aren't Masons, are they?"

"Money loves money. Maybe it's relevant, maybe not. The relevant thing is Thornton Jr. may have information I desire."

I didn't need to ask where he had gathered this data. Chuck Shepherd was the Wilson clan's pet investigator. He worked from an office in Seattle. Sober as a mortician, meticulous and smooth on the phone. I said, "Hermits aren't chatty folk."

"Enter Marvin Cortez, my favorite ambassador." Jacob leaned close enough to club me with his whiskey breath and squeezed my shoulder. "Two things. I want the location of this hominid, if there is a hominid. There probably isn't, but you know what I mean. Then, figure out if Thornton is connected to...the business with my uncle."

I raised my brows. "Does Shep think so?"

"I don't know what Shep thinks. I do know Teddy contacted Thornton. They briefly corresponded. A few weeks later, Teddy's gone."

"Damn, Jake, that's a stretch – never mind. How'd they make contact?"

Jacob shrugged. "Teddy mentioned it in passing. I wasn't taking notes."

"Ever call Thornton yourself, do any follow-up?"

"We searched Teddy's papers, pulled his phone records. No number for Thornton, no physical address, except for this card – the Weston Gallery, which is the one that has *Parallax Beta*. The director blew me off – some chump named Renfro. Sounded like a nut job, actually. I wrote Thornton a letter around Thanksgiving, sent it care of the gallery. He hasn't replied. I wanted the police to shake a few answers out of the gallery, but they gave me the runaround. Case closed, let's get some doughnuts, boys!"

"Turn Shep loose. A pro like him will do this a lot faster."

"Faster? I don't give a damn about faster. I want answers. The kind of answers you get by asking questions with a lead pipe. That isn't up Shep's alley."

I envisioned the investigator's soft, pink hands. Banker's hands. My own were broad and heavy, and hard as marble. Butcher's hands.

Jacob said, "I'll cover expenses. And that issue with King...."

"It'll dry up and blow away?" Rudolph King was a contractor on the West Side; he moonlighted as a loan shark, ran a pool hall and several neat little rackets from the local hippie college. I occasionally collected for him. A job went sour; he reneged on our arrangement, so I shut his fingers in a filing cabinet – a bit rough, but there were proprietary interests at stake. Jacob crossed certain palms with silver, saved me from making a return appearance at Walla Walla. Previously, I did nine months there on a vehicular assault charge for running over a wise-mouth pimp named Leon Berens. Berens had been muscling in on the wrong territory – a deputy sheriff's, in fact, which was the main reason I only did a short hitch. The kicker was, after he recovered, Berens landed the head bartender gig at the Happy Tiger, a prestigious lounge in the basement of the Sheraton. He was ecstatic because the Happy Tiger was in a prime spot three blocks from the Capitol Dome. Hustling a string of five hundred-dollar-a-night-call-girls for the stuffed shirts was definitely a vertical career move. He fixed me up with dinner and drinks whenever I wandered in.

"Poof."

Silence stretched between us. Jacob pretended to stare at his glass and I pretended to consider his proposal. We knew there was no escape clause in our contract. I owed him and the marker was on the table. I said, "I'll make some calls, see if I can track him down. You still want me to visit him...well, we'll talk again. All right?"

"Thanks, Marvin."

"Also, I want to look at Teddy's papers myself. I'll swing by in a day or two."

"No problem."

We ambled back to the party. A five-piece band from the Capitol Theatre was gearing up for a set. I went to locate more scotch. When I returned, Jacob was surrounded by a school of liberal arts piranhas, the lot of them swimming in a pool of smoke from clove cigarettes.

I melted into the scenery and spent three hours nursing a bottle of mineral water, avoiding eye contact with anyone who looked ready for conversation. I tried not to sneak too many glances at the photograph. No need to have worried on that score; by then, everyone else had lost complete interest.

Around midnight Carol keeled over beside the artificial tree. The guy in the Norwegian sweater moved on to a blonde in a shiny dress. I packed Carol in the car and drove home, grateful to escape another Jacob Wilson Christmas party without rearranging somebody's face.

2.

Nobody knew if Theodore Wilson was dead, it was simply the safe way to bet. One knife-bright October morning the Coast Guard had received a truncated distress signal from his yacht, *Pandora*, north of the San Juans. He'd been on a day trip to his lover's island home. Divers combed the area for two weeks before calling it quits. They found no wreckage, no body. The odds of a man surviving more than forty minutes in that frigid water were minimal, however. Teddy never slowed down to raise a family, so Jacob inherited a thirteen-million-dollar estate for Christmas. It should've been a nice present for me as well – I'd been Jake's asshole buddy since our time at State.

College with Jacob had been movie-of-the-week material – the blue-collar superjock meets the royal wastrel. Me on a full wrestling scholarship and Jacob starring as the fat rich boy who had discovered superior financial status did not always garner what he craved most – adulation. Thick as ticks, we shared a dorm, went on road trips to Vegas, spent holidays at the Wilson House. Eventually he convinced his globetrotting uncle to support my Olympic bid. It was a hard sell – the elder Wilson had no use for contemporary athletic competition. Descended from nineteenth-century New England gentry, he favored the refined pursuits of amateur archeology, ancient philology, and sailing – but young Jacob was glib and the deal was made. Never mind that I was a second-rate talent blown up on steroids and hype, or that two of my collegiate titles were fixed by thick-jowled Irishmen who drank boilermakers for breakfast and insisted wrestling was a pansy sport.

Teddy dropped me more than ten years ago. He lost a bucket of cash and a serious amount of face among his peers when I tanked in '90 before the Olympic Trials. The Ukrainian super heavyweight champion broke my back in two places during an exhibition match. Sounded like an elephant stepping on a stick of wet kindling.

Bye, bye, macho, patriotic career. Hello physician-prescribed dope, self-prescribed booze, and a lifetime of migraines that would poleax a mule.

Really, it was a goddamned relief.

I got familiar with body casts, neck braces, and pity. Lately, the bitter dregs of a savings account kept a roof over my head and steak in my belly. A piecemeal contract to unload trucks for a couple Thurston County museums satisfied a minor art fetish. Mama had majored in sculpture, got me hooked as a lad. Collecting debts for the local "moneylenders" was mainly a hobby – just like dear old Pop before somebody capped him at a dogfight. I was a real Renaissance man.

I met Carol while I was politely leaning on her then-boyfriend, a BMW salesman with a taste for long-shot ponies and hard luck basketball teams. Carol worked as a data specialist for the department of corrections. She found the whole failed-athlete turned arm-breaker routine erotic. What should've been a weekend fling developed into a bad habit that I hadn't decided the best way to quit.

The day after the party I asked her what she thought of Jacob's photograph. She was stepping out of the shower, dripping hair wrapped in a towel. "What photograph?" she asked.

I stared at her.

She didn't smile, too busy searching for her earrings. Probably as hungover as I was. "Oh, that piece of crap his uncle bought off that crazy bitch in Seattle. I didn't like it. Piece of crap. Where are my goddamned earrings."

"Did you even look at it?"

"Sure."

"Notice anything unusual?"

"It was unusually crappy. Here we go." She retrieved her earrings from the carpet near her discarded stockings. "Why, he try to sell it to you? For god's sake, don't buy the ugly thing. It's crap."

"Not likely. Jacob wants me to do a little research."

Carol applied her lipstick with expert slashes, eyed me in her vanity while she worked. "Research, huh?"

"Research, baby," I said.

"Don't do anything too stupid." She shrugged on her coat, grabbed an umbrella. It was pouring out there.

"Yeah," I said.

"Yeah, right. And don't buy that crappy photo." She pecked my cheek, left me sneezing in a cloud of perfume and hairspray.

New Year's Eve sneaked up on me. I stopped dragging my feet and made calls to friends of friends in the Bay Area, hoping to get a line on the enigmatic Mr. Thornton. No dice. However, the name triggered interesting matches on the Internet. According to his former associates, a couple of whom were wards of the federal penal system, Thornton had been a flower child; an advocate of free love, free wine, and free thinking. Yeah, yeah, yeah.

Shep's intelligence was more thorough. After quitting grad school Thornton organized a commune in San Francisco in the '60s, penned psychedelic tracts about the nature of faith and divine cosmology, appeared on local talk radio and did cameos in film documentaries. He'd also gotten himself charged with kidnapping and contributing to the delinquency of minors. Disgruntled parents accused him of operating a cult and brainwashing runaway teens. Nothing stuck. His house burned down in '74 and the commune disbanded, or migrated; reports were fuzzy.

Thornton resurfaced in 1981 to purchase *Parallax Beta* at an estate sale in Manitoba. Its owner, a furrier named Robespierre, had come to an unfortunate fate – Robespierre got raving drunk at a party, roared off in his brand-new Italian sports car and plunged into a ravine. Authorities located the smashed guardrail, but no further trace of the car or its drunken occupant.

Thornton's relatives were either dead or had disowned him. There was a loyal cousin in Cleveland, but the lady suffered from Alzheimer's, thus tracking him through family was a no-go. Shep confirmed getting stonewalled by the Weston Gallery. Ah, a dead end; my work here was done.

Except, it wasn't.

It began as the traditional New Year's routine. I drank and contemplated my navel about a wasted youth. I drank and contemplated the gutted carcass of my prospects. I drank and contemplated what *Parallax Alpha* was doing to my peace of mind.

Initially, I wrote it off as interest due on multiple fractures and damaged nerves. My lower back went into spasms; pain banged its Viking drum. I chased a bunch of pills with a bunch more eighty-proof and hallucinated. With sleep came ferocious nightmares that left welts under my eyes. *Dinosaurs trumpeting, roaches clattering across the hulks of crumbling skyscrapers. Dead stars in a dead sky. Skull-yellow planets caught in amber – a vast, twinkling necklace of dried knuckles. The beast in the photograph opening its mouth to batten on my face.* I was getting this nightmare, and ones like it, with increasing frequency.

I wasn't superstitious. Okay, the series had a bizarre history that got stranger the deeper I dug; bad things dogged its owners – early graves, retirement to asylums, disappearances. And yeah, the one picture I had viewed gave me a creepy vibe. But I wasn't buying into any sort of paranormal explanation. I didn't believe in curses. I believed in alcoholism, drug addiction, and paranoid delusion. Put them in a shaker and you were bound to lose your marbles now and again.

Then one evening, while sifting Teddy's personal effects – going through the motions to get Jacob off my back – I found a dented ammo box. The box was stuffed with three decades' worth of photographs, although the majority were wartime shots.

Whenever he had a few drinks under his belt, Jacob was pleased to expound upon the grittier side of his favorite uncle. Jolly Saint Teddy had not always been a simple playboy multimillionaire. Oh, no, Teddy served in Vietnam as an intelligence officer; spooks, the boys called them. Predictable as taxes, really – he'd recently graduated from Dartmouth and there was a war on. A police action, if you wanted to get picky, but everybody knew what it was.

The snapshots were mainly of field hijinks with the troops and a few of Saigon R&R exploits. From what I could discern, when they were in the rear areas, all the intelligence guys dressed like Hollywood celebrities auditioning for a game show – tinted shooting glasses, Hawaiian shirts, frosty Coke bottles with teeny umbrellas at hand, a girl on each arm; the whole bit. Amusing, in a morbid sense. One of the field shots caught my attention and held it. It was not amusing in any sense.

The faded caption read, *Mekong D. 1967.* A platoon of marines decked out in full combat gear, mouths grinning in olive-black faces. Behind them were two men dressed in civilian clothes. I had no problem recognizing Anselm Thornton from Shep's portfolio, which included newspaper clippings, class albums from Texas A&M, and a jittery videotaped chronicle of the beatniks. Thornton's image was fuzzy – a pith helmet obscured his eyes, and a bulky, complicated camera was slung over one shoulder; sweat stains made half-moons under his armpits. Had he been with the press corps? No, the records didn't lie. During Nam, Thornton had been dropping LSD and poaching chicks outside of Candlestick Park.

Teddy, the old, exquisitely corpulent Teddy I knew, stood near him, incomprehensibly juxtaposed with these child-warriors. He wore a double-breasted suit a South American tailor had made recently. The suit restrained a once powerful frame sliding to blubber. Below a prominent brow, his face shone a mottled ivory; his eyes were sockets. His mouth gaped happily, smoldering with dust and cobwebs. A structure loomed beyond the marines. Screened by foliage, a battered marquee took shape. The marquee spelled AL D IN. The building was canted at an alarming angle; greasy smoke mushroomed from the roof.

That gave me pause. The Aladdin used to be Teddy's residence of choice when he visited Vegas. It was in a back room of that sacred hotel he once shook hands with his hero, the inestimable Dean Martin – who, in his opinion, was the better half of the Lewis & Martin act – during a high-stakes poker game reserved for the crème de la crème of big-shot gamblers. Teddy didn't qualify as a whale, as they referred to those suckers who routinely lost half a mil in one night, but he dropped his share of iron at the tables, and he always did have a knack for being at the heart of the action. I squinted at that photo until my eyes crossed – it was the Aladdin, no question. Yet an Aladdin even Teddy might not have recognized. Gray smudges in the windows were faces gazing down upon the razed jungle. Many of them were laughing or screaming.

I couldn't figure out what the hell I was seeing. I pawed through the box by the light of a Tiffany lamp while a strong winter rain bashed at the windows. More of the same; nearly three hundred pictures, all out of kilter, many in ways I never did quite understand. The latest seemed to contain medical imagery – some kind of surgery in progress. Overexposed, they formed a ruddy patina that was maddeningly obscure: Teddy's face streaked with blood as someone stitched his scalp in near darkness; coils of achromatic motion and pale hands with thick, dirty nails; a close-up of a wound, or a flower's corona; white, pink and black. It was impossible to identify the action.

I stopped looking after that, hedged around the issue with Jacob, asked him in an oblique way if his uncle might've known Thornton, during the halcyon days. Jacob was skeptical; he was certain such a fact would've come to light during Teddy's quest for the Imago Sequence. I didn't tell him about the ammo box; at that point it seemed wiser to keep my mouth shut. Either I was losing my sanity, or something else was happening. Regardless, the pattern around Jacob's inherited art piece was woven much tighter than I had suspected. The whole mess stank and I could only speculate how ripe it would become.

3.

Drove to Bellevue for an interview with Mrs. Florence Monson Chin, previous owner of Parallax Alpha. Her family had placed her in Grable, the best that money, a heap of money, could buy. Intimates referred to it as the Grable Hotel or Club Grable. These days, her presence there was an open secret thanks to the insatiable press. No matter; the hospital had a closed-doors policy and an iron fist in dealing with staff members who might choose to blab. Any news was old news.

Mrs. Chin was heiress to the estate of a naturalized Chinese businessman who'd made his fortune breeding rhesus monkeys for medical research. His associates called him the Monkey King. After her elderly husband passed on,

Mrs. Chin resumed her debutante ways, club-hopping from Seattle to the French Riviera, screwing bullfighters, boxers, and a couple foreign dignitaries, snorting coke and buying abstract art – the more abstract, the more exquisitely provincial, the better. The folks at Art News didn't take her seriously as a collector, but it seemed a black AmEx card and a mean streak opened plenty of doors. She partied on the wild and wooly side of high society right up until she flipped her wig and got clapped in the funny farm.

I knew this because it was in all the tabloids. What I didn't know was if she would talk to me. Jacob made nice with her father, got me a direct line to her at the institution. She preferred to meet in person, but gave no indication she was particularly interested in discussing Parallax Alpha. She didn't sound too whacko on the phone, thank god.

Grable loomed at the terminus of a long gravel lane. Massive and Victorian, the institution had been freshly updated in tones of green and brown. The grounds were hemmed by a fieldstone wall and a spiral maze of orchards, parks, and vacant farmland. I'd picked a poor time of year to visit; everything was dead and moldering.

The staff oozed courtesy; it catered to a universally wealthy and powerful clientele. I might've looked like a schlep; nonetheless, far safer to kiss each and every ass that walked through the door. An androgynous receptionist processed my information, loaned me a visitor's tag and an escort named Hugo. Hugo deposited me in a cozy antechamber decorated with matching wicker chairs, an antique vase, prints of Mount Rainier and Puget Sound, and a worn Persian rug. The prints were remarkably cheap and crappy, in my humble opinion. Although I was far from an art critic. I favored statues over paintings any day. I twiddled my thumbs and pondered how the miracle of electroshock therapy had been replaced by cable television and self-help manuals. The wicker chair put a crick in my neck, so I paced.

Mrs. Chin sauntered in, dressed in a superfluous baby-blue sports bra with matching headband and chromatic spandex pants. Her face gleamed, stiff as a native death mask; her rangy frame reminded me of an adolescent mummy without the wrapper. I read in Us that she turned forty-five in the spring; her orange skin was speckled with plum-dark liver spots that formed clusters and constellations. She tested the air with predatory tongue-flicks. "Mr. Cortez, you are the most magnificently ugly man I have seen since Papa had our gardener deported to Argentina. Let me tell you what a shame that was."

"Hey, the light isn't doing you any favors either, lady," I said.

She went into her suite, left the door ajar. "Tea?" She rummaged through kitchen drawers. A faucet gurgled and then a microwave hummed.

"No thanks." I glanced around. It was similar to the antechamber, except

more furniture and artwork – she liked O'Keeffe and Bosch. There were numerous oil paintings I didn't recognize; anonymous nature photographs, a Mayan
calendar, and a smattering of southwestern pottery. She had a nice view of the
grounds. Joggers trundled cobble paths; a peacock fan of pastel umbrellas cluttered the commons. The place definitely appeared more an English country club
than a hospital. "Great digs, Mrs. Chin. I'm surprised they let you committed
types handle sharp objects." I stood near a mahogany rolltop and played with a
curved ceremonial knife that doubled as a paperweight.

"I'm rich. I do whatever I want." She returned with cups and a Tupperware
dish of steaming water. "This isn't a prison, you know. Sit."

I sat across from her at a small table with a centerpiece of wilted geraniums
and a fruit bowl containing a single overripe pear. A fat bluebottle fly crept about
the weeping flesh of the pear.

Mrs. Chin crumbled green tea into china cups, added hot water, then honey
from a stick with an expert motion, and leaned back without touching hers.
"Hemorrhoids, Mr. Cortez?"

"Excuse me?"

"You look uncomfortable."

"Uh, back trouble. Aches and pains galore from a misspent youth."

"Try shark cartilage. It's all the rage. I have a taste every day."

"Nummy. I'll pass. New Age health regimens don't grab me."

"Sharks grow new teeth," Mrs. Chin said. "Replacements. Teeth are a problem for humans – dentistry helps, but if an otherwise healthy man has them
all removed, say because of thin enamel, he loses a decade, perhaps more. The
jaw shortens, the mouth cavity shrinks, the brain is fooled. A general shutdown
begins to occur. How much happier our lives would be, with the shark's simple
restorative capability." This spooled from her tongue like an infomercial clip.

"Wow." I gave her an indulgent smile, took a cautious sip of tea. "You didn't
slip any in here, did you?"

"No, my stash is far too expensive to waste on the likes of you, Mr. Cortez.
Delightful name – are you a ruthless, modern-day conqueror? Did you come to
ravish my secrets from me?"

"I'm a self-serving sonofabitch, if that counts for anything. I don't even speak
Spanish. English will get you by in most places, and that's good enough for me.
What secrets?"

"I'm a sex addict."

"Now that's not exactly a secret, is it?" It wasn't. Her exploits were legendary
among the worldwide underground, as I had learned. She was fortunate to be
alive. "How do they treat that, anyway?"

"Pills, buckets of pills. Diversion therapy. They replace negative things with

positive things. They watch me – there are cameras everywhere in this building. Does the treatment work?" Here she winked theatrically. "I am permitted to
exercise whenever I please. I love to exercise – endorphins keep me going."

"Sad stuff. Tell me about *Parallax Alpha*." I produced a notebook, uncapped
a pen.

"Are you so confident that I will?" she said, amused.

"You're a lonely woman, I've a sympathetic ear. Consider it free counseling."

"Pretty. Very pretty. Papa had to sell a few of my things, balance the books.
Did you acquire the photograph?"

"A friend of mine. He wants me to find out more about it."

"You should tell your friend to go to hell."

"Really."

"Really." She picked up the pear, brushed the fly off, took a large bite. Juice
glistened in her teeth, dripped from her chin. She dabbed it with a napkin. Very
ladylike. "You don't have money, Mr. Cortez."

"I'm a pauper, it is true."

"Your friend has many uses for a man like you, I'm sure. Well, the history of
the *Imago Sequence* is chock full of awful things befalling rich people. Does that
interest you?"

"I'm not overly fond of the upper class. This is a favor."

"A big favor." Mrs. Chin took another huge bite, to accent the point. The lump
traveled slowly down her throat – a pig disappearing into an anaconda. "I purchased *Parallax Alpha* on a lark at a seedy auction house in Mexico City. That was
years ago; my husband was on his last legs – emphysema. The cigarette companies are making a killing in China. I was bored; a worldly stranger invited me to
tour the galleries, take in a party. I didn't speak Spanish either, but my date knew
the brokers, landed me a fair deal. The joke was on me, of course. My escort was
a man named Anselm Thornton. Later, I learned of his connection to the series.
You are aware that he owns the other two in the collection?"

"I am."

"They're bait. That's why he loans them to galleries, encourages people with
lots of friends to buy them and put them on display."

"Bait?"

"Yes, bait. The photographs radiate a certain allure; they draw people like
flies. He's always hunting for the sweetmeats." She chuckled ruefully. "I was
sweet, but not quite sweet enough to end up in the fold. *Alpha* was mine, though.
Not much later, I viewed *Beta*. By then the reaction, whatever it was, had started
inside me, was consuming me, altering me in ways I could scarcely dream. I
craved more. God, how I begged to see *Imago*! Anselm laughed – laughed, Mr.
Cortez. He laughed and said that it was too early in the game for me to rein-

tegrate. He also told me there's no Imago. No Imago, no El Dorado, no Santa Claus." Her eyes were hard and yellow. "The bastard was lying, though. Imago exists, perhaps not as a photograph. But it exists."

"Reintegrate with what, Mrs. Chin?"

"He wouldn't elaborate. He said, 'We are born, we absorb, we are absorbed. Therein lies the function of all sentient beings.' It's a mantra of his. Anselm held that thought doesn't originate in the mind. Our brains are rather like meaty receivers. Isn't that a wild concept? Humans as nothing more than complicated sensors, or mayhap walking sponges. Such is the path to ultimate, libertine anarchy. And one might as well live it up, because there is no escape from the cycle, no circumvention of the ultimate, messy conclusion; in fact, it's already happened a trillion times over. The glacier is coming and no power will hold it in abeyance."

I didn't bother writing any of that down; I was plenty spooked before she came across with that booby-hatch monologue. I said, "It sounds like extremely convenient rationale for psychopathic behavior. He dumped you after your romp?"

"Frankly, I'm a lucky girl. Anselm deemed me more useful at large, spreading his influence. I brought Parallax Alpha stateside – that was the bargain, my part in the grand drama. Life went on."

"You got together in Mexico?"

"Yes. The resort threw a ball, a singles event, and Roy Fulcher made the introductions. Fulcher was a radical, a former chemist – Caltech, I believe. Struck me as a naturalist gone feral. A little bird informed me the CIA had him under surveillance – he seemed primed to blow something up, maybe spike a city reservoir. At the outset I suspected Fulcher was approaching me about funding for some leftist cause. People warned me about him. Not that I needed their advice. I had oodles of card-carrying revolutionaries buzzing in my hair at the time. Soon, I absolutely abhorred the notion of traveling in Latin America. Fuck the guerillas, fuck the republic, I just want a margarita. Fulcher wasn't after cash, though. He was Anselm's closest friend. A disciple."

"Disciple, gotcha." I scribbled it in my trusty notebook. "What's Thornton call his philosophy? Cultist Christianity? Rogue Buddhism? Crystal worship? What's he into?"

She smiled, stretched, and tossed the remains of her fruit in a waste basket shaped like an elephant foot. "Anselm's into pleasure. I think it fair to designate him the reigning king of sybarites. I was moderately wicked when I met him. He finished me off. Go mucking about his business and he'll do for you too."

"Right. He's Satan, then. How did he ruin you, Mrs. Chin? Did he hook you on drugs, sex, or both?"

Her smile withered. "Satan may not exist, but Anselm surely does. Drugs were never the issue. I could always take them or leave them, and it's more profound than sex. I speak of a different thing entirely. There exists a quality of corruption you would not be familiar with – not on the level or to the degree that I have seen, have lived." She stopped, studied me. Her yellow eyes brightened. "Or, I'm mistaken. Did you enjoy it? Did you enjoy looking at *Parallax Alpha*? That's the first sign. It's a special person who does; the kind Anselm drools over."

"No, Mrs. Chin. I think it sucks."

"It frightened you. Poor baby. And why not? There are things to be frightened of in that picture. Enlightenment isn't necessarily a clean process. Enlightenment can be filthy, degenerate, dangerous. Enlightenment is its own reward, its own punishment. You begin to see so much more. And so much more sees you."

I said, "I take it this was in the late eighties, when you met Thornton? Rumor has it he's a hermit. Not much of a high-society player. Yet you say he was in Mexico, doing the playboy shtick."

"Even trapdoor spiders emerge from their lairs. Anselm travels in circles that will not publicize his movements."

"How would I go about contacting him? Maybe get things from the horse's mouth."

"We're not in touch. But those who wish to find him...find him. Be certain you wish to find him, Mr. Cortez."

"Okay. What about Fulcher? Do you know where he is?"

"Oh, ick. Creepy fellow. I pretended he didn't exist, I'm afraid."

"Thanks for your time, Mrs. Chin. And the tea." I started to rise.

"No more questions?"

"I'm fresh out, Mrs. Chin."

"Wait, if you please. There's a final item I'd like to show you." She went away and returned with a slim photo album. She pushed it across the table and watched me with a lizard smile to match her lizard eyes. "Can I trust you, Mr. Cortez?"

I shrugged.

She spoke softly. "The staff censors my mail, examines my belongings. There are periodic inspections. Backsliding will not be tolerated. They don't know about these. These are of my vacation in Mexico; a present from Anselm. Fulcher took them from the rafters of the cathedral. Go on, open it."

I did. There weren't many photos and I had to study them closely because each was a section of a larger whole. The cathedral must've been huge; an ancient vault lit by torches and lanterns. Obviously Fulcher had taken pains to get the sequence right – Mrs. Chin instructed me to remove eight of them from the protective plastic, place them in order on the table. An image took root and unfolded. A strange carpet, stained rose and peach, spread across shadowy counterchange tiles, snaked around immense gothic pillars and statuary. The carpet gleamed and blurred in patches, as if it were a living thing.

"That's me right about there," Mrs. Chin tapped the third photo from the top. "Thrilling, to enact the writhing of the Ouroboros!"

"Jesus Christ," I muttered. At least a thousand people coupled upon the cathedral floor. A great, quaking mass of oiled flesh, immortalized by Fulcher's lens. "Why did you show me this?" I looked away from the pictures and caught her smile, cruel as barbed wire. There was my answer. The institution was powerless to eradicate *all* of her pleasures.

"Good-bye, Mr. Cortez. Good-bye, now."

Leaving, I noticed another overripe pear in the fruit bowl, as if Mrs. Chin had replaced it by sleight of hand. A fly sat atop, rubbing its legs together, wearing my image in its prism eyes.

I wasn't feeling well.

I awoke at 2 A.M., slick and trembling, from yet another nightmare. My head roared with blood. I rose, trying to avoid disturbing Carol, who slept with her arm shielding her eyes, my dog-eared copy of *The Prince* clutched in her fingers. I staggered into the kitchen for a handful of aspirin and a glass of cold milk. There was a beer left over from dinner, so I drank that too. It was while standing there, washed in the unearthly radiance of the refrigerator light, that I realized the orgy in Mrs. Chin's photographs had been orchestrated to achieve a specific configuration. The monumental daisy chain made a nearly perfect double helix.

4.

In the middle of January I decided to cruise down to San Francisco and spend a weekend beating the bushes.

I met Jacob for early dinner on the waterfront at an upscale grill called The Marlin. Back in the day, Teddy treated us there when he was being especially avuncular, although he had preferred to hang around the yacht club or fly to Seattle, where his cronies played. Jacob handed me the Weston Gallery's business card and a roll of cash for expenses. We didn't discuss figures for Thornton's successful interrogation. The envelope would be fat and the goodwill of a wealthy, bored man would continue to flow freely. Nor did he question my sudden eagerness to locate the hermit art collector. Still, he must have noticed the damage to my appearance that suggested worse than a simple New Year's bender.

Following dinner, I drove out in the country to a farmhouse near Yelm for tequila and cigars with Earl Hutchinson, a buddy of mine since high school.

He'd been a small, tough kid from Iowa; a so-called bad seed. He looked the part: slicked hair, switchblade in his sock, a cigarette behind his ear, a way of standing that suggested trouble. Hutch hadn't changed, only drank a little more and got harder around the eyes.

We relaxed on the porch; it was a decent night with icy stars sprinkled among the gaps. Hutch was an entrepreneur; while I was away in college he hooked up in the arms trade – he'd served as an artillery specialist in the Army, forged connections within the underbelly of America's war machine. He amassed an impressive stockpile before the anti-assault weapon laws put the kibosh on legal sales; there were dozens of AK-47s, M16s, and Uzis buried in the pasture behind his house. I'd helped him dig.

These days it was guard dogs. He trained shepherds for security, did a comfortable business with local companies. I noticed his kennels were empty except for a brood bitch named Gerta and some pups. Hutch said demand was brisk, what with the rise of terrorism and the sagging economy. Burglaries always spiked during recessions. Eventually the conversation swung around to my California trip. He walked into the house, came out with a .357 and a box of shells. I peeled four hundred bucks from my brand new roll, watched him press the bills into his shirt pocket. Hutch poured more tequila and we finished our cigars, reminiscing about happy times. Lied about shit, mainly.

I went home and packed a suitcase from college, bringing the essentials – winter clothes, pain pills, toiletries. I watered the plants and left a terse message on Carol's answering service. She'd flown to Spokane to visit her mother. She generally found a good reason to bug out for the high country when I got piss-drunk and prowled the apartment like a bear with a toothache.

I told her I'd be gone for a few days, feed the fish. Then I headed south.

The truth is, I volunteered for the California job to see the rest of the *Imago Sequence*. As if viewing the first had not done ample harm. In addition to solving Teddy's vanishing act, I meant to ask Thornton some questions of my own.

I attempted to drive through the night. Tough sledding – my back knotted from hunching behind the wheel. A dose of vicodin had no effect. I needed sleep. Unfortunately, the prospect of dreaming scared the hell out of me.

I drove as long as my nerve held. Not fast, but methodically as a nail sinking into heartwood, popping Yellowjackets and blasting the radio. In the end the pain beat me down. I took a short detour on a dirt road and rented a motel room south of Redding. I tried to catch a couple hours of rest. It was a terrible idea.

Parallax Alpha ate its way into my dreams again.

The motel ceiling jiggled, tapioca pudding with stars revolving in its depths. The blackened figure at *Parallax Alpha*'s center seeped forth. I opened my mouth, but my mouth was already a rictus. The ceiling swallowed me, bones and all.

— I squatted in a cavernous vault, chilled despite the rank, humid darkness pressing my flesh. Stench burrowed into my nose and throat. Maggots, green meat, rotten bone. Thick, sloppy noises, as wet rope smacking rock drew closer. A cow gave birth, an eruption. The calf mewled – blind, terrified. Old, old water dripped. An army of roaches began to march; a battalion of worms plowed into a mountain of offal; the frenetic drone of flies in glass, an embryonic bulk uncoiling in its cyst –

I awakened, muscles twitching in metronome to the shuttering numbers of the radio clock. Since Christmas, my longest stretch of uninterrupted sleep was three hours and change. I almost relished the notion of a grapeshot tumor gestating in my brain as the source of all that was evil. It didn't wash; too easy. So said my puckered balls, the bunched hackles of my neck. Paleontologists, anthropologists, ordained priests, or who-the-hell-ever could debate the authenticity of Ammon's handiwork until the cows came home. My clenched guts and arrhythmic heart harbored no doubt that he had snapped a photo of someone or something truly unpleasant. Worse, I couldn't shake the feeling that Mrs. Chin was correct: it had looked right back at me. It was looking for me now.

I got on the road; left a red fantail of dust hanging.

Midmorning crawled over the Frisco skyline, gin blossom clouds piling upon the bay. I drove to the address on the card, a homely warehouse across from a Mexican restaurant and a mortgage office that had been victimized by graffiti artists, and parked in the alley. Inside the warehouse were glass walls and blue shadows broken by giant ferns.

I lifted a brochure from a kiosk in the foyer; a slick, multicolored pamphlet with headshots of the director and his chief cronies. I slipped it into my blazer pocket and forged ahead. The lady behind the front desk wore a prison-orange jumpsuit. Her hair was pulled back so tightly it forced her to smile when she shook my hand. I asked for Director Stanley Renfro and was informed that Mr. Renfro was on vacation.

Could I please speak to the acting director? She motioned me beyond shadowbox panels to the rear of the gallery where a crew of Hispanic and Vietnamese day laborers sweated to dismantle an installation of a scale city park complete with fiberglass fruit trees, benches, and a working gothic fountain. I picked my way across the mess of tarps, coax, and sawdust. Motes hung in the too-bright wash of stage lights. A Teutonic symphony shrilled counterpoint to arc welders.

Acting director Clarke was a lanky man with a spade-shaped face. A serious whitebread bastard with no interest in fielding questions about Thornton or his photograph. Clarke was sated with the power rush of his new executive position; I sensed I wouldn't be able to slip him a few bills to grease the rails and I'd already decided to save breaking his head as a last resort.

I used charm, opening with a throwaway remark about the genius of Maurice Ammon.

Clarke gave my haggard, sloppy self the once-over. "Ammon was a hack." His eyes slightly crossed and he talked like a man punching typewriter keys. "Topless native women suckling their babies; bone-through-the-nose savages leaning on spears. Tourist swill. His specialty."

"Yeah? Don't tell me the Weston Gallery is in the business of showcasing hacks?"

"We feature only the highest caliber work." Clarke paused to drone pidgin Spanish at one of the laborers. When he looked up at me again his sneer hardened. "I dislike the *Imago Sequence*. But one cannot deny its...resonance. Ammon got lucky. Doesn't overcome a portfolio of mediocrity."

No, he didn't like the series at all. I read that plainly from the brief bulge of his eyes similar to a horse getting a whiff of smoke for the first time. The reaction seemed reasonable. "A three-hit wonder." I tried to sound amiable.

It was wasted. "Are you a cop, Mr. Cortez?"

"What, I look like a cop to you?"

"Most citizens don't have so many busted knuckles. A private eye, then."

"I'm a tourist. Do you think Ammon actually photographed a fossilized caveman?"

"That's absurd. The so-called figures are geological formations. Ask the experts."

"Wish I had nothing else to do with my life. You don't buy it, eh?"

"The hominid theory is titillation." He smirked. "It does sell tickets."

"He got bored with native titties and went for abstract art? Sure looks like a troglodyte to me."

"Well, pardon my saying you don't know squat about photography and I think you're here on bad business. Did the toad send you?"

I chuckled. "You've met Teddy."

"Never had the pleasure. I saw him in September, sniffing around the photo, practically wetting his pants. Figured he was trying to collect the set. I'll tell you exactly what Renfro told him: *Parallax Beta* is not for sale and its owner is not interested in discussing the matter."

"Renfro said that to Teddy, did he? Seems I'm chasing my tail then." He had said what I hoped to hear. "By the way, where did Mr. Renfro go for his vacation? Somewhere warm, I hope."

Clarke's sneer broadened. "He's on sabbatical." From the pleasure in his tone he did not expect his former patron to return.

"Well, thanks for your time."

"Adios, Mr. Cortez. Since you came for a peek at *Parallax Beta*, stop by the Natural History display."

"Blessings to you and your children, Herr Director." I went where he pointed, trying to act casual. The prospect of viewing the second photograph filled me with elation and dread. There it was, hanging between the Grand Tetons and the caldera of slumbering Mt. Saint Helens.

Parallax Beta was the same photograph as *Alpha*, magnified tenfold. The amber background had acquired a coarser quality; its attendant clots and scars were more distinct, yet more distinctly ambiguous. They congealed to form asteroid belts, bell-shaped celestial gases, volcanic moons. The hominid's howling mouth encompassed the majority of the picture. It seemed capable of biting off my head, of blasting my eardrums with its guttural scream.

My vision tunneled and I tore myself away with the convulsive reflex of a man awakened from a dream of falling. *Panpipes, clashing cymbals, strobes of meteoric rain. Dogs snarling, a bleating goat. Buzzing flies, worms snuggling in musty soil.* All faded as I lurched away, routed from the field.

I made it to the lobby and drank from the water fountain, splashing my face until the floor stopped tilting. The lady in the jumpsuit perched behind her desk, vulture-talons poised near the phone. She extended another wintry smile as I retreated from the building into the hard white glare.

Eleven A.M. and next to zero accomplished, which meant I was basically on schedule. I was an amateur kneecap man, not a P.I. My local connections were limited to a bookie, a sports agent who might or might not be under indictment for money laundering, and the owner of a modest chain of gymnasiums. I adjourned to a biker grill called the Hog and downed several weak Bloody Marys with a basket of deep-fried oysters. The lunch crowd consisted of two leathery old-timers sipping draft beer, their Harley Davidson knockoffs parked on the curb; a brutish man in a wife-beater T-shirt at the bar doing his taxes on a short form; and the bartender who had so much pomade in his hair it gleamed like a steel helmet. The geriatric bikers were sniping over the big N.F.C. championship game coming up between the Niners and the Cowboys.

Between drinks, I borrowed the bartender's ratty phonebook. Half the pages were ripped out, but I found a listing for S. Renfro, which improved my mood for about three seconds. I tried ringing him from the pay phone next to the men's room. A recorded message declared that the number was not in service, please try again. Following Hog tradition, I tore out the page and saved it for later.

I called Jacob collect. After he accepted charges, I said, "Were you around Teddy before he disappeared?"

"Eh? We've been over this."

"Be nice, I'm slow."

Several static-laden beats passed. Then, "Um, not so much. Teddy's always been secretive, though."

"Okay, was he *more* or *less* secretive those last few weeks?"

He coughed in a phlegmy way that suggested I had prodded him from the slumber of the indolent rich. "I don't know, Marv. I got used to him sneaking around. What's going on?"

"I haven't figured that out yet. Did his habits change? And I mean even an iota."

"No – wait. He dressed oddly. Yeah. Well, more than usual, if you want to split hairs."

"I'm listening."

"Give me a sec...." Jacob cursed, knocked something off a shelf, cursed again. A metallic snick was followed by a scratchy drag into the receiver. "He wore winter clothes a lot at the end. Inside, too, the few times I saw him. You know – sock cap, mackinaw, and boots. He looked like a Canadian longshoreman. Said he was cold. But, what's that? Teddy dressed for safari half the time. He was eccentric."

"Thin blood. Too many years in the tropics," I said.

"You have anything yet?"

"Nope. I'm just trying to cover all the bases." I wondered if dear, departed Theodore had suffered night sweats, if he had ever lain in bed staring at a maw of darkness that grinned toothless as a sphincter. I wondered if Jacob did.

Jacob said, "You don't think he was mixing with a rough element, right?"

"Probably not. He was going batty, fell into the drink. Stuff like this happens to seniors. They find them wandering around race tracks or shopping malls. Happens every day."

"Keep digging anyway."

"I'll hit you back when I find more. Bye, bye." I broke the connection, rubbed sweat from my cheek. I needed a shave.

The last call was to my bookie friend. I took the Cowboys and the points because I hoped to counter the growing sense of inevitability hanging over my head like Damocles's least favorite pig sticker. Come Sunday night I owed the bookie five hundred bucks.

5.

Stanley Renfro's house drank the late afternoon glow. Far from imposing, as I had half expected; simply one of many brick and timber colonials bunkered in the surrounding hills. It was painted in conservative tones and set back from the street, windows blank. A blue sedan was parked in the drive, splattered with enough seagull shit to make me suspect it hadn't moved lately. Half a dozen rolled newspapers decomposed on the shaggy lawn. The grass was shin-high and climbing.

I did not want to walk up the block and enter that house.

My belly churned with indigestion. A scream had recently interrupted my fitful doze. This scream devolved into the dwindling complaints of a bus horn. Minutes later when the sodium lamps caught fire and Renfro's house remained black, I decided he was dead.

This leap of intuition could not be proved by yellow papers or flourishing weeds. *Nah, the illustrious director might be taking a nap. No need to turn the lights on. Maybe he's not even inside. Maybe he's in Borneo stealing objets d'art from the natives. He left his car because a crony gave him a lift to the airport. He forgot to cancel the newspaper. Somebody else forgot to cut the grass.* Sure. The house reminded me of a corpse that hadn't quite begun to fester. I retrieved a flashlight from the glove compartment. Thick, and made of steel, like cops use. It felt nice in my hand.

I climbed from the Chrysler, leaned against the frame until my neck loosened and I could rotate my head without catching a fireworks show. No one appeared to notice when I hiked through Renfro's yard, although a small dog barked nearby. The alarm system was cake – since it was predicated on pressure, all I needed to do was smash a kitchen window and climb through without disturbing the frame. This turned out to be unnecessary. The power was down and the alarm's emergency battery had died.

The kitchen smelled foul despite its antiseptic appearance. Street light spread my shadow into monstrous proportions. Water drooled around the base of the refrigerator. Distant traffic vibrated china in its cabinet. Everything reeked of mildew and decaying fruit.

I clicked on the flashlight as I proceeded deeper into the house. The ceilings were low. I determined within a few steps that the man was a bachelor. That relieved me. Beyond the kitchen, a narrow hall of dusky paneling absorbed my light beam. The décor was not extraordinary considering it belonged to the director of an art gallery – obscure oil paintings, antique vases, and ceramic sculptures. Undoubtedly the truly expensive bric-a-brac was stashed in a safe or strong room. I didn't care about that; I was hunting for a name, a name certain to be scribbled in Renfro's personal files.

The shipwrecked living room was a blow to my composure. However, even before I entered that demolished area, my wind was up. I felt as a man tiptoeing through a diorama blown to life size. As if the outer reaches of the house were a façade that had not quite encompassed the yard.

Mr. Renfro had been on a working vacation, by the evidence. Mounds of wet dirt were heaped around a crater. Uprooted boards lay in haphazard stacks. Sawed joists gleamed like exposed ribs. The pit was deep and ugly – a cavity. I turned away and released a sluice of vodka, tomato juice, and oyster chunks. Purged, I felt better than I had in days.

I skirted the destruction, mounted the stairs to the second floor. Naked footprints scarred the carpet, merging into a muddy path – the trail a beast might pound with its blundering mass. If Renfro made the prints, I figured him for around six feet, two hundred forty. Not quite in my league, but hefty enough that I was happy to grip the sturdy flashlight. A metal bucket was discarded on the landing. Inside the upper bathroom, the clawfoot tub had cracked, overflowing dirt and nails. The sink was shattered. Symbols had been scrawled above the toilet with mud, but the flowery paper hung in shreds. I deciphered the letters MAG and MMON. A cockroach clambered up the wall, fell, started again. Its giant, horned silhouette crossed mine. I didn't linger.

I peeked in the master bedroom to be thorough. It too was victim of hurricane savagery. The bed was stripped, sheets wadded on the floor amid drifts of clothes. A set of designer luggage had barely survived; buckles and zippers sprung, meticulously packed articles disgorged like intestines. I got the distinct impression Renfro had planned a trip before whatever happened, happened.

Renfro had converted the spare bedroom to an office. Here were toppled oak file cabinets, contents strewn and stomped. My prize was a semi-collapsed desk, buried in a landslide of paper. Its sides bore gouges and impact marks. Thankfully Renfro hadn't filled this room with dirt. I searched for his Rolodex amid the chaos, keeping an eye on the door. The house was empty, obviously the house was empty. Renfro wasn't likely to be lurking in a closet. He wasn't likely to come shambling into the office, caked with mud and blood and fondling a hatchet. I still kept an eye on the door.

A drawer contained more file hangers. Inside the R–T folder was an index card with A. THORNTON (*Imago Colony*) written in precise block letters, a Purdon address which was probably a drop box, a list of names that meant nothing to me, and an unmarked cassette tape. Actually the label had been smudged. I stuck the card and the tape in my pocket. On impulse I checked the W's and found a listing for T. WILSON. *Parallax Alpha* was penned in the margin. Below that, in fresher ink – *Provender?*

Mission accomplished, I was eager to saddle up and get the hell out of Tombstone. Then my light illuminated the edge of a wrinkled photograph of Stanford lacrosse players assembled on a field. A dated shot, but I recognized a younger Renfro from the brochure in my pocket. He knelt front and center, sporting a permed Afro and a butterfly collar. His eyes and mouth were holes.

They reminded me of how Teddy's mouth looked in his war pictures. They also reminded me of the pit Renfro had excavated in his living room. Behind the team, where campus buildings should logically be, reared the basalt ridge of a mountain. A flinty spine wreathed by primordial steam.

This was Teddy's photo collection redux. And there were more delights. I considered vomiting again.

I stared for a bit, turning the photo this way and that. Concentration was difficult, because my fingers shook. I sorted the papers again, including the pile on the floor, examining the various photographs and postcards that were salted through the general mess. Some framed, some not. Wallet-sized to the kind Grandma hangs above the mantle. This time I actually *looked* and beheld a pattern that my subconscious had recognized already. Each picture was warped, each was distorted. Each was a fake, a fabrication designed to unnerve the viewer. What other purpose could they serve?

I checked for splice marks, hints of computer grafting, as if my untrained eye could've helped. Nothing to explain the mechanics of the hoax. The terrain was wrong in all of these. Very wrong. The sky was not quite the same sky we walked around under every day. No, the sky in the more peculiar photos appeared somewhat viscous with bubbles and spot discoloration – the sky was a solid. As a matter of fact, it kind of resembled amber. Shapes that might've been blimps hovered at the periphery, pressed against the fabric of the sky.

This was enough spooky bullshit for me. I beat feet.

Downstairs, I hesitated at the pit. I shined my lonely beam into the gloom. It was about twelve feet deep; the sides crumbled and seeped groundwater. A nasty thought had been ticking in my brain. *Where is Renfro? In the hole, of course.*

Which suggested he was hiding – or *lying in wait.* I didn't actually want to find him either way. Thornton's information was in my pocket. Assuming it panned out, there were many hours of driving ahead. But the nasty thought was ticking louder, getting closer. *Why is Renfro digging a hole under his very nice house? Wow, I wonder if it's related to his screwed up picture collection? And, oh, do you think it has anything to do with a certain photograph on loan to his precious gallery? Do you suppose he spent long, long hours in front of that picture, fixated, neglecting his duties until his people sent him on a little vacation? Don't call us, we'll call you.*

There was a lot of debris at the bottom of that hole. A lot of debris and the light was dimming as its batteries gave up the ghost and I couldn't be one hundred percent sure, but I glimpsed an earthen lump down there, right where the darkness thickened. A man-sized lump. At its head was a damp depression in which a small object glinted. When I hit it with the light, it flickered. Blinked, blinked.

★

6.

I wanted to turn around and bolt for home, get back to my beer and cartoons. I headed for Purdon instead. A Mastodon sinking in a tar pit.

Purdon was a failed mill town several hours northeast of San Francisco – victim of the rise of environmentalism in the latter '90s. A mountainous region bracketed by a national park and a reservation. Rural and impoverished as all hell. Plenty of pot plantations, militia compounds, and dead mining camps; all of it crisscrossed with a few thousand miles of logging roads slowly being eaten by forest. An easy place to vanish from the planet.

My mind had been switched off for the last hundred miles.

I switched it off because I was tired of thinking about the events at Renfro's house. Tired of considering the implications. It occurred to me, not for the first time, that I had fallen down the rabbit hole and would awaken at any moment. Unfortunately, I had brought a couple of the suspect photos and they remained steadfastly bizarre. Combined with Teddy's, did this not suggest a supernatural force at work?

Thoughts like that are why I shut my mind off.

Better to stick with problems at hand. Problems such as motoring into the sticks looking for a man I had seen in ancient clippings and a jerky movie frame shot three decades prior. A man who was probably a certifiable lunatic if he had owned the Imago Sequence for so many years. Whether he might know the whereabouts of a petrified hominid, or the truth about the disappearance of a thoroughly modern human, no longer seemed important. The only matter of importance was finding a way to kill the nightmares. And if Thornton couldn't help me? Best not to scrutinize that possibility too closely. I could almost taste the cold, oily barrel of my revolver.

I played Renfro's tape. The recording was damaged – portions were garbled, others were missing entirely, comprised of clicking and deep sea warbles. The intelligible segments featured a male lecturer. " – satiation is the natural inclination. One is likely to spend centuries glutting primitive appetites, wreaking havoc on enemies, and so forth. What then? That depends on the personality. Few would seek the godhead, I think. Such a pursuit would require tremendous imagination, determination...resources. Provender would be an issue. It is difficult to conceive the acquisition of so much ripe flesh. No, the majority will be content with leisurely hedonism – "

The Chrysler groaned as it climbed. Night paled and the rain slackened into gray drizzle. Big hills, big trees, everything dripping and foggy. Signs grew sparse and the road fell apart. I had to pay attention lest my car be hurled into a ravine.

" – consumption of accelerated brainmatter being one proven catalyst. Immersion in a

protyle sink is significantly more efficacious, albeit infinitely more perilous. Best avoided."
Laughter. The recording petered to static.

I reached Purdon in time for church. Instead, I filled my tank at the Union 76 next to the defunct lumber mill, washed and changed clothes in the cramped bathroom. At the liquor store I bought a bottle of cheap whiskey. Here was my indemnity from coming nightmares. Then I ate a huge breakfast at the Hardpan Café. The waitress, who might also have been the proprietor, was a shrewd-eyed Russian. There were a lot of Russian immigrants in the area, I discovered. She didn't care for my looks, but she kept my coffee cup level and her thoughts to herself while I stared out the window and plotted my next move.

Not much to see – narrow streets crowded with warped 1920s salt box houses. FOR LEASE signs plastered dark windows. A few people, mostly hungover men, prowled the sidewalks. Everybody appeared to wear flannel and drive dented pickups. Most of the trucks had full gun racks.

I asked the Russian woman about finding a room and was directed to the Pine Valley Motel, which was less lovely than it sounded – unless you were thinking pine box, and then, yeah, that was more accurate, in an esthetic sense. The motel sprawled in a gravel lot at the edge of town, northernmost wing gutted by a recent fire and draped with rust-stained tarps. Mine was the sole car parked in front.

A stoic senior citizen missing two fingers of his right hand took my money and produced the key. His stained ballcap read: PURDON MILL – AN AMERICAN COMPANY! For fun, I asked if he knew anything about Anselm Thornton or the Imago Colony and received a glassy stare as he honked his nose into a handkerchief.

The walls of No. 32 were balsa-thin and the bed creaked ominously, but I didn't see any cockroaches. I counted myself lucky as I cracked the seal on the whiskey. I made it to within a pinky of the bottom before the curtain dropped.

Ants.

I shared a picnic with a woman who was the composite of several women, all of them attractive, all of them wanton yet motherly, like the new Betty Crocker. She spoke words that held no weight and so fluttered away on the breeze with a vapor trail of pollen. Our feast was laid upon the requisite checkerboard blanket beneath a flowering tree with the grass and the sun and all that. With all that and the chirping birds and the painfully blue sky and the goddamned ants; I didn't notice the ants until the woman held a slice of bread to my lips and as I opened my mouth to accept the bread I saw an ant trapped in the honey. Too late, my mouth closed and I swallowed and I looked down and beheld them everywhere upon the checker cloth, these ants. Formicating. I rose up, a behemoth enraged, and trampled them in shallow puffs of dust. They died in their numbers, complaining in small voices as their works were conculcated – their wagon trains and caravans, their miniature Hippodromes and coliseums, their monuments and toy superstructures, all crashed, all toppled, all ablaze. I threw my head back to bellow curses and noticed the sun had become a pinhole. The hole openedopenedopened –

Open.

I stared at the ceiling and realized that I now slept with my eyes wide and glazed. Marbles, the last of my marbles.

Shadows flowed swiftly along the decrepit wallpaper of No. 32, shrinking from the muzzy glare of the sun as it wallowed behind clouds. The thermostat was set at body temperature and the room steamed. I didn't recall waking to do that. I had slept for eighteen hours. *Eighteen hours!* It was a bloody miracle! I dressed, avoiding the mirror.

There were various stratagems available, a couple of them clever. I wasn't feeling clever, though. In fact, my skull felt like a pot of mush.

I flashed a snapshot of Teddy at the locals, finally got a bite from the mechanic at the gas station. He remembered Teddy from the previous September – *Heavy guy, yeah; drivin' a foreign car, passin' through. North, I suppose, 'cause he asked where Little Egypt was. We get that a lot. Tourists want to fool around the mines. Ain't shit-all left, though. I checked his brakes – these roads are hell on brakes. He paid cash.*

No surprises, the jigsaw was taking its form.

I measured the dwindling girth of my money clip and dealt a portion of it to Rod, the pimply badger of a clerk at the post office. It went down smoothly after I told him I was working for a family who believed their baby girl had joined a cult. Oh, this sweaty, mutton-chopped fellow became a regular Samaritan once the folding green was in his pocket. He came across with the goods – names and descriptions of the people who regularly accessed Thornton's box. He'd never seen Thornton, didn't know much about him and didn't want to. The Imago Colony? Zip. Thornton's group numbered about forty, although who knew? – what with tourist season and the influx of visitors come spring. They occupied mining claims somewhere on Little Egypt; kept to themselves. Mormons, or some shit. Weird folk, but nobody had heard about them causing trouble before. He let me look at a topographical map that showed Little Egypt was, in fact, a sizable chunk of real estate. Thornton's camp could be any one of a dozen claims scattered throughout the area. I slipped him another fifty bucks to keep mum about our conversation.

Satisfied, I retreated to the Hardpan Café, which commanded an unobstructed view of the post office. I settled in to wait for my hippie friends to make the scene. The Russian lady was overjoyed.

*

Thornton's people arrived on Thursday. Two rough men dressed in greatcoats; they drove around town in a clanking two-ton truck with a canvas top. A military surplus vehicle capable of serious off-road travel. The U.S Army Star was mud-splattered.

I compared them to my list. One, a redhead, was a nobody. The other man was middling sized, with a dented forehead, pebbly eyes and a long beard that would've made Fidel Castro jealous. Roy Fulcher, larger and uglier than life. Still playing henchman to Thornton in the new century. Loyal as a dog; how sweet.

If any of the locals tipped the men that I had been asking about their operation, it was not evident. They nonchalantly gathered supplies while I lurked in the background. Toward evening Fulcher pointed the truck north and rumbled off with a load of dry goods, fuel, and mail. I trailed.

Eventually, the truck turned onto a gravel road. A bullet-riddled sign read: LITTLE EGYPT RD. The metal pole was bent nearly double, victim of unknown violence. Rough country here; patches of concrete-hard snow gleamed under scraggly trees. In a few miles gravel gave way to a mud track and the ruts were too deep for the Chrysler. I pulled over, shouldered a satchel I'd bought at the Purdon Thrifty Saver and started walking, carefully picking my way as twilight grew moss and the stars glittered like caltrops. As the air cooled, mist cloaked the branches and brambles.

The hills got steep fast, draining the strength from my legs. My back protested. I shook most of the bottle of aspirin into my mouth to stay on the safe side, and rested frequently. When the track forked, I shined my flashlight to orient on the freshest ruts. It wasn't difficult; it was like following a bulldozer up the mountain. I clicked the light off quickly, hoping to conceal my position, and continued trudging.

I checked my watch to gauge the mileage and discovered it had died at 6:32 P.M. Much later, my legs got too heavy and I slumped under a lonely pine. Clouds snuffed the stars.

7.

The gray light swam as it brightened; rocks and brush solidified all around. Two inches of snow dusted the landscape like the face of a corpse.

My back had seized up. It hurt in a profound way. *Like a bitch*, as my pop would've said. The aspirin was gone, the whiskey too. It seemed impossible that I would ever stand. But I rose, among a shower of black motes and silvery comets. Rose with the chuffing sob of a steer as it is goaded onto the gangway. Then I hugged my homely little tree, pissed on my boots and trembled with nausea. I needed a drink.

The road curved upward in a series of switchbacks. The snow disintegrated to brown sludge. I staggered along the shoulder, avoiding the quagmire. My feet got wet anyway. I clutched at exposed roots and outcroppings. A bird scolded me.

Cresting a saddle in the hills, I gazed upon the flank of a mountain about a quarter-mile off. Shacks were scattered beneath the crags – tin roofs bled orange tracks in the snow. The truck Fulcher had driven was parked alongside two battered jeeps near a Quonset hut. Wood smoke coiled above the camp, chugged forth from several stacks. A knot of muddy pigs huddled in a paddock. Nothing else moved.

My glance fell upon a trio of silhouetted formations farther along the mountainside; too far to discern clearly. Pylons? The instant I spotted them a whisper of unease urged me to look elsewhere. To flee, yes. I patted the bulk of the revolver in my pocket and the whispers slithered away.

I gulped air and wished I'd thought to bring field glasses for this expedition. Keeping to the brush, I swung a wide northwest circle. As I drew closer to the pylons, it registered that about a dozen jutted randomly above the stony field. Crows danced atop them, squawking their hideous argot. An unpleasant sensation of primitive familiarity rooted me in my tracks. The objects were made of milled poles planted at angles like king-sized x's, each twice the height of a man. Symbols were carved into them. Latin? The farthest structure had something caught at its apex – a bundle of rags.

"Marvin!"

I turned. A man in a billowing poncho strode from the direction of the camp. He waved and I waved back automatically. The brush must not have concealed me so well after all. He walked swiftly, a stop-motion figure on grainy film. The haze had a spaghetti-western effect – it made him taller and shorter by turns and cast his face in gloom.

"Mr. Thornton?" I said when he halted before me. God, he was tall. I was no midget and I had to crane my neck at him.

"Welcome to the Pleasure Dome. Glad you could make it. We seldom receive visitors during the winter season." He sounded British and wore an Australian-style drover's hat pulled low over jagged brows and scaly eyes. Potbellied and thick through the hips, yet gangly and muscular the way a well-fed raptor is muscular. His enormous hands hung loosely. A thin-lipped mouth threatened to bisect his broad, sallow face. Lots and lots of stained crooked teeth were revealed by his huge smile. "It has you, I see. Ticktock go the mitochondria – a nova in bloom. Marvelous, marvelous."

I stared at him and decided he was far too spry for a fellow pushing seventy-five. His movements were quick and powerful. His doll-smooth flesh radiated youthful heat. "Who told you I was coming?" I suspected someone at the Weston Gallery had phoned with the news. Were there phones up here?

Thornton hesitated as if he actually meant to answer the question. "Come back to the house. The ground is unsafe."

"Unsafe how?"

"Not all the shafts are properly sealed. Holes everywhere. Periodically someone disappears – they come poking around for souvenirs or gold and...well, one misstep is all it takes. Teenagers, usually. Or tourists."

I nodded in idiot silence, grappling with my instincts – my mind was a cacophony of ghostly exhortations to rap this man's head while we were away from his presumed horde of disciples, to put him on his knees with the gun barrel under his jaw and pry loose the answers to a dozen pertinent questions. I recalled the lumpish shape at the bottom of Renfro's hole, how it shuddered and quaked, and my hand dipped into my pocket –

"How's Jacob, anyway?" Thornton had already turned his back. Maybe he was grinning. His dry, Victorian accent quavered up the register toward that of a crone's.

"Jacob." It seemed to be getting darker by the second in that desolate valley.

"The fellow who sent you to break my legs and whatnot. He misses his uncle. Kidding, kidding. Do you miss Teddy? Does anyone? It would be decent."

"You know Jacob?"

"Not really. His uncle and I were friends, once. Teddy lived on the edge of my circle. I never gathered the impression he spoke of me to anyone...uninitiated. Jacob would not suit my purposes."

"I'm here to find out what happened to Teddy."

"Truly? I supposed you came because of the *Sequence*."

"See, I'm kind of stuck on the chicken or the egg theory. I'll take whatever I can get. So give."

"Teddy vanished. A boating accident, wasn't it?"

"After visiting you."

"Teddy was a big boy. Big enough for both of us. Remove your hand from the gun, Marvin. Harm me and you'll never get what you came for."

My lungs burned. "Harm you. There's no reason. Is there?"

"For some men, there is always a reason. It's what you do well, hurting. You're a terrier. I know everything about you, Marvin. I smell meanness cooking in your blood. The blood on your hands. I ask, do you want blood from me, or knowledge? Here is a crossroads."

"I want to know about the photographs. I need to understand what's happening to me." I said this simply, even humbly. I removed my hand from the revolver.

"It's not only happening to you. It's happening to everyone, everywhere. You're tuned in to the correct frequency, and therein lies the difference." Thornton twisted his oversized head to regard me without shifting his shoulders. His face was milky. A face of unwholesome flexibility; and yes, his grin fetched to mind sickles and horns. "Let's amble – we'll do lunch, we'll chat. I'll show you my gallery. It's an amazing gallery. I'll show you *Imago*. You'll enjoy it, Marvin. You'll sleep again. Sleep without nightmares." He was walking before he finished, beckoning with a casual twitch of his hand. His oilskin poncho slithered in his wake not unlike a tail.

I followed on wooden legs. Crows argued behind us.

The Quonset hut was so old its floor was a sunken mass of caramelized wood and dirt. An arch in the rear opened to darkness. Moth-eaten banners of curiously medieval design hung from the rafters, casting fluttery shadows upon the long table where I mechanically chewed a ham sandwich and drank a sour beer that Roy Fulcher had fetched. Thornton had departed, promising a swift return. He asked Fulcher to attend to my needs.

Light oozed through window glass that sagged and pooled at the bottom of rotten frames. Crates made pyramids against the walls, alongside boxes, barrels, and stacks of curling newspapers. Homey.

Fulcher watched me eat. His features were vulpine and his lank beard was stained yellow-brown around the mouth. He smelled ripe. Farther off, a group of fellow colonists played at a ping-pong table. They cast sly glances our way and chuckled with suppressed brutality. Four men, two women, ages indeterminate. They were scrawny, haggard and unwashed. Several more came and went, shuffling. Zombies but for a merry spark in their eyes, satisfied smirks.

I said, "Here's the million-dollar question – where's the caveman buried?"

"Caveman? I don't think there's a caveman." Fulcher's was an earthy accent, a nasal drawl that smacked of coal mines and tarpaper shanties.

"All this trouble and no caveman?"

"Sorry."

"It's okay. Jacob will get over it," I said. "I don't suppose you'll tell me where Ammon took the *Imago Sequence*? That won't hurt anything, if there's no caveman."

Fulcher leaned in. "Take a spoon and dig a hole in your chest. That's where he made his pictures."

I pushed my plate aside. I wiped my lips with a dingy cloth towel. I stared at him, long and steadily. I said, "If you won't talk about Ammon, tell me about your colony. Love what you've done with the place. What do you guys do for fun in these parts?" I'd cultivated a talent for reading people, weighing them at a glance, separating shepherds from sheep. It was nothing special; a basic survival technique – but it came up dry now. These people confounded my expectations. Was I in a commune or a militia compound? Were these hippie cultists, leftwing anarchists, or something else? I gave one of the more brazen ping-pong players – the redhead from town – a hard look. Fulcher had called him Clint. Clint's grin vanished and he concentrated on his game. Human, at least.

"You know," Fulcher said.

"I hate word games, Roy. They make me hostile."

"Ask Anselm."

"I'm asking you."

"It brought you to us – one from multitudes. You still question what our work is here?"

"It? If you mean the *Imago Sequence*, then yeah, I'm full of questions."

"Anselm will answer your *questions* in due course."

"Well, Roy, problem is, I'm kind of stupid. People usually need to repeat stuff."

Fulcher's expression grew rigid. "You don't want to see. Surprise – it's too late. The fictions you've invented, your false assumptions, your pretenses, will soon be blown apart. I doubt it will profit you in the least. You're a thug."

"Story of my life; nobody likes me. I guess you'd be willing to show me the big picture. Shoot me down with your intellectual superiority."

"Anselm will show you the cosmic picture, Mr. Cortez."

"Isn't it customary for you religious zealots to have pamphlets lying around? Betcha there's a printing press somewhere in this Taj Mahal. Surely you've got propaganda for the recruits? And beads? I like beads."

"No pamphlets, no recruits. This is *Imago Colony*. Religion doesn't apply."

"Oh, no? What's with all the faux Roman crucifixes in the back forty?"

"The crucifixes? Those are authentic. Anselm imported them."

I tried to wrap my mind around that concept. The implications eluded me. I said, "Bullshit. What the hell for?"

"The obvious – sport. Anselm has exotic tastes. He enjoys aspects of cultural antiquity."

"Yeah, so I hear. And he has a thing about bugs, I guess; sort of similar to his mentor. Seems to be a reliable pattern with lunatics. An imago is an insect, right?"

"It's symbolic."

"Oh. I thought the bug thing was cute."

"An imago is not *any* insect. The final instar of an insect, its supreme incarnation. Care for another beer?"

"I'm good." I gestured at the ping-pong tournament. "Weedy crowd, Roy.

Somebody told me there were forty, fifty of you in this camp."

"Far less, these days. Attrition."

"Uh-huh."

"You've come during harvest season, Mr. Cortez. That's what we do in the cold months. The others are engaged, those who remain. Things will quicken in the spring. People seem to be more driven to enlightenment during sandal weather. Spiritualists, nature enthusiasts, software engineers on holiday with wives and kiddies. We get all kinds."

"Thornton is off to play plantation overseer, eh? I wonder what you kids harvest in these parts – poppies? Opium is Afghanistan's chief export – ask the Taliban what it paid for its military hardware, the light bills in its palaces. The climate around here is about goddamned ideal. You'd be millionaires. I've got a couple pals, line you right out for a piece of the pie."

Fulcher rubbed his dented brow, smiled. "What wonderful irony! We do love to trip. You have me there. Poppies, that's very funny. I almost miss those days. I stick with cigarettes anymore."

"Lay your gimmick on me."

"Evolution."

"You and everybody else."

"What do people want?" Fulcher raised his grimy hand to forestall my answer. "What do people truly want – what would induce a man to sell his soul?"

"To be healthy, wealthy, and wise," I said with mild sarcasm. Mild because as I uttered the punch line to the children's rhyme, coldness began to unfold in my bones. The tumblers in my head were turning again.

"Bravo, Mr. Cortez. Power, wisdom, immortality." His expression altered. "We have found something that will afford us...longevity, at least. With longevity comes everything else."

"The Fountain of Youth?" *In the deep mountain woods a mossy statue spurted black water. Congregations of hillbillies in coveralls bathed in its viscid pool. A bonfire, a forest of uncured pelts swaying. A piper.* I shuddered. "Dancing girls, winning lotto tickets?"

"A catalyst. A mechanism that compresses aeons of future human evolution. Although future is a relative term."

"Ammon's photographs." It seemed obvious. Everything seemed patently obvious, except that the room was undulating and I couldn't figure out who was playing the flute. A panpipe, actually; high, thin, discordant. It pierced my brain.

Fulcher ignored the music. He flushed, warming to my edification. "The *Imago Sequence* is a trigger. If you've got the right genes, you might already be a winner."

I rubbed my ear; the pipe raised unpleasant specters to mind, set them gibbering. *The monstrous hominid opened its mouth wider, wider.* "How does that shit work?"

"Take a picture of God, tack it on the wall and see who bows. Recognition is the key. It doesn't make a difference what you comprehend intellectually, only what stirs on a cellular level, what awakens when it recognizes the wellspring of creation."

"Don't tell me you believe the caveman is God."

"I said there's no caveman. Look deeper, friend. Reality lies beyond the surface. It's not the Devil in the details, it's God."

"Aha! You *are* a bunch of Christian cultists."

"We do not exist to worship an incomprehensible being. A being which assuredly lacks the means to appreciate slavish devotion."

"Seems pointless to have a god at all, when you put it like that."

"Do you supplicate plutonium? Do you sing hymns to uranium? We bask in the corona of an insensate majesty. In its sway we seek to lay the foundation blocks of a new city, a new civilization. We're pioneers. Our frontier is the grand wasteland between Alpha and Omega."

"Will you transform into a being of pure energy and migrate to Alpha Centauri?"

"Quite opposite. Successful animal organisms are enduring organisms. Enduring organisms are extremely basic, extremely efficient. Tarantulas. Scorpions. Reptiles. Flies."

"Don't forget cockroaches. They're going to inherit the Earth." I laughed, began coughing. The room wobbled. "So Thornton is what – the messiah helping you become the best imago you can be?"

"Anselm is the Imago. We are maggots. We are provender."

"I get it. He does the transcending and you get the slops."

"It is good to have a purpose in life. To be an integral part of the great and terrible cycle." Fulcher shook his head. "As I serve him, he served Ammon, and Ammon served the one before him down through time gone to dust. '*By sating the image of the Power they fulfill their fleshly contract. By suckling the teat of godliness the worthy shall earn their reward.*' Thus it is written in a book much more venerable than the Bible. For we who survive to remake ourselves in the image of the Power, all risks are acceptable."

"Reverend Jones rides again! Pass the grape Kool-Aid!"

"Hysterical, much?"

"Naw, just lately." I took a breath. "I wonder though, what does a guy do after he reaches the top of the ol' ladder? Live in a cave and compose epic poetry? Answer riddles? Pick up a sword and lay waste to Rome?"

"Caligula was one of us, actually."

I didn't know what to say to that. I plowed ahead. "Well?"

"Basic organisms require basic pleasures."

"Basic pleasures?" The chilly sensation linked hands with vertigo and did a Scottish jig. I was as a figurine in that enormous room.

"Subsistence and copulation. That's what the good life boils down to, my friend. Eating and fucking. Whoever you want, whatever you want, whenever you want."

The mouth opening, opening –

"Power to the people." I was slurring. Why was I slurring?

"Ready to go?" Fulcher rose, still smiling through his matted beard. We walked through the tall archway. He lightly gripped my elbow to steady me. One beer and I was drunk as a sailor on the third day of shore leave. The corridor expanded in the best Escher fashion, telescoping into infinite shadow. There were ragged tapestries at intervals, disfigured statues, a well-trammeled carpet with astrological designs. The corridor branched and branched again at grand arches marred by ages of smoke. At one fork, a kerosene lamp swung on a sooty chain. Behind a massive iron door the piping shrilled, died, shrilled. Hoarse screams of the primordial sex act, exhausted sobs, laughter and applause. Mrs. Chin's photograph haunted me.

"The gallery," Fulcher said.

I recognized the musk upon him, finally. For a horrible moment I thought we would go through that door. We continued down the other hall.

Fulcher brought me to a dingy chamber lit by a single dirty bulb in an overhead cage. The room was windowless and bare except for a large chair made of wood and iron. The chair had arm straps and leg shackles; an artifact from the Spanish Inquisition. It was not difficult to picture the fallen bishops, the heretical nobles who had shrieked in its embrace.

"Please, make yourself comfortable." Fulcher helped me along with a shove.

I slumped in the strange chair, my head heavy as a wrecking ball, and watched as he produced a nasty looking bowie knife and expertly sliced off my clothes. When he encountered the revolver he emptied the cylinder, slid the weapon into his waistband without comment. He cinched my arms and legs; his fingers glowed, dragging tracers as they adjusted buckles and straps. Seemingly he had grown extra arms. I could only gawk at this phantasm; I felt quite docile. "Wow, Roy. What was in my beer? I feel terrific."

"One should hope. You ingested five hundred milligrams of synthetic mescaline – enough to launch a rhinoceros into orbit."

"Party foul, and on the first date too. I thought you didn't do dope anymore."

"I dabble in the manufacturing end of the spectrum. Frankly, all that meta-physical mumbo-jumbo about hallucinogens affecting perception in a meaning-ful way is wishful thinking. Poor Huxley." Fulcher stepped back, surveyed his handiwork while rolling a cigarette. The yellow flare of his lighter painted his face, made him a devil. "Oh, except for you. You're special. You've seen *Alpha* and *Beta*. As my pappy would say, you've got the taint, boy." He blurred around the edges. With each inhalation the cherry of his cigarette brightened, became Jupiter's red sore.

I noticed the walls were metallic – whorls whorled, pits and pocks formed. Condensation trickled. Smoke made arabesques and demons. The walls were a tapestry from a palace in Hell.

The panpipe started wheedling again and Thornton entered the room on cue. He pushed a rickety hospital tray with a domed cover. The cover was scalloped, silver finish flaking. A maroon handprint smeared its curve.

"This is a bad sign," I said.

Thornton was efficient. He produced an electric razor and shaved a portion of my head to stubble, dug a thumb under my carotid artery and traced veins in my skull with a felt-tip pen. He tweaked my nose in a fatherly manner, stripped off his coat and rolled his sleeves to the elbows. His skin gleamed like coral, cast faint reflections upon the walls and ceiling. Shoals of phantom fish scattered above, regrouped and swam into an abyss; a superhighway and its endless traf-fic looped beneath my feet; it rippled and collapsed into a trench of unimagina-ble depths.

I watched him remove a headpiece from the tray – a clumsy framework of clamps and screws; a dunce cap with a collar. Parts had never been cleaned. I wanted to scream when he fitted it over my head and neck, locked it in place with a screwdriver. I sighed.

Fulcher stubbed his cigarette, produced a palm-sized digital camera and aimed it at me. He gave Thornton a thumbs-up.

Thornton selected a scalpel from the instruments on the tray, weighed it in his hand. "Teddy was a friend – I would never use him as provender, but neither could I set him on the path to Olympus. There's limited room in the boat, you see. Weak, genetically flawed, but a jolly nice fellow. A gentleman. Imagine my disappointment when he showed up on my doorstep last fall. Not only had the old goat bought *Parallax Alpha*, he'd viewed *Beta* as well. He demanded to see *Imago*. As if I could simply snap my fingers and show him. Wouldn't listen to reason, wouldn't go home and fall to pieces quietly like a good boy. So I enlight-ened him. It was out of my hands after that. Now, we come to you." He sliced my forehead, peeled back a flap of skin. Fulcher taped it down.

"What?" I said. "What?"

Thornton raised a circular saw with a greasy wooden handle. He attached it to a socket in my headpiece. "Trephination. An ancient method to open the so-called Third Eye. Fairly crude; Ammon taught me how and a Polynesian tribe showed him – he wasn't a surgeon either. He performed his own in a Bangkok opium den with a serrated knife and a corkscrew while a stoned whore held a mirror. Fortunately, medical expertise is not a requisite in this procedure."

The dent in Fulcher's brow drew my gaze. I sighed again, saddened by wisdom acquired too late in the day.

Thornton patted me kindly. His touch lingered as a caress. "Don't fret, it's not a lobotomy. You wished to behold *Imago*, this is the way. What an extraordinary specimen you are, Marvin, my boy. Your transformation will be a most satisfying conquest as I have not savored in years. I am sure to delay your reintegration for the span of many delightful hours. I will have compensation for your temerity."

"Mr. Thornton," I gasped; trembled with the effort of rolling my eye to meet his. "Mrs. Chin said the glacier is coming. I dream it every night; flies buzzing in my brain. It's killing me. That's why I came."

Thornton nodded. "Of course. I've seen it a thousand times. Everyone who has crawled into my lair wanted to satisfy one desire or another. What will satisfy you, O juicy morsel? To hear, to know?" He yawned. "Would you be happy to learn there is but one God and that all things come from Him? Existence is infinitely simple, Marvin – cells within cells, dreams within dreams, from the molten Fingertip of God Almighty, to the antenna of a roach, on this frequency and each of a billion after. Thus it goes until the circuit completes its ambit of the core, a protean-reality where dwells an intellect of surpassing might, yet impotent, bound as it is in the well of its own gravity. Cognition does not flourish in that limitless quagmire, the cosmic repository of information. The lightning of Heaven is reduced to torpid impulses that spiral outward, seeking gratification by osmosis. And by proxy. We are bags of nerves and electrolytes, fragile and weak, and we decompose so quickly. Which is the purpose, the very cunning design. Our experiences are readily digested to serve the biological imperative of a blind, vast sponge. Does it please you? Do you require more?"

A spike glinted within the ring of saw-teeth. Thornton casually pressed this spike into my skull, seated it with a few taps of a rubber mallet. He put his lips next to my ear. His breath reeked copper. "The prophets proclaim the end is near. I'll whisper to you something they don't know – the world ended this morning as you were sleeping, half-frozen on the mountainside. It ended aeons before your father squirted his genetic material into your mother. It will end tomorrow as it ends every day, same time, same station." He started cranking.

Listening to the rhythmic burr of metal on bone, I was thankful the mescaline had soldered my nerve endings. Thornton divided and divided until he crowded the room. Pith helmets, top hats, arctic coats, khakis, corporate suits, each double dressed for a singular occasion, each one animated by separate experience, but all of them smiling with tremendous pleasure as they turned the handle, turned the handle, turned the handle. Their faces sloughed, dough swelling and splitting. Beneath was something raw, and moist, and dark.

I glimpsed the face of the future and failed to comprehend its shape. Blood poured into my eyes. The panpipe went mad.

8.

The world ends every day.

Picture me walking in a rock garden under the dipping branches of cherry blossom trees. I love stones and there are heavy examples scattered across the garden; olive-bearded, embedded in the tough sod. God's voice echoes as through a gigantic gramophone horn, but softly from the lead plate of sky, and not God, it's Thornton guiding the progression, driving an auger into my skull while the music plays. Push it aside, keep moving toward a mound in the distance....

No Thornton, auger, no music; only God, the garden, and I. Where is God? Everywhere, but especially in the earth, the dark, warm earth that opens as a cave mouth in the side of a hill. God calls from the hill, in voices of grinding rock and gurgling water.

I walk toward the cave. Sleet falls, captured betwixt burning and freezing precisely as I am caught. Nor is the sleet truly sleet. A swirl of images falling, million-million shards fractured from a vast hoary mirror. There am I, and I and I a million million times, broken, melting....

I walk through God's rock garden, trampling incarnations of myself....

Watery images flickered on the wall. A home movie with the volume lowered. Choppy because the cameraman kept adjusting to peer over the shoulder of a tall figure who attended a third person in the awful chair – my chair. The victim was not I; it was a mirror casting a false reflection. And it wasn't a movie in the strictest sense; I detected no camera, nor aperture to project the film. More hallucinations then. More something.

Teddy's face, trapped in the conical helm; his feet scuffed and rattled the shackles. Thornton blocked the view, elbow pumping with the practiced ease of a farmer's wife churning butter. Muffled laughter, walnuts being cracked. The image went dark, but the dim sounds persisted.

Claustrophobia gagged me. I was still strapped in the chair, the helm fixed to my head. There was a hole in my head. My right eye was crusted and blind. I shuddered with chills. How much time had passed? Where had Fulcher and Thornton gone? Had they shown me *Imago* as promised? My memories balked.

As my faculties reengaged, my fear swelled. They had shredded my clothes, confiscated my belongings, tortured me. They would kill me. That was scarcely my fear. I dreaded what else would happen first.

The wall brightened with new images. *Sperm wriggled, hungry and fast. A wasp made love to a tarantula, thrusting, thrusting with its stinger. Mastiffs flung themselves upon a threshing stag, dangled from its antlers like ornaments. Fire ants swarmed over a gourd half-buried in desert earth –*

Fulcher drifted through the door, Clint at his heel. I remained limp when Fulcher scrutinized me briefly; he flashed a penlight in my good eye, checked my pulse. He murmured to his partner, and began unbuckling my straps. Clint hung back, perhaps to guard against a revival of my aggressive philosophy. Even so, he appeared bored, distracted.

I did not stir until Fulcher freed my arms. It occurred to me that the mescaline cocktail must've worn off because I wasn't feeling docile anymore. Nothing was premeditated; my mind was well below a rational state. I pawed his face – weakly, a drunken gesture, which he brushed aside. I became more insistent, got a fistful of his beard on the next half-hearted swipe, my left hand slithered behind his neck. Fulcher pried at my wrist, twisted his head. Frantic, he braced his boot against the chair and tried to push off. His back bowed and contorted.

A ghostly spider mounted a beetle; they clinched.

Growing stronger, more purposeful, I yanked him into my lap, and his beard ripped, but that was fine. I squeezed his throat and vertebrae popped the way it happens when you lift a heavy salmon by the tail. Stuff separates.

Clint tried to pull Fulcher, exactly as a man will pull a comrade from quicksand. Failing, he snatched up a screwdriver and stabbed me in the ribs. No harm, my ribs were covered with a nice slab of gristle and suet. Punch a side of beef hanging from a hook and see what you get.

A truck careened across a strange field riddled with holes. The vehicle juked and jived and nose-dived into the biggest hole of them all –

I dropped Fulcher and staggered from the chair. Clint stabbed me in the shoulder. I laughed; it felt good. I palmed his face, clamped down with full strength. He bit me, began a thick, red stream down my arm. He choked and gargled. Bubbles foamed between my finger webs. I waltzed him on tiptoes and banged his head against a support beam. Bonk, bonk, bonk, just like the cartoons. Just like Jackson Pollack. I stopped when his facial bones sort of collapsed and sank into the general confusion of his skull.

I fumbled with the screws of my helm, gave it up as a hopeless cause. I left the cell and wandered along the hall, trailing one hand against the rough surfaces. People met me, passed me without recognition, without interest. These people were versions of myself. I saw *a younger me dressed in a tropical shirt and a girl on my* arm; *me in a funeral suit and a sawed-off shotgun in my hand; another me pale and bruised, a doughnut brace on my neck, hunched on crutches; still another me, gray-haired, dead drunk, wild glare fixed upon the middle distance.* And others, too many others coming faster until it hurt my eyes. They flowed around me, collided, disappeared into the deep, lightless throat of the hall until all possibilities were lost.

Weight shifted within the bowels of Thornton's Pleasure Dome. A ponderous door was flung wide and a chorus of damned cries echoed up the corridors. The muscles between my shoulder blades tightened. I picked up the pace.

The main area was deserted but for a woman sweeping ashes from the barrel stove and a sturdy man in too-loose long johns eating dinner at a table. The woman was an automaton; she regarded me without emotion, resumed her mechanical duties. The man put aside his spoon, considering whether to challenge me. He remained undecided as I stumbled outside, bloody and birth-naked. The icy breeze plucked at my scalp, caused my wound to throb with the threat of a migraine. I was in a place far removed from such concerns.

A better man would've set a match to the drums of diesel, blown the place to smithereens Hollywood style. No action star, I headed for the vehicles.

Twilight cocooned the valley. The sky was smooth as opal. A crimson band pulsed at the horizon – the sun elongated to its breaking point. Clouds scudded from invisible distances, flew by at unnatural velocity.

"Don't go," Thornton said. A whisper, a shout.

I glanced back.

He filled the doorway of the Quonset hut, which was tiny, was receding. His many selves had merged, yet flickered beneath his skin, ready to burst forth. His voice had relinquished its command, now waned fragile, as it traveled across the gulf to find me. "You're opening doors without any idea of where they lead. It's a waste. Sweet God, what a waste!"

I kept walking, limping.

"Marvin!" A hot lash of hatred and appetite throbbed from his dwindling voice. "Say hello to Teddy!" He shrank to a speck, was lost.

A fleet of canvas-top trucks shimmered upon an island in a sea of velvet. They warped and ran with the fluidity of quicksilver, a kaleidoscope revolving around the original. I picked the closest truck and dragged myself inside. Keys dangled from the ignition. The helm was too tall for the cab; I was forced to drive with my head on my shoulder. Fresh blood seeped from the wound and obscured my vision.

The truck bucked and crow-hopped as I clanged gears, stomped the accelerator and sent it hurtling across the rugged valley. One road multiplied, became three roads, now six. Now, I was off the road, or the road had melted. Bizarre changes were altering the scenery, toying with my feeble perception. The moun-

tains doubled and redoubled and underwent the transformations of millennia
– a range exploding forward, rounding and shortening, another backward, rear-
ing into a toothy crown – in the span of heartbeats. It was a rough ride.

I found the knob for the headlights in time to illuminate the sinkhole a few
dozen yards ahead. A rapidly widening maw. I slammed the brakes. The cab
exploded with dust and smoking rubber. There was a tin-can-under-a-boot
crunch and the truck yawed, paused at the rim and toppled in, nose-first. I performed a lazy belly flop through the windshield.

I didn't lose consciousness, unfortunately. I bounced and felt bones crack
along old fault lines. Eventually I stopped with a terrific jolt; a feather mattress
dropped on a cavern floor. At least the truck didn't come down on top of me
– it had lodged in a bottleneck. Its engine shrieked momentarily, sputtered and
died. I stared up at the rapidly dulling headlights, as bits of sensation returned
to my extremities. Ages passed. When I finally managed to gain my knees, the
world was in darkness. What was broken? Ribs, definitely. A sprained knee that
swelled as I breathed. Possibly a bone in my back had snapped; insufficient to
immobilize me, yet neither could I straighten fully. Cuts on my face and hands.
The pain was minor, and that worried me. Why not worse? I had landed in deep,
spongy moss, was nearly buried from the impact. It sucked at me as I clambered
to solid footing.

The darkness wasn't complete. Aqueous light leaked from slimy surfaces,
the low ceiling of sweating rock. As my vision adjusted I saw moss claimed
everything. Stinking moss filled crevices and fissures, was habitat of beetles and
other things. Sloppy from the eternal drip of water, it squelched between my
toes, sucked my ankles. This was a relatively small cave, with a single chimney
jammed by the crashed truck. This wasn't a mine shaft; my animal self was positive about that. Nor did it require much heavy thinking to conclude that climbing out of there was impossible. I couldn't raise my left arm above waist level. A
single note from the panpipe came faintly. From below. A voice might have murmured my name – I was gasping too loudly and it did not repeat.

A fissure split the rear of the cave, a cramped tunnel descended. Mastering
my instincts, I followed it down. The cool air warmed, was soon moist as a panting mouth. Pungent odors clogged my nostrils, watered my eyes. Gradually, the
passage widened, opening into a larger area, a cavern of great dimensions. The
light strengthened, or my eyes got better, because pieces of the cavern joined as
Mrs. Chin's photos had joined. And I beheld *Imago*.

Here was the threshold of the Beginning and End.

The roof was invisible but for the tips of gargantuan stalactites, all else shrouded. Moss, more moss, a garden, a forest of moss. But was it moss? I doubted that. Moss didn't quiver where it met flesh, didn't contract as a muscle contracts.

The walls glistened; they glowed not unlike the glow which seeped from Thornton's skin. Shadows of the world dwelt in the walls. Those most familiar to me rose from the depths like champagne bubbles. I passed Teddy's yacht near the surface, its lines quite clean despite being encased. Further along, a seaplane was suspended on high, partially obscured by gloom. It hung, fossilized, an inverted crucifix. There were faces, a frieze of ghastly spectators massed in the tiers of an amphitheater. I averted my gaze, afraid of who I might see pithed in the bell jar. Deeper, inside folds of rock that was not rock, were glimpses of Things to Come. Houses, onion domes and turrets, utopian skylines, the graceful arcs of bridges, rainforests and jagged mountains. And deeper, deeper yet, solar systems of pregnant globes of smothered dirt and vine, and charred stars in endless procession.

I caught myself humming The Doors' "This Is The End." I stood upon a shattered slope, weeping and laughing, and humming the song of death. Thinking probably the same thoughts any lesser primate does when confronted with apocalyptic forces. To these I added, *Damn you, anyway, Jacob! You can shove this favor in your big, flabby ass!* And, *I wonder if Carol is feeding the fish?*

Before me lay the cavern's boundary; another translucent wall. This area was subtly different; it bulged with murky reefs of dubious matter – I conjured the image of coiled organs, the calcified ganglia of some Biblical colossus. Dead roots slithered from an abyss to end abysses – a primordial sea from which all life had been egurgitated. My ears popped with a sudden pressure change. I detected movement.

I tried to run, but my legs were unresponsive, as if they had fallen asleep, and the moss shifted beneath my nerveless feet, dumped me on my ass. I flailed down the slope, which I realized was a funnel, or a trough. This occurred with excruciating slowness, but it was impossible to halt my weight once it got moving. Wherever my skin made contact with the moss I lost sensation. This was because the moss that was not moss stung with tiny barbs, stung me as a jellyfish stings. My legs, my back, right hand, then left, until everything from the neck down was anesthetized.

At the bottom, by some trick of geometry, I pitched forward to lie spreadeagle against the curve of the wall. The rock softened, was vaguely gelatinous. I began to sink. Despite my numbed state, it was cold compared to the rank jungle of a cavern. Frigid.

As I sank into the wall, I thought, *Not a wall, a membrane.* Engulfed in amber jelly, tremendous pressure built upon my body, flattened my features. Wrenching my head to free it from imminent suffocation, to scream as an animal screams, dying alone in the wilderness, I saw a blossom of fire in the near distance. An abrupt blue-white flare that seemed to expand forever, then shrink into itself. I opened my mouth, opened my mouth –

The second flash was far smaller, far more remote. It faded swiftly.

I don't know if there was a third.

Magic in a Certain Slant of Light

Deborah Coates

Deborah Coates (*www.iknowiknow.org*) lives in Ames, Iowa, with her two Rottweilers, John Henry and Charming Billie. Billie is her current tracking dog; John Henry is "retired." She is "interested in dogs, knowledge, intelligence, the social aspects of computing, group-forming networks, communication, trust, culture, agriculture, Western science, Native science, writing, teaching, and aliens. Some days some of these things are peripherally related to information technology, the field in which she currently works." She has published occasional stories over the past decade in *The Magazine of Fantasy & Science Fiction*, *SciFiction*, *Strange Horizons*, the SFFnet anthologies *Between the Darkness and The Fire* and *The Age of Reason*, and the young-adult anthology *A Starfarer's Dozen*.

"Magic in a Certain Slant of Light" was published in *Strange Horizons* and this is its first appearance in print. It is a well-executed romantic story about a scientist with the power of precognition.

"If you could wish for something magical, what would you wish for?" Jeff asks Nora as he enters the kitchen.

Jeff has been gone all day, helping a friend fix the plumbing in his basement. There's no "Hello," or "How was your day?" Just Jeff, in the doorway, asking about magic. "It can't be about yourself," he continues. "I mean, like making yourself immortal. Or about world peace. It has to be – "

"Talking dogs," Nora says.

Jeff smiles in that way he has that seems to change his face. He's wearing faded jeans and a sweatshirt that's been washed so many times its cuffs are all unraveled; it's a change from pin-striped suits and crisp white shirts. "You know, Dexter made a dog talk once and it didn't work out like he figured it would. That dog was annoying."

"Well, I don't know how to tell you this" – Nora chops onions under running water, then transfers them to the frying pan on the stove – "but I don't rely on *Dexter's Laboratory* for my scientific knowledge."

"Talking dogs are not scientific."

"Yeah, magical." Nora turns the heat up on the pan and looks through the cupboards for the spices that she needs. She swears that they're never where she put them, no matter how often she returns them to their proper place. "That's what we were talking about, right? Magic? You tell me, what would you wish for?"

"Zeppelins," he says without hesitation.

"Uhm, zeppelins actually exist."

He stands in the kitchen doorway, slouched against the frame, and she knows that he will leave her. There is something in the way he looks, a shadow in his eye, that wasn't there yesterday or even this morning. And it almost kills her, like being stabbed right through the heart, because he's the only one she ever really loved.

"Zeppelins," he says, crossing to her and putting his arms around her waist from behind as she turns back to the stove, "are a collective figment of the imagination."

"Zeppelins are totally possible. Plus, you can ride in one."

He kisses the back of her neck and it feels like the soft brush of sun-warmed honey. "Bring me a zeppelin," he says. His words murmur against her skin as he talks and she can feel his smile through the small hairs along the nape of her neck. "Then I'll believe you."

"Bring me a talking dog."

He pulls her away from the stove and kisses her again, this time on the lips. After a minute, she turns off the stove and they go into the bedroom where they make love under the covers for hours until hunger drives them back to the kitchen at midnight to eat cold noodles and ice cream from the container. Then he kisses her again with lips that taste like vanilla beans and curry and laughs when she wrinkles her nose at him. He plants a line of kisses along her nose and down her chest, setting up a cool shiver along her spine. She wants him more than ever, wants him right now on the kitchen table. She grabs the waistband of his sweatpants to pull him toward her and kisses him so hard that it feels entirely possible for the two of them to meld completely.

But she still knows, before the year is through, that he will leave her.

The students in Physics 101 call her Dr. No, as in Dr. Nora, but also Dr. Knows-All-Sees-All, and possibly the James Bond villain, because she can tell Susan in the twelfth row back to stop necking with her boyfriend, Gianni, without ever looking up from her notes. She tells them it's just fun with mirrors; half-seen images that reflect against the whiteboard and the metal edges of things in the room. They don't tell her what she doesn't even know herself, that no matter where they sit, whether she's looked up from her notes or has her head turned to the whiteboard, she knows where each and every student sits and calls on them by name.

Today's lecture is on thermal energy and she's given it enough times before that she only half-thinks about it as she talks. Her eyes scan the room, her right hand writes notes, mostly on the overhead, but sometimes on the board. She thinks about Jeff and wonders what he's doing. He works at a small but very prestigious law firm downtown. Indications are that he will make partner soon and she wonders if that will be it, the thing that makes him leave her. Occasionally she thinks that she will ask him – *I know that you will leave,* she'll say, *but I don't know why.*

"Nora Holt! Where have you been keeping yourself?"

In the faculty dining hall, Sara Long, professor of English, approaches Nora's table. She wears flowing clothes that sweep back from her body when she walks as if she's always facing into the wind. Many years ago at another university, Sara and Nora were roommates, an unlikely mismatched pair, but they have remained friends ever since, eventually meeting up again when they both got professorships here.

Nora smiles up at her. "I don't think I'm the one who's been hiding," she says. "I eat here every day."

Sara is pregnant but she doesn't know it yet. Nora can tell by the glow of her skin and the extra bit of brightness in her eye. She was married last year to a man seven years younger than herself and she radiates happiness down to her toes.

"How's the research going?" Sara asks her.

"It's a dead end," Nora says. Though she knows it will be at least six months before she proves this, she can see it in the way her charts shade over time, in the way light refracts when she enters her lab, in results that aren't quite anything yet, except a trend she has no name for.

Back in her office, Nora sits at her desk and attempts to map out her relationship with Jeff. He is not the first lover she has ever lost. It is not the first time she has ever known. Nora always knows; she reads the smallest signs. But Jeff is the first one who will break her heart.

They met at a party just over a year and a half ago, the kind of thing Nora never goes to. She doesn't pay much attention to him at first; he is too tall, too thin, too well-dressed. She likes short, straight-shouldered men who wear loose-fitting blue jeans and clay-colored polo shirts. Late in the evening, past the time when Nora's usually politely bowed out, she finds herself next to him leaning against the railing of the backyard deck listening to the increasingly desperate laughter of three women in the living room whose husbands will divorce them before the year is over.

"My name is Jeff," he says to her.

At the very same moment, Nora says, "Leslie Walker is about to explode all over her husband."

"Literally explode?" Jeff asks.

Nora looks at him for what may be the first time that evening. "It will be very messy," she says with a straight face, "and they will be picking pieces out of the carpet for months."

Jeff grins, but before he can say anything further, Leslie Walker, who is standing by the open sliding glass doors, suddenly shouts in the kind of angry voice that simply stops every other conversation in the room, "Jack, you son of a bitch! You shut up! Shut up right now or I'll kill you where you stand!"

Jeff lays his hand on Nora's bare arm. "How did you know?" he asks her.

"Know what?" Nora asks him.

"That she would do that?"

"I could tell by the tone of her voice, by the way she was standing, by the other conversations in the room around her."

"You couldn't tell by the other conversations," Jeff says.

Nora looks at him. His hand is still on her arm. "Right," she says, "I meant the unspoken tensions."

"Ah," he says, "the unspoken tensions." And she is sure he doesn't notice that his hand runs down her arm and his thumb gently strokes her wrist.

He doesn't say much of anything else to her; five minutes later he's saying his goodbyes to the host and hostess and offering to drive Jack Walker home. Nora watches him walk out the door, not-quite-guiding Jack's unsteady progress, and isn't sure why she's watching him or why she can still feel a tingle across the bones of her wrist as if he's somehow been in contact with more than just her skin. There are eight bones in the wrist – pisiform, triquetrum, lunate, hamate, capitate, trapezoid, trapezium, and scaphoid. The scaphoid is the one that usually breaks. Nora doesn't know which one is tingling – it's possible they all are – maybe it's muscle or nerve instead of bone. But it's a new feeling for Nora, warm and cold, both at once. She isn't sure she likes it.

He's too tall, she tells herself, too thin and too well-dressed. She doesn't want him. She doesn't picture him standing at the base of her bed, pulling a faded red T-shirt off over his head. She doesn't imagine him touching her, making her whole body tingle the way her wrist does. She doesn't. He's not her type at all.

At dinner, Jeff brings up talking dogs again.

"Say I could invent talking dogs," he says. He's still wearing his shirt and tie from work though the tie is loose and hanging crooked. Jeff, the professional, always looks perfectly put together, perfectly cool when he leaves the house in the morning to go to work. Nora prefers Jeff at home, slouched and casual, like a secret only she has access to.

"Okay, see," she says to him, leaning on the table, "if you invent them it's not magical. It's science."

"If science says they can't exist," Jeff counters, "and I still manage to invent them..."

"If science says they can't exist, you can't invent them," Nora tells him. "Science makes life simple. Things that can't happen don't."

"Science makes life simple for you, you mean," Jeff says, but with a smile that erases any bite the words might have.

No, Nora wants to tell him, it doesn't. It doesn't make life simple at all.

"What about my zeppelin?" he asks later. "I hope you're working on that."

"Zeppelins exist," Nora says somewhat absentmindedly, working out a problem for tomorrow's class.

"Where's the magic?" Jeff asks her.

And it doesn't occur to Nora until later that he might have left off talking about zeppelins right then.

Nora goes running in the morning. She used to run every day, back before Jeff, before she had anything much to think about besides science and her next class and maybe ducking committee meetings. Now, she runs once a week, maybe. She enjoys it. She can feel the world open up when she runs. Possibilities become endless. It's only after she stops, after she takes a quick shower and dresses for the work day, that she knows that Jeff will leave her, that her department chair is going to announce his retirement in the next three weeks, that she will catch three students cheating on her next exam.

Between classes, she gets on the Internet and searches for "the science of love" and then doesn't visit any of the websites her search pulls up.

"Why do men leave women?" she asks Jeff that night after dinner is over and the dishes are washed. She asks it as if it's a big question – all men and all women and all the things they do – as if it has nothing to do with them. They are sitting on the couch together, she against one arm and he propped against the other, their legs intertwined.

Jeff is reading the evening paper and his reply is absentminded. "Which men?"

"Any men. Ever." Nora is exasperated. It has taken courage and planning to ask this question, as if asking manifests reality. And he isn't taking her seriously.

Jeff folds down the newspaper. "People leave," he says seriously. "Men. Women. It's all the same. They leave because they leave. Most of them think they can explain it – we never agreed on anything, he was too controlling, she never listened. But nearly always the real reason is both smaller and larger than any of those things. It's – "

"Research says," Nora begins earnestly.

"Oh, research." Jeff shrugs and the motion rustles his paper. "Research can tell you anything."

Nora bites her tongue on a long speech about scientific method and framing questions and double blinds and statistics because she knows it won't help the current situation.

"I'm still working on that talking dog thing," Jeff says five minutes later from behind the paper.

Nora doesn't really hear him. She's thinking about what he said – "she never listened." What was that about? Does he mean her? If she asked him, she knows he would say it was just an example. But it must be true. Why else would he say it? She thinks she listens. She intends to listen. But maybe she doesn't. Maybe this is why he leaves her.

"What did you just say?" she asks him, a shade of desperation in her voice.

"What?" He lowers the paper.

"What did you just say?"

"About what?"

"Never mind."

The next morning as Jeff is tying his tie, he asks her casually, "If I bring you a talking dog, will you get me my zeppelin?"

Nora's throat is suddenly dry; she has to clear it before she speaks. This is it, she thinks, the test she will fail, the path by which he will leave her. "Zeppelins are easy," she says.

"That's what you think," Jeff replies.

Nora thinks she sees a zeppelin directly overhead as she's driving to her office, a blinding flash of silver that makes her stop flat in the middle of the road and climb out of her car. She stares up at the sky as if staring is the answer, until a battered orange pickup truck, swinging wide around the corner, almost takes her arm off.

She is more absentminded than usual in her morning class. One of the students asks her how time works in a black hole and she tells him that "time" and "black" and "hole" are all just symbols of actions and objects. "In a way, they can be whatever you want," she says.

"I don't think that's right," he says cautiously. "I mean, the book says – "

"Yes," she says hastily, "of course." She can't tell him that she was thinking about Jeff, wondering whether he was playing word games with her, cleverly redefining "I'm leaving you" into zeppelins and talking dogs.

After class, instead of heading back to her office, she exits the building and crosses the busy quadrangle to the low, ivy-covered brick building that houses the English department. Though it won't be announced for at least six months, Nora knows that the Provost is maneuvering to demolish the three old buildings that house English, Foreign Languages, and History. She knew at convocation by the way he leaned on the podium, by the words he used to welcome them back, by the interplay of shadows on the wall just past his shoulder. She finds Sara in her office sitting cross-legged in a battered leather arm chair, talking to one of her students, who is perched nervously on the edge of a straight-backed chair. "Look, it's quite simple really," Sara is saying to the student. "Find out what your character wants most, and then take it away from them."

"What?" the student asks, a frown creasing her earnest forehead.

"What will they do?" Sara asks. "When what they want most in the world is gone, what will your character do?"

Nora stands in the doorway, her breath caught in her throat. Jeff cannot possibly be what she wants most in the world. She wants the Nobel Prize, an endowed chair, the next great radical rewriting of the rules of the universe. She wants...oh god, she wants to own her place in the world.

A memory six years gone flashes into Nora's head: her first postdoc in Finland. "Why would you want to go there?" her mother asked her nearly every time they talked on the telephone in the weeks before she left.

"For the lights," Nora told her.

"The lights? What lights? Are you insane?"

"I mean the research," Nora said.

"All right, then," said her mother.

Nora has been telling people she means the research ever since.

She's halfway down the stairs when Sara catches up with her. "Nora," she calls, "did you want to talk?"

"What do you think a zeppelin costs?" Nora asks her.

"Millions," Sara answers without hesitation, the only evidence of surprise a half-raised eyebrow.

Nora nods as if considering. "What about a talking dog?"

"I don't think you can actually buy one of those," Sara tells her.

Nora looks up the stairs at Sara. There is a crispness in the air, as if winter is coming early. Nora can feel her life, her careful, controlled, scientific life sliding down through the soles of her feet and tumbling, broken, down the stairs.

"I don't want Jeff to leave me," she says as if that's what their conversation has been about all along.

Sara appears more stunned by this uncharacteristic confession than by talk of zeppelins and talking dogs. She recovers quickly, though, and descends the stairs to grasp Nora's shoulder. "Oh, honey. I don't think he'd – why would he leave you?"

"I don't know."

"Then you don't know that he'll leave."

When Nora doesn't answer, Sara sighs and says, "Look, just ask him."

Nora understands that asking would be simple for Sara. "What's up?" Sara would say. "Are you leaving me or what?" But for Nora it would be like ripping her own heart from her chest – because what if the answer is something she can't fix? "The thing is," Nora says, "if I don't ask, then I can't get the wrong answer. Like Schrödinger's cat, you know."

"Is that the cat that doesn't die unless you look at it?"

Nora rolls her eyes. "Sort of."

"You need to get over the science thing," Sara says prosaically. "Thought experiments are not going to help you here."

Nora knows that this conversation will eventually inspire Sara to write a series of short stories dealing with the domestic lives of scientists, played out against the background of historic events. Characters will lose what they want most in all the world and science will not help them win it back.

"Science explains the world to us," Nora says.

"How's that idea working out for you?" Sara asks wryly.

"I have to go now," Nora says, backing away.

"Just ask him," Sara says to the back of Nora's head as she hurries out the door.

Nora sees flashes of silver in the sky when she's walking across campus, when she's in the parking lot getting into her car, when she's driving through downtown. She stops, gets out of her car and looks up at the sky. Red light from the setting sun slants across the clouds. Nothing silver, nothing big, nothing like an airship. She looks away and there it is – a flash of silver – out of the corner of her eye, just out of sight, just out of reach.

Nora gets back in her car and drives to the park, where she parks in the nearly empty lot and walks out into the middle of the open green. She stands there for twenty-seven minutes until the sun has completely faded from the sky, until the shadows have spread from horizon to horizon, until the moon rises.

Nora leaves her car behind and walks across the park. The moon is three-quarters full and the light it casts is so silver that it turns the shadows blue. There's a nip in the air, like the promise of winter, but the breeze is warm. She crosses a dry creek bed and climbs the bank to a large open field. She puts her hand down on a half-liter plastic soda bottle someone has tossed and picks it up. Nora has never walked this way before, though she knows where her home is from here, like a beacon lit by rooftops. Scattered throughout the field are tall stalks of dried grass that look silver in the moonlight.

In the center of the field, Nora drops to her knees and gathers silvery dry stalks of grass in her hands. The moon shadows and brightens as clouds like wispy cobwebs filter across the sky. Nora winds strands of grass around the plastic bottle in her hands, weaves silver in and out, length to length. She discovers to her surprise that she is crying, as if what she's doing is both destroying and creating the world.

When she's finished she holds the long cylinder, woven all around with grass from the field, up to the moonlight. It is very light and seems to nearly float in the soft breeze. It glows like bioluminescent plankton, like the afterglow of rocket engines, like the eyes of wolves in wilderness. She walks the rest of the way home, which seems to take longer than it should, carrying her prize gently in her hands.

She comes to the house from the back and stands for a moment on the porch looking into the kitchen through the window. Jeff is standing at the counter, his jacket off and his tie askew. His hands are flat against the counter and his head is hanging as if he's staring at his own hands. Nora wonders what he's thinking. Is he wondering where she is or has he not yet noticed that she's gone?

She wipes dried tears from her cheeks, takes a deep breath and walks into the kitchen, holding her woven-grass-soda-bottle-zeppelin in one hand behind her back. Jeff looks up when the door opens and smiles, that breathtaking smile that Nora can scarcely bear – it slams her heart like a hammer, like a promise and a threat, and she's not sure which one's a good thing.

"Where have you – " Jeff begins.

"I brought you something," Nora says at the same time. She brings it out from behind her back and shows him what she's created. "Your zeppelin."

There's a moment of silence. Jeff takes the grass and soda bottle creation and holds it at arm's length, turning it slightly in his hands.

"You may have to squint," Nora says, tilting her head to the side. "Or look at it in moonlight, maybe."

Jeff just stands there silently and looks at the object in his hands. It looks so crude, just broken stalks of grass, that Nora wants to cry. She has rarely been so foolish – so fooled – because it really looked, out in the moonlight, like something magic and silver and –

Jeff takes her hand and pulls her outside.

On the open back porch, moonlight slants across the whitewashed plank floor. Jeff holds the woven-grass-soda-bottle in the open palm of his right hand. In the moonlight the awkward strands of dried grass seem to knit themselves together into a smooth whole that swallows the shape-holding soda bottle and becomes something that encompasses the world, something so right in the space and time in which it exists that it becomes more than its components, an extension of the moonlight, and seems to float on its own just above Jeff's hand.

Jeff stares at it for several minutes, his other hand still clasping Nora's as if the connection is as important as the silver object in his hand. Eventually, he sets the zeppelin carefully on a rail post and brushes Nora's hair gently away from her face. He doesn't say anything, just kisses her. Nora wraps her arms tightly around his neck and kisses him fiercely back.

Sometime later, he says, "I haven't had a lot of luck with the dog thing yet."

Nora laughs. "Don't worry about it," she says.

Nora knows that within the next six months Jeff will take on a pro bono property case for a family in Montana he's never met. He will hike through three canyons on the border between Montana and Canada with a local survey crew, lose track of the arbitrary lines between one country and the next, and find an entire valley that no one has ever mapped. He will return from that trip with a dog that never barks or cries, though occasionally, when the two of them have been arguing about money or chores or other things that don't actually matter, the dog will jump onto the kitchen table and stare at them each in turn until they are forced to see the world reflecting back at them through its eyes.

Single White Farmhouse

Heather Shaw

Heather Shaw (journalscape.com/heather) lives in Oakland, California with her husband Tim Pratt ("we were married last October 1st." And see Pratt story note, earlier in this book). They co-edit the 'zine, *Flytrap*. "I grew up in the Midwest (Indiana) and moved out to California after college in 1997 to pursue, well, life outside the Midwest." She has been published in *Polyphony*, *Strange Horizons*, *Fortean Bureau*, and the anthology, *Nine Muses*.

"Single White Farmhouse" was published, as was the VanderMeer piece, in *Polyphony* 5. The fantastic sometimes animates and personifies, as in this gorgeously absurd story about a sentient house that gets on the Internet and then gets out of hand. It is an amusing counterpoint to the Anne Harris story earlier in this book.

OUR HOUSE'S FRISKY NATURE only became a problem after we'd wired her for the Internet. Before that our pretty white farmhouse's shameful ways had only led to a new doghouse or shed every few months, but we owned a lot of land and there was always room for her offspring. My family even had a decent side business selling off her pups, as she had a reputation for sturdy, handsome buildings capable of growing to many times their birth footage.

Sometimes, such as after the old barn burned down, she'd consent to be bred with buildings we picked out for her. To get Dad's new red barn we introduced her to Farmer Pierce's shiny silo and after creaking about how big and shiny he was, she took him like he was nothing but a chicken coop. The barn was a difficult birth – her floorboards groaned and she rocked on her foundations – but she was very proud of Barny when he was born, as he was nearly full size.

Us kids were the ones wanting Internet access out at the farm. My older brother and I were both in high school and it was a long way back into town just to do our homework after supper. It also meant I couldn't sneak off to see my boyfriend while I was supposed to be at the library, which was why Mom joined us in convincing Dad to agree to the wiring. Dad said the house had been good to us – over the years, she'd grown from a one-bedroom cabin to a lovely two-story, six-bedroom farmhouse with a wrap-around porch and fireplace. Dad said it just wasn't nice to go threading wires between her walls after she'd given us a roof over our heads for so long, but he finally gave in.

Not one of us would have predicted the 'net sex.

The house consented to the wiring, and as soon as it was done she explored it carefully, like you or I would poke at a new tooth filling. Wasn't long before any unused terminal would be flashing from her zooms around the Internet. New bookmarks were always appearing in the browser files – architecture sites, construction sites, even some redecorating, *Better Homes and Gardens*-type sites were piling up in the history. Dad was disgusted by this, called it "house porn," which made me and my brother giggle.

It wasn't long before the house started spending all her time in chat rooms, flirting with buildings in far-off places such as New York and San Francisco. She left photos of the buildings she met on the desktop, and for a while we were all pretty proud of our little farmhouse. Every day a different landmark would send its picture: the Empire State Building, the Eiffel Tower, the Space Needle. Once she left a triptych of the Sydney Opera House, the Palace of Fine Arts, and the Taj Mahal on screen, and when Dad saw it he cursed, going on about how it was bad enough her catting around with skyscrapers online, but he wasn't living in a lesbian house, and she'd better lay off the other girl houses. She got real sad and shrunken after being yelled at like that, and we lost both our guest bedrooms over the fight. But she did lay off the other girls.

Wasn't long after that when she figured out how to order things over the 'net. Mom had been paying bills online, as it was a lot easier than writing a dozen checks every month, and the house picked up on it and snagged our credit card numbers.

At first it seemed like the only consequence of the house having access to the 'net and our credit cards was that we'd never have to worry about maintenance again. Exterminators showed up early one morning at our door. "Hi. Got a work order saying you've got a 'termite invasion in the southwest corner of the basement.'"

Dad scratched his head, torn between anger that he hadn't ordered this man to come out and pride over the farmhouse. Pride won out.

"Let me take you down there."

A little bit later, the exterminator was the one scratching his head as he had Dad sign off on the rather small bill.

"Sir, I don't know how she knew there were termites down there. It was just a pregnant queen and some workers...they didn't even have time to eat much, let alone set up their colony. I ain't never seen nothing like it; most houses don't notice till the infestation is much further along. Your house saved you hundreds of dollars of damage and I just can't figure out how she knew. She's got a lot upstairs, eh?"

Mom and I groaned and Dad made some evasive "aw shucks" noises, paid the man and showed him out. The man shook his head the whole way back to his truck.

Back inside, Dad stood in the foyer and said to the house, "Well, I guess that was all right, seeing as how you saved us money. Next time you ask first, though, you hear?"

Our house had never communicated directly with him, not even once we got her e-mail, so this was sort of a futile request. Mom always said it was because being silent was a powerful choice for certain women, but I thought she was just shy with people. She was starting to open up to me, though, gossiping with me over guys I met online, discussing the far-away big cities where they lived and, sometimes, the buildings they lived in. She was very popular online by then, a big flirt in the building scene, and pretty enough to pull it off.

She was clever, too. She waited until a school day when Mom was in town shopping and Dad was out in the back forty to have the house painters come. By the time everyone was home again, she was gleaming fresh white, her shutters painted a sultry shade of smoky blue. Sure enough, there was a hefty charge on the credit cards for a rush paint job.

Dad was livid about it, but instead of shrinking on him she gave back one of the guest rooms, Dad's favorite one, with all the furniture intact, and he forgave her.

Since I'd helped her pick the shutter shadow, I was relieved she got away with it. She was looking beautiful.

"She's learning fast," Mom said. She looked around in worry. "If you were my daughter, House, I'd be wanting to meet the young men you talk to and set curfews about now. These aren't the nice local boy-buildings you grew up with; you be careful, you hear?"

Mom was pretty proud of the house, though. When the gardeners showed up at the door a few days later, she not only let them landscape the front yard, but she paid them cash out of the cookie jar and told Dad she'd done it herself. Dad was a little skeptical about Mom's ability to carry and lay in the curving cobblestone path, let alone the flowering plum tree, but he let it go.

When Dad claimed that the new solar panels were his idea, my brother and I just rolled our eyes. It was cool to be off the grid, sure, but the house got away with everything!

I didn't tell them about my increasing communication with the house. She was getting to be a good friend of mine, actually, since she seemed to be the only one who realized how boring it was out on the farm or even in town. Looking back over those e-mails, I guess I should've realized what she was planning, but at the time I thought we were just daydreaming together.

By this time the house was looking very nice indeed. Her paint was fresh, the lawn green, and her window boxes overflowing with colorful flowers. She flattered Ma by sending her an e-mail asking for new lacy curtains in all the front windows. Ma bragged for a solid week about the house choosing to e-mail her instead of contacting a fancy interior designer.

When the house was all spiffed up and ready, I took pictures of her and scanned them into the computer system.

Turns out she'd been chatting online with a fancy skyscraper in San Francisco, and he had been pressuring her to send along a photo. She conveyed this to me while I was supposed to be doing my homework in my bedroom.

"Ah, so that's what you're up to! You should've told me sooner! Did he at least send you a picture of himself first?"

The screen fluttered and a photo of the San Francisco skyline flashed on the screen.

"Which one?"

The photo zoomed in on a tall pointy skyscraper in the right hand corner.

"Holy shit! That's the TransAmerica Pyramid! It's famous! Way to go Housey!"

The lights in the bedroom dimmed and took on a rosy hue.

"Oh, quit blushing! We all know around here you're the best. Wait till he opens his shutters on you. If he wasn't in love before, he will be then."

The lights in the room fluttered excitedly as they brightened.

I sighed. "I'm jealous. I'd give anything to have a really sexy, sophisticated boyfriend instead of some farm dweeb who happens to be good at football and who my mom won't let me have any fun with anyway."

The lights dimmed and the floorboards sighed as a map flashed onto the screen. There was a star on our farm and another on San Francisco. A blue dotted line started at the farm and inched its way slowly to the coastal city.

"Yeah...that's true. A long-distance relationship sucks. After a while, letters aren't enough and you just want to rub skin...er, walls." The house groaned. "Poor Housey."

A few days later we heard a great creaking and groaning as the house rocked up from her foundations. Shutters flapped as her chicken legs unfolded beneath her.

We were shocked that she did this while we were all home, inside. Houses were notoriously shy about getting up and mating in front of humans. Dad ran out on the front porch, grabbing at the railing so he wouldn't fall off. The chicken legs had lifted the bottom step a clear fifteen feet off the ground.

"What the hell do you think you're doing?" Dad roared as the house took an unsteady step. It had been months since she'd moved last, and we'd never seen her so much as stand up in front of us before this. "I won't tolerate you mating while we're inside! You stop and let us off right now!"

Tilting back first so Dad slid down across the front porch and through the doorway, the house slammed the door shut, closing us inside. She took another step, then another, faster and faster until she was running across the landscape at a blurring speed.

When I gave her hell for not at least warning me that she was kidnapping us, she cringed and tried to distract me by pointing out that she'd waited until the crops were all in, and had picked a day after Mom had done a big grocery shopping run so we'd have food for the trip. Not that cooking is easy in a jogging house. Mom joked that the eggs flipped themselves, but it didn't take long before most of our meals were prepared in the microwave. Mom also wouldn't let any of us chop, saying we'd cut ourselves when the house leaped over the next creek, so we ate a lot of cereal and grits and had to tear off our meat in chunks. All the glassware was kept safely stowed away, so we had to use plastic cups. Dad hated this, saying the milk tasted funny in anything other than glass.

We passed a big cathedral in a small city the next state over, and when I made "hey-hey, check him out" noises about him, the house told me, rather primly, that cathedrals weren't sexual buildings, and that they were immaculately conceived. I wondered about that all afternoon.

Despite the cool new scenery just outside our windows, we were all getting grumpy, being cooped up together in a jolting house. After a few days, the house started sleeping during the day and traveling at night, probably to appease us. It was nice to have stillness, though for the first few hours every morning everyone staggered as if we'd been at sea for months, and toward the end of the eight hours everyone got jumpy, waiting for the house to start moving again. It still felt like we were at the mercy of the house, and for me it was weird not having her awake to chat with, so nothing felt normal.

"What I don't understand," Mom whispered on the fourth day of the trip while the house was sleeping, "is why she took us with her while running away." We were somewhere in the desert by then, and it was so hot we didn't do much but lay around in our summer clothes. The air conditioning automatically shut off to conserve energy while the house was asleep, so the still hours were practically pointless. It was too hot to do anything but sleep and we'd all gotten used to being rocked while we slept.

Dad grinned at us kids. "If you're gonna run off, don't take us with you."

He was trying to be funny, but my brother snorted and I rolled my eyes.

"Dad!" I said, "Don't you get it? Housey's attached to us. She has to follow her heart, but she doesn't want to leave her family behind. I think it's sweet."

Mom and Dad exchanged a glance. My brother asked, "What the hell do you mean, 'follow her heart'?"

"Don't swear." Mom said. She always nagged more when she was too hot, even though it just made everyone more miserable.

"She's running off to see her shiny hot skyscraper in San Francisco! That one she's been chatting with?"

"You mean one of those online buildings has lured her out to – " Dad sputtered. "She's taking us out to the land of fruits and nuts?"

"We're going to San Fran? Cool!" my brother said.

"Oh, my goodness," Mom said. She kind of looked excited.

Dad stood up and pounded on the wall, waking the house before Mom could stop him. "Listen up, 'Housey'! Hear me good! There ain't no way in HELL you're taking my family out where all those 'people' live!" He even made the finger quotes when he said "people."

"Daddy!"

"Be nice, dear!" Mom said.

Dad muttered. "God damn liberal political correct..." He looked back up at the ceiling toward the entryway, which was usually where he looked when he spoke to the house directly. "You see what you done? You can't take my family there. My kids ain't going to see that. No way."

There was a pause and a sound like wind through floorboards while the house considered. Then the windows slammed down and all the outside locks in the house clicked closed with an audible "Clack!"

No one moved. Dad's eyes swiveled over to Mom's. I wondered if I looked as scared as my brother. Finally, I went over and tried to open the window. It wouldn't budge. Without speaking, my brother, Mom, and finally Dad all came over and tried, without success. We moved soundlessly from one door or window until all outside entrances had been tested. Not one had moved an inch.

I glared at my father. "Great, thanks a lot Dad. Now we can't even get fresh air in here."

Dad mustered up his pride. "I think the house is agreeing with me that you all don't need to be catting around...that city."

Things were pretty tense after that. Everyone had been kind of curious about where Housey was going the whole trip. I'd been barely able to contain my excitement, let alone my internet searches on cool stuff to do there. I spent the rest of the trip using this information to try and persuade my father that there were educational things to do other than going to drag queen shows, but even after I won him over the house showed no signs of opening up. She seemed piqued with us, as much as a house can, and it was strange for her to have a side in a family argument. My brother tried to freak me out by telling me that my bedroom was making creaking sounds, like it was going to disappear during the night. I hate it when he's a jerk like that.

We finally crossed the Sierra Nevadas and ran downhill through the valley toward the San Francisco Bay Area. We stayed one day on a big cattle farm that was all mud and no grass. The house seemed distressed by seeing cows staggering through the mud and scared a bunch of them by setting down in their midst for the day. The sound of cattle outside our window woke us before the stillness did. We left with one calf fenced in by Housey on the big porch. Housey let Mom open the kitchen window to feed it the last of our oats. Dad eyed the calf and muttered something about the difference between peace offerings and theft, but you could tell he was somewhat pleased by the house's thoughtfulness.

The next morning we got to Oakland. If we'd thought Housey was upset by the cattle, it was worse in Oakland, where the houses seemed unnaturally still and colorless in many neighborhoods as we moved out of the hills. It took us a while to figure out that they were dead houses, full of people – crammed full of people in some places – but empty of their own spark of life. Housey shuddered and creaked, and even though it wasn't raining, the roof leaked. My brother made gagging noises to show his displeasure over the mildew smell. Me, I hugged my knees and rocked back and forth on my bed as I looked at the sad shells of houses outside my window.

"It's like a graveyard." Mom said to Dad, standing next to him at the big picture window in the front room. The house was moving slowly, almost reverently, along the streets. We watched people going into a particularly decrepit house and my parents shook their heads. "Can't people afford to put these to rest and buy some pups?"

"Don't know where they'd get 'em." Dad said. "Probably expensive to buy 'em out here where most of the buildings are long dead."

A little later he said, "At least we don't have to worry about her slumming."

All day long Housey moved slowly to the bay, and she swam across to San Francisco as the sun set orange and yellow and pink above the water, which was dark silver with the approaching night. It was one of the most beautiful things I've ever seen. The houses were too close together in Oakland for us to sit down and rest anyway, not that we had hopes of room in a good neighborhood in San Francisco. We settled down on a vacant pier early so that Housey could get a night of "beauty rest" before meeting her skyscraper the next morning.

She rose early, and opened all her windows to let fresh air in for the first time in days. Mom's lace curtains fluttered in the salty breeze, and everyone went out on the porch and breathed deeply.

I was the first to wrinkle my nose. "Smells like...like fish!"

"Yuck!"

"Hm." Dad looked toward the water. "Probably low tide."

Mom waved a hand in front of her face and looked back toward the house. "You might want to move inland if your intention is to smell pretty, sweetheart."

Housey moved carefully inland, letting the wind whistle through her boards, making a merry little tune. Her excitement was palpable, and combined with the novelty of being allowed outside, it elevated everyone's spirits.

The city itself was a maze of narrow streets, and it was obvious that even the early morning traffic was annoyed by something as big as Housey wandering down the streets at such a slow pace. As we entered the business district, the honking got bad enough that we all went inside to let Housey pick up the pace.

We plastered our faces against the windows as we came out of the financial district into Chinatown. The streets were lined with strange shops and red buildings shaped like pagodas and a lot of the signs were in Chinese. "Holy shit, Mom, look! It's like being in China."

"Language – oh, my! Look! How strange and wonderful – " We were passing a little stall overflowing with beautiful Asian black lacquer boxes and huge paper fans and lanterns and a bin of leopard-print slippers for only $3 a pair. "Look at the weird little shops! Oh, I wish I could stop and shop!"

As if on cue, the house stopped and kneeled down. There wasn't a basement to fold her legs into, so she had to gently lean forward to make the porch touch the ground.

"You're letting us off?" Dad asked from the porch. The house flapped her shutters toward the pointy skyscraper down the street. "You coming back for us?"

Once we were all outside the house nodded.

"Do you want me to come along, for moral support?" I asked. The house considered for a moment, then nodded again and knelt down to let me back on.

"Sweetheart, get back here!" Dad scolded.

"It's a girl thing, Dad. Don't worry, she won't let anything bad happen to me."

"I don't want you on board while that house – does her thing! Especially not with a skyscraper!"

"Da-ad! Jeez!" I couldn't believe him sometimes. "I'm just going along so she can meet him! What kind of house do you think we live in? She's not going to mate right away with a building she just met!"

Dad seemed embarrassed by this and muttered something like, "Be good, then," and wandered off with Mom and my brother to explore.

The house and I went up the street, stopping at the foot of the big, pointy skyscraper. He was really tall, though not as tall as some of the other buildings we'd just passed in the financial district, where the Bank of America building had made Housey titter like a young schoolhouse, but he was kind of arrow-shaped, and I guess that pointy bit at the top was really hot to other buildings. I watched from my bedroom window as Housey fluttered her shutters at him. The shining building did not move. Housey creaked and groaned, demurely at first, then louder and louder until I finally suggested, "Try sending him an IM."

The terminal flashed as the message was sent. A short while later, words appeared on the screen and I read them out loud, "'You're here in the City? Now?'"

"Uh-oh." I said, glancing out at the still-oblivious skyscraper. "Oh, Housey, I'm sorry sweetie, but that's not him out there. Find out which building he really is."

Turns out that another skyscraper – Housey called it, "a stumpy, artsy tower down the street, on a hill," but it was actually the Coit Tower – had sent along the TransAmerica Pyramid's photo as his own, hoping to impress Housey. After hearing the news, Housey walked us slowly into North Beach to see the real facade behind her internet lover, and her lights went dim when she looked up the hill and saw the much smaller, and much less shiny, reality. She looked longingly toward Chinatown where we could still see the TransAmerica Pyramid glinting in the sunlight.

"Don't you like him, Housey?" I asked about the Coit Tower. "Think about it – he's all romantic, up on that hill like that! He's a landmark, too – just an older one."

The tower on the hill bent hopefully down toward the pretty white farmhouse at his feet, and she shuddered all over in response. I obviously don't get what's sexy to buildings, because I think the Coit Tower is pretty good looking – and famous! Coit slumped, obviously distressed. I read countless apologies from him flooding over the terminal, but Housey was deleting them almost too fast for me to read.

"Oh, Housey, look how sad he is! He was just insecure about his size and age! Why don't you give him a chance?"

Housey flashed a picture of my quarterback boyfriend, then a picture of the chess club president who had sent me countless, and eventually annoying, love e-mails last year.

I sighed. "OK, point taken."

Housey flashed me another message.

I looked at the screen in surprise, then smiled up at the House. "Yes, yes, ok, lying is bad, too." I hugged a wall as best I could. "Sorry Housey."

After a moment, a photo of the Palace of Fine Arts flashed on the screen.

"Oooh, yeah, of course I remember her! She wrote you back? Excellent! You should totally go see her."

A photo of Dad flashed on the screen.

"Tell you what – you drop me in Haight-Ashbury and let me explore the City for awhile on my own – and don't tell Dad where I was – and I won't tell Dad about that pretty lady you're going to go see in the Presidio. Deal?"

The lights flickered in assent and we skipped off toward the ocean.

Read It in the Headlines!

Garth Nix

Garth Nix (publisher site: *www.garthnix.co.uk*) lives in a beach suburb of Sydney, Australia, with his wife Anna, a publisher, and son Thomas Henry. He worked in a bookshop, then as a book publicist, a publisher's sales representative, and editor. Along the way he was also a part-time soldier in the Australian Army Reserve, serving in an Assault Pioneer platoon for four years. Garth left publishing to work as a public relations and marketing consultant from 1994–1997, till he became a full-time writer in 1998. He did that for a year before joining Curtis Brown Australia as a part-time literary agent in 1999. In January 2002 Garth went back to being a dedicated writer again, despite his belief that full-time writing explains the strange behavior of many authors. His fantasy novels are published as children's books in some countries, as adult books in others.

"Read It in the Headlines!" was published in *Daikaiju! Giant Monster Tales*, an original anthology of giant monster stories edited by Robert Hood and Robin Pen, in Australia. Told entirely as tabloid newspaper headlines, it is no longer than it needs to be, and pure enjoyment.

ARCHAEOLOGISTS ENTER FORBIDDEN TOMB!

ARCHAEOLOGISTS FLEE FORBIDDEN TOMB!
TOMB FORBIDDEN FOR GOOD REASON

GUARDIAN CREATURE
'DEFINITELY WILL NOT LEAVE' ANCIENT TOMB,
SAY ARCHAEOLOGISTS

GUARDIAN CREATURE LEAVES TOMB!
EXPERTS RE-CHECK TOMB TEXTS

PUBLIC SAFETY ANNOUNCEMENT
NORTH OF RIVER: LEAVE NOW

NAVY WILL STOP GUARDIAN CREATURE

"IT TUNNELLED RIGHT UNDER THE RIVER!"

"GEECEE" KILLS 18
NAVY KILLS 2,117

PUBLIC SAFETY ANNOUNCEMENT:
LIST OF SUBURBS TO BE EVACUATED

GENERAL NASHER:
"WE WILL DESTROY THAT THING!"

GEECEE ON RAMPAGE!

PROTESTORS DISRUPT GENERAL'S FUNERAL

PUBLIC SAFETY ANNOUNCEMENT:
NEW EVACUATIONS

PROFESSOR PENHOOD:
CREATURE NEEDS 'GOOD' HEART

THREE HEARTS OR THREE TOES?
TRANSLATION DISPUTED

GEECEE HEADING SOUTH-WEST

GEECEE FIVE-TOED SAYS STOMPING SURVIVOR

WHAT DOES IT WANT? THE PUBLIC ASKS

IT WANTS THE ARCHAEOLOGISTS!

MISSILE ATTACK KILLS 856
GEECEE UNHARMED

CREATURE RESPONSE TACTICS CRITICISED

PROFESSOR PENHOOD SAYS GEECEE HAS HEART OF IRON

IRON AND GOLD HEARTS MUST BE SWAPPED,
SAYS PENHOOD

GEECEE KILLS THIRD-LAST ARCHAEOLOGIST

ARCHAEOLOGISTS FERRISH AND DANCER APOLOGISE TO CITY

DANCER GOES DOWN GEECEE GULLET
FERRISH HIDDEN FOR OWN SAFETY

GEECEE DIGS UP SECRET BASE BELOW CITY!

RESIDENTS PROTEST EXISTENCE OF SECRET NUCLEAR ARSENAL:
GEECEE DIGGING CONTINUES

PROFESSOR PENHOOD RETURNS FROM TOMB

SIX TON HEART OF GOLD MOVED TO HELIBASE

DR FERRISH DEAD. IS THIS THE END?

PENHOOD SAYS RELATIVES OF ARCHAEOLOGISTS AT RISK

GEECEE MAKES GOULASH OF THIRD COUSIN

IT THINKS WE'RE ALL RELATED!

MASS PANIC.
MAYOR URGES CALM.

PROFESSOR TO DROP HEART BY HELICOPTER

HELICOPTER SPAT OUT OF SKY!
PENHOOD SURVIVES CRASH!

HEART RETRIEVED FROM
SMASHED HELI IN CRUSHED DELI

HEART ATTACK!
ARMOURED SEMI TO SMASH INTO GEECEE!

EJECTION SEAT SLIM CHANCE FOR HERO PROF.

PROF'S FIANCÉE RETURNS RING

PUBLIC SAFETY ANNOUNCEMENT:
GET OUT OF THE CITY!

H-HOUR FOR HOT-ROD HEART TRANSPLANT

DID HEART HIT?

PLUME OF SMOKE AND DUST 5KM HIGH
PENHOOD'S PARACHUTE NOT SEEN

PENHOOD EMERGES FROM RUINS!

IT WORKED!

SUCCESS?
GEECEE DORMANT DOWNTOWN

MAYOR, CITIZENS FURIOUS WITH PENHOOD
BILLIONS LOST IN REAL ESTATE VALUES

HI-TECH PERIMETER GOES UP AROUND CITY CENTRE

PENHOOD SUED BY PROPERTY OWNERS, CITY,
REAL ESTATE ORGANISATIONS

INVESTIGATIVE COMMISSION EMPANELLED:
PROFESSOR PENHOOD ARRESTED

PROSECUTORS DEMAND LIFE IMPRISONMENT OF PENHOOD

PENHOOD SENTENCED TOMORROW

MYSTERIOUS GOUT OF
RADIOACTIVE STEAM IN CHANNEL

GIANT UNDERWATER SHADOW
MOVING TOWARDS CITY!

GET GEECEE TO GUARD US! DEMANDS FRIGHTENED PUBLIC

PENHOOD RELEASED!

PUBLIC SAFETY ANNOUNCEMENTS:
Ten Page List....

Niels Bohr and the Sleeping Dane

Jonathon Sullivan

Jonathon Sullivan lives in Farmington Hills, Michigan, with his wife Marilyn. Jonathon Sullivan, MD, Ph.D., practices Emergency Medicine at Detroit Receiving Hospital, and conducts cerebral resuscitation research at Wayne State University. His fiction has appeared in the anthologies *Bones of the World* and *Monolith 6*, and in *3SF*, *Strange Horizons*, and *Escape Pod* (*www.escapepod.org*), where the author serves on the editorial staff.

"Niels Bohr and the Sleeping Dane" was published in Strange Horizons. It is an excellent story of Jewish magic and escaping the Nazis, intertwined with a story about physics. To see Kronborg Castle and meet The Sleeping Dane, go to: *www.copenhagenpictures. dk/kronborg.html*.

THE GESTAPO had imposed curfews and roadblocks for the first time since the occupation of Denmark. They stopped our train at Helgoland, where the tidy streets of Copenhagen blend into the sparse woods and open gray sky of coastal Zealand. An ss captain and two men with short rifles clambered into our car. They demanded papers from every passenger, and I knew that by nightfall my father and I would be on another train, bound for darkness.

The man who sat across from us was also a Jew, but he would not go to the camps with us. Niels Henrik David Bohr would remain in Denmark, or perhaps he would be sent to Berlin. But he would be no less a prisoner.

The black uniforms and burnished weapons cut into the reality of the railcar like nightmares. You could hear the shared thought of everyone aboard: Not here. Not in Copenhagen. There's some mistake.

The Danes had lived with a monster in their house for two years, and they had learned to ignore it. The monster looked like them. It seemed to be housebroken. It kept out of sight, hiding under the bed while Denmark slept. But finally, inevitably, the monster had emerged, and it was ravenous.

Looking for us.

The ss captain was a handsome young man, square-jawed and blue-eyed, Hitler's Aryan ideal in the flesh. But his pale complexion reminded me of a wax doll. His ink-black uniform, with its red armband and skull insignia – the regalia of death – enhanced his pallor. In his eyes I saw the deep hunger that drives a man to devour his fellows. He evaluated the passengers, his head cranking from side to side with each click of his black leather boots, as if clockwork connected his legs to his neck.

He stopped a few rows away from us, to examine a young couple. Speaking in curt, inflected Danish, he demanded their papers. The man, a swarthy fellow with curly black hair, rummaged nervously in a satchel.

The captain put up his hand. "That's all right," he said. "It won't be necessary."

The man nodded with relief.

"You are *Juden*, yes?" The captain smiled.

One of the most vivid memories of my life is how the air on the bus changed at that moment, suddenly cloying and thick. A smell of quiet panic, like sweat and rotten meat.

The young man blanched. "I am a Danish citizen," he said, voice quavering.

The officer's expression was not so much a smile as a gash cut into his face. "You are a subject of the German Reich," he said. He made a command with his fingers: *on your feet.* The young man stood, and he and his wife were led off the bus. The woman carried an infant bundled in blue wool.

I have often wondered what became of that family. Did they die at Theresienstadt? Dachau? Auschwitz? I still have nightmares about the look in that young woman's eyes.

The captain approached us. His gaze settled on me for a moment, then passed to my father.

The Danish resistance had told us we must pass for everyday people. Papa had retorted that we were people, every day, but he hadn't really argued. He had shaved that majestic, iron-gray beard, trading his broad-brimmed black hat and dark coat for the dress of a *goy*.

Papa had strange gifts. But I could not imagine he would deceive the pale *Hauptsturmführer*. My father's essence would shine through the rumpled khaki trousers and thick sweater of green wool, and any fool would see him as a rabbi of the *Hassidim*.

Who could look at my father and fail to see what he was? Until the day I die, his will be the human face of Yahweh: fierce but serene, severe but kind, deeply etched with sadness and humor, encompassing the mystery of opposites that are one. Brilliant, forceful *Chockhmah* and dark, gentle *Binah* united in *Tiferet*, the living heart of Israel that is the center of the universe. No man who met my father, Jew or Gentile, failed to be awed by him. Least of all me.

When he saw Papa, the *Hauptsturmführer* frowned.

Papa said, "Good morning."

The captain nodded, his frown slowly unwinding. "Good morning. *Heil Hitler.*"

He quickly looked away from Papa's eyes, and next gave a cursory glance to the brother and sister seated next to us. With their light brown hair and sullen expressions, the two teenagers could not possibly have looked more generically and ethnically Danish. They were, in fact, armed members of the threadbare Danish resistance. They didn't get a second look.

The captain turned to scrutinize the three people in the seat facing ours. A frumpy man with unruly red hair pretended to look out the window. Hans Nielsen was the father of the two young partisans. Next to him sat an elegant woman in her mid-fifties, with a slender neck and fine Nordic features.

Beside her, directly across from me, sat the father of the modern atom.

Bohr had a paunch, but he was still a lanky man, with that characteristic Danish angularity and length of bone. His brown suit fit him with a balanced, casual elegance. His features had sagged beneath the weight of the occupation, the constant threat from the Nazis who circled him like hyenas, waiting for him to go too far in his vocal defense of Danish culture against the Reich. Thick-lipped, balding, and aged – he should have been ugly. But the intelligence was there, quiet and profound, like clean water pouring out of a rocky cave. I like to think that, even if I had not known him as the man who had resurrected the corpse of Rutherford's atom and made it dance to the strange music of Planck and Einstein, I would have loved him the moment I saw him.

"Herr Doktor Bohr!" The captain's cruel smile returned. "What a relief. We've been very concerned about you."

Hans, the frumpy man at the window, forced himself to look, a film of defeat in his eyes. The two young partisans next to Papa stared at the floor. I thought of the weapons beneath their coats. In their stillness I could sense a gathering, desperate violence.

Bohr sighed, looked up at the Gestapo captain with calm resignation, and took his wife's hand. He started to get up.

"You are mistaken, sir," Papa said.

I wanted to scream at him: No! This creature has already passed us over and now you beg for his attention!

I was nineteen years old. I had followed Bohr's career for half my life, with something bordering on worship. A terrible miracle of circumstance had finally brought me into his presence. But at that moment his life meant nothing next to my own. Niels Bohr was already a prisoner of the Third Reich – nothing could stop that now, save some desperate stupidity from Hans and his children. Papa's action could only put us on a boxcar to Theresienstadt.

The Gestapo captain gave Papa another nervous glare. "What did you say?"

"I said you are mistaken. This is my brother-in-law, Karl Gervuld. This woman is my sister, Frieda."

The captain's features hardened, but Papa's stare held him prisoner. "This man's face is known throughout the world," he said, uncertainty creeping into his voice. "This man is Niels Bohr and he will be taken into protective custody."

"Take a closer look," Papa said.

The captain obeyed: Bohr was unmistakable. He shook his head, frowning. "I'm...quite sure..."

It won't work, Papa. You're killing us.

"Look at me."

The captain turned. Confusion and fear grew in his eyes.

"This is my brother-in-law, Karl Gervuld." Papa's belly tensed in and out beneath his sweater. I could almost see the power surging between Papa's *Tiferet* and the captain's *Yesod*.

"It would be *embarrassing* if you presented him to your superiors as somebody he is not. You wouldn't want to be *embarrassed!*"

"I..."

"This is my brother-in-law, Karl Gervuld."

The captain licked his lips. "I should see his papers. Yours too."

The young man next to Papa reached into his coat, tensing for action. I thought of the last time Papa had tried this. My mother had died anyway.

"That won't be necessary," Papa said. *"This is my brother-in-law, Karl Gervuld."*

By now, everyone was staring at Papa, except for the two ss men checking papers a few rows up. Bohr himself was transfixed by the motion of Papa's belly, pumping in and out like a bellows. The partisans watched like mystified children. And I could see from the young captain's face that Papa's eyes had become the center of his universe.

The German's jaw slackened, then snapped shut. His glassy eyes came back into focus. His hand went to rest on his holster, and I knew that Papa had failed again.

But the captain turned away, and did not look at us again. He swaggered back the way he had come, hand at his holster in a posture of Prussian authority. He ordered his men off the train, and moments later we were clattering up the Zealand coast toward Elsinore.

Nobody spoke for a long time. I stared at my knees, running the episode over and over.

Eight years earlier, Papa's power had failed to save Mama from the brownshirts. But even before that I had begun to doubt whether I could follow his path to knowledge.

I looked over at him. He sat with eyes half-closed, as if he were drunk.

No. I refused to regret my decisions. I refused to feel guilty for taking my own path. But for not having the courage to tell him...for that I could feel guilty. And I did.

"Sir?" Bohr reached over to touch Papa's knee. "We're grateful for...whatever it was you did. I thought for sure we would..." He shook his head. His wife managed a thin smile. She had not let go of her husband's arm.

Papa put out his hand to shake with Bohr and his wife. "I'm Itzak Goldblum. My son, David."

"My wife, Margrethe. Oh. I'm, uh..."

"Yes, I know." Papa shrugged. "But you certainly look like my brother-in-law Karl."

Bohr's eyes twinkled. "Do you have a brother-in-law?"

Papa smiled at Margrethe. "I don't even have a sister."

The Bohrs laughed. Niels looked over at me and smiled. "Nice to meet you, David."

I shook that noble hand and gawked at him, trying to think of something to say.

"Forgive him," Papa said. "If his brain were working now, he'd tell you that he's a great admirer of yours."

Bohr nodded. "Well...I'm honored." A polite dismissal of the schoolboy. He turned back to Papa. "I have to ask you. What did you do to that Gestapo man?"

"Barely a man," Papa said, shrugging. "A real man I could not have managed. He was more of a *golem*."

Bohr frowned. "I beg your pardon?"

"A *golem*. A fairy-tale monster, yes? An empty creature of wood or clay that can be filled with the will of another. A strong man cannot be manipulated so easily. But a *golem*..."

Margrethe leaned forward to listen. The two partisans were whispering with their father. Bohr shifted in his seat to retrieve a pipe from his pocket. "A *golem*."

"A man like that," Papa said, "is empty. You just have to know how to fill him. Dress him up in an imposing uniform, fill his head with grand ideas, and point him at a target. The *poor* Germans."

Bohr, tamping tobacco into the bowl, shook his head. "The poor Germans?"

Papa shrugged. "They've become a nation of *golem*. To make a *golem* of clay is a sin, a mortal sin. To make a *golem* of a man, is that any better? Perhaps God will punish me, although I didn't create that creature. Hitler has tapped into the unconscious, the world of dreams."

Bohr lit his pipe. "You sound like Herr Doktor Freud."

Papa reached up to stroke his beard, found it missing, scratched his chin. "Yes. Well, there's little that's new in Freud, except for the words."

Bohr took exception, and they got into a friendly argument over whether Freud was a scientist or metaphysician. It was exhilarating to watch the two most important men in my life joust and find each other worthy. And maddening, because I wasn't part of it. I could quote every word Bohr had ever published, almost verbatim. But for now I was just the boy.

By the time we passed the low hills of Klampenborg, halfway to Elsinore, I was seething. Papa was doing it deliberately. Another ploy to keep me in his world. Out of Bohr's. Almost before I could read, Papa had taught me that numbers were God's brick and mortar. To his lasting chagrin, I'd followed that teaching in a different direction than he'd intended. While he sought mystery and beauty in the Torah and Sefir Yetzirah, I had found my own truth in the writings of Bohr and Dirac, Heisenberg and Born.

"Of course," Papa said as the argument wound down, "I'm just an old rabbi. There's nothing I can point to and say: There's my proof. Herr Freud, he's in the same boat. But a man like you, you can put a handle on wisdom, no?"

Bohr shook his head. "I'm not sure what you mean."

Papa looked up, begging the roof for patience. "He's not sure what I mean! You are the man who discovered the atoms, no?"

Bohr shifted uncomfortably.

Hans leaned forward, over Margrethe's lap. "Not everybody on this goddamn train is known to us," he said. "I know the cat's out of the bag, but you could still keep it down to a dull roar."

He sat back and shook his head at his two children.

"He didn't discover the atom," I told Papa in a whisper. "He described the atom, in terms of Planck's quantized energy."

"Ahhh," Papa said. "A description."

"A description," I said, "that predicts atomic spectra, including the Zeeman perturbations, to the nanometer. A description that rescues the Rutherford atom from its own angular momentum. A description that explains the periodic table with a few quantum numbers."

Bohr shrugged. "An imperfect description," he said. But he was smiling at me.

"Ah! Numbers!" Papa shook his finger in affirmation. "Yes, I knew it would come down to numbers."

Bohr's grin widened. "Why is that?"

"Because everything does! My tradition also describes the universe with numbers."

"I am half-Jewish, you know," Bohr said. "In middle school, I dabbled in the Kabbalah."

"And what did you learn from dabbling in the Kabbalah?" Papa looked at Bohr, but I knew he was speaking to me.

Bohr shrugged. "Not much."

"Not much, because you *dabbled*! But in science you did not dabble. There you gave your all, and you learned a great deal. Am I wrong?"

"I suppose that's true." Bohr's pipe unfurled an aromatic veil that hid his expression from me.

"My son, he dabbles in everything," Papa said. "He dabbles in physics. He dabbles in the Talmud and the *Zohar*. Any more dabbling, he ends up a *nebbish*."

The conversation aborted. There was only the clattering of the tracks and the whispers of the partisans. Bohr puffed at his pipe and pretended to look at his feet.

It was Margrethe who saved me. Margrethe Bohr, who challenged me with her steely Nordic eyes and a look on her face...a look she might have given her own son Kristian, had she not lost him in an accident. A look my mother might have given me, had my father not lost her to the brownshirts. The secret message on her face was one of empathy, but not pity. A tiny nod and a curl of her lips that said: *Are you going to let these two old men dismiss you like that? Fight!*

"I never dabble," I said. "Not in Kabbalah. Not in physics."

Bohr fidgeted. Papa waved a dismissive hand and snorted.

I reached into my coat for the only scrap of paper I had: the letter from Cambridge. I unfolded it and turned it over quickly, so Papa could not read it. I set it on my knee, blank side up, and began to sketch out the Tree of Life: ten Holy *Sefirot* connected by twenty-two paths.

"My father," I said, "is an international authority on the *Zohar* and *Sefir Yetzirah*. In his last book, *The Song of Adam Kadmon*, he says, 'The *Sefirot* are not things.'"

Bohr, whose old friend Heisenberg had once said the same of atoms, sat up and looked at my drawing.

"The *Sefirot*, the ten nodes of existence, are numbers – like everything else," I said. "As my father writes, they are musical notes sung by God. Thus, vibrations. Vibration implies frequency. Frequency implies energy. The *Sefirot* are the 'quantum numbers,' if you'll forgive me, that describe all creation."

Bohr smiled. The expression was indulgent, but not patronizing. And I had his attention.

"The right branch of the Tree is creative, impulsive, masculine, positive. The left is receptive, nurturing, feminine, negative. The duality reconciles in the middle trunk, the synthesis of opposites that drives all creation. The Tree is a map of the Universe."

Bohr shook his head, but he kept listening.

I kept scribbling. "For example, in *Adam Kadmon* my father maps the Tree onto human physiology. Catabolism, motor processes, and the sympathetic nervous system appear on the right – all the functions that involve action, the release of energy. Anabolism, sensory processes and parasympathetic activity map to the left side." Then I pointed with my pen at *Tiferet*, the *Sefirot* in the center of the Tree, the one that connected to all the others.

"The heart?" Bohr offered.

"Ah, he sees!" Papa said.

I shook my head. "No, I don't think that's right."

"What?" Papa leaned over to look at my drawing. "*Mishegos!* Of course it's right!"

I hesitated, but then I caught Margrethe out of the corner of my eye again.

"No," I said, and continued scribbling. "The heart is a circulatory organ. It belongs at *Nezah*, on the lower left trunk. No, *Tiferet* is Beauty, the thing created. Balance, integration, essence."

"And so," Bohr asked, "what is the *Tiferet* of human physiology, young David?"

I flushed under Papa's withering glare. "The central nervous system," I said, and wrote it in. "The brain and spinal cord."

Bohr's pipe had gone cold from neglect. Papa chewed on his lower lip and stared at my drawing.

"We can also map the atom," I said. Across the top of the page I wrote n, l, m, s. "These are the four quantum numbers that underlie the structure of matter. Shell, subshell, magnetic, spin. But to describe matter, we also need to describe the electric force that binds electrons to the nucleus, and the force that holds the nucleus together. We need mass and charge..."

I kept talking, kept scribbling, my hands and brain working together in a storm of delight.

When I finished, Papa shook his head. "Huh. My son a *knaker*. Mr. Big Shot."

A smile grew on Bohr's thick lips, and he took the paper from my hand, so he didn't have to look at it upside-down. I was afraid Papa would read the other side.

"This is really quite beautiful," Bohr said.

Papa stared at me, and my delight intertwined with my dread. I had not told him of the scholarship I had won to study physics at Cambridge, recently announced in the *Letters*. I had avoided confronting him by telling myself it didn't matter. We had lost everything in Germany. Everything. Now Denmark was a mess, and if the resistance couldn't get us across the Elsinore Sound and into Sweden I might never go to university at all. So I willed myself to stop worrying about it, to bask in that perfect moment when the two men I loved and admired most looked at me with new eyes and nodded their heads with wonder and respect.

Bohr studied my drawing for a long time. I don't think he wanted to give it back.

Hans had made arrangements with the engineer, who stopped the train a kilometer shy of Elsinore Station. Seventeen Jews, including the Bohrs, disembarked at this unscheduled stop. Hans and his children led us to a nearby bus stand. There we caught a ride to Kronborg Castle, where Claudius had murdered Hamlet's father and Hamlet had murdered Claudius.

The fortress of stone and timber overlooks the Elsinore Sound at its narrowest point. From this vantage, Denmark had once imposed her will on all naval traffic through the Baltic. But Danish power had long since ebbed, and Kronborg Castle, with its wide moats and towers topped with spires of bluing copper, had become a museum. The Nazis had not closed the castle, just as they had not interfered in most aspects of Danish life – until now.

The bus pulled up to a wide bridge of wood and iron, half a kilometer from the castle. Our party joined a dozen sightseers who had already gathered around a tour guide. She was a plump woman with thick glasses and the bearing of a schoolmistress. While she collected the tour fee she lectured us in a nasal, singsong voice. Stay with me. The tour must end on time, because of the curfew. No photos. Don't touch.

Hans stood behind Papa and me. "She is our contact," he told us. "But you stay with me, not her, understand? Just before the tour enters the courtyard we split off and go to the old stables."

He moved on, whispering into other ears, including Bohr's. Hans's son and daughter stood on either side of the group, scanning the area.

My gaze kept wandering past the gorgeous mass of the castle, across the gray waters of the Sound, to the swelling of land on the other side.

Sweden. Neutral Sweden.

Our guide led us through a wooden gate and over a cobblestone footpath to the castle, lecturing all the way. Somebody built this in that year, over there was the residence of so-and-so. As we approached Kronborg, the majesty of the structure became more imposing, and for a moment I forgot our peril. I had seen my share of German castles – outside our home town of Heidelberg sits a seventeenth-century ruin of lichened stone. But Kronborg was huge, well-preserved, and graceful. The sun broke through the clouds, and I craned my neck to watch the spires rise into the bright sky. It was a perfect moment. I looked over at Papa, and he smiled.

We crossed the moat, our feet drumming the ancient drawbridge like the hooves of cattle. The guide continued her jabbering, leading us into a broad cobblestone courtyard, with a grand fountain at the center. I was sorry I wouldn't get to see more. But now Hans gave us a grim nod over his shoulder. As the rest of the group filtered into the sunlit courtyard, the Jews split off and took their own path into hiding.

As usual, I thought.

Hans and his children led us down a narrow path that ran along the outer moat and into the abandoned stables, a labyrinth of rotting wood set into the castle's eastern wall. There was no lighting here, and as we followed Hans into a maze of abandoned stalls my mood darkened.

Soon we were deep within the entrails of the castle. Hans led us through a broad wooden door and down a narrow staircase. We emerged into utter darkness.

A yellow flicker from his electric torch cut into the black like a firefly, moving crazily through the void. Then the light of a candle mounted on the wall began to etch out our surroundings. Hans lit two more, illuminating a place of despair.

"Looks like a dungeon," Papa said, and everybody turned to frown at him. Papa was always willing to say things people would rather not hear.

"Catacombs," Hans said. "But the dungeons aren't far."

The chamber was oppressively small. Rough stone curved just overhead, damp and ugly. Bohr had to stoop. Gravel and dirt crunched beneath our feet. The walls were abrasive and bare – even lichen refused to grow in this place.

But one creature did dwell here. Seated on a throne of rock against one wall, an eight-foot-tall viking slept with his chin on his chest, a broadsword across his knees. The statue of gray stone was exquisite and menacing. Even in repose, the warrior's features were implacable and noble. His legs were as thick as my torso. He wore a simple helmet and a tunic of mail, but his thick arms were bare. A massive shield sat propped against his thigh.

"Why do they keep this down here?" I asked Hans. "It's beautiful."

"Holger Danske sleeps here," he said matter-of-factly, as if I were an idiot.

"Well, now we know, don't we?" Papa said.

"We'll be here a few hours," Hans said, settling into a dark corner. "Try to rest. You especially, Doktor Bohr. Sweden is just a way station for you."

"I understand," Bohr said, and like everybody else he began searching for a stretch of wall. He removed his coat and spread it over the dirt so Margrethe could sit. He lit his pipe, and the sweet aroma was a great improvement. Some in our group whispered among themselves, but the close walls of the catacomb magnified every sound, and so for a long time there was only silence and, finally, the sound of Hans's snoring.

I, too, was exhausted. I sat beside Papa in the gravel beneath the stone warrior. Soon I joined Holger Danske in sleep.

I dreamed of my father's bookstore, in the Jewish quarter of Heidelberg. The brownshirts had come. One stood out front to trumpet his epithets, wearing sandwich boards that said *Warning! Germans Don't Buy From Jews!* While I tended the shop, four men came inside to ransack the shelves and break the windows. They beat me with fists and clubs, doubling me over with pain and shame. My parents came down the stairs from our apartment. My mother screamed and rushed to my side. The leader pushed her away, called her a whore.

The other three brownshirts converged on Papa, but they stepped back without laying a hand on him. He transfixed them with those dark eyes full of power, his belly rippling beneath his coat.

"You need to go now," he said, and they turned away.

But the leader had his own iron, his own malignant strength. He was too deep or too shallow for Papa's power to fill him. He cursed at his men, mocking them. He struck with his club, and Papa crumpled to the floor. Like cowardly dogs emboldened by blood, the others took his example. While they beat Papa, the leader kicked me in the face. As I lay choking on my own blood, he seized my mother by her hair and dragged her toward the street.

To be met at the doorway by Neils Henrik David Bohr. The Bohr I knew from books and photos. The young, gangly Bohr who had gone to England in 1911 to change the world.

He held up his atom of spinning orbitals, vibrating with latent energy. His fingers broke it apart, and released a brilliance that blinded the Nazis and dispelled them like a vapor.

When the brilliance faded, only Papa and I remained. My mother was gone.

The catacomb was dark enough to nourish the dream a few minutes into waking. Papa had taught me to cling to my dreams and interrogate them – they were wisdom from *Yesod*, or even from *Da'at*, and not to be discarded without examination.

My eyes adjusted slowly. Bohr and my father sat together at the stone feet of Holger Danske. Their low voices echoed off the walls.

"I promise," Bohr was saying. "I did my best work at Cambridge. And I still have friends there. It won't be difficult."

His words intertwined with my dream, a good fit. But not difficult? If the resistance managed to get Bohr to England, his task would be difficult in the extreme.

It was no secret that Bohr might be instrumental in splitting the atom for the Allies – if Heisenberg didn't beat him to it. My father's path might lead to wisdom, and a sort of ineffable power. But Bohr's path, the path I had chosen, led to a more reliable power, the kind of power that might rescue humanity from the grip of the Axis.

My father, bloody and helpless, splayed on the floor with his tattered books. Bohr at the doorway, splitting his atom to dispel evil.

The dream faded. Neither path would bring Mama back to me.

"He's awake," Papa said. "Welcome back! Better you shouldn't sleep, if you're going to be so fitful."

I went to sit with them. Everybody else sat quietly, except the two young partisans who stood at the entrance to the catacomb, smoking. Hans had abandoned his corner.

Bohr followed my gaze. "He left at nightfall, to check the area. He should be returning soon."

I nodded, rubbing the sleep from my eyes. A long silence ensued. I realized I had interrupted something.

Papa looked up at Holger Danske.

"My son is right. It's a strange thing to find in such a place."

"This is where he belongs," Bohr said. "Holger Danske is our national hero. The Sleeping Dane, we call him. This statue was put here in 1911, just before I went to England. The Sleeping Dane fought many battles for Denmark abroad. But eventually he grew weary of war. He came back to Elsinore, and fell asleep on this spot." Bohr lit his pipe again, and I smiled. He seemed unable to speak without a pipe in his hand.

"They say he is the final defender of Denmark. When invaders come, the Sleeping Dane will awaken to save us." Bohr gave Papa a fatalistic smile. "But still he sleeps. So much for legends."

Papa looked up at Holger Danske for a long time. Finally he said: "You're wrong, Doktor Bohr. The Sleeping Dane is *awake*."

Bohr shook his head, bemused.

"The occupation has been almost painless up to now." Papa scratched at his bare chin. "You Danes have had it easy. The Germans pretend to respect your neutrality, and you pretend you still have something to respect."

Bohr frowned, then nodded. "Yes, I'm afraid so."

"But since the rumors started two days ago, that the Nazis would round us up like cattle, what have you seen? The King's government refuses to cooperate and resigns in protest. The newspapers speak out against the Nazis, when they would do better to keep silent. The Danish people take us in to hide us from the Gestapo. Hans and his children risk their lives to smuggle us to Sweden. The Sleeping Dane is awake, Herr Doktor Bohr. You should be proud of your people."

Bohr stared at Holger Danske. His chin quivered, and again I sensed how heavily the occupation had weighed on him.

He put out his arm to clasp Papa's shoulder. "I'm glad we met, Rabbi."

Hans emerged from the shadows. He looked grim. "I need everyone's attention."

Everybody stirred, groaning at the cold in their muscles.

"The Gestapo is on the castle grounds," Hans said.

Muttered fear echoed through the catacomb. Margrethe put her hands over her mouth. Bohr went to put his arms around her.

Hans waved us into quiet. "Unless more are on the way, it's unlikely they'll find us before the rendezvous. It's a small detail – our friend from this morning and a half-dozen troops. But in half an hour we'll have to cross 500 meters of open ground under a full moon down to the beach. We'll be exposed. If we're lucky, they'll still be searching the castle proper."

"How did they know?" somebody asked.

"Considering what happened this morning," Hans said, "we're lucky we made it this far. We hadn't anticipated the search at Helgoland. I suspect the *Hauptsturmführer* came to his senses." He looked over at us.

Papa shrugged. "I should solve *all* your problems? Nobody's perfect."

Hans managed a grim smile, then disappeared with his son. His daughter stayed with us. She produced a Luger and checked the chamber and magazine. We watched her with mute terror.

Papa withdrew a bundle of cloth from the pocket of his wrinkled khakis. As he unfolded it, I saw what it was: his *tallis*. He wrapped the prayer shawl over his shoulders.

"Hear, O Israel." Barely a whisper, but in that awful place it still carried my father's power.

We all went to him, all except the girl.

"Hear, O Israel. The Lord Our God, the Lord is One..." As my father intoned the *Shema*, and repeated it twice, my heart slowed and my terror ebbed. I looked at the others, saw the calm seep into their faces.

Such power. No, I had made the right choice. I knew: I did not have my father's gifts.

Hans reappeared, alone. His forehead glistened with effort and fear. "More ss have arrived," he said. "They're dispersing over the castle grounds."

Silence.

"I'll go," Bohr said.

Hans frowned, licking his lips. He was thinking about it.

"They're looking for me," Bohr said. "As far as they know, it's just Margrethe and I. If we surrender, perhaps they'll leave."

The rest of us voiced our protest, but Bohr held up his hands. "They won't harm us!" he said. "Margrethe is...Aryan, and I'm only half-Jewish. And I'm valuable. They think they can use me."

"Which is exactly why it won't do," Hans said. "And it doesn't solve the problem of getting the rest of us down to the shore. No, thank you, Doktor."

Bohr shook his head. I thought he would weep.

"My son is watching for the boat," Hans said. "When he gets the signal from the Sound, we'll just have to run for it. Stretch your muscles."

He lit a cigarette and turned away from us. I saw his daughter ask a question with her eyes.

Hans shook his head. This was no time for lies.

We weren't going to make it.

As the group gathered at the opening of the catacomb, I went to join Papa. He stood apart from the rest, at the foot of the Sleeping Dane, fingering his tallis.

My decision didn't matter now. This path, that path. Telling him the truth would only hurt him, gaining nothing.

I looked over at Bohr, standing with the others, Margrethe's face in his chest. And then at my father, praying silently.

The truth gains nothing? The thought struck from within, like the stinging shame of a well-deserved slap. For Bohr, for my father, there had never been anything but truth.

"There's something I have to tell you, Papa," I said, pushing against the words. "Important."

He spread his arms and rolled his eyes at the ceiling. "Gevalt! Important, he says!" His voice dropped into a coarse whisper. "The Nazi wolves are at the door and they'll be tearing out our throats any minute! We need to talk about something else?"

"Yes. Because the wolves are at the door, and we may not have another chance. Don't make this harder for me, Papa."

His face settled into its true nature, kind and sad. "You would not be a Rabbi. You would not study the word of God."

I took a deep breath. "Not as you do, no."

"No. You would go to Cambridge and study the word of Bohr under your fancy scholarship."

My heart skipped. "You knew?"

"Am I a schmuck? Of course I knew! I knew about Cambridge, I knew about the scholarship, I knew about the paper you published in the contest from the fancy journal to win the scholarship." He half-closed his eyes, as when he recited scripture. "Correlating Experimental Lithium Spectra with Bohr Model Predictions of Valence Angular Momenta by David Goldblum." He managed a smile. "Such language! Yes, I knew."

I gaped at him.

"What I did *not* know," he said, "was when you would work up the courage to tell me, or whether you'd just elope with your books and go *shlepping* off into the night!" He gave me an affectionate slap on the cheek.

"It doesn't look like I'll be *shlepping* anywhere," I said.

"I'm afraid you're right. But you told me anyway, and you didn't have to. You faced me like a man. *As* a man."

I took a deep, shuddering breath. "You're not angry? Disappointed?"

Again he questioned the roof. "If he's so smart, Lord, how can he be such a *putz*?" He glowered at me. "Of *course* I'm angry and disappointed! What, you think I'm not paying attention? Just because my son makes his own decisions doesn't mean I have to be *happy* about them!"

Hans's son appeared at the opening, breathing hard. "The SS are moving this way," he said. "The boat hasn't signaled yet, but I can see her moving up the Sound. We can't wait."

"Let's move," Hans said.

Papa took my face in his hands and kissed me. "You are my gift to the world," he said. "Now...let's run for our lives."

The next few moments were a blur of jostling bodies, cold rock, and black fear. By the time we emerged from the stables, the moonlight that washed over the castle grounds seemed like midday brilliance. The ground sloped gently, 500 meters to the water. A fishing boat waited just offshore.

"Do you see it?" Hans asked us. "There are dinghies waiting on the beach. At my signal, run as fast as you can, and don't stop. No matter what happens, you keep running."

I took Papa's hand.

"No," he said. "Better not. I'll try to keep up. Do as the man says."

"Now!"

We sprinted into the night like terrified deer. I took Papa's arm again, but he twisted away and pushed me. My fear took over then, my legs pumping away at the turf like pistons.

We covered perhaps two hundred meters, spreading out in a panicky Gaussian distribution before the first shouts, the first gunshots, the first blood. Hans's daughter fell in front of me, her lower back bursting into a dark spray of gore. I stopped to help her up, but her limbs were flaccid. When I saw her eyes, I knew she was dead. More shots rang out, and I saw others fall.

I stumbled back to my feet, and looked over my shoulder for Papa. He should have been behind me, but by now I was the last straggler.

"David!" A strong hand seized my arm and spun me around.

It was Bohr. He had come back for me.

"What are you doing, boy? Run!"

"Where's my father?" I cried.

More gunshots, closer. We turned, and saw at least ten ss running toward us across the green. There were more assembling on the walls above the moat.

"Halt! Halt!"

We turned to run, but the ground at our feet boiled under a rain of bullets, and we cowered with our hands in the air.

"Niels!" Margrethe's voice came from direction of the shore, where the others were piling into dinghies.

"Damn," Bohr muttered, and raised his hands a little higher.

It was over. Because of me.

The sporadic *pop-pop-pop* of gunfire erupted into a hailstorm. I expected to die at that moment. Instead I heard shouting. Screams. Terror and confusion. From the ss troops.

Bohr and I turned to look, our hands still in the air.

The Sleeping Dane was awake.

He still had the color of stone, but his massive limbs were supple with life. The arc of his broadsword passed through two ss men, cleaving them at the waist. The sword continued its orbit, swinging overhead and then dropping vertically, biting through a soldier's helmet to split him like firewood. In the moonlight I saw the *Hauptsturmführer* step forward to empty his sidearm into the Dane's chest. Holger Danske swung his shield, and the captain fell into a misshapen heap twenty yards away.

More ss spilled onto the field. Their rifles might as well have been quarterstaffs. The Dane stood rooted to one spot, legs spread wide like the roots of an oak. But the sword never ceased swinging, like an electron switching between orbitals – horizontal, vertical, oblique. Body parts and blood spread over the ground. And still the ss kept coming.

I caught sight of Papa, at the opening of the stables beneath the east wall, his *tallis* hanging from his shoulders, arms stretching into the night, waving about to animate the limbs of Holger Danske. I screamed at him, but he could not have heard me over the din of gunfire.

And then he died, as a black bird spread its liquid wings across his chest. But his *golem* kept cutting and killing, fully roused to bloodlust.

"He's gone," Bohr said. "Come on!"

I couldn't move. I couldn't breathe.

"David."

I couldn't even wail.

"David!" Bohr shook me so hard that I bit my tongue. "Come on!"

The gunfire ceased as the remaining ss finally retreated. We ran to the shoreline and splashed into the icy water of the Sound. We had to swim a few yards to catch up to one of the dinghies. The others dragged us out of the water and somebody wrapped his jacket about my wet shoulders. My teeth chattered, and it was good to be numb with cold, nothing but cold.

They pulled us aboard the fishing boat a few minutes later. I stood alone, still shivering. I saw Hans and his boy fall to their knees, embracing each other with quiet grief. Margrethe was in Bohr's arms, shaking with relief and rage. My fellow Jews stood at the railing and wailed for those who had fallen.

As the boat turned her prow toward Sweden, I went aft for a last look at Kronborg Castle. The Dane stood in the moonlight with carnage at his feet. His shoulders slumped. The tip of his sword dragged in the dirt. Weariness seeped into his stony flesh. He shuffled toward the stables. Before he stooped into the darkness, he lay aside his shield and went down on one knee. He draped Papa's body over a massive shoulder. Then Holger Danske took up his shield and returned to his rest.

Presently I realized that Bohr and Margrethe were standing next to me. They didn't say anything trite or useless. Margrethe took my hand.

"Your father made arrangements with me," Bohr said. For a moment he could not speak. "Just in case. I have an audience with the King of Sweden tomorrow. After that, they will put me on a plane to England. You'll come with me."

I shook my head.

"Your father told me the scholarship would pay your tuition," he said. "But you'll need room and board. A good advisor. Many other things. It won't be difficult. I have friends at Cambridge. He made me promise."

It was only then that I wept, my hands tearing at the damp fabric of my shirt. Margrethe took me into her arms, as a mother might.

As I write this, I have at hand the drawing I made for my Papa and Niels Bohr, sixty years ago. It is yellowed and cracked from age and overhandling. Today, as on many days, I have taken it out to consult it, to make refinements, to seek inspiration, or simply to remember.

Beneath the drawing sits a recent letter from the Nobel Academy, congratulating me for the work I did in the seventies on the topological analysis of 10-dimensional quantum-observer interfaces. In recent years, the neuroscientists have appropriated that work, as part of a fundamental new theory of consciousness. My father's gift to the world.

Soon I will return to Sweden for the first time since that night. I will go by way of Denmark, to visit the one who sleeps beneath Kronborg Castle. In Stockholm I will shake hands with a King. For a few moments the world will be mine. The world will listen.

When I speak, it will not be of physics, or Kabbalah, or the nobility of science, or the power of faith. I will speak of my father, Rabbi Itzak Josef Goldblum, and my other father, Niels Henrik David Bohr. I will speak of my debt to them, and how my life and work have been nothing, nothing but my effort to be worthy of them both.

Mortegarde

Liz Williams

Liz Williams (*www.arkady.btinternet.co.uk*) lives in Brighton, England. She has a Ph.D. in History and Philosophy of Science from Cambridge and she is the daughter of a part-time conjuror and a Gothic novelist. She has been publishing fantasy and science fiction in *Asimov's*, *Interzone*, *Realms of Fantasy*, and *The Third Alternative* among others, more than forty stories since the turn of the century, and was co-editor of the anthology *Fabulous Brighton*. Her novels are *The Ghost Sister*, a *New York Times* Notable Book of 2001; *Empire of Bones* (2002), nominated, as was the first, for the Philip K. Dick Award; *The Poison Master* (2002); *Nine Layers of Sky* (2003), and *Banner of Souls* (2004). Her first story collection, *The Banquet of the Lords of Night*, was published in 2005.

"Mortegarde" was published in *Realms of Fantasy*. It is a strange and colorful tale of alternate universe travel, fantasy, and medical science. A human doctor is invited to give a medical presentation on his theory of the blood in the universe of the Wyverns.

I HAD JUST COME from attendance upon the Queen when the summons arrived from Mortegarde. A dark bird brought it, a bird like a raven but with snow-white legs and a crimson bill, and a bright gaze betokening intelligence. I half expected it to speak, but it only dropped the scroll at my feet before my own front door. There was no doubt that the scroll had been meant for me: it bore my name on the outside – DR. GWILLIAM ANSTRUTHER, in large, straggling letters, as though written by someone unversed in the practice.

I picked up the scroll and ushered the bird inside. It strode down the hallway as though it were the master of the place, not I, and turned smartly through the door of my consulting chamber. Wondering how it had known where to go, I followed it. The bird watched as I sat down at the desk and unfastened the scroll.

I knew immediately that it had come from another world upon the Tree. Its smell was different: not the dry crackle of our own reed paper, speaking of sun on the marshes, but of iron and fire and ash. It hissed as I unscrolled it, and the words inscribed upon it were written not in indigo or black, but in sharp red letters like wounds. I knew where it came from even before I read the word: MORTEGARDE.

Every child knows that there are as many spheres that hang upon the World Tree as there are apples in an orchard in Gildermonth. Some, in both the higher levels toward the stars and the lower reaches of the Great Root, cannot sustain humankind for long. The air of such spheres curdles or boils within the lungs, or splinters against the skin. I have seen a traveler, brought back from a high sphere by a Gatespeaker, and the thing that lay smoldering upon the shew-stone mirror was barely recognizable as a human being, rather a bunch of twisted twigs with a round rim at one end, where a gaping mouth seemed to have consumed its own head. As the College watched, aghast, its tongue sizzled away with a sound like a sigh and the Gatespeaker did not need to add a further warning. Then the civil war had come, bringing more local horrors, and few cared to go exploring elsewhere in such times.

I had wanted to investigate the corpse, but they would not let me. This was only one of many such nuisances, caused by changing times and a new religion that believed in the sanctity of the flesh. How are we to explore the limits of existence if human squeamishness holds us back? How would I have completed my work on the vital spirits of the organism if I had been subject to such spiritual qualms? The flesh is a machine that contains the spirit, nothing more. It is like saying that a kick to the wall of my house damages me. But I digress. It is easy to become obsessed by other people's foolishness.

Of the world of Mortegarde itself, I knew no more than the common run of superstition and legend, brought by explorers upon the Terra Arbor to entertain the credulous and the gullible. Yet perhaps they told us no more than the truth – there were wonders enough upon the Tree after all, and maybe the tales of the iron palaces and the clever-tongued beasts that lived within them were truth indeed.

As I stood staring down at the scroll, the red words shifted and changed until they formed phrases in my own language of Berechamur: "Come. You are needed."

There was no signature, only a scored mark in the paper like the touch of a claw. The final unraveling of the scroll proved my undoing. A shining sliver fell out and when, reflexively, I snatched at it, the thing burned its way into my palm. The room filled with the stench of scorched flesh as I doubled up, clutching my hand. The agony ebbed quickly, leaving only soreness and shock in its wake, but when I opened up my palm I found a thick new ridge of bone, marbled with silver. I stared at it in horror and fascination. It was an arboreal key.

I knew I would need a Gatespeaker to travel safely, otherwise the key might simply snatch me up the Tree with no regard for my well-being en route. I therefore made arrangements for the following morning, and spent much of the night studying this addition to my hand. If only one could invent an engine to look within the flesh, unlock the mysteries of bone and sinew without the messy recourse to the dissecting table... I longed to look inside my hand, see what was happening there, how the key had melded itself to the bones and the skin. At last, frustrated, I took myself off to bed.

★

"You have little choice," the Gatespeaker said. Her scarred lips mangled the words, making her hard to comprehend. Gently, she turned my hand between her own so that the striations within the key flashed in the late light. We were sitting in my study, the windows fastened against the winter cold. "If you do not use the key, it will begin to seek a Gate of its own accord. It will grow inward, infesting your flesh, devouring you from within."

"How interesting!" But, I had to concur, almost certainly fatal.

"An irony, that."

"What do you mean?"

The Gatespeaker smiled. "Only that the man they call 'Scalpel Anstruther,' for his enthusiasm for the methods of dissection, is now in danger of dissection himself, from within."

"I'm aware of my nickname," I said, stiffly. "Medical humor, nothing more. Now, about this key."

"Only use will diminish it," the Gatespeaker went on.

"And it will take me to Mortegarde?"

"Probably."

I stared at her. "Only 'probably'?"

"It came from Mortegarde and thus is likely to return there. But these things are never wholly certain. The weather of the World Tree is strange and filled with vagaries, your passage can be affected by it. But as I have said, you have little choice."

"So what should I do?" I asked her reluctantly. I did not like the idea of Gate travel, though the notion of exploring the Tree possessed, I must admit, a certain eldritch appeal.

"You must take this to a Gate, to which I will speak, and then you will travel through."

"There is said to be a Gate near here, in Badelem. Is that true?"

"In the old Basilica." The Gatespeaker paused and her long, sad face grew sadder yet.

"An evil place," I said. "The place where the war started."

"You are not a religious man?" the Gatespeaker asked, mildly.

"Of course not. I am a scientist. I believe in what I can experience and see. And besides, who could be, after the ruin that they have brought us to? The Basilica is an unholy place."

The Gatespeaker sighed. "Plenty still follow the path, as I'm sure you know. And gates do not choose. There are portals and rifts everywhere, opening and closing like the wounds of the world. Perhaps there is even one in this room – but stable Gates are rare and it is better to travel thus. I will accompany you to the Gate and speak the prayers to the Tree for your safe passage. We can do no more."

I looked down at my own changed hand. Tomorrow, I thought with mingled apprehension and excitement, I could be in Mortegarde.

When the time came, I hastened through the streets. Many were still half-ruined, damaged by mortar fire and shot, and I cursed the superstitions that had brought us to such a pass and interrupted my work. I went up the rain-wet steps and through the bloodwood doors of the Basilica. The wind slammed them shut behind me as thunder peeled out across Badelem. The Gatespeaker was waiting for me, standing in a shaft of lamplight like a flame in the dark. When she saw me she turned away without speaking, scarlet skirts hissing over the stone flags, but not before I had seen the great thorn that pierced her lips, fastening them shut – a thorn from the World Tree itself, or so it was said.

She beckoned me up a set of spiral stairs that led into the dome of the Basilica, a shattered shell ever since a firebolt from the conflict had broken it like an egg. The Council of Badelem had not had the money to repair it, but the branched candelabras, the delicate leaves that hung from the painted ceiling, and the great gilded column of the trunk that rose from floor to ceiling remained intact. Potential looters were too afraid of the Gate, it seemed, of where it led, and of what might come through it. I followed the Gatespeaker along the narrow walkway of a golden branch, until we stood close to the trunk itself. I felt a cold, wet drop slide down my cheek and looked up to see a rift in the dome, a cloud-race of sky. The Gatespeaker turned her mute face to me, eyes lost in wells of pain and shadow, and pointed to a slit in the gilt bark. I knew that this was only a representation of the World Tree itself, microcosm reflecting macrocosm, but as I stepped hesitantly closer to the trunk, a dark glitter fractured from deep within the rift and I grew cold and dizzy, as though I stood on the very edge of the Tree and the drop into the Maw.

The Gatespeaker tore the thorn from her lips and spoke a single, terrible word through welling blood. "Now!"

She had gone through such pain for me that I hesitated no longer. Behind me, I heard her freed voice crying out the runic payers in the oldest tongue of Badelem and I slammed my altered hand against the rift.

Immediately, I was snatched up into a storm. Clouds, lightning, the marbled moon were ripped away and I fell upward into the World Tree. I saw its branches crimson in the light of a circlet of suns, the pulsing veins whirling below me in the unfolding landscape of a leaf, as the howl of the World Tree's weather caught me up and tore me through to Mortegarde.

*

Hard to speak of first impressions, the glimpses gained through the black mist of midnight and the red fog of dawn as I traveled from the Gate. The conjuration of the key brought me out onto the top of a pillar of iron, some miles from the city that I was to come to know as Anrush. Tiny pellets of metal rolled across the surface, making my steps perilous. Beyond, a storm was raging, the wind whipping my hair from its binding and half blinding me. The ground tilted far below, making me dizzy, but I still tried to explore my new surroundings.

Moments later, I fell over a large metal cage. A voice like a bell spoke into my ear. "Get in." I looked around, but no one was visible. Climbing into the cage, however, was preferable to trying to remain upright and as soon as I did so, the cage lifted up from the surface of the pillar and bowled over the edge. It was almost as bad as the journey up the World Tree, yet an intriguing experience, all the same. My yell was lost in the wind, sucked so thoroughly from my throat that I thought I might never speak again. Then I was dangling a few feet from the ground. A carriage – a round thing of metal slats interspersed with scaled leather – was waiting on a path of glossy black earth. Two great beasts with hunched shoulders waited between the shafts. One of them swung its head around as I hastened toward the carriage. I caught sight of black, coiled horns like polished glass, an immense yellow eye. Then I stepped into the carriage. Soft darkness fell around me, and the smell of fire. I sank into a seat, panting, and felt the carriage stir into movement beneath me.

"How was your journey?" – a small whispering voice. It was female.

"Well enough," I tried to say, but the words would not come. I tried again and this time spoke.

"I am Shirre," the small voice said.

"I should like to see you," I ventured, and an obliging light flared up. I found myself gazing into a narrow, shining face. She was beautiful: a classically delineated profile, curved lips, her hair as dark red as a smoldering fire, the eyes concealed behind lenses of jet. Her breasts were bare, and slightly scaled. Then the resemblance to a woman was lost in a coil of snake tail and two long, gloved hands, on which she balanced on the edges of the seat.

"You are a siren," I breathed. Her lips twitched.

"Why, how kind. But in fact, my heritage is all wyvern, truly of Anrush and Mortegarde. And I am a physician, like yourself."

I nearly exclaimed, "But you are female!" but held my tongue in time. Many things would be different here, to say the least of it. I must not fear new things.

"I have worked in the College of Chirugeons for seven years now, ever since I completed my schooling. I come from the mountains," she confided, as though I would know what she was talking about.

"I myself was born in the city, in Badelem. I live there now."

"Ah," the wyvern said. "Then you will find Anrush a familiar place."

"Is it possible to release the blinds? I should like to see where we are."

She snapped the blinds of the carriage open. "Then see. We are entering it now."

I looked out upon a massive Gate, arising from blood-red earth. The metal of which it was made was bright with heat, seeming to boil and bubble in unceasing configuration. It looked nothing like any Gate on my world. I felt the heat as the carriage passed through: reaching out to sear my face like a hissing kiss. Then we were through into a street of black iron mansions. Steam rose from vents in the paving and I could see the glow of fires deep within windows. There was no sign of any vegetation. Sweat trickled down the back of my neck.

"We have prepared a special place for you," Shirre said. "It is a room packed with a particular kind of icy stone, brought down from the high crags. I think it will be more to your liking." She leaned forward anxiously as she spoke, clearly eager for me to feel at home.

"I'm sure that I shall appreciate it greatly," I said, though at the moment the choice seemed to be between boiling or freezing. "Tell me, Madame Shirre. Why have you brought me here?"

"Why, to address our College," the wyvern said. "News of your expertise has reached us, tales told down the branches of the Tree. It is our College's understanding that you have many revolutionary new theories – about the blood, for instance."

"Indeed," I said. In a moment, the heat and discomfort were forgotten in that other heat, the glow of science and knowledge. I began to expound upon my latest theory: that the blood is not, as commonly supposed, infected by the element of fire but contains many small particulates akin to benevolent spirits, which girdle the body and converse with one another, carrying messages to the vital organs of consciousness such as the liver, and which are cooled by the influence of the brain. Some of these particulates, I believe, perform a military function, and attack malign influences that infect the body through the weakness of the will.

I have seldom had such a receptive audience – not only was there the dreadful religious issue, which silenced my work until recent years, but the more staid and elderly members of my own Institute were prone to scoff – and my recounting took us all the way to the doors of a mansion which, so Shirre informed me, was the home of her own College.

The chamber which I had been allotted was at the back of the mansion. I was taken to it through a labyrinth of passages, but as I stepped from the carriage a second wyvern, a small, twisted dark thing with the unmistakably subservient demeanor of slave or servant, hastened up to me with a pair of clogs, made out of some unknown substance, and a woven coat.

"These will protect you from the worst of the heat in the house," Shirre assured me. "Do not touch the walls with your bare flesh on the way to the chamber. We ourselves are used to the heat," she added, apologetically.

The clogs were too big, obliging me to proceed in a kind of slow shuffle. I hoped I would not have to go anywhere in a hurry during my stay. And it was a relief finally to reach the stone-ice room. The room had a single window, which looked out onto a racing torrent and a high arched bridge. A haunch of charred meat and a jug of water stood on a table, and Shirre insisted that it was safe for me to eat and drink. I could not tell where the meat originated: it was fibrous and curiously textured, but flavorsome enough.

When she had gone, I spent some time staring out of the window at the torrent below, illuminated by lamps that formed hazy pools of light in the waterglow, and then I lay down on the hard couch and slept. It did not seem long before the red day dawned.

When I next awoke, Shirre was by the side of the bed, anxiously balancing on a long curl of tail. For a moment, I thought I was still in the middle of a nightmare.

"Please, take time to collect yourself," Shirre said. "In the early afternoon, you are requested to defend your theories before the College."

"Defend?"

Her beautiful mouth smiled. "I meant, of course, 'deliver.' My facility with your language is not so great, sometimes."

There was water for washing, and it did not take me long to prepare. I wrenched the window open, and let in a blast of heat that I immediately regretted. Hauling it shut again, I stared out at the crimson sky. Perhaps this would be the sum of it, and then I could go home. But the scientist in me approved: I felt like a bee, soaring through the branches of the World Tree to pollinate Mortegarde with knowledge. And thus I donned my clogs and followed Shirre to the Debating Chamber with enthusiasm.

It was filled with wyverns. Most of them were male: with grave, beautiful countenances. Some had silvered scales, and I wondered whether this was a sign of age. Shirre fluttered to the podium, moving with quick, sinuous movements of her lower tail: she looked top-heavy, and it seemed impossible that she could balance or move, but she did. Wyvern anatomy was beginning to fascinate me.

The audience was very still as I delivered my theories, listening attentively with none of the restless fidgeting that I had come to expect from my own Institute. Their eyes were green and golden, like lamps, and they seemed not to blink, but only gazed. I took them through the precepts of my theory of the blood, explaining the issue of animating particulates, and spent some time in disassembly of the notion of fire as an aspect of this most vital fluid.

At the end of the talk, I asked whether there were any questions. A great silver wyvern in the front row raised a hand, balancing perilously, or so it seemed to me, upon a single palm.

"What do you know, Doctor, of the beliefs of Mortegarde?"

"I fear I know very little."

"Then you do not know of our myth of origin, which tells of how Aissh the First went to the great volcano of Kharth, and in sacrificing himself for his people was reborn with the inspiriting principle of fire within his blood?"

"I did not know that tale," I said. "But I am most interested to hear of it." Best to be polite.

"It is no tale!" the wyvern thundered. His voice filled the chamber, resounding with echoes. "It is the truth of all that we are. We are the people of fire and flame, and to claim otherwise is arrant heresy!"

One of the old guard, then. I shifted uneasily upon the podium. A second wyvern, sitting some distance away, interrupted smoothly. "Gheiss, you cannot expect someone from another world to be aware of our beliefs. Doctor, now that you have heard this tale, might I ask whether you would consider it as a possibility for the basis of scientific practice?"

Courtesy urged me to answer yes, but then I thought of Badelem, of my city so recently shattered by religious ideology and faction, superstition that had nearly caused the downfall of our civilization. I could not, in all integrity, tell him that I believed in this myth of origin.

"No," I said. "I cannot. The scientific method must proceed by exploration and examination, not by fable. I fear that I regard all essences of spirit to have a physical explanation."

I feared an outcry, but they were silent. After a moment, the second wyvern said, "Most interesting. I'm sure we would all like to thank Doctor Anstruther for his fascinating new perspective."

This sounded smooth and reasonable enough, but the outburst had agitated me. I had not, I thought, come all the way along the World Tree in order to experience more of the same treatment that I had formerly received at home. I was relieved to see that there was none of the usual kind of socializing that follows these lectures. Instead the wyvern physicians all filed out in silence and Shirre showed me back to my chamber.

"I hope I did not offend anyone," I said.

"Not at all. Some people are a little more – outspoken – about their beliefs than others."

"Well, I have encountered the same thing, but I should not have liked to have given offense."

"Dr. Anstruther – your theories. How did you come about them?"

"Why, by experiment."

"On living things?"

"Very rarely. Most of my work was carried out upon dead matter, of many varying kinds. Some was human – this is permitted in my own world – " only a small lie here " – but much of it was animal." I paused. "Might I ask whether I am to give any other talks while I am here?"

Shirre appeared momentarily flustered. "I do not know. I believe so, but I must check with the College."

"Of course," I said. "Perhaps you would be so kind as to bring me some material on the beliefs of your people, if it can be translated?"

"I will bring you a speaking scroll, of course," Shirre said. She appeared relieved, doubtless because I could clearly amuse myself and she would not have to spend the time entertaining me. I wondered about her life. Was she wed, did she have small wyverns of her own? Or were these folk's lives so utterly removed from my own?

Later, she brought me the scroll and I read through the myths of origin. As I had suspected, they were nothing more than superstition, and possibly allegorical. They reminded me of the fables of the Last and First Hours, which had brought such ruin to my own city, and after a while I threw them across the couch in disgust and went to look out of the window at the Mortegarde night instead. I did not sleep well.

In the morning, Shirre once more came to me and explained that later that day, I was to address a much wider audience.

"The College feels that their presence alone is a little narrow," she told me. "They would like you to put your views to a more extensive section of society – indeed, to the aristocracy itself."

"I'm flattered, I told her. "And it's good to see the upper echelons taking such an interest in science." But I was not sure that I believed her. My own recent experience had led me to mistrust people's ability to prefer reason and experience to their own blind faith, and I was beginning to feel that Mortegarde might not be as strange as it appeared in this respect.

I was, however, keen to see more of Anrush and as we rumbled along I peered through the windows of the carriage with intense interest. More iron mansions, and here there were gardens between them that seemed composed of mere spikes and spines of trees, as scaled as the beasts that pulled the carriage. But soon the view was blotted out by a fall of hot hail and Shirre pulled the blinds closed once more. A harsh, sere land, this world. I could see why there was such an emphasis on fire and flame.

At length, we reached the place where I was to deliver my lecture. It turned out to be a large hall, with seats arranged in circular rows around a deep central pit: an amphitheater, in short. The theater was filled with wyverns and I could see that these were not the common run of people, but encrusted with jewels and gems, their scales burnished to a dragon's shine. There seemed to be different varieties: some were as green as the ocean, others were the mottled scarlet and black of salamanders. I observed them with interest, and their eyes were all affixed on me.

Once more, I delivered my lecture. And the same thing happened again. This time, an elderly female wyvern, whose eyes were filmed with the bloom of cataract, rose on her tail and asked me whether I had had time to study the myth of origin. Uneasily, I replied.

"Yes. I consider it a most meaningful metaphor."

"But do you think it to be true?" the wyvern persisted. I thought for a long, hard moment. A lie might get me out of a difficult situation, and yet – ruined Badelem rose before my inner sight.

"I'm afraid that I do not."

There was a pause. My words seemed to hang in the chamber, echoing. And I realized that I had made a dreadful mistake, but one that I could not regret.

"Then we shall prove it to you," the wyvern said. Suddenly, two of them were on either side of me: huge gray presences, with blades.

"No!" I cried. "Wait, I – "

One of them whipped out a tail and brought me crashing to the floor. I lay there, dazed, and when they laid their long clawed hands on me I started to struggle, but it was too late. They picked me up and I felt something very cold enter my arm, the coldest thing I had sensed since coming to Mortegarde.

I awoke strapped to a table, naked beneath a sheet. Shirre was perched on its edge, with a dissecting scalpel in her hand. Beyond her, I saw a sea of faces: eyes glowing, anticipatory.

"...necessary to drain the entire body of blood," she was saying, "in order to observe the inflammatory effects. The drained blood will undergo full elemental testing, to prove that the living flame is contained in all beings, and that the inspiriting principle of the Tree emanates from Mortegarde itself." There was a light in her reptilian eyes that I had not seen in her before, but which I recognized immediately. It was the derangement of faith. I had seen it plenty of times myself, in Badelem.

"Wait," I tried to say again, but they had gagged me. I endeavored to move my legs, but could not. I tensed my fists and found an unfamiliar sharpness: the key. The hand in which the key had become embedded was on the other side to

Shirre, and her long, smooth back was turned. Very slowly, so that she could not see any movement beneath the sheet, I began to saw at the binding with the edge of the key. I did not know how I would get out of the dissecting hall, naked and unarmed as I was, before a host of wyverns. I could not even walk on the hot floor in my own shoes. But if I could not convince them of their errors, I was at least determined not to die without putting up some kind of fight. I sawed at the binding, covert and frantic, as Shirre talked on. She betrayed a depth of fanaticism that she had never revealed to me, but then, she was not human and I did not understand her. When she turned back to me, my hand was almost free.

"The first cut should ably demonstrate my earlier points," she said. I wrenched my hand free of the binding, but it was too late. The scalpel came down, drawing a long incision in my flesh.

The pain was blazing and intense. I cried out, jerking my free hand up, and clapped it to my abdomen. I had forgotten about the key. I felt it penetrate my flesh, screaming down through nerve and fat and jarring on bone.

And the key worked.

I was traveling inward, down through my own body. I saw the red walls of my own self as I turned inside out, glimpsing the slow pulse of organs and the white shelves of bone, the beat of arteries and the long branched tree of my own spine. Microcosm and macrocosm, I thought through the pain. I was like the Tree itself, journeying through the body that reflects the world.

We do not need Gates, I know that now. We can travel the Tree whenever we choose, as long as we are prepared to pay its bloody price. But knowledge has always had a high cost, as the Gatespeaker herself might say, through her scarred lips. I did not see the Tree as I fell, only my own interior, and I came out, injured but whole, in my own study chamber before a congregation of startled students. I wept to see them, and am not ashamed to admit it.

It took me a week to recover. When the stitches were removed, and the brood-maggots that they had placed in my wound had done their work, I was deemed strong enough to be told that I had not returned from Mortegarde alone. The wyvern Shirre, sensing my escape, had coiled around me as I vanished into my own flesh, but instead of preventing my flight, she had returned with me. The cold of Badelem had stunned her, but the Institute had made a thorough investigation of her and was continuing to do so.

They asked me to undertake the dissection. I thought of all that she had done to me, all that she was, the light of blind and superstitious faith that had blazed from her inhuman eyes as she stood over me on the dissecting table. I agreed to the dissection.

The procedure was to be undertaken in public for the edification of all. I rejoiced that science was once more in the ascendant, that knowledge again held sway. But as I was preparing for the dissection in the back regions of the surgical amphitheater, preoccupied with such thoughts, I caught sight of myself in a mirror. And I saw to my horror that the light that had blazed behind the wyvern's eyes, now lit my own.

I looked at myself for a long time, staring until the light faded and died. And then I walked, very slowly, into the ring of the amphitheater. Shirre lay on the dissection table, her hands and tail strapped securely down. She stared at me defiantly. She knew what to expect, or thought she did. And it was then that I drew the duty surgeons aside, and instructed them to let her go.

Inside Job

Connie Willis

Connie Willis (www.sftv.org/cw/) lives in Greeley, Colorado. If H.L. Mencken was the "sage of Baltimore," then Willis is the Sage of Greeley. She is an excellent and entertaining writer whose characteristic genre is SF. She has won many awards and is one of the leading SF writers of her generation who came into prominence in the 1980s. Her most famous novel is perhaps *Doomsday Book*, part of a body of stories and novels about time travel. Her three story collections to date are *Fire Watch*, *Impossible Things*, and *Miracle and Other Christmas Stories*. One of her characteristic modes is comedy, especially romantic "screwball" comedy in the manner of 1940s Hollywood movies, updated.

"Inside Job" was published in *Asimov's* and as a small press book, in 2005. It revolves around channeling the ghost of H. L. Mencken and the practice of debunking. It even has three rules: the three rules of skeptics are: "Extraordinary claims require extraordinary evidence"; "If it seems too good to be true, it probably is"; and, "By their fruits shall ye know them." It has dames, dates, wordplay, skepticism, fantasy, romance, fun, and a paradox to resolve.

> *Nobody ever went broke underestimating the intelligence of the American people.*
>   — H. L. MENCKEN

"IT'S ME, ROB," Kildy said when I picked up the phone. "I want you to go with me to see somebody Saturday."

Usually when Kildy calls, she's bubbling over with details. "You've *got* to see this psychic cosmetic surgeon, Rob," she'd crowed the last time. "His specialty is liposuction, and you can *see* the tube coming out of his sleeve. And that's not all. The fat he's supposed to be suctioning out of their thighs is that goop they use in McDonald's milkshakes. You can smell the vanilla! It wouldn't fool a five-year-old, so of course half the women in Hollywood are buying it hook, line, and sinker. We've *got* to do a story on him, Rob!"

I usually had to say, "Kildy – Kildy – Kildy!" before I could get her to shut up long enough to tell me where he was performing.

But this time all she said was, "The seminar's at one o'clock at the Beverly Hills Hilton. I'll meet you in the parking lot," and hung up before I could ask her if the somebody she wanted me to see was a pet channeler or a Vedic-force therapist, and how much it was going to cost.

I called her back.

"The tickets are on me," she said.

If Kildy had her way, the tickets would always be on her, and she can more than afford it. Her father's a director at Dreamworks, her current stepmother heads her own production company, and her mother's a two-time Oscar winner. And Kildy's rich in her own right – she only acted in four films before she quit the business for a career in debunking, but one of them was the surprise top grosser of the year, and she'd opted for shares instead of a salary.

But she's ostensibly my employee, even though I can't afford to pay her enough to keep her in toenail polish. The least I can do is spring for expenses, and a barely known channeler shouldn't be too bad. Medium Charles Fred, the current darling of the Hollywood set, was only charging two hundred a séance.

"*The Jaundiced Eye* is paying for the tickets," I said firmly. "How much?"

"Seven hundred and fifty apiece for the group seminar," she said. "Fifteen hundred for a private enlightenment audience."

"The tickets are on you," I said.

"Great," she said. "Bring the Sony videocam."

"Not the little one?" I asked. Most psychic events don't allow recording devices – they make it too easy to spot the earpieces and wires – and the Hasaka is small enough to be smuggled in.

"No," she said, "bring the Sony. See you Saturday, Rob. Bye."

"Wait," I said. "You haven't told me what this guy does."

"Woman. She's a channeler. She channels an entity named Isis," Kildy said, and hung up again.

I was surprised. We don't usually waste our time on channelers. They're no longer trendy. Right now mediums like Charles Fred and Yogi Magaputra and assorted sensory therapists (aroma-, sonic-, auratic-) are the rage.

It's also an exercise in frustration, since there's no way to prove whether someone's channeling or not, unless they claim to be channeling Abraham Lincoln (like Randall Mars) or Nefertiti (like Hanh Nah). In that case you can challenge their facts – Nefertiti could not have had an affair with Alexander the Great, who wasn't born till a thousand years later, and she was not Cleopatra's cousin – but most of them channel hundred-thousand-year-old sages or high priests of Lemuria, and there are no physical manifestations.

They've learned their lesson from the Victorian spiritualists (who kept getting caught), so there's no ectoplasm or ghostly trumpets or double-exposed photographic plates. Just a deep, hollow voice that sounds like a cross between Obi-Wan Kenobi and Basil Rathbone. Why is it that channeled "entities" all have British accents? And speak King James Bible English?

And why was Kildy willing to waste fifteen hundred bucks – correction, twenty-two fifty; she'd already been to the seminar once – to have me see this Isis? The channeler must have a new gimmick. I'd noticed a couple of people advertising themselves as "angel channelers" in the local psychic rag, but Isis wasn't an angel name. Egyptian channeler? Goddess conduit?

I looked "Isis-channeler" up on the net. At first I couldn't find any references, even using Google. I tried skeptics.org and finally Marty Rumboldt, who runs a website that tracks psychics.

"You're spelling it wrong, Rob," he e-mailed me back. "It's Isus."

Which should have occurred to me. The channelers of Lazaris, Kochise, and Merlynn all use variations on historical names (probably from some fear of spiritual slander lawsuits), and more than one channeler's prone to "inventive" spellings: Joye Wildde. And Emmanual.

I Googled "Isus." He – bad sign, the channeler didn't even know Isis was female – was the "spirit entity" channeled by somebody named Ariaura Keller. She'd started in Salem, Massachusetts (a breeding ground for psychics), moved to Sedona (another one), and then headed west and worked her way down the coast, appearing in Seattle, the other Salem, Eugene, Berkeley, and now Beverly Hills. She had six afternoon seminars and two week-long "spiritual immersions" scheduled for L.A., along with private "individually scheduled enlightenment audiences" with Isus. She'd written two books, *The Voice of Isus* and *On the Receiving End* (with links to amazon.com), and you could read her bio: "I knew from childhood that I was destined to be a channel for the Truth," and extracts from her speeches: "The earth is destined to witness a transforming spiritual event," on-line. She sounded just like every other channeler I'd ever heard.

And I'd sat through a bunch of them. Back at the height of their popularity (and before I knew better), *The Jaundiced Eye* had done a six-part series on channelers, starting with M. Z. Lord and running on through Joye Wildde, Todd Phoenix, and Taryn Kryme, whose "entity" was a giggly six-year-old kid from Atlantis. It was the longest six months of my life. And it didn't have any impact at all on the business. It was tax evasion and mail fraud charges that had put an end to the fad, not my hard-hitting exposés.

Ariaura Keller didn't have a criminal record (at least under that name), and there weren't many articles about her. And no mention of any gimmick. "The electric, amazing Isus shares his spiritual wisdom and helps you find your own inner-centeredness and soul-unenfoldment." Nothing new there.

Well, whatever it was that had gotten Kildy interested in her, I'd find out on Saturday. In the meantime, I had an article on Charles Fred to write for the December issue, a book on intelligent design (the latest ploy for getting creationism into the schools and evolution out) to review, and a past-life chiropractor to go see. He claimed his patients' backaches came from hauling blocks of stone to Stonehenge and/or the pyramids. (The pyramids had in fact been a big job, but over the course of three years in business he'd told over two thousand patients they'd gotten their herniated discs at Stonehenge, every single one of them while setting the altar stone in place.)

And he was actually credible compared to Charles Fred, who was having amazing success communicating highly specific messages from the dead to their grieving relatives. I was convinced he was doing something besides the usual cold reading and shills to get the millions he was raking in, but so far I hadn't been able to figure out what, and every lead I managed to come up with went nowhere.

I didn't think about the "electric, amazing Isus" again till I was driving over to the Hilton Saturday. Then it occurred to me that I hadn't heard from Kildy since her phone call. Usually she drops by the office every day, and if we're going somewhere calls three or four times to reconfirm where and when we're meeting. I wondered if the seminar was still on, or if she'd forgotten all about it. Or suddenly gotten tired of being a debunker and gone back to being a movie star.

I'd been waiting for that to happen ever since the day just over eight months ago when, just like the gorgeous dame in a Bogie movie, she'd walked into my office and asked if she could have a job.

There are three cardinal rules in the skeptic business. The first one is, "Extraordinary claims require extraordinary evidence," and the second one is, "If it seems too good to be true, it probably is." And if anything was ever too good to be true, it's Kildy. She's not only rich and movie-star beautiful, but intelligent, and, unlike everyone else in Hollywood, a complete skeptic, even though, as she told me the first day, Shirley MacLaine had dandled her on her knee and her own mother would believe anything, "no matter how ridiculous, which is probably why her marriage to my father lasted nearly six years."

She was now on Stepmother Number Four, who had gotten her the role in the surprise top grosser "that made almost as much money as *Lord of the Rings* and enabled me to take early retirement."

"Retirement?" I'd said. "Why would you want to retire? You could have – "

"Starred in *The Hulk III*," she said, "and been on the cover of the *Globe* with Ben Affleck. Or with my lawyer in front of a rehab center. I know, it was tough to give all that up."

She had a point, but that didn't explain why she'd want to go to work for a barely making-it magazine like *The Jaundiced Eye*. Or why she'd want to go to work at all.

I said so.

"I've already tried the whole 'fill your day with massages and lunch at Ardani's and sex with your trainer' scene, Rob," she said. "It was even worse than *The Hulk*. Plus, the lights and makeup *destroy* your complexion."

I found that hard to believe. She had skin like honey.

"And then my mother took me to this luminescence reading – she's into all those things, psychics and past-life regression and intuitive healing, and the guy doing the reading – "

"Lucius Windfire," I'd said. I'd been working on an exposé of him for the last two months.

"Yes, Lucius Windfire," she'd said. "He claimed he could read your mind by determining your Vedic fault lines, which consisted of setting candles all around you and 'reading' the wavering of the flames. It was obvious he was a fake – you could see the earpiece he was getting his information over – but everybody there was eating it up, especially my mother. He'd already talked her into private sessions that set her back ten thousand dollars. And I thought, somebody should put him out of business, and then I thought, that's what I want to do with my life, and I looked up 'debunkers' online and found your magazine, and here I am."

I'd said, "I can't possibly pay you the kind of money you're – "

"Your going rate for articles is fine," she'd said and flashed me her better-than-Julia-Roberts smile. "I just want the chance to do something useful and sensible with my life."

And for the last eight months she'd been working with me on the magazine. She was wonderful – she knew everybody in Hollywood, which meant she could get us into invitation-only stuff, and heard about new spiritual fads even before I did. She was also willing to do anything, from letting herself be hypnotized to stealing chicken guts from psychic surgeons to proofreading galleys. And fun to talk to, and gorgeous, and much too good for a small-time skeptic.

And I knew it was just a matter of time before she got bored with debunking and went back to going to premieres and driving around in her Jaguar, but she didn't. "Have you ever *worked* with Ben Affleck?" she'd said when I told her she was too beautiful not to still be in the movies. "You couldn't *pay* me to go back to that."

She wasn't in the parking lot, and neither was her Jaguar, and I wondered, as I did every day, if this was the day she'd decided to call it quits. No, there she was, getting out of a taxi. She was wearing a honey-colored pantsuit the same shade as her hair, and designer sunglasses, and she looked, as always, too good to be true. She saw me and waved, and then reached back in for two big throw pillows.

Shit. That meant we were going to have to sit on the floor again. These people made a fortune scamming people out of their not-so-hard-earned cash. You'd think they could afford chairs.

I walked over to her. "I take it we're going in together," I said, since the pillows were a matching pair, purple brocade jobs with tassels at the corners.

"Yes," Kildy said. "Did you bring the Sony?"

"Yeah," I said. "I still think I should have brought the Hasaka."

She shook her head. "They're doing body checks. I don't want to give them an excuse to throw us out. When they fill out the nametags, give them your real name."

"We're not using a cover?" I asked. Psychics often use skeptics in the audience as an excuse for failure: the negative vibrations made it impossible to contact the spirits, etc. A couple of them had even banned me from their performances, claiming I disturbed the cosmos with my nonbelieving presence. "Do you think that's a good idea?"

"We don't have any choice," she said. "When I came last week, I was with my publicist, so I had to use my own name, and I didn't think it mattered – we never do channelers. Besides, the ushers recognized me. So our cover is, I was so impressed with Ariaura that I talked you into coming to see her."

"Which is pretty much the truth," I said. "What exactly is her gimmick, that you thought I should see her?"

"I don't want to prejudice you beforehand." She glanced at her Vera Wang watch and handed me one of the pillows. "Let's go."

We went into the lobby and over to a table under a lilac-and-silver banner proclaiming "Presenting Ariaura and the Wisdom of Isus" and under it, "Believe and It Will Happen." Kildy told the woman at the table our names.

"Oh, I loved you in that movie, Miss Ross," she said and handed us lilac- and-silver nametags and motioned us toward another table next to the door, where a Russell Crowe type in a lilac polo shirt was doing security checks.

"Any cameras, tape recorders, videocams?" he asked us.

Kildy opened her bag and took out an Olympus. "Can't I take one picture?" she pleaded. "I won't use the flash or anything. I just wanted to get a photo of Ariaura."

He plucked the Olympus neatly from her fingers. "Autographed 8x10 glossies can be purchased in the waiting area."

"Oh, *good*," she said. She really should have stayed in acting.

I relinquished the videocam. "What about videos of today's performance?" I said after he finished frisking me.

He stiffened. "Ariaura's communications with Isus are not performances. They are unique glimpses into a higher plane. You can order videos of today's experience in the waiting area," he said, pointing toward a pair of double doors.

The "waiting area" was a long hall lined with tables full of books, videos, audio-tapes, chakra charts, crystal balls, aromatherapy oils, amulets, Zuni fetishes, wisdom mobiles, healing stones, singing crystal bowls, amaryllis roots, aura cleansers, pyramids, and assorted other New Age junk, all with the lilac-and-silver Isus logo.

The third cardinal rule of debunking, and maybe the most important, is "Ask yourself, what do they get out of it?" or, as the Bible (source of many scams) puts it, "By their fruits shall ye know them."

And if the prices on this stuff were any indication, Ariaura was getting a hell of a lot out of it. The 8x10 glossies were $28.99, thirty-five with Ariaura's signature. "And if you want it signed by Isus," the blond guy behind the table said, "it's a hundred. He's not always willing to sign."

I could see why. His signature (done in Magic Marker) was a string of complicated symbols that looked like a cross between Elvish runes and Egyptian hieroglyphics, whereas Ariaura's was a script "A" followed by a formless scrawl.

Videotapes of her previous seminars – Volumes 1–20 – cost a cool sixty apiece, and Ariaura's "sacred amulet" (which looked like something you'd buy on the Home Shopping Network) cost nine hundred and fifty (box extra). People were snapping them up like hotcakes, along with Celtic pentacles, meditation necklaces, dreamcatcher earrings, worry beads, and toe rings with your zodiac sign on them.

Kildy bought one of the outrageously priced stills (no signature) and three of the videos, cooing, "I just loved her last seminar," gave the guy selling them her autograph, and we went into the auditorium.

It was hung with rose, lilac, and silver chiffon floor-length banners and a state-of-the-art lighting system. Stars and planets rotated overhead, and comets occasionally whizzed by. The stage end of the auditorium was hung with gold mylar, and in the center of the stage was a black pyramid-backed throne. Apparently Ariaura did not intend to sit on the floor like the rest of us.

At the door, ushers clad in mostly unbuttoned lilac silk shirts and tight pants took our tickets. They all looked like Tom Cruise, which would be par for the course even if this wasn't Hollywood.

Sex has been a mainstay of the psychic business since Victorian days. Half the appeal of early table-rapping had been the filmy-draperies-and-nothing-else clad female "spirits" who drifted tantalizingly among the male séance goers, fogging up their spectacles and preventing them from thinking clearly. Sir William Crookes, the famous British chemist, had been so besotted by an obviously fake medium's sexy daughter that he'd staked his scientific reputation on the medium's dubious authenticity, and nowadays it's no accident that most channelers are male and given to chest-baring Rudolph-Valentino-like robes. Or, if they're female, have buff, handsome ushers to distract the women in the audience. If you're drooling over them, you're not likely to spot the wires and chicken guts or realize what they're saying is nonsense. It's the oldest trick in the book.

One of the ushers gave Kildy a Tom Cruise smile and led her to the end of a cross-legged row on the very hard-looking floor. I was glad Kildy had brought the pillows.

I plopped mine next to hers and sat down on it. "This had better be good," I said.

"Oh, it will be," a fifty-ish redhead wearing the sacred amulet and a diamond as big as my fist said. "I've seen Ariaura, and she's wonderful." She reached into one of the three lilac shopping bags she'd stuck between us and pulled out a needlepoint lavender pillow that said, "Believe and It Will Happen."

I wondered if that applied to her believing her pillow was large enough to sit on, because it was about the same size as the rock on her finger, but as soon as they'd finished organizing the rows, the ushers came around bearing stacks of plastic-covered cushions (the kind rented at football games, only lilac) for ten bucks apiece.

The woman next to me took three, and I counted ten other people in our row, and eleven in the row ahead of us shelling out for them. Eighty rows times ten, to be conservative. A cool eight thousand bucks, just to sit down, and who knows how much profit in all those lilac shopping bags. "By their fruits shall ye know them."

I looked around. I couldn't see any signs of shills or a wireless setup, but, unlike psychics and mediums, channelers don't need them. They give out general advice, couched in New Age terms.

"Isus is absolutely astonishing," my neighbor confided. "He's so *wise!* Much better than Romtha. He's responsible for my deciding to leave Randall. 'To thine inner self be true,' Isus said, and I realized Randall had been *blocking* my spiritual ascent – "

"Were you at last Saturday's seminar?" Kildy leaned across me to ask.

"No. I was in Cancun, and I was just decimated when I realized I'd missed it. I made Tio bring me back early so I could come today. I desperately need Isus's wisdom about the divorce. Randall's claiming Isus had nothing to do with my decision, that I left him because the pre-nup had expired, and he's threatening to call Tio as – "

But Kildy had lost interest and was leaning across *her* to ask a pencil-thin woman in the full lotus position if she'd seen Ariaura before. She hadn't, but the one on her right had.

"Last Saturday?" Kildy asked.

She hadn't. She'd seen her six weeks ago in Eugene.

I leaned toward Kildy and whispered, "What happened last Saturday?"

"I think they're starting, Rob," she said, pointing at the stage, where absolutely nothing was happening, and got off her pillow and onto her knees.

"What are you doing?" I whispered.

She didn't answer that either. She reached inside her pillow, pulled out an orange pillow the same size as the "Believe and It Will Happen" cushion, handed it to me, and arranged herself gracefully on the large tasseled one. As soon as she was cross-legged, she took the orange pillow back from me and laid it across her knees.

"Comfy?" I asked.

"Yes, thank you," she said, turning her movie-star smile on me.

I leaned toward her. "You sure you don't want to tell me what we're doing here?"

"Oh, look, they're starting," she said, and this time they were.

A Brad Pitt lookalike stepped out on stage holding a hand mike and gave us the ground rules. No flash photos (even though they'd confiscated all the cameras). No applause (it breaks Ariaura's concentration). No bathroom breaks. "The cosmic link with Isus is extremely fragile," Brad explained, "and movement or the shutting of a door can break that connection."

Right. Or else Ariaura had learned a few lessons from EST, including the fact that people who are distracted by their bladders are less likely to spot gobbledygook, like the stuff Brad was spouting right now:

"Eighty thousand years ago Isus was a high priest of Atlantis. He lived for three hundred years before he departed this earthly plane and acquired the wisdom of the ages – "

What ages? The Paleolithic and Neolithic? Eighty thousand years ago we were still living in trees.

" – he spoke with the oracle at Delphi, he delved into the Sacred Writings of Rosicrucian – "

Rosicrucian?

"Now watch as Ariaura calls him from the Cosmic All to share his wisdom with you."

The lights deepened to rose, and the chiffon banners began to blow in, as if there was a breeze behind them. Correction, state-of-the-art lighting and fans.

The gale intensified, and for a moment I wondered if Ariaura was going to swoop in on a wire, but then the gold mylar parted, revealing a curving black stairway, and Ariaura, in a purple velvet caftan and her sacred amulet, descended it to the strains of Holst's *Planets* and went to stand dramatically in front of her throne.

The audience paid no attention to the "no applause" edict, and Ariaura seemed to expect it. She stood there for at least two minutes, regally surveying the crowd. Then she raised her arms as if delivering a benediction and lowered them again, quieting the crowd. "Welcome, Seekers after Divine Truth," she said in a peppy, Oprah-type voice, and there was more applause. "We're going to have a wonderful spiritual experience together here today and achieve a new plane of enlightenment."

More applause.

"But you mustn't applaud me. I am only the conduit *through* which Isus passes, the vessel he fills. Isus first came to me, or, rather, I should say, through me, five years ago, but I was afraid. I didn't want to believe it. It took me nearly a whole year to accept that I had become the focus for cosmic energies beyond the reality we know. It's the wisdom of his highly evolved spirit you'll hear today, not mine. If..." a nice theatrical pause here "...he deigns to come to us. For Isus is a sage, not a servant to be bidden. He comes when he wills. Mayhap he will be among us this afternoon, mayhap not."

In a pig's eye. These women weren't going to shell out seven hundred and fifty bucks for a no-show, even if this was Beverly Hills. I'd bet the house Isus showed up right on cue.

"Isus will come only if our earthly plane is in alignment with the cosmic," Ariaura said, "if the auratic vibrations are right." She looked sternly out at the audience. "If any of you are harboring negative vibrations, contact cannot be made."

Uh-oh, here it comes, I thought, and waited for her to look straight at the two of us and tell us to leave, but she didn't. She merely said, "Are all of you thinking positive thoughts, feeling positive emotions? Are you all believing?"

You bet.

"I sense that every one of you is thinking positive thoughts," Ariaura said. "Good. Now, to bring Isus among us, you must help me. You must each calm your center." She closed her eyes. "You must concentrate on your inner soul-self."

I glanced around the audience. Over half of the women had their eyes shut, and many had folded their hands in an attitude of prayer. Some swayed back and forth, and the woman next to me was droning, "Om." Kildy had her eyes closed, her orange pillow clasped to her chest.

"Align...align..." Ariaura chanted, and then with finality, "Align." There was another theatrical pause.

"I will now attempt to contact Isus," she said. "The focusing of the astral energy is a dangerous and difficult operation. I must ask that you remain perfectly quiet and still while I am preparing myself."

The woman next to me obediently stopped chanting "Om," and everyone opened their eyes. Ariaura closed hers and leaned back on her throne, her ring-covered hands draped over the ends of the arms. The lights went down and the music came up, the theme from Holst's "Mars." Everyone, including Kildy, watched breathlessly.

Ariaura jerked suddenly as if she were being electrocuted and clutched the arms of the throne. Her face contorted, her mouth twisting and her head shaking. The audience gasped. Her body jerked again, slamming back against the throne, and she went into a series of spasms and writhings, with more shaking. This went on for a full minute, while "Mars" built slowly behind her and the spotlight morphed to pink. The music cut off, and she slumped lifelessly back against the throne.

She remained there for a nicely timed interval, and then sat up stiffly, staring straight ahead, her hands lying loosely on the throne's arms. "I am Isus!" she said in a booming voice that was a dead ringer for "Who dares to approach the great Oz?"

"I am the Enlightened One, a servant unto that which is called the Text and the First Source. I have come from the ninth level of the astral plane," she boomed, "to aid you in your spiritual journeys."

So far it was an exact duplicate of Romtha, right down to the pink light and the number of the astral plane level, but next to me Kildy was leaning forward expectantly.

"I have come to speak the truth," Isus boomed, "to reveal to thou thine higher self."

I leaned over to Kildy and whispered, "Why is it they never learn how to use 'thee' and 'thou' correctly on the astral plane?"

"Shh," Kildy hissed, intent on what Isus was saying.

"I bring you the long-lost wisdom of the kingdom of Lemuria and the prophecies of Antinous to aid thee in these troubled days, for thou livest in a time of tribulation. The last days these are of the Present Age, days filled with anxiety and terrorist attacks and dysfunctional relationships. But I say unto ye, thou must not look without but within, for thee alone are responsible for your happiness, and if that means getting out of a bad relationship, make it so. Seek you must your own inner isness and create thou must thine own inner reality. Thee art the universe."

I don't know what I'd been expecting. *Something*, at least, but this was just the usual New Age nonsense, a mush of psychobabble, self-help tips, pseudo-scripture, and *Chicken Soup for the Soul*.

I sneaked a glance at Kildy. She was sitting forward, still clutching her pillow tightly to her chest, her beautiful face intent, her mouth slightly open. I wondered if she could actually have been taken in by Ariaura. It's always a possibility, even with skeptics. Kildy wouldn't be the first one to be fooled by a cleverly done illusion.

But this wasn't cleverly done. It wasn't even original. The Lemuria stuff was Richard Zephyr, the "Thou art the universe" stuff was Shirley MacLaine, and the syntax was pure Yoda.

And this was Kildy we were talking about. Kildy, who never fell for anything, not even that devic levitator. She had to have a good reason for shelling out over two thousand bucks for this, but so far I was stumped. "What exactly is it you wanted me to see?" I murmured.

"Shh."

"But fear not," Ariaura said, "for a New Age is coming, an age of peace, of spiritual enlightenment, when you – doing here listening to this confounded claptrap?"

I looked up sharply. Ariaura's voice had changed in midsentence from Isus's booming bass to a gravelly baritone, and her manner had, too. She leaned forward, hands on her knees, scowling at the audience. "It's a lot of infernal gabble," she said belligerently.

I glanced at Kildy. She had her eyes fixed on the stage.

"This hokum is even worse than the pretentious bombast you hear in the chautauqua," the voice croaked.

Chautauqua? I thought. What the – ?

"But there you sit, with your mouths hanging open, like the rubes at an Arkansas camp meeting, listening to a snakecharming preacher, waiting for her to fix up your romances and cure your gallstones – "

The woman next to Kildy glanced questioningly at us and then back at the stage. Two of the ushers standing along the wall exchanged frowning glances, and I could hear whispering from somewhere in the audience.

"Have you yaps actually fallen for this mystical mumbo-jumbo? Of course you have. This is America, home of the imbecile and the ass!" the voice said, and the whispering became a definite murmur.

"What in the – ?" a woman behind us said, and the woman next to me gathered up her bags, stuffed her "Believe" pillow into one of them, stood up, and began to step over people to get to the door.

One of the ushers signaled someone in the control booth, and the lights and Holst's "Venus" began to come up. The emcee took a hesitant step out onto the stage.

"You sit there like a bunch of gaping primates, ready to buy anyth – " Ariaura said, and her voice changed abruptly back to the basso of Isus, " – but the Age of Spiritual Enlightenment cannot begin until each of thou beginnest thy own journey."

The emcee stopped in midstep, and so did the murmuring. And the woman who'd been next to me and who was almost to the door. She stood there next to it, holding her bags and listening.

"And believe. All of you, casteth out the toxins of doubt and skepticism now. *Believe* and it will happen."

She must be back on script. The emcee gave a sigh of relief, and retreated back into the wings, and the woman who'd been next to me sat down where she'd been standing, bags and pillows and all. The music faded, and the lights went back to rose.

"Believe in thine inner Soul-Self," Ariaura/Isus said. "Believe, and let your spiritual unenfoldment begin." She paused, and the ushers looked up nervously. The emcee poked his head out from the gold mylar drapes.

"I grow weary," she said. "I must return now to that higher reality from whence I cameth. Fear not, for though I no longer share this earthly plane with thee, still I am with thou." She raised her arm stiffly in a benediction/Nazi salute, gave a sharp shudder, and then slumped forward in a swoon that would have done credit to Gloria Swanson. Holst's "Venus" began again, and she sat up, blinking, and turned to the emcee, who had come out onstage again.

"Did Isus speak?" she asked him in her original voice.

"Yes, he did," the emcee said, and the audience burst into thunderous applause, during which he helped her to her feet and handed her over to two of the ushers, who walked her, leaning heavily on them, up the black stairway and out of sight.

As soon as she was safely gone, the emcee quieted the applause and said, "Copies of Ariaura's books and videotapes are available outside in the waiting area. If you wish to arrange for a private audience, see me or one of the ushers," and everyone began gathering up their pillows and heading for the door.

"Wasn't he *wonderful?*" a woman ahead of us in the exodus said to her friend. "So authentic!"

> Is Los Angeles the worst town in America, or only next to the worst? The
> skeptic, asked the original question, will say yes, the believer will say no.
> There you have it.
>   — H. L. MENCKEN

★

Kildy and I didn't talk till we were out of the parking lot and on Wilshire, at which point Kildy said, "Now do you understand why I wanted you to see it for yourself, Rob?"

"It was interesting, all right. I take it she did the same thing at the seminar you went to last week?"

She nodded. "Only last week two people walked out."

"Was it the exact same spiel?"

"No. It didn't last quite as long – I don't know how long exactly, it caught me by surprise – and she used slightly different words, but the message was the same. And it happened the same way – no warning, no contortions, her voice just changed abruptly in midsentence. So what do you think's going on, Rob?"

I turned onto LaBrea. "I don't know, but lots of channelers do more than one 'entity.' Joye Wildde does two, and before Hans Lightfoot went to jail, he did half a dozen."

Kildy looked skeptical. "Her promotional material doesn't say anything about multiple entities."

"Maybe she's tired of Isus and wants to switch to another spirit. When you're a channeler, you can't just announce, 'Coming soon: Isus II.' You've got to make it look authentic. So she introduces him with a few words one week, a couple of sentences the next, et cetera."

"She's introducing a new and improved spirit who yells at the audience and calls them imbeciles and rubes?" she said incredulously.

"It's probably what channelers call a 'dark spirit,' a so-called bad entity that tries to lead the unwary astray. Todd Phoenix used to have a nasty voice break in in the middle of White Feather's spiel and make heckling comments. It's a useful trick. It reinforces the idea that the psychic's actually channeling, and anything inconsistent or controversial the channeler says can be blamed on the bad spirit."

"But Ariaura didn't even seem to be aware that there *was* a bad spirit, if that's what it was supposed to be. Why would it tell the audience to go home and stop giving their money to a snake-oil vendor like Ariaura?"

A snake-oil vendor? That sounded vaguely familiar, too. "Is that what she said last week? Snake-oil vendor?"

"Yes," she said. "Why? Do you know who she's channeling?"

"No," I said, frowning, "but I've heard that phrase somewhere. And the line about the chautauqua."

"So it's obviously somebody famous," Kildy said.

But the historical figures channelers did were always instantly recognizable.

Randall Mars's Abraham Lincoln began every sentence with "Four score and seven years ago," and the others were all equally obvious. "I wish I'd gotten Ariaura's little outburst on tape," I said.

"We did," Kildy said, reaching over the backseat and grabbing her orange pillow. She unzipped it, reached inside, and brought out a micro-videocam. "Ta-da! I'm sorry I didn't get last week's. I didn't realize they were frisking people."

She fished in the pillow again and brought out a sheet of paper. "I had to run to the bathroom and scribble down what I could remember."

"I thought they didn't let people go to the bathroom."

She grinned at me. "I gave an Oscar-worthy performance of an actress they'd let out of rehab too soon."

I glanced at the list at the next stoplight. There were only a few phrases on it: the one she'd mentioned, and "I've never seen such shameless bilge," and "you'd have to be a pack of deluded half-wits to believe something so preposterous."

"That's all?"

She nodded. "I told you, it didn't last nearly as long last time. And since I wasn't expecting it, I missed most of the first sentence."

"That's why you were asking at the seminar about buying the videotape?"

"Uh-huh, although I doubt if there's anything on it. I've watched her last three videos, and there's no sign of Entity Number Two."

"But it happened at the seminar you went to and at this one. Has it occurred to you it might have happened *because* we were there?" I pulled into a parking space in front of the building where *The Jaundiced Eye* has its office.

"But – " she said.

"The ticket-taker could have alerted her that we were there," I said. I got out and opened her door for her, and we started up to the office. "Or she could have spotted us in the audience – you're not the only one who's famous. My picture's on every psychic wanted poster on the West Coast – and she decided to jazz up the performance a little by adding another entity. To impress us."

"That can't be it."

I opened the door. "Why not?"

"Because it's happened at least twice before," she said, walking in and sitting down in the only good chair. "In Berkeley and Seattle."

"How do you know?"

"My publicist's ex-boyfriend's girlfriend saw her in Berkeley – that's how my publicist found out about Ariaura – so I got her number and called her and asked her, and she said Isus was talking along about tribulation and thee being the universe, and all of a sudden this other voice said, 'What a bunch of boobs!' She said that's how she knew Ariaura was really channeling, because if it was fake she'd hardly have called the audience names."

"Well, there's your answer. She does it to make her audiences believe her."

"You saw them, they already believe her," Kildy said. "And if that's what she's doing, why isn't it on the Berkeley videotape?"

"It isn't?"

She shook her head. "I watched it six times. Nothing."

"And you're sure your publicist's ex-boyfriend's girlfriend really saw it? That you weren't leading her when you asked her questions?"

"I'm sure," she said indignantly. "Besides, I asked my mother."

"She was there, too?"

"No, but two of her friends were, and one of them knew someone who saw the Seattle seminar. They all said basically the same thing, except the part about it making them believe her. In fact, one of them said, 'I think her cue cards were out of order,' and told me not to waste my money, that the person I should go see was Angelina Black Feather." She grinned at me and then went serious. "If Ariaura was doing it on purpose, why would she edit it out? And why did the emcee and the ushers look so uneasy?"

So she'd noticed that, too.

"Maybe she didn't warn them she was going to do it. Or, more likely, it's all part of the act, to make people believe it's authentic."

Kildy shook her head doubtfully. "I don't think so. I think it's something else."

"Like what? You don't think she's really channeling this guy?"

"No, of *course* not, Rob," she said indignantly. "It's just that...you say she's doing it to get publicity and bigger crowds, but as you told me, the first rule of success in the psychic business is to tell people what they want to hear, not to call them boobs. You saw the woman next to you – she was all ready to walk out, and I watched her afterward. She didn't sign up for a private enlightenment audience, and neither did very many other people, and I heard the emcee telling someone there were lots of tickets still available for the next seminar. Last week's was sold out a month in advance. Why would she do something to hurt her business?"

"She's got to do something to up the ante, to keep the customers coming back, and this new spirit is to create buzz. You watch, next week she'll be advertising 'The Battle of the Ancients.' It's a gimmick, Kildy."

"So you don't think we should go see her again."

"No. That's the worst thing we could possibly do. We don't want to give her free publicity, and if she did do it to impress us, though it doesn't sound like it, we'd be playing right into her hands. If she's not, and the spirit *is* driving customers away, like you say, she'll dump it and come up with a different one. Or put herself out of business. Either way, there's no need for us to do anything. It's a nonstory. You can forget all about her."

Which just goes to show you why I could never make it as a psychic. Because before the words were even out of my mouth, the office door banged open, and Ariaura roared in and grabbed me by the lapels.

"I don't know what you're doing or how you're doing it!" she screamed, "but I want you to stop it right now!"

> *He has a large and extremely uncommon capacity for provocative*
> *utterance....*
> — H. L. MENCKEN

I hadn't given Ariaura's acting skills enough credit. Her portrayal of Isus might be wooden and fakey, but she gave a pretty convincing portrayal of a hopping-mad psychic.

"How *dare* you!" she shrieked. "I'll sue you for everything you own!"

She had changed out of her flowing robes and into a lilac-colored suit Kildy told me later was a Zac Posen, and her diamond-studded necklace and earrings rattled. She was practically vibrating with rage, though not the positive vibrations she'd said were necessary for the appearance of spirits.

"I just watched the video of my seminar," she shrieked, her face two inches from mine. "How *dare* you hypnotize me and make me look like a complete fool in front of – "

"Hypnotize?" Kildy said. (I was too busy trying to loosen her grip on my lapels to say anything.) "You think Rob hypnotized you?"

"Oh, don't play the innocent with me," Ariaura said, wheeling on her. "I saw you two out there in the audience today, and I know all about you and your nasty, sneering little magazine. I know you nonbelievers will stop at nothing to keep us from spreading the Higher Truth, but I didn't think you'd go this far, hypnotizing me against my will and making me say those things! Isus told me I shouldn't let you stay in the auditorium, that he sensed danger in your reality, but I said, 'No, let the unbelievers stay and experience your presence. Let them know you come from the Existence Beyond to help us, to bring us words of Higher Wisdom,' but Isus was right, you were up to no good."

She removed one hand from a lapel long enough to shake a lilac-lacquered fingernail at me. "Well, your little hypnotism scheme won't work. I've worked too hard to get where I am, and I'm not going to let a pair of narrow-minded little unbelievers like you get in my way. I have no intention – Higher Wisdom, my foot!" she snorted. "Higher Humbug is what I call it."

Kildy glanced, startled, at me.

"Oh, the trappings are a lot gaudier, I'll give you that," Ariaura said in the gravelly voice we'd heard at the seminar.

As before, the change had come without a break and in midsentence. One minute she had had me by the lapels, and the next she'd let go and was pacing around the room, her hands behind her back, musing, "That auditorium's a lot fancier, and it's a big improvement over a courthouse lawn, and a good forty degrees cooler." She sat down on the couch, her hands on her spread-apart knees. "And those duds she wears would make a grand worthy bow-wow of the Knights of Zoroaster look dowdy, but it's the same old line of buncombe and the same old Boobus Americanus drinking it in."

Kildy took a careful step toward my desk, reached for her handbag and did something I couldn't see, and then went back to where she'd been standing, keeping her eyes the whole time on Ariaura, who was holding forth about the seminar.

"I never saw such an assortment of slack-jawed simians in one place! Except for the fact that the yokels have to sit on the floor – and pay for the privilege! – it's the spitting image of a Baptist tent revival. Tell 'em what they want to hear, do a couple of parlor tricks, and then pass the collection plate. And they're still falling for it!" She stood up and began pacing again. "I knew I should've stuck around. It's just like that time in Dayton – I think it's all over and leave, and look what happens! You let the quacks and the crooks take over, like this latter-day Aimee Semple McPherson. She's no more a seer than – of allowing you to ruin everything I've worked for! I..." She looked around bewilderedly. "...what?... I..." She faltered to a stop.

I had to hand it to her. She was good. She'd switched back into her own voice without missing a beat, and then given an impressive impersonation of someone who had no idea what was going on.

She looked confusedly from me to Kildy and back. "It happened again, didn't it?" she asked, a quaver in her voice, and turned to appeal to Kildy. "He did it again, didn't he?" and began backing toward the door. "Didn't he?"

She pointed accusingly at me. "You keep *away* from me!" she shrieked. "And you keep away from my seminars! If you so much as *try* to come near me again, I'll get a restraining order against you!" she said and roared out, slamming the door behind her.

"Well," Kildy said after a minute. "That was interesting."

"Yes," I said, looking at the door. "Interesting."

Kildy went over to my desk and pulled the Hasaka out from behind her handbag. "I got it all," she said, taking out the disk, sticking it in the computer dock, and sitting down in front of the monitor. "There were a lot more clues this time."

She began typing in commands. "There should be more than enough for us to be able to figure out who it is."

"I know who it is," I said.

Kildy stopped in mid-keystroke. "Who?"

"The High Priest of Irreverence."

"Who?"

"The Holy Terror from Baltimore, the Apostle of Common Sense, the Scourge of Con Men, Creationists, Faith-Healers, and the Booboisie," I said. "Henry Louis Mencken."

In brief, it is a fraud.
— H. L. MENCKEN

"H. L. Mencken?" Kildy said. "The reporter who covered the Scopes trial?" (I told you she was too good to be true.)

"But why would Ariaura channel him?" she asked after we'd checked the words and phrases we'd listed against Mencken's writings. They all checked out, from "buncombe" to "slackjawed simians" to "home of the imbecile and the ass."

"What did he mean about leaving Dayton early? Did something happen in Ohio?"

I shook my head. "Tennessee. Dayton was where the Scopes trial was held."

"And Mencken left early?"

"I don't know," I said, and went over to the bookcase to look for *The Great Monkey Trial*, "but I know it got so hot during the trial they moved it outside."

"That's what that comment about the courthouse lawn and its being forty degrees cooler meant," Kildy said.

I nodded. "It was a hundred and five degrees and 90 percent humidity the week of the trial. It's definitely Mencken. He invented the term 'Boobus Americanus.'"

"But why would Ariaura channel H. L. Mencken, Rob? He *hated* people like her, didn't he?"

"He certainly did." He'd been the bane of charlatans and quacks all through the twenties, writing scathing columns on all kinds of scams, from faith-healing to chiropractic to creationism, railing incessantly against all forms of "hocus-pocus" and on behalf of science and rational thought.

"Then why would she channel him?" Kildy asked. Why not somebody sympathetic to psychics, like Edgar Cayce or Madame Blavatsky?"

"Because they'd obviously be suspect. By channeling an enemy of psychics, she makes it seem more credible."

"But nobody's ever heard of him."

"You have. I have."

"But nobody else in Ariaura's audience has."

"Exactly," I said, still looking for *The Great Monkey Trial*.

"You mean you think she's doing it to impress us?"

"Obviously," I said, scanning the titles. "Why else would she have come all the way over here to give that little performance?"

"But – what about the Seattle seminar? Or the one in Berkeley?"

"Dry runs. Or she was hoping we'd hear about them and go see her. Which we did."

"I didn't," Kildy said. "I went because my publicist wanted me to."

"But you go to lots of spiritualist events, and you talk to lots of people. Your publicist was there. Even if you hadn't gone, she'd have told you about it."

"But what would be the point? You're a skeptic. You don't believe in channeling. Would she honestly think she could convince you Mencken was real?"

"Maybe," I said. "She's obviously gone to a lot of trouble to make the spirit sound like him. And think what a coup that would be. 'Skeptic Says Channeled Spirit Authentic'? Have you ever heard of Uri Geller? He made a splash back in the seventies by claiming to bend spoons with his mind. He got all kinds of attention when a pair of scientists from the Stanford Research Institute said it wasn't a trick, that he was actually doing it."

"Was he?"

"No, of course not, and eventually he was exposed as a fraud. By Johnny Carson. Geller made the mistake of going on the *Tonight Show* and doing it in front of him. He'd apparently forgotten Carson had been a magician in his early days. But the point is, he made it onto the *Tonight Show*. And what made him a celebrity was having the endorsement of reputable scientists."

"And if you endorsed Ariaura, if you said you thought it was really Mencken, she'd be a celebrity, too."

"Exactly."

"So what do we do?"

"Nothing."

"Nothing? You're not going to try to expose her as a fake?"

"Channeling isn't the same as bending spoons. There's no independently verifiable evidence." I looked at her. "It's not worth it, and we've got bigger fish to fry. Like Charles Fred. He's making way too much money for a medium who only charges two hundred a performance, and he has *way* too many hits for a cold-reader. We need to find out how he's doing it, and where the money's coming from."

"But shouldn't we at least go to Ariaura's next seminar to see if it happens again?" Kildy persisted.

"And have to explain to the L.A. *Times* reporter who just happens to be there why we're so interested in Ariaura?" I said. "And why you came back three times?"

"I suppose you're right. But what if some other skeptic endorses her? Or some English professor?"

I hadn't thought of that. Ariaura had dangled the bait at four seminars we knew of. She might have been doing it at more, and *The Skeptical Mind* was in Seattle, Carlyle Drew was in San Francisco, and there were any number of amateur skeptics who went to spiritualist events.

And they would all know who Mencken was. He was the critical thinker's favorite person, next to the Amazing Randi and Houdini. He'd not only been fearless in his attacks on superstition and fraud, he could write "like a bat out of hell." And, unlike the rest of us skeptics, people had actually listened to what he said.

I'd liked him ever since I'd read about him chatting with somebody in his office at the *Baltimore Sun* and then suddenly looking out the window, saying, "The sons of bitches are gaining on us!" and frantically beginning to type. That was how I felt about twice a day, and more than once I'd muttered to myself, "Where the hell is Mencken when we need him?"

And I'd be willing to bet there were other people who felt the same way I did, who might be seduced by Mencken's language and the fact that Ariaura was telling them exactly what they wanted to hear.

"You're right," I said. "We need to look into this, but we should send somebody else to the seminar."

"How about my publicist? She said she wanted to go again."

"No, I don't want it to be anybody connected with us."

"I know just the person," Kildy said, snatching up her cell phone. "Her name's Riata Starr. She's an actress."

With a name like that, what else could she be?

"She's between jobs right now," Kildy said, punching in a number, "and if I tell her there's likely to be a casting director there, she'll definitely do it for us."

"Does she believe in channelers?"

She looked pityingly at me. "Everyone in Hollywood believes in channelers, but it won't matter." She put the phone to her ear. "I'll put a videocam on her, and a recorder," she whispered. "And I'll tell her an undercover job would look great on her acting resume. Hello?" she said in a normal voice. "I'm trying to reach Riata Starr. Oh. No, no message."

She pushed "end." "She's at a casting call at Miramax." She stuck the phone in her bag, fished her keys out of its depths, and slung the bag over her shoulder. "I'm going to go out there and talk to her. I'll be back," she said and went out.

Definitely too good to be true, I thought, watching her leave, and called up a friend of mine in the police department and asked him what they had on Ariaura.

He promised he'd call me back, and while I was waiting I looked for and found The Great Monkey Trial. I looked up Mencken in the index and started through the references to see when Mencken had left Dayton. I doubted if he would have left before the trial was over. He'd been having the time of his life, pillorying William Jennings Bryan and the creationists. Maybe the reference was to Mencken's having left before Bryan's death. Bryan had died five days after the trial ended, presumably from a heart attack, but more likely from the humiliation he'd suffered at the hands of Clarence Darrow, who'd put him on the stand and fired questions at him about the Bible. Darrow had made him, and creationism, look ridiculous, or rather, Bryan had made himself look ridiculous. The cross-examination had been the high point of the trial, and it had killed him.

Mencken had written a deadly, unforgiving eulogy of Bryan, and he might very well have been sorry he hadn't been in at the kill, but I couldn't imagine Ariaura knowing that, even if she had taken the trouble to look up "Boobus Americanus" and "unmitigated bilge," and research Mencken's gravelly voice and explosive delivery.

Of course she might have read it. In this very book, even. I read the chapter on Bryan's death, looking for references to Mencken, but I couldn't find any. I backtracked, and there it was. And I couldn't believe it. He hadn't left after the trial. When Darrow's expert witnesses had all been disallowed, Mencken had assumed that the trial was all over except for assorted legal technicalities and had gone back to Baltimore. Mencken hadn't seen Darrow's withering cross-examination. He'd missed Bryan saying man wasn't a mammal, his insisting the sun could stand still without throwing the Earth out of orbit. He'd definitely left too soon. And I was willing to bet he'd never forgiven himself for it.

> To me, the scientific point of view is completely satisfying, and it has been so as long as I remember. Not once in this life have I ever been inclined to seek a rock and refuge elsewhere.
> — H. L. MENCKEN

"But how could Ariaura know that?" Kildy said when she got back from the casting call.

"The same way I know it. She read it in a book. Did your friend Riata agree to go to the seminar?"

"Yes, she said she'd go. I gave her the Hasaka, but I'm worried they might confiscate it, so I've got an appointment with this props guy at Universal who worked on the last Bond movie to see if he's got any ideas."

"Uh, Kildy...those gadgets James Bond uses aren't real. It's a movie."

She shot me her Julia-Roberts-plus smile. "I said *ideas*. Oh, and I got Riata's ticket. When I called, I asked if they were sold out, and the guy I talked to said, 'Are you kidding?' and told me they'd only sold about half what they usually do. Did you find out anything about Ariaura?"

"No," I said. "I'm checking out some leads," but my friend at the police department didn't have any dope on Ariaura, not even a possible alibi.

"She's clean," he said when he finally called back the next morning. "No mail fraud, not even a parking ticket."

I couldn't find anything on her in *The Skeptical Mind* or on the Scam-watch website. It looked like she made her money the good old American way, by telling her customers a bunch of nonsense and selling them chakra charts.

I told Kildy as much when she came in, looking gorgeous in a casual shirt and jeans that had probably cost as much as *The Jaundiced Eye*'s annual budget.

"Ariaura's obviously not her real name, but so far I haven't been able to find out what it is," I said. "Did you get a James Bond secret videocam from your buddy Q?"

"Yes," she said, setting the tote bag down. "And I have an idea for proving Ariaura's a fraud." She handed me a sheaf of papers. "Here are the transcripts of everything Mencken said. We check them against Mencken's writings, and – what?"

I was shaking my head. "This is channeling. When I wrote an exposé about Swami Vishnu Jammi's fifty-thousand-year-old entity, Yogati, using phrases like 'totally awesome' and 'funky' and talking about cell phones, he said he 'transliterated' Yogati's thoughts into his own words."

"Oh." Kildy bit her lip. "Rob, what about a computer match? You know, one of those things where they compare a manuscript with Shakespeare's plays to see if they were written by the same person."

"Too expensive," I said. "Besides, they're done by universities, who I doubt would want to risk their credibility by running a check on a channeler. And even if they did match, all it would prove is that it's Mencken's words, not that it's Mencken."

"Oh." She sat on the corner of my desk, swinging her long legs for a minute, and then stood up, walked over to the bookcase, and began pulling down books.

"What are you doing?" I asked, going over to see what she was doing. She was holding a copy of Mencken's *Heathen Days*. "I told you," I said, "Mencken's phrases won't – "

"I'm not looking up his phrases," she said, handing me *Prejudices* and Mencken's biography. "I'm looking for questions to ask him."

"Him? He's not Mencken, Kildy. He's a concoction of Ariaura's."

"I know," she said, handing me *The Collectible Mencken*. "That's why we need to question him – I mean Ariaura. We need to ask him – her – questions like, 'What was your wife's maiden name?' and 'What was the first newspaper you worked for?' and – are any of these paperbacks on the bottom shelf here by Mencken?"

"No, they're mysteries mostly. Chandler and Hammett and James M. Cain."

She straightened to look at the middle shelves. "Questions like, 'What did your father do for a living?'"

"He made cigars," I said. "The first newspaper he worked for wasn't the *Baltimore Sun*, it was the *Morning Herald*, and his wife's maiden name was Sarah Haardt. With a 'd' and two 'a's.' But that doesn't mean I'm Mencken."

"No," Kildy said, "but if you didn't know them, it would prove you weren't." She handed me *A Mencken Chrestomathy*. "If we ask Ariaura questions Mencken would know the answers to, and she gets them wrong, it proves she's faking."

She had a point. Ariaura had obviously researched Mencken fairly thoroughly to be able to mimic his language and mannerisms, and probably well enough to answer basic questions about his life, but she would hardly have memorized every detail. There were dozens of books about him, let alone his own work and his diaries. And *Inherit the Wind* and all the other plays and books and treatises that had been written about the Scopes trial. I'd bet there were close to a hundred Mencken things in print, and that didn't include the stuff he'd written for the *Baltimore Sun*.

And if we could catch her not knowing something Mencken would know, it would be a simple way to prove conclusively that she was faking, and we could move on to the much more important question of why. If Ariaura would let herself be questioned.

"How do you plan to get Ariaura to agree to this?" I said. "My guess is she won't even let us in to see her."

"If she doesn't, then that's proof, too," she said imperturbably.

"All right," I said, "but forget about asking what Mencken's father did. Ask what he drank. Rye, by the way."

Kildy grabbed a notebook and started writing.

"Ask what the name of his first editor at the *Sun* was," I said, picking up *The Great Monkey Trial*. "And ask who Sue Hicks was."

"Who was she?" Kildy asked.

"He. He was one of the defense lawyers at the Scopes trial."

"Should we ask him – her what the Scopes trial was about?"

"No, too easy. Ask him..." I said, trying to think of a good question. "Ask him what he ate while he was there covering the trial, and ask him where he sat in the courtroom."

"Where he sat?"

"It's a trick question. He stood on a table in the corner. Oh, and ask where he was born."

She frowned. "Isn't that too easy? Everyone knows he's from Baltimore."

"I want to hear him say it."

"Oh," Kildy said, nodding. "Did he have any kids?"

I shook my head. "He had a sister and two brothers. Gertrude, Charles, and August."

"Oh, good, August's not a name you'd be able to come up with just by guessing. Did he have any hobbies?"

"He played the piano. Ask about the Saturday Night Club. He and a bunch of friends got together to play music."

We worked on the questions the rest of the day and the next morning, writing them down on index cards so they could be asked out of order.

"What about some of his sayings?" Kildy asked.

"You mean like, 'Puritanism is the haunting fear that someone, somewhere, may be happy?' No. They're the easiest thing of all to memorize, and no real person speaks in aphorisms."

Kildy nodded and bent her beautiful head over the book again. I looked up Mencken's medical history – he suffered from ulcers and had had an operation on his mouth to remove his uvula – and went out and got us sandwiches for lunch and made copies of Mencken's "History of the Bathtub" and a fake handbill he'd passed out during the Scopes trial announcing "a public demonstration of healing, casting out devils, and prophesying" by a (made-up) evangelist. Mencken had crowed that not a single person in Dayton had spotted the fake.

Kildy looked up from her book. "Did you know Mencken dated Lillian Gish?" she asked, sounding surprised.

"Yeah. He dated a lot of actresses. He had an affair with Anita Loos and nearly married Aileen Pringle. Why?"

"I'm impressed he wasn't intimidated by the fact that they were movie stars, that's all."

I didn't know if that was directed at me or not. "Speaking of actresses," I said, "what time is Ariaura's seminar?"

"Two o'clock," she said, glancing at her watch. "It's a quarter till two right now. It should be over around four. Riata said she'd call as soon as the seminar was done."

We went back to looking through Mencken's books and his biographies, looking for details Ariaura was unlikely to have memorized. He'd loved baseball. He had stolen Gideon Bibles from hotel rooms and then given them to his friends, inscribed, "Compliments of the Author." He'd been friends with lots of writers, including Theodore Dreiser and F. Scott Fitzgerald, who'd gotten so drunk at a dinner with Mencken he'd stood up at the dinner table and pulled his pants down.

The phone rang. I reached for it, but it was Kildy's cell phone. "It's Riata," she told me, looking at the readout.

"Riata?" I glanced at my watch. It was only two-thirty. "Why isn't she in the seminar?"

Kildy shrugged and put the phone to her ear. "Riata? What's going on?... You're kidding!... Did you get it? Great...no, meet me at Spago's, like we agreed. I'll be there in half an hour."

She hit "end," stood up, and took out her keys, all in one graceful motion. "Ariaura did it again, only this time as soon as she started, they stopped the seminar, yanked her off-stage, and told everybody to leave. Riata got it on tape. I'm going to go pick it up. Will you be here?"

I nodded absently, trying to think of a way to ask about Mencken's two-fingered typing, and Kildy waved goodbye and went out.

If I asked, "How do you write your stories?" I'd get an answer about the process of writing, but if I asked, "Do you touch-type?" Ariaura —

Kildy reappeared in the doorway, sat down, and picked up her notebook again. "What are you doing?" I asked, "I thought you were – "

She put her finger to her lips. "She's here," she mouthed, and Ariaura came in.

She was still wearing her purple robes and her stage makeup, so she must have come here straight from her seminar, but she didn't roar in angrily the way she had before. She looked frightened.

"What are you doing to me?" she asked, her voice trembling. "And don't say you're not doing anything. I saw the videotape. You're – that's what I want to know, too," the gravelly voice demanded. "What the hell have you been doing? I thought you ran a magazine that worked to put a stop to the kind of bilgewater this high priestess of blather spews out. She was at it again today, calling up spirits and rooking a bunch of mysticism-besotted fools out of their cold cash, and where the hell were you? I didn't see you there, cracking heads."

"We didn't go because we didn't want to encourage her if she was – " Kildy hesitated. "We're not sure what...I mean, who we're dealing with here...." she faltered.

"Ariaura," I said firmly. "You pretend to channel spirits from the astral plane for a living. Why should we believe you're not pretending to channel H. L. Mencken?"

"Pretending?" she said, sounding surprised. "You think I'm something that two-bit Jezebel's confabulating?" She sat down heavily in the chair in front of my desk and grinned wryly at me. "You're absolutely right. I wouldn't believe it either. A skeptic after my own heart."

"Yes," I said. "And as a skeptic, I need to have some proof you're who you say you are."

"Fair enough. What kind of proof?"

"We want to ask you some questions," Kildy said.

Ariaura slapped her knees. "Fire away."

"All right," I said. "Since you mentioned fires, when was the Baltimore fire?"

"Aught-four," she said promptly. "February. Cold as hell." She grinned. "Best time I ever had."

Kildy glanced at me.

"What did your father drink?" she asked.

"Rye."

"What did you drink?" I asked.

"From 1919 on, whatever I could get."

"Where are you from?" Kildy asked.

"The most beautiful city in the world."

"Which is?" I said.

"Which is?" she roared, outraged. "Bawlmer!"

Kildy shot me a glance. "What's the Saturday Night Club?" I barked.

"A drinking society," she said, "with musical accompaniment."

"What instrument did you play?"

"Piano."

"What's the Mann Act?"

"Why?" she said, winking at Kildy. "You planning on taking her across state lines? Is she underage?"

I ignored that. "If you're really Mencken, you hate charlatans, so why have you inhabited Ariaura's body?"

"Why do people go to zoos?"

She was good, I had to give her that. And fast. She spat out answers as fast as I could ask questions about the *Sun* and the *Smart Set* and William Jennings Bryan.

"Why did you go to Dayton?"

"To see a three-ring circus. And stir up the animals."

"What did you take with you?"

"A typewriter and four quarts of Scotch. I should have taken a fan. It was hotter than the seventh circle of hell, with the same company."

"What did you eat while you were there?" Kildy asked.

"Fried chicken and tomatoes. At every meal. Even breakfast."

I handed her the bogus evangelist handbill Mencken had handed out at the Scopes trial. "What's this?"

She looked at it, turned it over, looked at the other side. "It appears to be some sort of circular."

And there's all the proof we need, I thought smugly. Mencken would have recognized that instantly. "Do you know who wrote this handbill?" I started to ask and thought better of it. The question itself might give the answer away. And better not use the word "handbill."

"Do you know the event this circular describes?" I asked instead.

"I'm afraid I can't answer that," she said.

Then you're not Mencken, I thought. I shot a triumphant glance at Kildy.

"But I would be glad to," Ariaura said, "if you would be so good as to read what is written on it to me."

She handed the handbill back to me, and I stood there looking at it and then at her and then at it again.

"What is it, Rob?" Kildy said. "What's wrong?"

"Nothing," I said. "Never mind about the circular. What was your first published news story about?"

"A stolen horse and buggy," she said and proceeded to tell the whole story, but I wasn't listening.

He didn't know who the handbill was about, I thought, because he couldn't read. Because he'd had an aphasic stroke in 1948 that had left him unable to read and write.

> *I had a nice clean place to stay, madam, and I left it to come here.*
> — INHERIT THE WIND

"It doesn't prove anything," I told Kildy after Ariaura was gone. She'd come out of her Mencken act abruptly after I'd asked her what street she lived on in Baltimore, looked bewilderedly at me and then Kildy, and bolted without a word. "Ariaura could have found out about Mencken's stroke the same way I did," I said, "by reading it in a book."

"Then why did you go white like that?" Kildy said. "I thought you were going to pass out. And why wouldn't she just answer the question? She knew the answers to all the others."

"Probably she didn't know that one and that was her fallback response," I said. "It caught me off-guard, that's all. I was expecting her to have memorized pat answers, not – "

"Exactly," Kildy cut in. "Somebody faking it would have said they had an aphasic stroke if you asked them a direct question about it, but they wouldn't have...and that wasn't the only instance. When you asked him about the Baltimore fire, he said it was the best time he'd ever had. Someone faking it would have told you what buildings burned or how horrible it was."

And he'd said, not "1904" or "oh-four," but "aught-four." Nobody talked like that nowadays, and it wasn't something that would have been in Mencken's writings. It was something people said, not wrote, and Ariaura couldn't possibly –

"It doesn't prove he's Mencken," I said and realized I was saying "he." And shouting. I lowered my voice. "It's a very clever trick, that's all. And just because we don't know how the trick's being done doesn't mean it's not a trick. She could have been coached in the part, including telling her how to pretend she can't read if she's confronted with anything written, or she could be hooked up to somebody with a computer."

"I looked. She wasn't wearing an earpiece, and if somebody was looking up the answers and feeding them to her, she'd be slower answering them, wouldn't she?"

"Not necessarily. She might have a photographic memory."

"But then wouldn't she be doing a mind-reading act instead of channeling?"

"Maybe she did. We don't know what she was doing before Salem," I said, but Kildy was right. Someone with a photographic memory could make a killing as a fortuneteller or a medium, and there were no signs of a photographic memory in Ariaura's channeling act – she spoke only in generalities.

"Or she might be coming up with the answers some other way," I said.

"What if she isn't, Rob? What if she's really channeling the spirit of Mencken?"

"Kildy, channelers are fakes. There are no spirits, no sympathetic vibrations, no astral plane."

"I know," she said, "but his answers were so – " She shook her head. "And there's something about him, his voice and the way he moves – "

"It's called acting."

"But Ariaura's a terrible actress. You saw her do Isus."

"All right," I said. "Let's suppose for a minute it is Mencken, and that instead of being in the family plot in Louden Park Cemetery, his spirit's floating in the ether somewhere, why would he come back at this particular moment? Why didn't he come back when Uri Geller was bending spoons all over the place, or when Shirley MacLaine was on every talk show in the universe? Why didn't he come back in the fifties when Virginia Tighe was claiming to be Bridey Murphy?"

"I don't know," Kildy admitted.

"And why would he choose to make his appearance through the 'channel' of a third-rate mountebank like Ariaura? He *hated* charlatans like her."

"Maybe that's why he came back, because people like her are still around and he hadn't finished what he set out to do. You heard him – he said he left too early."

"He was talking about the Scopes trial."

"Maybe not. You heard him, he said, 'You let the quacks and the crooks take over.' Or maybe – " she stopped.

"Maybe what?"

"Maybe he came back to help you, Rob. That time you were so frustrated over Charles Fred, I heard you say, 'Where the hell is H. L. Mencken when we need him?' Maybe he heard you."

"And decided to come all the way back from an astral plane that doesn't exist to help a skeptic nobody's ever heard of."

"It's not *that* inconceivable that someone would be interested in you," Kildy said. "I...I mean, the work you're doing is really important, and Mencken – "

"Kildy," I said. "I don't believe this."

"I don't either – I just...you have to admit, it's a very convincing illusion."

"Yes, so was the Fox Sisters' table-rapping and Virginia Tighe's past life as an Irish washerwoman in 1880s Dublin, but there was a logical explanation for both of them, and it may not even be that complicated. The details Bridey Murphy knew all turned out to have come from Virginia Tighe's Irish nanny. The Fox Sisters were cracking their *toes*, for God's sake."

"You're right," Kildy said, but she didn't sound completely convinced, and that worried me. If Ariaura's Mencken imitation could fool Kildy, it could fool anybody, and "I'm sure it's a trick. I just don't know how she's doing it," wasn't going to cut it when the networks called me for a statement. I had to figure this out fast.

"Ariaura has to be getting her information about Mencken from someplace," I said. "We need to find out where. We need to check with bookstores and the library. And the Internet," I said, hoping that wasn't what she was using. It would take forever to find out what sites she'd visited.

"What do you want me to do?" Kildy asked.

"I want you to go through the transcripts like you suggested and find out where the quotes came from so we'll know the particular works we're dealing with," I told her. "And I want you to talk to your publicist and anybody else who's been to the seminars and find out if any of them had a private enlightenment audience with Ariaura. I want to know what goes on in them. Is she using Mencken for some purpose we don't know about? See if you can find out."

"I could ask Riata to get one," she suggested.

"That's a good idea," I said.

"What about questions? Do you want me to try to come up with some harder ones than the ones we asked him – I mean, her?"

I shook my head. "Asking harder questions won't help. If she's got a photographic memory, she'll know anything we throw at her, and if she doesn't, and we ask her some obscure question about one of the reporters Mencken worked with at the *Morning Herald*, or one of his *Smart Set* essays, she can say she doesn't remember, and it won't prove anything. If you asked me what was in articles I wrote for *The Jaundiced Eye* five years ago, I couldn't remember either."

"I'm not talking about facts and figures, Rob," Kildy said. "I'm talking about the kinds of things people don't forget, like the first time Mencken met Sara."

I thought of the first time I met Kildy, looking up from my desk to see her standing there, with her blonde hair and that movie-star smile. Unforgettable was the word, all right.

"Or how his mother died," Kildy was saying, "or how he found out about the Baltimore fire. The paper called him and woke him out of a sound sleep. There's no way you could forget that, or the name of a dog you had as a kid, or the nickname the other kids called you in grade school."

Nickname. That triggered something. Something Ariaura wouldn't know. About a baby. Had Mencken had a nickname when he was a baby? No, that wasn't it –

"Or what he got for Christmas when he was ten," Kildy said. "We need to find a question Mencken would absolutely know the answer to, and if he doesn't, it proves it's Ariaura."

"And if he does, it still doesn't prove it's Mencken. Right?"

"I'll go talk to Riata about getting a private audience," she said, stuffed the transcripts in her tote, and put on her sunglasses. "And I'll pick up the videotape. I'll see you tomorrow morning."

"Right, Kildy?" I insisted.

"Right," she said, her hand on the door. "I guess."

★

*In the highest confidence there is always a flavor of doubt – a feeling, half
instinctive and half logical, that, after all, the scoundrel may have something up his sleeve.*

    – H.L. MENCKEN

After Kildy left, I called up a computer-hacker friend of mine and put him to
work on the problem and then phoned a guy I knew in the English department
at UCLA.

"Inquiries about Mencken?" he said. "Not that I know of, Rob. You might try
the journalism department."

The guy at the journalism department said, "Who?" and, when I explained,
suggested I call Johns Hopkins in Baltimore.

And what had I been thinking? Kildy said Ariaura had started doing Mencken
in Seattle. I needed to be checking there, or in Salem or – where had she gone
after that? Sedona. I spent the rest of the day (and evening) calling bookstores
and reference librarians in all three places. Five of them responded, "Who?" and
all of them asked me how to spell "Mencken," which might or might not mean
they hadn't heard the name lately, and only seven of the thirty stores stocked any
books on him. Half of those were the latest Mencken biography, which for an
excited moment I thought might have answered the question, "Why Mencken?"
(the title of it was *Skeptic and Prophet*), but it had only been out two weeks. None
of the bookstores could give me any information on orders or recent purchases,
and the public libraries couldn't give me any information at all.

I tried their electronic card catalogues, but they only showed currently checked-
out books. I called up the L.A. Public Library's catalogue. It showed four Mencken
titles checked out, all from the Beverly Hills branch.

"Which looks promising," I told Kildy when she came in the next morning.

"No, it doesn't," she said. "I'm the one who checked them out, to compare
the transcripts against." She pulled a sheaf of papers out of her designer tote.
"I need to talk to you about the transcripts. I found something interesting.
I know," she said, anticipating my objection, "you said all it proved was that
Ariaura – "

"Or whoever's feeding this stuff to her."

She acknowledged that with a nod. " – all it proved was that whoever was
doing it was reading Mencken, and I agree, but you'd expect her to quote him
back verbatim, wouldn't you?"

"Yes," I said, thinking of Randall Mars's Lincoln and his "Four score and
seven..."

"But she doesn't. Look, here's what she said when we asked him about William Jennings Bryan: 'Bryan! I don't even want to hear that mangy old mounte-

bank's name mentioned. That scoundrel had a malignant hatred of science and sense.'"

"And he didn't say that?"

"Yes and no. Mencken called him a 'walking malignancy' and said he was 'mangy and flea-bitten' and had 'an almost pathological hatred of all learning.' And the rest of the answers, and the things she said at the seminars, are like that, too."

"So she mixed and matched his phrases," I said, but what she'd found was disturbing. Someone trying to pull off an impersonation would stick to the script, since any deviations from Mencken's actual words could be used as proof it wasn't him.

And the annotated list Kildy handed me was troubling in another way. The phrases hadn't been taken from one or two sources. They were from all over the map – "complete hooey" from *Minority Report*, "buncombe" from *The New Republic*, "as truthful as Lydia Pinkham's Vegetable Compound" from an article on pedagogy in the *Sun*.

"Could they all have been in a Mencken biography?"

She shook her head. "I checked. I found a couple of sources that had several of them, but no one source that had them all."

"That doesn't mean there isn't one," I said, and changed the subject. "Was your friend able to get a private audience with Ariaura?"

"Yes," she said, glancing at her watch. "I have to go meet her in a few minutes. She also got tickets to the seminar Saturday. They didn't cancel it like I thought they would, but they did cancel a local radio interview she was supposed to do last night, and the week-long spiritual immersion she had scheduled for next week."

"Did she give you the recording of Ariaura's last seminar?"

"No, she'd left it at home. She said she'd bring it when we meet before her private audience. She said she got some really good footage of the emcee. She swears from the way he looked that he's not in on the scam. And there's something else. I called Judy Helzberg, who goes to every psychic event there is – Remember? I interviewed her when we did the piece on shamanic astrologers – and she said Ariaura called her and asked her for Wilson Amboy's number."

"Wilson Amboy?"

"Beverly Hills psychiatrist."

"It's all part of the illusion," I said, but even I sounded a little doubtful. It was an awfully good deception for a third-rate channeler like Ariaura. There's somebody else in on it, I thought, and not just somebody feeding her answers. A partner. A mastermind.

After Kildy left I called Marty Rumboldt and asked him if Ariaura had had a partner in Salem. "Not that I know of," he said. "Prentiss just did a study on witchcraft in Salem. She might know somebody who would know. Hang on. Hey, Prentiss!" I could hear him call. "Jamie!"

Jamie, I thought. That had been James M. Cain's nickname, and Mencken had been good friends with him. Where had I read that?

"She said to call Madame Orima," Marty said, getting back on the phone, and gave me the number.

I started to dial it and then stopped and looked up "Cain, James M." in Mencken's biography. It said he and Mencken had worked on the *Baltimore Sun* together, that they had been good friends, that Mencken had helped him get his first story collection published: *The Baby in the Icebox*.

I went over to the bookcase, squatted down, and started through the row of paperbacks on the bottom shelf...Chandler, Hammett... It had a red cover, with a picture of a baby in a high chair and a...Chandler, Cain...

But no red. I scanned the titles – *Double Indemnity*, *The Postman Always Rings Twice*... Here it was, stuck behind *Mildred Pierce* and not red at all. *The Baby in the Icebox*. It was a lurid orange and yellow, with pictures of a baby in its mother's arms and a cigarette-smoking lug in front of a gas station. I hoped I remembered the inside better than the outside.

I did. The introduction was by Roy Hoopes, and it was not only a Penguin edition, but one that had been out of print for at least twenty years. Even if Ariaura's researcher had bothered to check out Cain, it would hardly have been this edition.

And the introduction was full of stuff about Cain that was perfect – the fact that everyone who knew him called him Jamie, the fact that he'd spent a summer in a tuberculosis sanitarium and hated Baltimore, Mencken's favorite place.

Some of the information was in the Mencken books – Mencken's introducing him to Alfred A. Knopf, who'd published that first collection, the *Sun* connection, Cain and Mencken's rivalry over movie star Aileen Pringle.

But most of the facts in the introduction weren't, and they were exactly the kind of thing a friend would know. And Ariaura wouldn't, because they were details about Cain's life, not Mencken's. Even a mastermind wouldn't have memorized every detail of Cain's life or those of Mencken's other famous friends. If there wasn't anything here I could use, there might be something in Dreiser's biography, or F. Scott Fitzgerald's. Or Lillian Gish's.

But there was plenty here, like the fact that Cain's brother Boydie had died in a tragic accident after the Armistice, and Cain's statement that all his writing was modeled on *Alice in Wonderland*. That was something no one would ever guess from reading Cain's books, which were all full of crimes and murderers and a beautiful, calculating woman who seduced the hero into helping her with a scam and then turned out to be working a scam of her own.

Not exactly the kind of thing Ariaura would read, and definitely the kind of thing Mencken would have. He'd bought "The Baby in the Icebox" for the *American Mercury* and told Cain it was one of the best things he'd ever written. Which meant it would make a perfect source for a question, and I knew just what to ask. To anyone who hadn't heard of the story, the question wouldn't even make sense. Only somebody who'd read the story would know the answer. Like Mencken.

And if Ariaura knew it, I'd – what? Believe she was actually channeling Mencken?

Right. And Charles Fred was really talking to the dead and Uri Geller was really bending spoons.

It was a trick, that was all. She had a photographic memory, or somebody was feeding her the answers.

Feeding her the answers.

I thought suddenly of Kildy saying, "Who *was* Sue Hicks?" of her insisting I go with her to see Ariaura, of her saying, "But why would Ariaura channel a spirit who yells at her audiences?"

I looked down at the orange-and-yellow paperback in my hand. "A beautiful, calculating woman who seduces the hero into helping her with a scam," I murmured, and thought about Ariaura's movie-star-handsome ushers and about scantily clad Victorian spirits and about Sir William Crookes.

Sex. Get the chump emotionally involved and he won't see the wires. It was the oldest trick in the book.

I'd said Ariaura wasn't smart enough to pull off such a complicated scam, and she wasn't. But Kildy was. So you get her on the inside where she can see the shelf full of Mencken books, where she can hear the chump mutter, "Where the hell is Mencken when we need him?" You get the chump to trust her, and if he falls in love with her, so much the better. It'll keep him off-balance and he won't get suspicious.

And it all fit. It was Kildy who'd set up the contact – I never did channelers, and Kildy knew that. It was Kildy who'd said we couldn't go incognito, Kildy who'd said to bring the Sony, knowing it would be confiscated, Kildy who'd taken a taxi to the seminar instead of coming in her Jaguar so she'd be at the office when Ariaura came roaring in.

But she'd gotten all of it on tape. And she hadn't had any idea who the spirit was. I was the one who'd figured out it was Mencken.

With Kildy feeding me clues from the seminar she'd gone to before, and I only had her word that Ariaura had channeled him that time. And that it had happened in Berkeley and Seattle. And that the tapes had been edited.

And she was the one who'd kept telling me it was really Mencken, the one who'd come up with the idea of asking him questions that would prove it – questions I'd conveniently told her the answers to – the one who'd suggested a friend of hers go to the seminar and videotape it, a videotape I'd never seen. I wondered if it – or Riata – even existed.

The whole thing, from beginning to end, had been a setup.

And I had never tumbled to it. Because I'd been too busy looking at her legs and her hair and that smile. Just like Crookes.

I don't believe it, I thought. Not Kildy, who'd worked side-by-side with me for nearly a year, who'd stolen chicken guts and pretended to be hypnotized and let Jean-Piette cleanse her aura, who'd come to work for me in the first place because she hated scam-artists like Ariaura.

Right. Who'd come to work for a two-bit magazine when she could have been getting five million a movie and dating Viggo Mortensen. Who'd been willing to give up premieres and summers in Tahiti and deep massages for me. Skeptics' Rule Number Two: If it seems too good to be true, it is. And how often have you said she's a good actress?

No, I thought, every bone in my body rebelling. It can't be true.

And that's what the chump always says, isn't it, even when he's faced with the evidence? "I don't believe it. She wouldn't do that to me."

And that was the whole point – to get you to trust her, to make you believe she was on your side. Otherwise you'd have insisted on checking those tapes of Ariaura's seminars for yourself to see if they'd been edited, you'd have demanded independently verifiable evidence that Ariaura had really canceled those seminars and asked about a psychiatrist.

Independently verifiable evidence. That's what I needed, and I knew exactly where to look.

"My mother took me to Lucius Windfire's luminescence reading," Kildy had said, and I had the guest lists for those readings. They were part of the court records, and I'd gotten them when I'd done the story on his arrest. Kildy had come to see me on May tenth and he'd only had two seminars that month.

I called up the lists for both seminars and for the two before that and typed in Kildy's name.

Nothing.

She said she went with her mother, I thought, and typed her mom's name in. Nothing. And nothing when I printed out the lists and went through them by hand, nothing when I went through the lists for March and April. And no ten-thousand-dollar donation on any of Windfire, Inc.'s financial statements.

Half an hour later Kildy showed up smiling, beautiful, full of news. "Ariaura's canceled all the private sessions she scheduled and the rest of her tour." She leaned over my shoulder to look at what I was doing. "Did you come up with a foolproof question for Mencken?"

"No," I said, sliding *The Baby in the Icebox* under a file folder and sticking them both in a drawer. "I came up with a theory about what's going on, though."

"Really?" she said.

"Really. You know, one of my big problems all along has been Ariaura. She's just not smart enough to have come up with all this – the 'aught-four' thing, the not being able to read, the going to see a psychiatrist. Which either meant she was actually channeling Mencken, or there was some other factor. And I think I've got it figured out."

"You have?"

"Yeah. Tell me what you think of this: Ariaura wants to be big. Not just seven-hundred-and-fifty-a-pop seminars and thirty-dollar videotapes, but *Oprah*, the *Today Show*, *Larry King*, the whole works. But to do that it's not enough to have audiences who believe her. She needs to have somebody with credibility say she's for real, a scientist, say, or a professional skeptic."

"Like you," she said cautiously.

"Like me. Only I don't believe in astral spirits. Or channelers. And I certainly wouldn't fall for the spirit of an ancient priest of Atlantis. It's going to have to be somebody a charlatan would never dream of channeling, somebody who'll say what I want to hear. And somebody I know a lot about so I'll recognize the clues being fed to me, somebody custom-tailored for me."

"Like H. L. Mencken," Kildy said. "But how would she have known you were a fan of Mencken's?"

"She didn't have to," I said. "That was her partner's job."

"Her part – "

"Partner, sidekick, shill, whatever you want to call it. Somebody I'd trust when she said it was important to go see some channeler."

"Let me get this straight," she said. "You think I went to Ariaura's seminar and her imitation of Isus was so impressive I immediately became a Believer with a capital B and fell in with her nefarious scheme, whatever it is?"

"No," I said. "I think you were in it with her from the beginning, from the very first day you came to work for me."

She really was a good actress. The expression in those beautiful blue eyes looked exactly like stunned hurt. "You believe I set you up," she said wonderingly.

I shook my head. "I'm a skeptic, remember? I deal in independently verifiable evidence. Like this," I said and handed her Lucius Windfire's attendee list.

She looked at it in silence.

"Your whole story about how you found out about me was a fake, wasn't it? You didn't look up 'debunkers' in the phone book, did you? You didn't go see a luminescence therapist with your mother?"

"No."

No.

I hadn't realized till she admitted it how much I had been counting on her saying, "There must be some mistake, I was there," or her having some excuse, no matter how phony: "Did I say the fourteenth? I meant the twentieth," or "My publicist got the tickets for us. It would be in her name." Anything. Even flinging the list dramatically at me and sobbing, "I can't believe you don't trust me."

But she just stood there, looking at the incriminatory list and then at me, not a tantrum or a tear in sight.

"You concocted the whole story," I said finally.

"Yes."

I waited for her to say, "It's not the way it looks, Rob, I can explain," but she didn't say that either. She handed the list back to me and picked up her cell phone and her bag, fishing for her keys and then slinging her bag over her shoulder as casually as if she were on her way to go cover a new moon ceremony or a tarot reading, and left.

And this was the place in the story where the private eye takes a bottle of Scotch out of his bottom drawer, pours himself a nice stiff drink, and congratulates himself on his narrow escape.

I'd almost been made a royal chump, and Mencken (the real one, not the imitation Kildy and Ariaura had tried to pass off as him) would never have forgiven me. So good riddance. And what I needed to do now was write up the whole sorry scam as a lesson to other skeptics for the next issue.

But I sat there a good fifteen minutes, thinking about Kildy and her exit, and knowing that, in spite of its off-handedness, I was never going to see her again.

> *What I need is a miracle.*
> — INHERIT THE WIND

I told you I'd make a lousy psychic. The next morning Kildy walked in carrying an armload of papers and file folders. She dumped them in front of me on my desk, picked up my phone, and began punching in numbers.

"What the hell do you think you're doing? And what's all this?" I said, gesturing at the stack of papers.

"Independently verifiable evidence," she said, still punching in numbers, and put the phone to her ear. "Hello, this is Kildy Ross. I need to speak to Ariaura." There was a pause. "She's not taking calls? All right, tell her I'm at *The*

Jaundiced Eye office, and I need to speak to her as soon as possible. Tell her it's urgent. Thank you." She hung up.

"What the hell do you think you're doing, calling Ariaura on my phone?" I said.

"I wasn't," she said. "I was calling Mencken." She pulled a file out of the middle of the stack. "I'm sorry it took me so long. Getting Ariaura's phone records was harder than I thought."

"Ariaura's phone records?"

"Yeah. Going back four years," she said, pulling a file folder out of the middle of the stack and handing it to me.

I opened it up. "How did you get her phone records?"

"I know this computer guy at Pixar. We should do an issue on how easy it is to get hold of private information and how mediums are using it to convince people they're talking to their dead relatives," she said, fishing through the stack for another folder. "And here are my phone records." She handed it to me. "The cell's on top, and then my home number and my car phone. And my mom's. And my publicist's cell phone."

"Your publicist's cell – ?"

She nodded. "In case you think I used her phone to call Ariaura. She doesn't have a regular phone, just a cell. And here are my dad's and my stepmother's. I can get my other stepmothers', too, but it'll take a couple more days, and Ariaura's big seminar is tonight."

She handed me more files. "This is a list of all my trips – airline tickets, hotel bills, rental car records. Credit card bills, with annotations," she said, and went over to her tote bag and pulled out three fat Italian-leather notebooks with a bunch of post-its sticking out the sides. "These are my dayplanners, with notes as to what the abbreviations mean, and my publicist's log."

"And this is supposed to prove you were at Lucius Windfire's luminescence reading with your mother?"

"No, Rob, I told you, I lied about the seminar," she said, looking earnestly through the stack, folder by folder. "These are to prove I didn't call Ariaura, that she didn't call me, that I wasn't in Seattle or Eugene or any of the other cities she was in, and never went to Salem." She pulled a folder out of the pile and began handing items to me. "Here's the program for Yogi Magaputra's matinee performance for May nineteenth. I couldn't find the ticket stubs and I didn't buy the tickets, the studio did, but here's a receipt for the champagne cocktail I had at intermission. See? It's got the date and it was at the Roosevelt, and here's a schedule of Magaputra's performances, showing he was at the Roosevelt on that day. And a flyer for the next session they gave out as we left."

I had one of those flyers in my file on mediums, and I was pretty sure I'd been at that séance. I'd gone to three, working on a piece on his use of funeral home records to obtain information on his victims' dead relatives. I'd never published the article – he'd been arrested on tax evasion charges before I finished it. I looked questioningly at Kildy.

"I was there researching a movie I was thinking about doing," Kildy said, "a comedy about a medium. It was called *Medium Rare*. Here's the screenplay." She handed me a thick bound manuscript. "I wouldn't read the whole thing. It's terrible. Anyway, I saw you there, talking to this guy with hair transplants – "

Magaputra's personal manager, who I'd suspected was feeding him info from the audience. I'd been trying to see if I could spot his concealed mike.

"I saw you talking to him, and I thought you looked – "

"Gullible?"

Her jaw tightened. "No. Interesting. Cute. Not the kind of guy I expected to see at one of the yogi's séances. I asked who you were, and somebody said you were a professional skeptic, and I thought, well, thank goodness! Magaputra was *patently* fake, and everyone was buying it, lock, stock, and barrel."

"Including your mother," I said.

"No, I made that up, too. My mother's even more of a skeptic than I am, especially after being married to my father. She's partly why I was interested – she's always after me to date guys from outside the movie business – so I bought a copy of *The Jaundiced Eye* and got your address and came to see you."

"And lied."

"Yes," she said. "It was a dumb thing to do. I knew it as soon as you started talking about how you shouldn't take anything anyone tells you on faith and how important independently verifiable evidence is, but I was afraid if I told you I was doing research for a movie you wouldn't want me tagging along, and if I told you I was attracted to you, you wouldn't believe me. You'd think it was a reality show or some kind of Hollywood fad thing everybody was doing right then, like opening a boutique or knitting or checking into Betty Ford."

"And you fully intended to tell me," I said, "you were just waiting for the right moment. In fact, you were all set to when Ariaura came along – "

"You don't have to be sarcastic," she said. "I thought if I went to work for you and you got to know me, you might stop thinking of me as a movie star and ask me out – "

"And incidentally pick up some good acting tips for your medium movie."

"Yes," she said angrily. "If you want to know the truth, I also thought if I kept going to those stupid past-life regression sessions and covens and soul retrieval circles, I might get over the stupid crush I had on you, but the better I got to know you, the worse it got." She looked up at me. "I know you don't believe me, but I didn't set you up. I'd never seen Ariaura before I went to that first seminar with my publicist, and I'm not in any kind of scam with her. And that story I told you the first day is the only thing I've ever lied to you about. Everything else I told you – about hating psychics and Ben Affleck and wanting to get out of the movie business and wanting to help you debunk charlatans and loathing the idea of ending up in rehab or in *The Hulk III* – was true." She rummaged in the pile and pulled out an olive green-covered script. "They really did offer me the part."

"Of the Hulk?"

"No," she said and held the script out to me. "Of the love interest."

She looked up at me with those blue eyes of hers, and if anything had ever been too good to be true, it was Kildy, standing there with that bilious green script and the office's fluorescent light on her golden hair. I had always wondered how all those chumps sitting around séance tables and squatting on lilac-colored cushions could believe such obvious nonsense. Well, now I knew.

Because standing there right then, knowing it all had to be a scam, that the *Hulk* script and the credit card bills and the phone bills didn't prove a thing, that they could easily have been faked and I was nothing more than a prize chump being set up for the big finale by a couple of pros, I still wanted to believe it. And not just the researching-a-movie alibi, but the whole thing – that H.L. Mencken had come back from the grave, that he was here to help me crusade against charlatans, that if I grabbed the wrist holding that script and pulled Kildy toward me and kissed her, we would live happily ever after.

And no wonder Mencken, railing against creationists and chiropractic and Mary Baker Eddy, hadn't gotten anywhere. What chance do facts and reason possibly have against what people desperately need to believe?

Only Mencken hadn't come back. A third-rate channeler was only pretending to be him, and Kildy's protests of love, much as I wanted to hear them, were the oldest trick in the book.

"Nice try," I said.

"But you don't believe me," she said bleakly, and Ariaura walked in.

"I got your message," she said to Kildy in Mencken's gravelly voice. "I came as soon as I could." She plunked down in a chair facing me. "Those goons of Ariaura's – "

"You can knock off the voices, Ariaura," I said. "The jig, as Mencken would say, is up."

Ariaura looked inquiringly at Kildy.

"Rob thinks Ariaura's a fake," Kildy said.

Ariaura switched her gaze to me. "You just figured that out? Of course she's a fake, she's a bamboozling mountebank, an oleaginous – "

"He thinks you're not real," Kildy said. "He thinks you're just a voice Ariaura does, like Isus, that your disrupting her seminars is a trick to convince him she's an authentic channeler, and he thinks I'm in on the plot with you, that I helped you set him up."

Here it comes, I thought. Shocked outrage. Affronted innocence. Kildy's a total stranger, I've never seen her before in my life!

"He thinks that you – ?" Ariaura hooted and banged the arms of the chair with glee. "Doesn't the poor fish know you're in love with him?"

"He thinks that's part of the scam," Kildy said earnestly. "The only way he'll believe I am is if he believes there is no scam, if he believes you're really Mencken."

"Well, then," Ariaura said and grinned, "I guess we'll have to convince him." She slapped her knees and turned expectantly to me. "What do you want to know, sir? I was born in 1880 at nine P.M., right before the police went out and raided ten or twenty saloons, and went to work at the *Morning Herald* at the tender age of eighteen – "

"Where you laid siege to the editor Max Ways for four straight weeks before he gave you an assignment," I said, "but my knowing that doesn't any more make me Henry Lawrence Mencken than it does you."

"Henry *Louis*," Ariaura said, "after an uncle of mine who died when he was a baby. All right, you set the questions."

"It's not that simple," Kildy said. She pulled a chair up in front of Ariaura and sat down, facing her. She took both hands in hers. "To prove you're Mencken you can't just answer questions. The skeptic's first rule is: 'Extraordinary claims require extraordinary evidence.' You've got to do something extraordinary."

"And independently verifiable," I said.

"Extraordinary," Ariaura said, looking at Kildy. "I presume you're not talking about handling snakes. Or speaking in tongues."

"No," I said.

"The problem is, if you prove you're Mencken," Kildy said earnestly, "then you're also proving that Ariaura's really channeling astral spirits, which means she's not – "

" – the papuliferous poser I know her to be."

"Exactly," Kildy said, "and her career will skyrocket."

"Along with that of every other channeler and psychic and medium out there," I said.

"Rob's put his entire life into trying to debunk these people," Kildy said. "If you prove Ariaura's really channeling – "

"The noble calling of skepticism will be dealt a heavy blow," Ariaura said thoughtfully, "hardly the outcome a man like Mencken would want. So the only way I can prove who I am is to keep silent and go back to where I came from."

Kildy nodded.

"But I came to try and stop her. If I return to the ether, Ariaura will go right back to spreading her pernicious astral-plane-Higher-Wisdom hokum and bilking her benighted audiences out of their cash."

Kildy nodded again. "She might even pretend she's channeling you."

"*Pretend!*" Ariaura said, outraged. "I won't allow it! I'll – " and then stopped. "But if I speak out, I'm proving the very thing I'm trying to debunk. And if I don't – "

"Rob will never trust me again," Kildy said.

"So," Ariaura said, "it's – "

A catch-22, I thought, and then, if she says that I've got her – the book wasn't written till 1961, five years after Mencken died. And "catch-22" was the kind of thing, unlike "Bible belt" or "booboisie," that even Kildy wouldn't have thought of, it had become such an ingrained part of the language. I listened, waiting for Ariaura to say it.

" – a conundrum," she said.

"A what?" Kildy said.

"A puzzle with no solution, a hand there's no way to win, a hellacious dilemma."

"You're saying it's impossible," Kildy said hopelessly.

Ariaura shook her head. "I've had tougher assignments than this. There's bound to be something – " She turned to me. "She said something about 'the skeptic's first rule.' Are there any others?"

"Yes," I said. "If it seems too good to be true, it is."

"And 'by their fruits shall ye know them,'" Kildy said. "It's from the Bible."

"The Bible..." Ariaura said, narrowing her eyes thoughtfully. "The Bible... how much time have we got? When's Ariaura's next show?"

"Tonight," Kildy said, "but she canceled the last one. What if she – "

"What time?" Ariaura cut in.

"Eight o'clock."

"Eight o'clock," she repeated, and made a motion toward her right midsection for all the world like she was reaching for a pocket watch. "You two be out there, front row center."

"What are you doing to do?" Kildy asked hopefully.

"I dunno," Ariaura said. "Sometimes you don't have to do a damned thing – they do it to themselves. Look at that High Muckitymuck of Hot Air, Bryan." She laughed. "Either of you know where I can get some rope?" She didn't wait for an answer. " – I'd better get on it. There's only a couple of hours to deadline – " She slapped her knees. "Front row center," she said to Kildy. "Eight o'clock."

"What if she won't let us in?" Kildy asked. "Ariaura said she was going to get a restraining order against – "

"She'll let you in. Eight o'clock."

Kildy nodded. "I'll be there, but I don't know if Rob – "

"Oh, I wouldn't miss this for the world," I said.

Ariaura ignored my tone. "Bring a notebook," she ordered. "And in the meantime, you'd better get busy on your charlatan debunking. The sons of bitches are gaining on us."

> One sits through long sessions...and then suddenly there comes a show so gaudy and hilarious, so melodramatic and obscene, so unimaginably exhilarating and preposterous that one lives a gorgeous year in an hour.
> – H.L. MENCKEN

An hour later a messenger showed up with a manila envelope. In it was a square vellum envelope sealed with purple wax and embossed with Isus's hieroglyphs. Inside were a lilac card printed in silver with "The pleasure of your company is requested..." and two tickets to the seminar.

"Is the invitation signed?" she'd asked.

She'd refused to leave after Ariaura'd departed, still acting the part of Mencken. "I'm staying right here with you till the seminar," she'd said, perching herself on my desk. "It's the only way I can prove I'm not off somewhere with Ariaura cooking up some trick. And here's my phone – " she'd handed me her cell – "so you won't think I'm sending her secret messages via text-message or something. Do you want to check me to see if I'm wired?"

"No."

"Do you need any help?" Kildy'd asked, picking up a pile of proofs. "Do you want me to go over these, or am I fired?"

"I'll let you know after the seminar."

She'd given me a Julia Roberts-radiant smile and retreated to the far end of the office with the proofs, and I'd called up Charles Fred's file and started through it, looking for leads and trying not to think about Ariaura's parting shot.

I was positive I'd never told Kildy that story, and it wasn't in Daniels's biography, or Hobson's. The only place I'd ever seen it was in an article in the *Atlantic Monthly*. I looked it up in Bartlett's, but it wasn't there. I Googled "Mencken – bitches." Nothing.

Which didn't prove anything. Ariaura – or Kildy – could have read it in the *Atlantic Monthly* just like I had. And since when had H. L. Mencken looked to the Bible for inspiration? That remark alone proved it wasn't Mencken, didn't it? On the other hand, he hadn't said "catch-22," although "conundrum" wasn't nearly as precise a word. And he hadn't said William Jennings Bryan, he'd said "that High Muckitymuck of Hot Air, Bryan," which I hadn't read anywhere, but which sounded like something he would have put in that scathing eulogy he'd written of Bryan.

And this wasn't going anywhere. There was nothing, short of a heretofore undiscovered manuscript or a will in his handwriting leaving everything to Lillian Gish – no, that wouldn't work. The aphasic stroke, remember? – that would prove it was Mencken. And both of those could be faked, too.

And there wasn't anything that could do what Kildy had told him – correction, told Ariaura she had to do: prove he was real without proving Ariaura was legit. Which she clearly wasn't.

I got out Ariaura's transcripts and read through them, looking for I wasn't sure what, until the tickets came.

"Is the card signed?" Kildy asked again.

"No," I said and handed it to her.

"'The pleasure of your company is requested...' is printed on," she said, turning the invitation over to look at the back. "What about the address on the envelope?"

"There isn't one," I said, seeing where she was going with this. "But just because it's not handwritten, that doesn't prove it's from Mencken."

"I know. 'Extraordinary claims,' but at least it's consistent with its being Mencken."

"It's also consistent with the two of you trying to convince me it's Mencken so I'll go to that seminar tonight."

"You think it's a trap?" Kildy said.

"Yes," I said, but standing there, staring at the tickets, I had no idea what kind. Ariaura couldn't possibly still be hoping I'd stand up and shout, "By George, she's the real thing! She's channeling Mencken!" no matter what anecdote she quoted. I wondered if her lawyers might be intending to slap me with a restraining order or a subpoena when I walked in, but that made no sense. She knew my address – she'd been here this very afternoon, and I'd been here most of the past two days. Besides, if she had me arrested, the press would be clamoring to talk to me, and she wouldn't want me voicing my suspicions of a con game to the L.A. Times.

When Kildy and I left for the seminar an hour and a half later (on our way out, I'd pretended I forgot my keys and left Kildy standing in the hall while I went back in, bound *The Baby in the Icebox* with Scotch tape, and hid it down behind the bookcase), I still hadn't come up with a plausible theory, and the Santa Monica Hilton, where the seminar was being held, didn't yield any clues.

It had the same "Believe and It Will Happen" banner, the same Tom Cruise-ish bodyguards, the same security check. They confiscated my Olympus and my digital recorder and Kildy's Hasaka (and asked for her autograph), and we went through the same crystal/pyramid/amulet-crammed waiting area into the same lilac-and-rose draped ballroom. With the same hard, bare floor.

"Oh, I forgot to bring pillows, I'm sorry," Kildy said and started toward the ushers and stacks of lilac-plastic cushions at the rear. Halfway there she turned around and came back. "I don't want to have had an opportunity to send some kind of secret message to Ariaura," she said. "If you want to come with me…"

I shook my head. "The floor'll be good," I said, lowering myself to the ground. "It may actually keep me in touch with reality."

Kildy sat down effortlessly beside me, opened her bag, and fumbled in it for her mirror. I looked around. The crowd seemed a little sparser, and somewhere behind us, I heard a woman say, "It was so bizarre. Romtha never did anything like that. I wonder if she's drinking."

The lights went pink, the music swelled, and Brad Pitt came out, went through the same spiel (no flash, no applause, no bathroom breaks) and the same intro (Atlantis, Oracle of Delphi, Cosmic All), and revealed Ariaura, standing at the top of the same black stairway.

She was exactly the same as she had been at that first seminar, dramatically regal in her purple robes and amulets, serene as she acknowledged the audience's applause. The events of the past few days – her roaring into my office, asking frightenedly, "What's happening? Where am I?" slapping her knees and exploding with laughter – might never have happened.

And obviously had been a fake, I thought grimly. I glanced at Kildy. She was still fishing unconcernedly in her bag.

"Welcome, Seekers after Divine Truth," Ariaura said. "We're going to have a wonderful spiritual experience together here today. It's a very special day. This is my one hundredth 'Believe and It Will Happen' seminar.'"

Lots of applause, which after a couple of minutes she motioned to stop.

"In honor of the anniversary, Isus and I want to do something a little different today."

More applause. I glanced at the ushers. They were looking nervously at each other, as if they expected her to start spouting Menckenese, but the voice was clearly Ariaura's and so was the Oprah-perky manner.

"My – *our* – seminars are usually pretty structured. They have to be – if the auratic vibrations aren't exactly right beforehand, the spirits cannot come, and after I've channeled, I'm physically and spiritually exhausted, so I rarely have the opportunity to just *talk* to you. But today's a special occasion. So I'd like the tech crew – " she looked up at the control booth " – to bring up the lights – "

There was a pause, as if the tech crew was debating whether to follow orders, and then the lights came up.

"Thanks, that's perfect, you can have the rest of the day off," Ariaura said. She turned to the emcee. "That goes for you, too, Ken. And my fabulous ushers – Derek, Jared, Tad – let's hear it for the great job they do."

She led a round of applause and then, since the ushers continued to stand there at the doors, looking warily at each other and at the emcee, she made shooing motions with her hands. "Go on. Scoot. I want to talk to these people in private," and when they still hesitated, "you'll still get paid for the full seminar. Go on." She walked over to the emcee and said something to him, smiling, and it must have reassured him because he nodded to the ushers and then up at the control room, and the ushers went out.

I looked over at Kildy. She was calmly applying lipstick. I looked back at the stage.

"Are you sure – ?" I could see the emcee whisper to Ariaura.

"I'm *fine*," she mouthed back at him.

The emcee frowned and then stepped off the stage and over to the side door, and the cameraman at the back began taking his videocam off its tripod. "No, no, Ernesto, not you," Ariaura said, "keep filming."

She waited as the emcee pulled the last door shut behind him and then walked to the front of the stage and stood there completely silent, her arms stiffly at her sides.

Kildy leaned close to me, her lipstick still in her hand. "Are you thinking the prom scene in *Carrie*?"

I nodded, gauging our distance to the emergency exit. There was a distant sound of a door shutting above us – the control room – and Ariaura clasped her hands together. "Alone at last," she said, smiling. "I thought they'd never leave."

Laughter.

"And now that they're gone, I have to say this – " She paused dramatically. "Aren't they *gorgeous*?"

Laughter, applause, and several whistles. Ariaura waited till the noise had died down and then asked, "How many of you were at my seminar last Saturday?"

The mood changed instantly. Several hands went up, but tentatively, and two hoop-earringed women looked at each other with the same nervous glance as the ushers had had.

"Or at the one two weeks ago?" Ariaura asked.

Another couple of hands.

"Well, for those of you who weren't at either, let's just say that lately my seminars have been rather...interesting, to put it mildly."

Scattered nervous laughter.

"And those of you familiar with the spirit world know that's what can happen when we try to make contact with energies beyond our earthly plane. The astral plane can be a dangerous place. There are spirits there beyond our control, false spirits who seek to keep us from enlightenment."

False spirits is right, I thought.

"But I fear them not, for my weapon is the Truth." She somehow managed to say it with a capital T.

I looked over at Kildy. She was leaning forward the way she had at that first seminar, intent on Ariaura's words. She was still holding her mirror and lipstick. "What's she up to?" I whispered to Kildy.

She shook her head, still intent on the stage. "It's not her."

"What?"

"She's channeling."

"Chan – ?" I said and looked at the stage.

"No spirit, no matter how dark," Ariaura said, "no matter how dishonest, can stand between me and that Higher Truth."

Applause, more enthusiastic.

"Or keep me from bringing that Truth to all of you." She smiled and spread out her arms. "I'm a fraud, a charlatan, a fake," she said cheerfully. "I've never channeled a cosmic spirit in my life. Isus is something I made up back in 1996, when I was running a pyramid scheme in Dayton, Ohio. The feds were closing in on us, and I'd already been up on charges of mail fraud in '94, so I changed my name – my real name's Bonnie Friehl, by the way, but I was using Doreen Manning in Dayton – and stashed the money in a bank in Chickamauga, Virginia, my home town, and then moved to Miami Beach and did fortune-telling while I worked on perfecting Isus's voice."

I fumbled for my notebook and pen. Bonnie Friehl, Chickamauga, Miami Beach –

"I did fortune-telling, curses mostly – 'Pay me and I'll remove the curse I see hanging over you' – till I had my Isus-impersonation ready and then I contacted this guy I knew in Vegas – "

There was an enormous crash from the rear. Ernesto had dropped his shoulder-held video camera and was heading for the door. And this needed to be on film. But I didn't want to miss anything while I tried to figure out how the camera worked.

I glanced over at Kildy, hoping she was taking notes, but she seemed transfixed by what was happening onstage, her forgotten mirror and lipstick still in her hands, her mouth open. I would have to risk missing a few words. I scrambled to my feet.

"Where are you going?" Kildy whispered.

"I've got to get this on tape."

"We are," she said calmly, and nodded imperceptibly at the lipstick and then the mirror. "Audio...and video."

"I love you," I said.

She nodded. "You'd better get those names down, just in case the police confiscate my makeup as evidence," she said.

"His name was Chuck Venture," Ariaura was saying. "He and I had worked together on a chain-letter scheme. His real name's Harold Vogel, but you probably know him by the name he uses out here, Charles Fred."

Jesus. I scribbled the names down: Harold Vogel, Chuck Venture –

"We'd worked a couple of chain-letter scams together," Ariaura said, "so I told him I wanted him to take me to Salem and set me up in the channeling business."

There was a clank and a thud as Ernesto made it to the door and out. It slammed shut behind him.

"Harold always did have a bad habit of writing everything down," Ariaura said chattily. "'You can't blackmail me, Doreen,' he said. 'Wanna bet?' I said. 'It's all in a safety deposit box in Dayton with instructions to open it if anything happens to me.'" She leaned confidingly forward. "It's not, of course. It's in the safe in my bedroom behind the portrait of Isus. The combination's twelve left, six right, fourteen left." She laughed brightly. "So anyway, he taught me all about how you soften the chumps up in the seminars so they'll tell Isus all about their love life in the private audiences and then send them copies of the audience videotapes – "

There were several audible gasps behind me and then the beginnings of a murmur, or possibly a growl, but Ariaura paid no attention –

" – and he introduced me to one of the orderlies at New Beginnings Rehab center, and the deep masseuse at the Willowsage Spa for personal details Isus can use to convince them he knows all, sees all – "

The growl was becoming a roar, but it was scarcely audible over the shouts from outside and the banging on the doors, which were apparently locked from the inside.

" – and how to change my voice and expression to make it look like I'm actually channeling a spirit from beyond – "

It sounded as though the emcee and ushers had found a battering ram. The banging had become shuddering thuds.

" – although I don't think learning all that junk about Lemuria and stuff was necessary," Ariaura said. "I mean, it's obvious you people will believe *anything*." She smiled beatifically at the audience, as if expecting applause, but the only sound (beside the thuds) was of cell phone keys being hit and women shouting into them. When I glanced back, everybody except Kildy had a phone clapped to their ear.

"Are there any questions?" Ariaura asked brightly.

"Yes," I said. "Are you saying you're the one doing the voice of Isus?"

She smiled pleasedly down at me. "Of course. There's no such thing as channeling spirits from the Great Beyond. Other questions?" She looked past me to the other wildly waving hands. "Yes? The woman in blue?"

"How could you lie to us, you – "

I stepped adroitly in front of her. "Are you saying Todd Phoenix is a fake, too?"

"Oh, yes," Ariaura said. "They're all fakes – Todd Phoenix, Joye Wildde, Randall Mars. Next question? Yes, Miss Ross?"

Kildy stepped forward, still holding the compact and lipstick. "When was the first time you met me?" she asked.

"You don't have to do this," I said.

"Just for the record," she said, flashing me her radiant smile and then turning back to the stage. "Ariaura, had you ever met me before last week?"

"No," she said. "I saw you at Ari – at my seminar, but I didn't meet you till afterward at the office of The Jaundiced Eye, a fine magazine, by the way. I suggest you all take out subscriptions."

"And I'm not your shill?" Kildy persisted.

"No, though I do have them," she said. "The woman in green back there in the sixth row is one," she said, pointing at a plump brunette. "Stand up, Lucy."

Lucy was already scuttling to the door, and so were a thin redhead in a rainbow caftan and an impeccably tailored sixty-year-old in an Armani suit, with a large number of the audience right on their tails.

"Janine's one, too," Ariaura said, pointing at the redhead. "And Doris. They all help gather personal information for Isus to tell them, so it looks like he 'knows all, sees all.'" She laughed delightedly. "Come up on stage and take a bow, girls."

The "girls" ignored her. Doris, a pack of elderly women on her heels, pushed open the middle door and shouted, "You've got to stop her!"

The emcee and ushers began pushing their way through the door and toward the stage. The audience was even more determined to get out than they were to get in, but I still didn't have much time. "Are all the psychics you named using blackmail like you?" I asked.

"Ariaura!" the emcee shouted, halfway to the stage and caught in the flood of women. "Stop talking. Anything you say can be held against you."

"Oh, hi, Ken," she said. "Ken's in charge of laundering all our money. Take a

bow, Ken! And you, too, Derek and Tad and Jared," she said, indicating the ushers. "The boys pump the audience for information and feed it to me over this,"
she said, holding up her sacred amulet.

She looked back at me. "I forgot what you asked."

"Are all the pyschics you named using blackmail like you?"

"No, not all of them. Swami Vishnu Jammi uses post-hypnotic suggestion,
and Nadrilene's always used extortion."

"What about Charles Fred? What's his scam?"

"Invest – " Ariaura's pin-on mike went suddenly dead. I looked back at the
melee. One of the ushers was proudly holding up an unplugged cord.

"Investment fraud," Ariaura shouted, her hands cupped around her mouth.
"Chuck tells his marks their dead relations want them to invest in certain stocks.
I'd suggest you – "

One of the ushers reached the stage. He grabbed Ariaura by one arm and tried
to grab the other.

" – suggest you check out Metra – " Ariaura shouted, flailing at him. "Metra-
con, Spirilink – "

A second usher appeared, and the two of them managed to pinion her arms.
"Crystalcom, Inc – " she said, kicking out at them " – and Universis. Find out
– " She aimed a kick at the groin of one of the ushers that made me flinch. "Get
your paws off me."

The emcee stepped in front of her. "That concludes Ariaura's presentation,"
he said, avoiding her kicking feet. "Thank you all for coming. Videos of – " he
said and then thought better of it " – personally autographed copies of Ariaura's
book, *Believe and* – "

"Find out who the majority stockholder is," Ariaura shrieked, struggling.
"And ask Chuck what he knows about a check forgery scam Zolita's running in
Reno."

" – *It Will Happen* are on sale in the..." the emcee said and gave up. He grabbed
for Ariaura's feet. The three of them wrestled her toward the wings.

"One last question!" I shouted, but it was too late. They already had her off
the stage. "Why was the baby in the icebox?"

> ...this is the last time you'll see me....
> – H. L. MENCKEN

"It still doesn't prove it was Mencken," I told Kildy. "The whole thing could be
a manifestation of Ariaura's – excuse me, Bonnie Friehl's – subconscious, produced by her guilt."

"Or," Kildy said, "there could have been a scam just like the one you postulated, only one of the swindlers fell in love with you and decided she couldn't go through with it."

"Nope, that won't work," I said. "She might have been able to talk Ariaura into calling off the scam, but not into confessing all those crimes."

"If she really committed them," Kildy said. "We don't have any independently verifiable evidence that she is Bonnie Friehl yet." But the fingerprints on her Ohio driver's license matched, and every single lead she'd given us checked out.

We spent the next two months following up on all of them and putting together a massive special issue on "The Great Channeling Swindle." It looked like we were going to have to testify at Ariaura's preliminary hearing, which could have proved awkward, but she and her lawyers got in a big fight over whether or not to use an insanity defense since she was claiming she'd been possessed by the Spirit of Evil and Darkness, and she ended up firing them and turning state's evidence against Charles Fred, Joye Wildde, and several other psychics she hadn't gotten around to mentioning, and it began to look like the magazine might fold because there weren't any scams left to write about.

Fat chance. Within weeks, new mediums and psychics, advertising themselves as "Restorers of Cosmic Ethics" and "the spirit entity you can trust," moved in to fill the void, and a new weight-loss-through-meditation program began packing them in, promising Low-Carb Essence, and Kildy and I were back in business.

"He didn't make any difference at all," Kildy said disgustedly after a standing-room-only seminar on psychic Botox treatments.

"Yeah, he did," I said. "Charles Fred's up on insider trading charges, attendance is down at the Temple of Cosmic Exploration, and half of L.A.'s psychics are on the lam. And it'll take everybody awhile to come up with new methods for separating people from their money."

"I thought you said it wasn't Mencken."

"I said it didn't prove it was Mencken. Rule Number One: Extraordinary claims require extraordinary evidence."

"And you don't think what happened on that stage was extraordinary?"

I had to admit it was. "But it could have been Ariaura herself. She didn't say anything she couldn't have known."

"What about her telling us the combination of her safe? And ordering everybody to subscribe to The Jaundiced Eye?"

"It still doesn't prove it was Mencken. It could have been some sort of Bridey Murphy phenomenon. Ariaura could have had a babysitter who read the Baltimore Sun out loud to her when she was a toddler."

Kildy laughed. "You don't believe that."

"I don't believe anything without proof," I said. "I'm a skeptic, remember? And there's nothing that happened on that stage that couldn't be explained rationally."

"Exactly," Kildy said.

"What do you mean, exactly?"

"By their fruits shall ye know them."

"What?"

"I mean it has to have been Mencken because he did exactly what we asked him to do: prove it wasn't a scam and he wasn't a fake and Ariaura was. And do it without proving he was Mencken because if he did, then that proved she was on the level. Which *proves* it was Mencken."

There was no good answer to that kind of crazy illogic except to change the subject, which I did. I kissed her.

And then sent the transcripts of Ariaura's outbursts to UCLA to have the language patterns compared to Mencken's writing. Independently verifiable evidence. And got the taped *Baby in the Icebox* out of its hiding place down behind the bookcase while Kildy was out of the office, took it home, wrapped it in tin foil, stuck it inside an empty Lean Cuisine box, and hid it – where else? – in the icebox. Old habits die hard.

UCLA sent the transcripts back, saying it wasn't a big enough sample for a conclusive result. So did Caltech. And Duke. So that was that. Which was too bad. It would have been nice to have Mencken back in the fray, even for a little while. He had definitely left too soon.

So Kildy and I would have to pick up where he left off, which meant not only putting "The sons of bitches are gaining on us" on the masthead of *The Jaundiced Eye*, but trying to channel his spirit into every page.

And that didn't just mean exposing shysters and con men. Mencken hadn't been the important force he was because of his rants against creationism and faith-healers and patent medicine, but because of what he'd stood for: the Truth. That's why he'd hated ignorance and superstition and dishonesty so much, because he loved science and reason and logic, and he'd communicated that love, that passion, to his readers with every word he wrote.

That was what we had to do with *The Jaundiced Eye*. It wasn't enough just to expose Ariaura and Swami Vishnu and psychic dentists and meditation Atkins diets. We also had to make our readers as passionate about science and reason as they were about Romtha and luminescence readings. We had to not only tell the truth, but make our readers *want* to believe it.

So, as I say, we were pretty busy for the next few months, revamping the magazine, cooperating with the police, and following up on all the leads Ariaura had given us. We went to Vegas to research the chain-letter scam she and Chuck Venture/Charles Fred had run, after which I came home to put the magazine to bed, and Kildy went to Dayton and then to Chickamauga to follow up on Ariaura's criminal history.

She called last night. "It's me, Rob," she said, sounding excited. "I'm in Chattanooga."

"Chattanooga, *Tennessee?*" I said. "What are you doing there?"

"The prosecutor working on the pyramid scheme case is on a trip to Roanoke, so I can't see him till Monday, and the school board in Zion – that's a little town near here – is trying to pass a law requiring intelligent design to be taught in the public schools. This Zion thing's part of a nationwide program that's going to introduce intelligent design state by state. So, anyway, since I couldn't see the prosecutor, I thought I'd drive over – it's only about fifty miles from Chickamauga – and interview some of the science teachers for that piece on 'The Scopes Trial Eighty Years Out' you were talking about doing."

"And?" I said warily.

"*And*, according to the chemistry teacher, something peculiar happened at the school board meeting. It might be nothing, but I thought I'd better call so you could be looking up flights to Chattanooga, just in case."

Just in case.

"One of the school board members, a Mr. – " she paused as if consulting her notes – "Horace Didlong, was talking about the lack of scientific proof for Darwin's theory, when he suddenly started ranting at the crowd."

"Did the chemistry teacher say what he said?" I asked, hoping I didn't already know.

"She couldn't remember all of it," Kildy said, "but the basketball coach said some of the students had said they intended to tape the meeting and send it to the ACLU, and he'd try to find out if they did and get me a copy. He said it was 'a very odd outburst, almost like he was possessed.'"

"Or drunk," I said. "And neither of them remembers what he said?"

"No, they both do, just not everything. Didlong apparently went on for several minutes. He said he couldn't believe there were still addlepated ignoramuses around who didn't believe in evolution, and what the hell had they been teaching in the schools all this time. The chemistry teacher said the rant went on like that for about five minutes and then broke off, right in the middle of a word, and Didlong went back to talking about how Newton's Second Law makes evolution physically impossible."

"Have you interviewed Didlong?"

"No. I'm going over there as soon as we finish talking, but the chemistry teacher said she heard Didlong's wife ask him what happened, and he looked like he didn't have any idea."

"That doesn't prove it's Mencken," I said.

"I know," she said, but it is Tennessee, and it is evolution. And it would be nice if it was him, wouldn't it?"

Nice. H. L. Mencken loose in the middle of Tennessee in the middle of a creationism debate.

"Yeah," I said and grinned, "it would, but it's much more likely Horace Didlong has been smoking something he grew in his backyard. Or is trying to stir up some publicity, à la Judge Roy Moore and his Ten Commandments monument. Do they remember anything else he said?"

"Yes, um...where is it?" she said. "Oh, here it is. He called the other board members a gang of benighted rubes...and then he said he'd take a monkey any day over a school board whose cerebellums were all paralyzed from listening to too much theological bombast...and right at the end, before he broke off, the chemistry teacher said he said, 'I never saw much resemblance to Alice myself.'"

"Alice?" I said. "They're sure he said Alice and not August?"

"Yes, because the chemistry teacher's name is Alice, and she thought he was talking to her, and the chairman of the school board did, too, because he looked at her and said, 'Alice? What the heck does Alice have to do with intelligent design?' and Didlong said, 'Jamie sure could write, though, even if the bastard did steal my girl. You better be careful I don't steal yours.' Do you know what that means, Rob?"

"Yes," I said. "How long does it take to get a marriage license in Tennessee?"

"I'll find out," Kildy said, sounding pleased, "and then the chairman said, 'You cannot use language like that,' and, according to the chemistry teacher, Didlong said...wait a minute, I need to read it to you so I get it right – it really didn't make any sense – he said, 'You'd be surprised at what I can do. Like stir up the animals. Speaking of which, that's why the baby was stashed in the icebox. Its mother stuck it there to keep the tiger from eating it.'"

"I'll be right there," I said.